THE WITCH HUNTER CHRONICLES

THE DEVIL'S FIRE

THE WITCH HUNTER CHRONICLES

THE DEVIL'S FIRE

STUART DALY

RANDOM HOUSE AUSTRALIA

A Random House book
Published by Random House Australia Pty Ltd
Level 3, 100 Pacific Highway, North Sydney NSW 2060
www.randomhouse.com.au

First published by Random House Australia in 2012

Addresses for companies within the Random House Group can be found at
www.randomhouse.com.au/offices.

National Library of Australia
Cataloguing-in-Publication Entry

Author: Daly, Stuart
Title: The devil's fire / Stuart Daly
ISBN: 978 1 74275 480 2 (pbk)
Series: Daly, Stuart. Witch hunter chronicles; 3
Target Audience: For secondary school age
Subjects: Witch hunting – Juvenile fiction
Dewey number: A823.4

Cover illustration and design by Sammy Yuen
Maps by Stuart Daly and Anna Warren
Internal design by Midland Typesetters
Typeset in 12/16 Minion by Midland Typesetters, Australia
Printed in Australia by Griffin Press, an accredited ISO AS/NZS 14001:2004
Environmental Management System printer

Random House Australia uses papers that are natural, renewable and recyclable
products and made from wood grown in sustainable forests. The logging and
manufacturing processes are expected to conform to the environmental regulations of
the country of origin.

To Belinda, for everything

Europe and the Mediterranean in 1666

The Holy Roman Empire in 1666

CHAPTER ONE

Standing knee-deep in water in the flooded medieval dungeon, I raise my pistol to my lips, kiss its polished barrel and pray hastily that our ambush works. I lean out of the cell, take aim down the tunnel and fire at the closest of the unsuspecting Dutch soldiers. He staggers back, holding his blasted chest.

My signal given, six English soldiers spring out of the adjacent cells that line the tunnel, level their muskets and pistols at the Dutchmen and blast away. Before the powdered flashes from our firearms have cleared, my fellow Hexenjäger Armand races out from one of the cells and tears into the startled Dutch soldiers, his mortuary blade and sabre moving with blinding speed. Three of the Dutchmen drop dead, clutching at wounds they never saw delivered.

Deftly dodging a swipe at his head with the butt of a musket, Armand weaves past two other soldiers before finding himself in front of a brutish Dutchman. This soldier's face is a butchered mess of scars – souvenirs collected from a life of fighting. Whipping up his pistol, the Dutchman takes aim at Armand's chest. But Armand is faster. The French duellist grabs hold of a nearby soldier who is fumbling with his musket and uses him as a human shield against the Dutchman's shot. Armand tosses the now-dead soldier towards the hulking figure standing before him, forcing the Dutchman to lose his balance in the water. Armand seizes the advantage and lunges forward, his sabre snaking out and punching through the side of his adversary. Collapsing to his knees, the brutish soldier lashes out desperately with the butt of his pistol, but Armand parries the attack aside and finishes him off with a savage slash across the throat.

Armand leaps to his left, shouldering into the nearest soldier, and sends him careening head-first into the tunnel wall, knocking him senseless. His eyes then lock on an advancing Dutchman, whose sword-arm is outstretched and held high. The point of the soldier's rapier is aimed at the Frenchman's face.

Facing an adversary trained in the Spanish school of swordplay, Armand adjusts his fighting technique accordingly and assumes a traversing stance, raising his sabre to counter the Dutchman's blade. Having parried aside the first three thrusts and assessed the quality of the soldier's fencing, Armand turns his fourth parry into a lightning-fast riposte, his sabre transformed into a *hiss* of death. The Dutchman is caught off-guard – and left with three hand-spans of steel protruding through his back.

Armand kicks the body free from his blade and twists to his left, narrowly avoiding a pistol shot from one of the two remaining soldiers. The duellist then streaks across the tunnel, crossing the distance to the remaining Dutchmen in less than a heartbeat. Feigning to his right, he lures one of them into a lunge that forces him to over-extend his attack. Armand springs forward and hammers the pommel of his mortuary blade into the man's temple with a sickening crack. Even before the soldier slumps unconscious into the waters of the flooded corridor, Armand spins on his heel and flicks out his sabre, its point stopping a hair's-breadth from the throat of the remaining Dutchman, pinning him against the dungeon wall.

Sheathing his mortuary blade, Armand unhooks the lantern hanging from the soldier's belt and attaches it to his own. 'Tell your comrades not to come down,' he snarls, forcing the terrified soldier back down the tunnel. 'All that awaits them here is death. Now go, before my blades decide to taste your blood!'

One of the English soldiers assigned to help us defend this section of the dungeon runs over to join Armand and shakes his head in awe. 'My God! Well done,' he says in stilted German, watching the Dutchman flee. 'Never before have I seen such skill with a sword!'

'Don't commend me for butchery,' Armand says dis-dainfully, his features looking twisted and demonic in the lantern-light. He bends down to wipe the blood from his sabre on the cloak of one of the fallen Dutchmen. 'Taking the lives of innocent soldiers gives me no pleasure. I am a Hexenjäger – a witch hunter. I wage war at a higher level, with the Devil's legions. Now let's move back before reinforcements arrive and I'm forced to spill more Dutch blood.'

No sooner has he said this than a dozen or so Dutch soldiers appear at the end of the tunnel, their muskets and pistols raised in preparation to fire. Calling for our English allies to take shelter in the cells, Armand races frantically towards me through the water, his head held low, a hand keeping his wide-brimmed hat in place. The *BLAM!* of firearms reverberates from the darkness at the far end of the passage, and musket balls zip past the French duellist. As he races into the cell where I am hiding, I lean out and discharge my remaining pistol at the Dutch soldiers, knocking one of them off his feet with a direct shot to the forehead. The rest respond with hasty shots as they retreat down the tunnel.

Armand sheaths his sabre and draws the long-barrelled flintlock pistols from his belt. 'Where are Christian and Francesca?' he roars over the report of gunfire.

'Somewhere up ahead with Captain Lightfoot,' I yell back. 'They have moved deeper into the dungeon. The Captain wants us to join Lieutenant Wolf. We're to hold the Dutch at bay, granting the Captain the time he needs to blast through to the gaol.'

Armand's eyes flash with alarm. 'What? I thought we'd

agreed against that. Didn't we say that it would make too much noise and alert the prison guards?'

'I know,' I say as I start to reload my pistols. 'But the Captain has changed his mind, and I can see his point. We no longer have time to carry through with our initial idea of chiselling through to the prison. We've lost the element of surprise – these dungeon tunnels are alive with Dutch city watch. We just have to hope that we can still break into the prison before the guards are alerted. The last thing we want is to get trapped down here, with the Dutch coming at us from both sides.'

Armand shakes his head. 'This has gone from bad to worse. But what can we do? We're stuck in this mess now. If Lightfoot wants to blast his way through, then so be it. I just hope to God he does it quickly, because I don't know how long we're going to be able to hold the Dutch off; I think the entire city watch has come down after us.'

My companions – Armand, Christian von Frankenthal and Francesca – had accompanied me to Rotterdam in the hope that my father, long thought dead, may have been captured by the Dutch some ten years ago and imprisoned within the Devil's Bowels: the notorious gaol lying in the very heart of the Dutch city-port. Having entered a war zone – with the Anglo–Dutch War in its second year – we had kept our numbers to a bare minimum, believing that stealth and secrecy would be best suited to this mission.

Armand had only recently been promoted to the rank of Lieutenant. Before setting off on this adventure, he had assured me that my resourcefulness, Francesca's skill with traps and locks, von Frankenthal's brute strength, as well as Armand's own skill with swords – not to mention his dashing good looks and charm, Armand had modestly added – would be more than adequate to deal with a handful of decrepit prison guards. If all went to plan, he bragged, we wouldn't even have to draw our blades.

Famous last words if you ask me. For here we are now, having formed an alliance with a much larger English force and engaged in a vicious skirmish with a Dutch patrol, deep in an abandoned dungeon.

We arrived in Rotterdam yesterday morning and took residence in a coaching inn on the outskirts of the city. Not long after our arrival, Armand – having stepped outside to observe which parts of the city were monitored by the city guards, and to make a mental note of the location of Dutch garrisons throughout the area – had a fortuitous encounter with a disgruntled former prison guard. Armand convinced the man that he was part of a French contingent sent to assist the Dutch in their war against the English, and managed to bring the former guard back to our inn to toast a speedy Dutch victory. Several flagons of claret later, the guard was well and truly inebriated, and he revealed a secret that gave hope to our cause of freeing my father.

Rotterdam's prison had been built earlier this century to replace an older medieval dungeon. This twisting labyrinth of tunnels, stairwells and cells was located beside the Meuse, the central river that flows through the city, and had been abandoned sometime last century due to constant flooding. Although built further back from the Meuse, the prison was connected to the old dungeon via a doorway. This had been bricked over in the past decade, but the guard believed that it would be possible for two or three men, equipped with mallets and crowbars, to sneak into the dungeon and break through to the prison. He had also revealed the location of a secret entrance to the medieval dungeon: a metal grate, hidden beneath a pier along the northern embankment of the Meuse.

If the guard's information was correct, the prison comprised of two levels: an upper level, which was reserved for prisoners of state; and a lower level, which was full to bursting with English soldiers and sailors, most of whom had been captured during recent naval engagements. But there were a few cells in the southern wing – the dampest, rat-infested, most Godforsaken section of the entire prison – which housed Spanish and German prisoners, some of whom had been shackled within their solitary cells for over a decade.

Several hours before the break of dawn this morning, Armand, von Frankenthal, Francesca and I decided to investigate the dungeon. We had no intention of staging our gaolbreak just yet, for we first needed to test the validity of the guard's information. Indeed, this morning's expedition was intended as nothing more than a reconnaissance mission.

Wrapped in the folds of our cloaks, we scurried through the deserted streets. Coming to the aforementioned pier, we climbed down the brick embankment – only to find a force of twenty or so soldiers concealed in the darkness near the entrance to the dungeon, treading water in the river, their firearms and gunpowder flasks held above their heads so as to keep them dry. Some were hanging onto the sides of a small rowboat, its contents hidden under an oilcloth cover, and atop which sat a man. His features were obscured beneath a wide-brimmed hat, and he was wrapped in a cloak. I detected the outline of a rapier and a brace of pistols strapped across his chest.

Believing that the former prison guard had betrayed us to the city watch and led us into a trap, our hands flew to our blades, and the stillness of the night was disturbed by the hiss of drawn steel. It quickly became apparent, however, that we had encountered a group of *English* soldiers; this observation being based on the curses they hurled at us in their native tongue.

For several anxious moments we tried to convince the startled soldiers that we were not working for the Dutch, but were members of the Hexenjäger, on a personal mission to rescue my father from the prison. Although Armand was fluent in English, his French accent alarmed the soldiers, who were suspicious that he may have been a French soldier allied to the Dutch. Fortunately, the man sitting atop the boat, who later introduced himself as Captain Lightfoot, believed our protestations, particularly after we revealed the crimson tabards concealed beneath our cloaks, proving that we were indeed members of the Hexenjäger.

Fluent in German and with a roguish twist to his lips, the Captain had reasoned that if we were allied with the Dutch then surely we would have made a greater effort to alert the enemy of their presence. Nonetheless, he had insisted that we would have to join his men until he had achieved his objective in Rotterdam: namely, to break into the Devil's Bowels to free over fifty recently captured English prisoners of war. He could not risk us being detected and captured by the Dutch, only to reveal his plan under the threat of torture.

He then explained that English spies in the Dutch Republic had learned that the enemy were planning to place all captured English soldiers and seamen in the holds of Dutch merchant vessels. This barbaric act was going to be committed as an attempt to dissuade the English from attacking Dutch ships, for fear of killing their own men. It was a response to the recent English raid on Terschelling, an island off the coast of the Dutch Republic, where over a hundred Dutch merchant vessels had been caught by surprise and destroyed. The English fleet had then sacked and plundered the town of West-Terschelling. It was a brutal, savage attack, word of which had even reached us in Saxony.

The English spy-network had also revealed that Rotterdam's gaol was to be emptied and the prisoners transported onto the vessels before the end of the week. Hence the English needed to strike whilst they still had the chance.

As a large fleet of English men-of-war and frigates lay ready for action in the Channel, trying to draw out the Dutch fleet, a small, hand-picked team of twenty-six soldiers was to infiltrate the gaol, free the prisoners and make their escape back down the Meuse, where they would rendez-vous with an English warship and be transported back home.

Seeing that we had similar goals, Armand declared that we would become allies of convenience, and that we would join our four blades with the twenty-five under Captain Lightfoot's command.

'It's time we moved,' Armand announces, noting that the Dutch soldiers have withdrawn, but alerted by the sound of splashing feet that carries from beyond the turn in the tunnel. 'It sounds as if there's a much larger force approaching, and we need to pull back. If they catch us here it will only be a matter of time before they overwhelm us.' He turns around and looks up the opposite end of the passage. 'But if we withdraw to the next bend in the tunnel, we can use that to our advantage, picking the Dutch off with our firearms and then pulling back to reload.'

He orders the six English soldiers hiding in the cells along the tunnel wall opposite us to cover our retreat with their pistols and muskets, and then we are off. Hoisting our legs through the water, we race back twenty yards before reaching the next turn in the dungeon, where we join a further six of our English allies. This team is led by Captain Lightfoot's second-in-command, Lieutenant Richard Wolf: a lean and wiry career soldier with eyes as black as olives, and wearing a scarred leather buff coat.

'We are to hold them off for as long as possible,' Wolf says in stilted German, his musket trained on the far end of the tunnel, to where the Dutch patrol will shortly appear. 'We're to buy the Captain the time he needs to blast through to the prison.'

'So I've heard,' Armand says, stepping aside to allow the six Englishmen who had covered our retreat to join us. 'I just hope we don't have to buy him too much time. There's a second patrol approaching, and it sounds much larger than the first. The longer we are stalled down here, more and more Dutch soldiers are going to rush into these tunnels like flood waters.'

An inner fire flashes in Lieutenant Wolf's eyes and he smiles ruefully. 'Then I hope you can swim, Frenchman?'

He then turns to his men and speaks in English, to which they respond by joining their voices in a low howl. One of the Englishmen says something, and receives an encouraging slap on the back from the Lieutenant in return.

'What did the Lieutenant say?' I ask Armand.

'He referred to his men as Dogs of War and asked them if they were prepared to wade through blood,' he explains. 'One of them responded that they would buy the Captain the time he needs, even if it means holding this position until these tunnels are wall to wall with dead Hogen Mogens.'

'Hogen Mogens?' I ask.

'It is a derogatory term used by the English to describe the Dutch.'

'And what of you, boy?' the Lieutenant says in German, turning towards me. 'Will you join us in a baptism of blood? Or do you want to stay back and reload my firearms?'

'Jakob's already had his baptism,' Armand says, quick to intervene. 'And believe me, he won't be relegated to loading your firearms. He's a fully initiated Hexenjäger. He'll fight by my side.'

Lieutenant Wolf looks me square in the eye and nods. 'It appears the Hexenjäger train their hounds from when they are pups, suckling them on the teats of war. But I will not be a hypocrite and hold your age against you. I was no older than you when I fought my first action at Maastricht. Besides, my blade is no sharper than yours.'

I'm about to respond, when one of the Englishmen – who had been standing at the end of the tunnel, looking around the corner – pulls his head back sharply, his expression grave. He says something to Lieutenant Wolf, whose eyes flash in alarm.

'What's happened?' I ask Armand, curious as to what has startled the stalwart soldier.

'It's the new patrol,' Armand explains, his look distant. He then turns to regard me, his eyes uncharacteristically narrow with concern. 'It might be best if you stay back and reload our firearms.'

'Why? What's happened?'

'The Dutch reinforcements have arrived, but they are

12

not Dutch,' Armand says. 'Yesterday, when I surveyed the city streets, I heard rumours that a contingent of French soldiers had been stationed in Rotterdam to assist the Dutch. And the rumours appear to be true, for a unit of Frenchmen are coming up the tunnel. But they are no ordinary soldiers.' He pauses. 'They are wearing the blue tabard of King Louis XIV's Grey Musketeers.'

He might as well have hit me with a sledgehammer, such is the impact of this announcement. I stare blankly at Armand, wondering how we will ever survive this mission.

The Grey Musketeers are the most revered fighting force in France – a handpicked unit of France's finest soldiers. Experts at close-quarters combat, they are always the first to enter battle and the last to leave. They are commanded by their sub-lieutenant, Charles Castelmore d'Artagnan: a Gascon with a reputation for bravery and whose daring escapades are the bread and butter of the Parisian gazettes.

And if he's leading the Musketeers who have entered the dungeon, I just hope he hasn't come to spread *us* across the next slice of bread he'll deliver to the Parisian newspapers.

CHAPTER TWO

'What do we do now?' I ask Armand, feeling like running away as fast as my legs can carry me.

'We have no option but to hold this position,' Armand returns. 'I need you to go back and warn the others. Tell the Captain that we will hold them off for as long as possible. Though I don't know how much time we will be able to buy him.'

'What about you?' I ask, not wanting to abandon my friend.

Armand smiles confidently. 'I've faced the Grey Musketeers before, back in Paris. It was the reason for my expulsion from the city. They are exceptional swordsmen, but I can hold my own against them.'

'I know the stories,' I say, thinking back to the tales I

had heard of when Armand was a Captain in Louis XIV's Royal Palace Cavalry. 'You fought six separate duels in one day with members of the Musketeers, winning each of them. But now there's an entire *patrol* heading our way. We came to see if my father is here and, if so, to rescue him; not to help some English Captain pursue his own goals.'

Armand shakes his head. 'We are committed now.' He produces his handkerchief from a pocket, kisses it tenderly and ties it to the pommel of his mortuary blade. 'Besides, I've never been one to run from a fight. There are also unsettled matters I need to resolve with some of the Grey Musketeers. With any luck, they will be down here.' He pats me on the shoulder. 'Now go, Jakob. Warn the others. Godspeed.'

Knowing that each passing second is vital to the success of our rescue mission, I race along the tunnel and pray that this night will not end in a bloodbath.

I have barely moved beyond the perimeter of light cast by Armand's lantern when it becomes too dark for me to proceed any further. I untie my lantern from the side of the pack slung over my back, light it with my tinder and flint, attach it to my belt and continue running. I haven't travelled far when I hear the sharp report of firearms as Lieutenant Wolf's soldiers engage the Grey Musketeers. I hasten along the passage, which turns left and right every thirty yards or so until, eventually, I reach the rest of our team.

Captain Lightfoot, Francesca and von Frankenthal are at the beginning of the tunnel, positioning gunpowder barrels in elevated alcoves on opposite sides of the dungeon wall. A group of English soldiers are using wooden beams to prop the petard – a bell-shaped explosive device usually attached to a castle gate and detonated by a fuse – against the bricked-in doorway that gives access to the prison.

'You're making enough noise to wake the dead, sloshing about like that,' von Frankenthal says, stepping away from the others to greet me, his massive frame accentuated by the full-length cloak he is wearing. He looks warily down the passage, to where the sounds of combat are all but a distant, muffled echo. 'It sounds as if there's one hell of a fight happening back there. I hope you've been keeping your head down. Perhaps it's better if you stay here with me from here on.'

As much as I appreciate his concern, von Frankenthal is becoming too over-protective of me. This is quite ironic, considering the rough start we had. Only a month before I joined the order, a seventeen-year-old initiate who had been placed under von Frankenthal's care had died during an ambush by witches. Having blamed himself for the initiate's death, it had taken von Frankenthal some time to accept his new charge of watching over me. And now that he has, I often feel as if I am constantly shadowed by him. It's not that I'm ungrateful. On the contrary, I feel secure – almost invulnerable at times – having the muscle-corded witch hunter constantly watching my back. But I also feel restricted. I'm actually amazed that he ever allowed me to stay back with Armand and Lieutenant Wolf in the first place.

Captain Lightfoot attaches a fuse to one of the sets of barrels. 'How goes the delaying action?' he asks, not looking up, focusing on the task at hand.

'Lieutenant Wolf is determined to hold his position for as long as possible,' I say. 'But there's a problem.'

The Captain's eyes snap up. 'I don't like problems. What is it?'

'The Dutch have had reinforcements arrive,' I say, the Captain hanging off my every word, 'and they are a company of the Grey Musketeers.'

Captain Lightfoot stares hard into my eyes, contemplating this latest information. He turns to four of his remaining twelve soldiers, clicks his fingers and points down the tunnel, directing them to support the Lieutenant. He gestures for me to join him and Francesca in preparing the fuses. 'Then we must hurry,' he says.

As the soldiers hasten down the tunnel, Francesca hands me a coil of twine and instructs me to cut off two lengths, each approximately one foot long.

'Why are we placing the barrels here?' I ask, producing a dagger from my top boot and cutting the requested lengths of cord.

'The Captain doesn't want any Dutch patrols coming into the gaols after us,' Francesca says. She uses the pommel of her dagger to make a small hole in the top of a barrel, and inserts one of the fuses. 'At the same moment we detonate the petard, we are going to ignite these barrels, bringing down this section of the tunnel, blocking any further Dutch patrols from reaching us.'

'But won't that alert every Dutch soldier in the city?' I ask.

'The entire city will be alerted to our presence the instant we blast our way into the gaol. If that's going to be the case, we might as well set off some other explosions and bring down the tunnel. Besides, we won't be going back that way. The Captain has studied maps of the dungeon, and he knows of another way out.'

'And what of Armand and everyone else?'

'We won't be leaving anybody behind,' Francesca says determinedly. 'We'll send a runner back to warn the others. No barrels will be detonated until they are all back here. You have my word on that.'

Reassured by her promise, I assist Francesca in preparing the barrels. Captain Lightfoot then calls for us to join him near the bricked-in section of wall.

'We are ready to go,' he announces. 'Once the fuses are lit, it will only take ten seconds or so before the petard and gunpowder barrels go up. We're going to take shelter beyond the next turn in the tunnel. There will be one hell of an explosion, so remember to cover your ears.' He looks at me. 'I'd say you'd be faster on your feet than the rest of us. I need you to go and tell Lieutenant Wolf that he is to pull back. The instant I see the Lieutenant and his men enter this tunnel, I am going to ignite the fuses . . .'

'Let me warn the others,' von Frankenthal says.

Captain Lightfoot shakes his head. 'No offence intended, but you'll be too slow. Jakob will go.'

I place the spare length of fuse I am holding in a pocket on the inside of my cloak. 'Wish me luck.'

'Be careful,' Francesca says.

I smile bravely in return and then I'm off, determined to pass on the message before Armand and Lieutenant Wolf are cut down by the Grey Musketeers.

CHAPTER THREE

The sounds of combat getting louder with each passing turn in the dungeon, I race through the tunnels until I make it back to where Armand and Lieutenant Wolf's soldiers are holding off the Grey Musketeers. I come to a grinding halt, shocked when I find the tunnel transformed into a scene of carnage.

Whereas I had last seen Lieutenant Wolf's Dogs of War standing proud and defiant, determined to hold their position for as long as possible, all that remains now are five wounded soldiers. They are gasping for air and leaning on their weapons. The smell of gunpowder hangs heavily in the air, and dead Englishmen and the odd Grey Musketeer lie floating in the water. Von Frankenthal was right – this was one *hell* of a fight.

'Where are Armand and Lieutenant Wolf?' I ask the

closest soldier, who stares blankly at me, not understanding a word I say.

My stomach knots as I look at the bodies, fearing that Armand must lie somewhere amongst them. But then I hear the squeal of steel on steel, coming from somewhere beyond the next bend in the dungeon.

Armand!

I race along the tunnel, hoping that I am not too late to save my friend. When I turn the corner, however, I realise that the situation is dire.

Armand is standing beside Lieutenant Wolf at the far end of the passage. They are hemmed up against the dungeon wall, attempting to hold at bay several dozen Grey Musketeers. The French soldiers are stalking around them like wolves toying with cornered prey.

I remove the lantern from my belt, dim its light and place it in an elevated alcove in the previous corridor. I then draw both of my pistols, take a deep breath to steady my nerves and sneak around the corner. I make my way stealthily down the tunnel, being careful not to disturb the knee-deep water and betray my presence. I stop at the edge of the perimeter of light cast by Armand's lantern and take aim at a Musketeer standing at the rear of the combatants; his magnificently plumed hat and the elaborate hilt of the sword hanging by his side distinguish him as an officer.

'Call off your men and let my friends go!' I yell, stepping boldly into the light. It takes every ounce of my willpower to stop the barrels of my raised pistols from trembling.

Surprised, the Musketeers turn towards me and, seeing the pistols trained on their commander, step warily away from Armand and Lieutenant Wolf. There is an anxious moment of silence. I swallow nervously. Then one of the Frenchmen lunges forward, his blade striking out at Armand, hoping to catch him off-guard.

But the Musketeer's blade never reaches Armand. At the exact moment the French soldier darts forward, I snap one of my pistols towards him and fire. Although I was aiming at the Musketeer's torso, I say a silent prayer when he staggers back to join his companions, clutching his injured thigh.

'I won't be so generous next time,' I snarl, levelling my remaining pistol at the Musketeer officer. 'The next shot takes off your commander's head! Now back away from my companions.'

I'm not too sure if any of the Musketeers understand German, but their commander – a man of perhaps forty years of age, and with the proud demeanour of a Gascon – considers me for some time before grinning ruefully and bowing in acquiescence. He says something in French, and the Musketeers withdraw to the far end of the tunnel.

Armand and Lieutenant Wolf race over to join me, and we start to make our way back up the passage. The Musketeer officer – the barrel of my pistol still trained on him – steps boldly forward and stares at Armand. He calls out again in French, causing Armand's eyes to narrow. Armand says something in return, his tone hostile, to which the Musketeer officer smiles derisively.

We reach the end of the tunnel, and it's just as we are about to turn into the next section of the dungeon that all hell breaks loose. As if some secret cue has been given, several of the Musketeers reach for the pistols tucked into their belts. Aiming my pistol at the first Musketeer to move, I fire a hasty shot that misses its mark. Then, as the deafening report of over a dozen firearms erupt in unison, I race after Armand and Lieutenant Wolf, balls whizzing past us and smacking into the tunnel walls.

Tearing into the next corridor, I pause to collect my lantern, attach it to my belt and continue running. It's not long before we catch up to the remnants of Lieutenant Wolf's soldiers. Offering them assistance, we hustle along the tunnel and disappear around the next turn.

'Move! Move! Move!' Armand yells, urging us onward, snatching a musket from one of the injured Englishmen and staying behind at the end of the tunnel to cover our retreat.

We have barely moved ten yards before – *BLAM!* – Armand fires the musket. Slinging the firearm over his shoulder, the French duellist races after us.

'That will stall the Musketeers for a few seconds,' he says. 'I took one out with a shot to the chest. But they will come after us – so move as if the Devil was at your heels!'

Lieutenant Wolf snarls something through clenched teeth, and the wounded remnants of his force stagger through the water, reaching the next turn in the dungeon. The Lieutenant stays behind, his pistol raised, waiting for the Musketeers to appear. We use this tactic for the next few sections of tunnel – one of us remaining behind to cover our retreat, their discharged firearms momentarily delaying the French – before we make it back to the section of the dungeon with the gunpowder barrels.

Only to find that Captain Lightfoot, von Frankenthal, Francesca and the remaining English soldiers are locked in a savage fight with a Dutch patrol at the far end of the passage.

'This isn't promising,' Armand says, pulling up alongside one of the sets of gunpowder barrels. 'Take everyone down to assist the Captain,' he says to Lieutenant Wolf, who orders his men to charge after him down the tunnel. Armand then looks my way. 'Jakob, I need you to stay here with me. Have you ever wondered what damage a couple of barrels of gunpowder can do to a wall? Well, we're about to find out.'

Armand must have forgotten that I am well and truly aware of the destructive power of ignited gunpowder barrels. I had almost been blown to shreds by one in the tunnel beneath Schloss Kriegsberg. Like a hit to the head with a hammer, that was something I do not want to experience again. There's not much say I have in the matter, however, as we might only have seconds before the Musketeers catch up to us.

Having taken position beside the barrels set in the alcove opposite Armand, I follow his lead and return my pistols to my belt and produce my tinder and flint.

'The Musketeers will be here any second now,' Armand says. 'But we only need to light one of these fuses. The blast from one of these sets of gunpowder barrels will be enough to set the others off. And we don't want to be standing around when that happens. We need to hightail it out of here as soon as one of us manages to ignite a fuse.'

My eyes darting back and forth between the fuse and the end of the tunnel, I work frantically with my tinder and flint, trying to catch a spark on the fuse.

'Mine's lit!' Armand yells after a few attempts.

We leap from the alcoves and race back up the tunnel, but we haven't even covered more than ten yards before we snap our heads around at the sound of splashing water. Several of the Musketeers burst into our section of the dungeon, their pistols raised in preparation to shoot.

'Move!' Armand cries, his head lowered to minimise the target he presents for the French soldiers.

There's a deafening *BLAM!* as the Musketeers discharge their pistols. Balls zip past us: one knocking the hat clear from Armand's head; a second ripping a hole through my cloak. Miraculously, none hit us, and we race back along the tunnel, believing we might somehow manage to survive this, when – *KABOOM!* – the powder kegs explode.

We are instantly caught in the incredible force of the dual explosions. Thrown down the corridor several yards, we land in the water near the bricked-in section of wall, saved from the hellish billowing wall of fire and smoke that roars above us. Staying under the water until the fire has passed, we clamber to our feet.

Armand collects his hat and looks back, inspecting the collapsed section of the dungeon. 'It worked!' he yells, his hearing – like mine – evidently affected by the explosion.

I look down the opposite end of the tunnel and realise that the explosion was so great that it even reached our companions. They are climbing to their feet, preparing to re-engage the remaining dozen or so Dutch soldiers. The smile from having survived the explosion vanishes from my lips the instant my attention is drawn to the petard propped up against the former doorway leading to the prison – its fuse *lit* by the furious blast of the gunpowder barrels.

'Run!' I scream, grabbing Armand by the arm and pulling him after me. 'The petard is about to explode!'

'What? The Devil take us!' Armand curses, and we bolt for dear life.

Barely four heartbeats pass before the petard detonates. A second massive explosion rips through the dungeon, hitting Armand and me with its full fury. Lifted off my feet, I am thrown through the air to slam – hard! – into the tunnel's brick wall.

I sink to my knees; the copper taste of blood in my mouth.

Darkness then takes me.

CHAPTER FOUR

I stir, dragged out of the misty darkness by a dull ache in my forehead. Reaching up, I discover that my head has been bandaged. I also find that I am lying on a bed in what appears to be a cabin aboard a moving ship. There's a chest over to the right and a cloak hanging from a hook on the back of the room's solitary door. A leadlight window set in the wall behind the bed allows orange light – suggesting that it must be sunset – to sway back and forth across the interior of the cabin.

I push myself up on an elbow and realise that I am wearing my undergarments. My clothing is folded at the end of the bed and my weapons are slung over a bedpost. I can also discern the distant sound of many cannons being fired; either that, or there is a distant storm approaching.

Wondering how I arrived here – and curious as to where *here* exactly is – I dress, taking care not to lose my balance, for I still feel light-headed from the injuries sustained in the dungeon. I am strapping on my weapons when the door opens and Francesca and Armand enter the cabin.

'Well, look who it is!' Armand announces with a broad smile and pats me on the shoulder. 'I wasn't expecting to see you on your feet just yet. That head of yours must be thicker than it looks.'

Francesca hurries past him to take me by the arm and directs me to sit on the bed. 'You shouldn't be moving about.' She lifts an edge of the bandage wrapped around my head to inspect the wound. 'You're lucky to have survived with merely a concussion and bruise. But you must rest.'

Armand shakes his head. 'Why does he get all your attention? You have barely left his side since we boarded this vessel. Need I remind you that I, too, was injured during the explosion?'

'You?' Francesca says dismissively. 'There's barely a scratch on you.'

'Barely a scratch!' Armand parts his cloak and lifts his tabard and shirt to reveal a purple bruise on his lower chest. 'What do you call this?'

Francesca arches her eyebrows sarcastically. 'Would you like me to kiss it better?'

Armand and I had first met the beautiful nineteen-year-old Italian during our mission to recover the Tablet of Breaking. Francesca's skills as one of the *Custodiatti* – the

Vatican's covert unit of professional tomb-robbers – had proved invaluable in leading us through the trap-riddled mausoleum lying at the bottom of the Dead Sea. She was so impressed by the Hexenjäger that she decided to leave the *Custodiatti* and join our order. She is still awaiting approval from the Vatican.

'As a matter of fact, yes, I would.' Armand points at his lips. 'And seeing that I was also hurt here, you can . . .'

'Stop right there.' Francesca raises a hand to interrupt the Frenchman. 'I'm not going to even entertain the thought.'

'Entertain what thought?' Armand asks, feigning ignorance. His eyes then widen in shock, and he shakes a finger at the Italian tomb-robber. 'Francesca! Well, I never! You must learn to control such thoughts.'

Francesca rolls her eyes. 'How do you feel?' she asks me, ignoring Armand.

Despite the pain in my head, I cannot help but laugh at Armand. 'Like I've been hit by von Frankenthal,' I say. 'But where are we? The last thing I remember is running away from the petard, and then the explosion. But we are now aboard a ship and, if I'm not mistaken, I can hear cannons being fired. What's happened?'

'The explosion from the petard threw you straight into the dungeon wall. It was one hell of a hit; you're lucky it didn't crack your skull,' Armand says. 'Not surprisingly, you were knocked unconscious. I was also thrown into the wall, but despite sustaining injuries that would have killed a less handsome man,' he boasts, with a sideways glance at Francesca, 'I carried you into one of the elevated alcoves, where von Frankenthal kept guard over you and the wounded. Captain Lightfoot's men then dispatched the remaining Dutch soldiers, and we entered the prison. Having fought our way past the guards, our English allies set about freeing their countrymen. Francesca and I ran ahead into the southern wing of the prison, where the Spanish and German prisoners were kept.'

'And did you find my father?' I ask hopefully, hanging off Armand's every word.

The Frenchman reaches out to place a hand on my shoulder, almost as if to brace me for what he is about to say. 'Those cells weren't even fit for rats, let alone human beings. We searched each and every cell, but we could not find your father. In the very last cell we checked, however, we found a very sick prisoner lying on the floor. He was a veteran German soldier from the wars in the Low Countries; the last of a company of dragoons that had been captured by the French outside Breda over a decade ago.'

'What?' I say, barely believing what I am hearing. 'So he was a member of my father's company?'

Armand nods. 'And he knew what had become of him.' He pauses, and his hold on my shoulder tightens. 'Apparently your father spent only one night in the Devil's Bowels. The next morning, he was taken from his cell to be executed. But it's now that this story gets interesting.'

'What do you mean?' I ask, a cold numbness overcoming me.

'A month or two after your father was taken from his

cell, another German soldier – who unfortunately only survived a month in the Devil's Bowels – was locked within the prison,' Armand continues. 'As it turned out, he also knew your father, having served under him in Flanders. What's interesting is that he informed the other prisoner that your father could not have possibly been executed, for he had seen your father, alive and well, the day after he had been taken prisoner.'

I shake my head in bewilderment. 'How can that be possible?'

'I don't know. But the plot gets even thicker.' Armand pauses and leans in close, as if what he is about to tell me is secret. 'The second prisoner had been taken captive by a company of French soldiers serving in the Low Countries. The prisoner had said that he had seen your father in the enemy French camp, coming out of a tent accompanied by Henri de la Tour d'Auvergne, Vicomte de Turenne, who is now marshal-general of France. Your father was not under arrest. On the contrary, Turenne appeared to be taking orders from *him*.'

I rise from the bed and stare hard into Armand's eyes. 'What? So he wasn't executed? My father is still alive!'

'Yes, according to the information we received,' Francesca says. 'But what do you make of all this?'

'I don't know what to think just at this moment,' I say, and pace the cabin. 'It seems that the deeper I dig into my father's past, the deeper the mystery gets. Up until a few months ago all I knew of him was that he had been a cavalry commander in the Low Countries, fighting alongside the

Spanish against the French. I also knew that he had lived for some time in Spain. But now I know that he not only had an affair with the cousin of the Marquis of Ayamonte, deep in the Andalusian region of southern Spain – and had two children with her – but he had been taken out of the Devil's Bowels to be executed, only to appear several months later in a French camp, giving orders to Turenne.' I pause and look at my friends. 'What's going on?'

Armand rubs his chin and clicks his tongue in thought. 'It doesn't sound promising. If the second prisoner's information is correct, then it appears that your father, although fighting for the Spanish, had at least one powerful ally in the French army. I hate to be the one to say it, but your father may have been working for the French.'

I stare at Armand for some time, cut by his words, yet knowing that he is probably speaking the truth. 'I need to see the prisoner who told you this,' I say at length. 'He may have more information.'

Francesca shakes her head. 'I'm sorry, but he refused to leave his cell. He wanted to remain behind to see the look on his captors' faces when they discovered that the gaol had been freed of prisoners. Besides, he was so emaciated and sick that I very much doubt he would have survived the journey back with us.' She smiles softly. 'Let's not dwell on this for now. You were unconscious for over fifteen hours. You must be famished. Let's have some food.'

'Fifteen hours!' I say. It's also only now that I realise that my original question hasn't been fully answered. 'Where are we?'

'After we freed the prisoners, we followed Captain Light-foot back through the dungeon and escaped into the Meuse, where we boarded some concealed skiffs and made our way out to the Channel,' Armand says. 'Once there, we boarded an English warship and sailed into deeper waters, where we joined up with an English fleet. It was then that a Dutch fleet came out to intercept us. I never knew ships could move so fast. With the wind behind them, they pursued us like hawks swooping out of the sky. Whilst the rest of the English ships turned back to engage the Dutch – the sounds of the distant sea battle you can still hear – we made our escape. And so, Jakob, the winds of fate are blowing us towards England.'

CHAPTER FIVE

Having decided to stretch my legs and take a look around the ship, we leave the cabin and find von Frankenthal up on deck. He is excited to see me – he hugs me so hard he almost crushes me to death. We then watch the distant sea battle for some time, fascinated by the orange flashes of cannon-fire lighting up the darkening horizon. At length, Lieutenant Wolf comes over to greet us, conveys his admiration in seeing me on my feet again, and informs us that Captain Lightfoot has requested that we dine with him tonight.

As we are following the Lieutenant to a doorway set in the stern of the quarter deck, I notice something on the opposite side of the ship. It appears to be a figure enveloped in shadow, like some spectre materialised from beyond the grave. Upon closer inspection I realise that it is in fact a woman, wrapped in the folds of a full-length black cloak. I shudder when, beneath her wide-brimmed black hat, I catch a glimpse of letters tattooed across her forehead, bringing back memories of Heinrich von Dornheim, the tattoo-covered witch hunter I had encountered in Schloss Kriegsberg.

Rather than observe the distant battle, the shadowy figure is carefully watching *us*, and a cold shiver runs across my skin when I suspect that she has been doing so the entire time that we have been on the deck. I also notice the wary glances the ship's crew pay her, and the way in which they avoid the section of the deck where she is standing, as if they – sea-hardened sailors who use language that could make even the Devil blush – have something to fear, almost as if Death itself is standing aboard the vessel.

I am about to draw my companions' attention to her, when Lieutenant Wolf opens the cabin door and ushers us inside. In contrast to the sparse furnishings of the cabin where I had rested, this room has the trappings of wealth: an ornately carved bookcase is set against a wall, crammed with sea charts and heavy leather volumes; several framed paintings of seascapes adorn the walls; gilded candelabra are set atop the polished surface of a central oak table.

Captain Lightfoot is sitting at the head of the table. I'm surprised to find that the two men sitting on either side of the Captain – one dressed in the lace and finery of lords and dukes; the other in a red cassock and with a large silver crucifix hanging from his neck – regard him with deference. When I see the portrait of Captain Lightfoot on the far wall, however, I exchange a suspicious glance with my companions.

'My Lords and Excellency, your guests have arrived,' Lieutenant Wolf announces in German, before exiting the cabin and closing the door behind him.

'If your real name is Captain Lightfoot then I'm the Queen of Sheba! What game are you playing at?' von Frankenthal demands of the Captain. 'And you,' he adds, pointing at the man sitting on Captain Lightfoot's left, 'we rescued you from the prison. But you were wearing sailor's clothing back then. Now you're decked out like the King of England!'

'Captain Lightfoot?' the lavishly dressed man says in stilted German, suppressing a grin as he twirls the edge of his moustache. He is perhaps the same age as the Captain, in his mid-forties, and his long black hair is tied back in a ponytail. A silk-embroidered cape is slung over his shoulder, and the cuffs of his shirt are accentuated with lace. Although this is an extravagance usually reserved for dandies, there is a devilish glint in his youthful eyes – a warning that he will not hesitate to draw the elaborately carved broadsword slung over the rear of his seat. 'It's been a long time since I have heard that name. When did you last use it? Now, let me think – wasn't it just after the fall of York?'

Captain Lightfoot smiles. 'Not York. But you are close. It was that time we almost got caught after the Battle of Naseby. They were good times.'

'They wouldn't have been too good had you been caught,' corrects the man with the pony tail. 'Even with a false name, I'm sure the Parliamentarians would have recognised your face. And I can't believe you risked your life to rescue *me* from the Devil's Bowels. What if you had been captured? The risk was too great.'

'But I wasn't caught, was I?' Captain Lightfoot returns. 'Besides, who else was going to save you? And that wasn't the first time I've had to pull you out of trouble. Remember when we were at Armentières and you were hit by a musket ball?'

The Captain's companion rubs his leg. 'How could I forget? It's not as if you don't take a private pleasure in reminding me of the incident, my dear Prince Rupert.'

'Prince Rupert!' I blurt, barely believing my ears. 'The German prince who left his homeland to command King Charles's cavalry forces during the English Civil War?'

The man with the pony tail makes an elaborate flourish at the Prince. 'And the same who, having been unfairly dismissed from the King's service, sailed as a privateer throughout the Caribbean, only to be reinstated as an Admiral of the English fleet and given command of the King's flagship, the *Royal Charles* – which you happen to be aboard.'

Prince Rupert gestures at his companion. 'And the same who, throughout all of his adventures – whether it be leading cavalry charges during the Civil War, or roving the Caribbean in search of Spanish treasure fleets – has been accompanied by his comrade-in-arms, Sir Robert Holmes, now Rear Admiral of the Red squadron.' Prince Rupert looks back at us. 'I am sorry for the subterfuge, but I could not risk letting the enemy know that I had snuck into Rotterdam. Our heads are much coveted by the Dutch and French – although, Robert's, I must say, is not as handsome as mine.'

'So this was all a ploy to rescue Sir Robert?' I ask, feeling as if we haven't just had the wool pulled over our eyes, but that an entire cartload of fleece has been shoved in our faces.

'No, it wasn't a ploy,' Prince Rupert says, and I immediately believe the sincerity in his voice. 'The Dutch were indeed planning on placing recently captured English soldiers in the hulls of Dutch merchant vessels. It just so happened that, unbeknownst to the Dutch, they had captured a Rear Admiral of the English fleet during a naval engagement last week. We are fortunate that Sir Robert had changed his clothing just before being captured, hiding his identity. Otherwise, all that would have been left to rescue might have been his head, stuck on a pole somewhere in the Dutch Republic.'

'I still cannot believe that the Dutch have resorted to such a base act as placing prisoners of war aboard their vessels,' Sir Robert says. 'What will they think of next?'

Prince Rupert raises his eyebrows and sighs. 'It seems that your raid on West-Terschelling has stirred the beehive somewhat. But enough of that for now ... I don't believe I have formally introduced our guests.'

He proceeds to introduce each of us in turn, his eyes lingering for some time on Francesca, obviously drawn by her beauty. 'You owe your life to them,' he says, looking back at Sir Robert. 'Without their assistance, I very much doubt we could have completed the rescue mission. This one in particular –' he points at Armand '– fights like a demon fresh out of Hell. Not even I would dare draw steel on him.' Prince Rupert pauses and clears his throat, signifying that the remaining man seated at the table – clad in the red cassock and with an upward curl to his top lip, giving the appearance of a permanent sneer – should pay attention. The man has paid us scant interest since we entered the cabin, his eyes focused on the goblet he rotates on the table between his thumb and forefinger. 'I should also point out, Your Excellency, that the men and boy are Hexenjäger. Although, I assume you had already surmised as much, based on the crimson tabards they wear beneath their cloaks.'

No sooner has Prince Rupert uttered these words than the man with the permanent sneer looks up and considers us with intense interest. 'Hexenjäger! This is indeed fortuitous,' he says in fluent German, licking his lips, as if we are some morsel he is about to taste. He looks us up and down before nodding in a satisfied manner. 'The Lord does indeed smile on us this day.'

'What difference does it make to you if we are Hexenjäger?' Armand asks warily, staring the man straight in the eye, bearing the authority of his newly appointed position as Lieutenant. 'It was merely circumstance that brought us together, and we will have our leave as soon as we land in England.'

The man rises from his seat. 'The fact that you are witch hunters is of the greatest interest to me. And the fact that you have been delivered to us on this very day can be considered as nothing less than providence.' He crosses over to us, leans in close and whispers, 'For England is about to wage war with the Devil and is in need of your services.'

CHAPTER SIX

P rince Rupert asks us to sit around the table before introducing the man with the sneer as Humphrey Henchman, the Bishop of London.

'He is not part of the normal company aboard this ship,' the Prince explains. 'He rendezvoused with the *Royal Charles* only an hour before we left the Dutch coast. He brings news of the greatest gravity; news that must be reported back to King Charles and the Archbishop of Canterbury. I'm sure, too, it is news that will be of great interest to a company of witch hunters, even those who are keen to return to the Holy Roman Empire.'

Armand folds his arms across his chest. 'What manner of danger is your country in?'

Sitting by his side, I shift uncomfortably, wary of what we may be dragged into, since we have already been tricked once by our present company. Bishop Henchman looks across at Prince Rupert, who nods in consent.

'Have you heard of the Codex Gigas?' the Bishop asks, his voice lowered, as if merely mentioning the name of the text is something that should be feared.

Armand looks at each of us in turn before shaking his head. 'No. None of us have.'

Bishop Henchman's eyes narrow. 'Then perhaps I should refer to the codex as it is more commonly known. Tell me, witch hunters, have you heard of the Devil's Bible?'

The candles in the cabin seem to flicker, yet there is no draught in the room.

The Devil's Bible! Who has not heard of this text?

It is the most infamous manuscript ever written. It was created in the thirteenth century by a monk who, as an act of penance for sins committed, copied the Bible. According to legend, he completed this task in a single night, but only because he was assisted by the Devil. In return, the Devil claimed the monk's soul.

What makes the codex truly unique is that the monk dedicated a page of the manuscript to a drawing of the Devil. There is also a section at the end of the manuscript containing spells for exorcising and summoning demons.

'We have heard of this text,' Armand says, his blue eyes betraying no emotion. 'But why do you ask?'

'It is a little-known fact that the forces of Sweden took possession of the Codex Gigas after sacking Prague in 1648,' Bishop Henchman explains. 'The text was taken to Sweden, where it has remained locked within a vault in the

Swedish National Library in Stockholm and guarded by an order of twenty elite warriors.'

Armand nods. 'The Brothers of the Sacred Trust were created for the specific task of guarding the Devil's Bible. They are commanded by Staffan Ostergaard, Sweden's most revered soldier.'

The Bishop toys with his goblet for a few seconds before he looks up at Armand, his expression grave. 'I have just returned from Stockholm. My three companions – who I will introduce shortly – and I had hoped to check how securely the codex was guarded. But we were too late, for six days ago it was stolen.'

Armand's eyes flash with alarm. 'By whom?'

'A lone swordsman,' the Bishop says. 'He slew four of the Brothers of the Sacred Trust in order to reach the codex. The swordsman was impervious to the guards' blades and firearms, which had been blessed by the Church. His eyes dripped blood, and he was accompanied by a massive hound.' The Bishop pauses, letting the gravity of this news settle into our bones. 'We know of this swordsman,' he continues, his voice little more than a whisper. 'He is one of the Sons of Cain.'

Armand leans forward and stares boldly at Bishop Henchman. 'You say this name as if we should have reason to be afraid. You forget that we are Hexenjäger. Now tell me, who are these Sons of Cain?'

Armand may be confident, but my knees – which are thankfully hidden beneath the table – are trembling like a tenor's tonsils.

'The Sons of Cain had their origin during the wave of violence that swept across England during the Civil War,' Bishop Henchman explains. 'Many atrocities were committed during the war; entire towns were often at the mercy of marauding soldiers who took up the banner of King or Parliament as a pretext to profiteer through pillage and plunder. Not even the Protestant Church was spared. It was seen as a centre of popish idolatry, with its bishops and altars modelled on Rome. All perceived signs of Catholicism were targeted: altars were desecrated, effigies of Christ were ripped from walls, and stained-glass windows were smashed.'

'And yet, I bet, as is so often the case, both Royalists and Parliamentarians claimed God was on their side,' von Frankenthal scoffs. 'The hypocrisy of man knows no bounds.'

'Morality becomes blurred during war,' Prince Rupert says, nodding in agreement. 'But it is the very nature of war that makes it unavoidable. Both soldiers and civilians – at least, those who are suspected of aiding and abetting the enemy – are legitimate targets of war. We can only hope that God turns a blind eye to the conduct of man during such times.'

I have heard that the Prince was criticised by both Parliamentarians and his own Royalist forces for the way in which he waged war across England during the Civil War. Having fought in the Thirty Years' War and trained in Continental warfare, he often allowed the soldiers under his command to loot indiscriminately from

44

Parliamentarian towns and households. Not surprisingly, he had been branded as the Devil incarnate by Parliamentarian propaganda.

'There were four Parliamentarian cavalry soldiers who rode with General Ireton's troop, and who took their hatred of the King and Church to the extreme, signing an unholy pact with the Devil to rid England of what they claimed to be a Papal plague,' Bishop Henchman continues, drawing the discussion back to its initial focus. 'According to legend, the pact was signed under an oak tree in a graveyard located several leagues south of London. The pact, signed on a leather satchel, was pinned to the trunk of the oak. It was finalised by a bloody act through which the Sons of Cain received their name: they each slew their younger brother and hung them in gibbets from the branches of the oak tree, which was henceforth known as the Hanging Tree. The remains of the brothers still hang in the gibbets. They are known as the Forsaken.

'The Sons of Cain were given unholy eternal life through their pact, but only as long as the satchel is pinned to the tree and the Forsaken are denied their last rites. But the Sons of Cain delved deep into the dark arts to gain other powers. They also summoned four Hell Hounds to guard the Hanging Tree.'

'Charming,' von Frankenthal remarks, his lips curled in distaste. 'And now you want us to deal with your problem?'

A reproachful look from Armand silences the witch hunter. 'Tell us more about these Sons of Cain.'

'They started their reign of terror in Yorkshire, destroying churches and preying on Royalist patrols at night time,' Prince Rupert says. 'Having slain their victims, they hung their bodies from trees bordering roadways as a warning to all supporters of King Charles. When they moved west they became bolder, engaging entire companies of soldiers. In the later years of the war, a Royalist infantry unit of over a hundred men was camped several miles outside Oxford, where the King – no longer safe in London, which had become a Parliamentarian stronghold – had taken residence. The Sons of Cain tore into the camp and slaughtered the unit, leaving only a sole survivor to spread word of their butchery. I rode out the following day to inspect the camp. Never before, in over thirty years of soldiery, have I seen such carnage.'

The Prince pauses for some time before continuing. 'Their leader, Alistair McClodden, is as wild and savage as the Highlands he hails from. He's a giant of a man, standing nearly as tall as our friend here.' He jerks his chin at von Frankenthal. 'He used the Civil War as a pretext to enact revenge against the Protestant Church for burning his mother as a witch. You should be warned: he has a particular hatred of witch hunters.'

That's just fantastic. What is the Prince going to tell us next? That one of the Sons of Cain has a particular dislike of sixteen-year-old boys named Jakob, and who wield Pappenheimer rapiers?

'They were often seen upon black horses, so it wasn't long before people started calling them the Four Riders of the Apocalypse,' Prince Rupert continues, driving another nail into my coffin of fear. 'Consumed by the Devil's hatred of humanity, the Sons of Cain started slaughtering all they came across, even the most devout of Parliamentarian Puritans. They were corrupted by the evil that coursed through their veins like poison – their skin turned the ghastly colour of plague victims and they bled from their eyes.'

A long silence greets his words. The world suddenly feels darker and menacing, and I focus on the wan light cast by the candelabra on the table. At length, I shift uncomfortably and clear my throat, drawing everyone's attention.

'Why hasn't anybody removed the satchel and given last rites to the bodies on the Hanging Tree?' I ask.

'Dozens have tried over the years, but all have failed,' Bishop Henchman says. 'Not even Witch Finder General Matthew Hopkins – the most infamous witch hunter in England during the period of the Civil War – could get within fifty yards of the Hanging Tree. He was forced to retreat after six of his companions were torn to shreds by the Hell Hounds that guard the cemetery. It is also rumoured that the Sons of Cain have a lair hidden somewhere within the cemetery, in which they rest in stone coffins.'

'But you want us to try,' Armand says matter-of-factly, resting back in his seat, his eyes locked on the surface of the table. 'You want the Hexenjäger to kill the Sons of Cain.'

The Bishop nods. 'That's correct.'

Armand clicks his tongue in thought for some time. 'We might help you,' he says and looks hard into the

Bishop's eyes. 'But only if we are told the *whole* story. You have failed to share with us, for instance, why the Sons of Cain stole the Devil's Bible. And I must warn you, do not try to deceive us.'

Bishop Henchman casts a furtive glance at Prince Rupert, as if seeking approval to answer Armand's question. The Prince nods.

'Last century,' Bishop Henchman begins, 'an English prophetess by the name of Mother Shipton made the following prophecy:

> From the Latviumus text
> The False Prophet spawned,
> Summoned by Cain's Brood,
> Between midnight's final stroke
> And the birth of dawn,
> Upon the Altar of Sun,
> Buried beneath Saint Mellitus's beheaded edifice,
> Fifty days since heaven's darkness,
> Spawned in the flames of the City of Gemini,
> Only just risen from rotting pestilence.'

Von Frankenthal screws up his nose. 'It seems a load of gibberish to me.'

Armand raises a hand, signalling for him not to interrupt. 'Riddles can be interpreted in many ways, my friend.' He then addresses Bishop Henchman. 'How have you interpreted the prophecy?'

'Perhaps it is best if I leave that up to one of the people

responsible for breaking the riddle,' the Bishop says, rising from his seat and crossing the cabin to open the door. A few moments later, he ushers into the room three black-clad figures who join us around the table.

One of them is the woman whom I had noticed watching us aboard the deck. Sitting only a few feet away from her, I can now clearly make out the Latin inscription tattooed across her forehead: *dies irae*.

Translation: Judgement Day.

The hilt of a blade juts out from beneath her cloak, its metal pommel in the form of an angel whose hands are joined in supplication. As the woman takes off her leather gloves and rests her hands on the table, I notice crucifixes tattooed on her knuckles. It is her eyes, however, to which I am drawn, for they resemble those of an elderly person, being rheumy and set in sunken, wrinkled sockets, yet the woman could not be any older than thirty.

One of her companions, a man in his mid-twenties, is similarly dressed in a black cloak, hat, breeches and doublet. Rather than have an inscription tattooed across his forehead, twin silver crucifixes dangle from piercings located at the edge of his eyebrows. His face has been powdered white, but his lips have been blackened. A phial, containing what appears to be blood, hangs from a silver chain around his neck. The heavy butts of two pistols protrude through the folds of his cloak, and he has a long-barrelled rifle propped against the table. He sits rigidly in his seat and his eyes dart around the room, as if he is in a state of constant distraction.

The third person is a man of perhaps sixty years of age, clad in the same clothing as his younger companions. A heavy leather volume – which I can only assume is a copy of the *Malleus Maleficarum*, the book of the witch hunter – is slung over his shoulder in a leather case, its surface scratched and worn. Beneath the shadow cast by his hat, thin wisps of grey hair frame a wrinkled forehead and piercing blue eyes, which quickly assess us and note the weapons jutting beneath our cloaks. Age may have left its withered signature in the man's skin, but he holds himself tall and proud, conveying strength and authority.

You don't need to be the sharpest blade in the armoury to tell that they are witch hunters.

Having introduced us as members of the Hexenjäger, Bishop Henchman jerks his chin towards the elderly witch hunter. 'This is Witch Finder Israel Blackwood,' he says, then gestures at the woman and man in turn. 'And this is Prayer and Dorian, members of the *Angeli Mortis*. Fortunately, they are fluent in German, having spent some time hunting witches in the Protestant states of the Holy Roman Empire.'

The *Angeli Mortis* – meaning Angels of Death in Latin – are England's most revered unit of witch hunters. Only last year some of their order came under investigation by the Protestant Church, accused of delving into the dark arts. All that the team of church officials could find, however, was that the *Angeli Mortis* had unlocked the deepest secrets of the *Malleus Maleficarum*. It is rumoured that some of them can converse with the dead.

It is to Witch Finder Israel Blackwood, one of the most experienced witch hunters in England, that I find my eyes drawn. Even as far away as Saxony, his exploits are talked of. A former companion of Witch Finder General Matthew Hopkins and John Stearne, he had hunted witches and warlocks across the entire length of England during the period of the Civil War. After Hopkins's death, he became somewhat of a recluse, spending almost a decade – if the rumours were true – living in a ruined Norman keep somewhere near Penzance, in the south-east of England, devoting his time to studying the *Malleus Maleficarum*. Then, some four years ago – coinciding with the time that Emperor Leopold created the Hexenjäger – Charles II, who was restored as the King of England in 1660, commissioned the creation of the *Angeli Mortis*. Naturally, Israel Blackwood was selected to lead the order, appointed the position of Witch Finder.

Bishop Henchman toys with his goblet again. 'The *Angeli Mortis* have been working on Mother Shipton's riddle for some time now. It has been a personal obsession of Witch Finder Blackwood's for the past twenty years, ever since the Sons of Cain signed their pact with the Devil.' He stops rotating the goblet, leans closer and stares at Armand, his features dark and foreboding. 'Many people have tried to interpret the riddle, witch hunter. But I believe that only Witch Finder Blackwood has been able to decipher its true meaning. He believes the prophecy heralds the coming of the Antichrist.'

CHAPTER SEVEN

'The first line of Mother Shipton's riddle – "From the Latviumus text" – refers to the Codex Gigas,' Witch Finder Blackwood explains, his voice sounding like the grinding wheels of a medieval torture device. 'The codex was created in the Monastery of Podlažice in Bohemia. The monastery, however, had been built on top of a much earlier Roman settlement called Latviumus. The second line – "The False Prophet spawned" – refers to the coming of the Antichrist, as prophesied in the Book of Revelation of John.

'The next three lines – "Summoned by Cain's Brood, between midnight's final stroke and the birth of dawn" – refer to the Sons of Cain using the Codex Gigas to summon the Antichrist between the hours of midnight and the rising sun. This ritual must be performed upon an "Altar of Sun, buried beneath Saint Mellitus's beheaded edifice", which refers to Saint Paul's Cathedral in London. Saint Mellitus was the founder of the cathedral, the steeple of which was struck by lightning in 1561. Legend has it that the cathedral was built atop an earlier pagan temple devoted to Mithras, the sun god. We have conducted extensive searches of the cathedral, particularly focusing on its crypt, but we are yet to find any evidence of an entryway to a subterranean temple. "The City of Gemini" refers to London, a city often associated with the zodiacal sign of Gemini. London has also just emerged from the plague – "only just risen from rotting pestilence".

'We also know that the Sons of Cain will attempt to summon the Antichrist this Sunday, being "fifty days since unnatural darkness", when an eclipse occurred. According to the prophecy, the Antichrist will be "spawned in the flames of the City of Gemini". London, it appears, will be consumed by a great fire, from which the Prince of Darkness will rise.'

Armand's eyes narrow. 'That means you only have three days to stop this from happening.'

Bishop Henchman nods gravely. 'We are on our way back from Stockholm, where the *Angeli Mortis* had hoped to assist the Brothers of the Sacred Trust in guarding the Devil's Bible. We had warned the Swedish authorities of the Sons of Cain some time ago, and they had assured us that they had taken the necessary precautions. But their precautions were evidently inadequate, and we were too late. The Devil's Bible has already fallen into the hands of the Sons of Cain, who are no doubt returning to London, from where they will use it to summon the Antichrist.' Bishop Henchman drums his bony fingers on the table and stares deep into Armand's eyes. 'And that is why we are in need of your help.'

Witch Finder Blackwood stares at Bishop Henchman and shakes his head. 'The *Angeli Mortis* work alone. And we most certainly will not work with Catholics.'

'Not this time,' the Bishop says, returning the Witch Finder's stare. 'The Hexenjäger are the finest witch hunters in the Holy Roman Empire. Had we time, we would send for more of them to come to our assistance. But we don't, and so we must be content with these few who the Lord has sent our way. And I would not question their ability. Some of the Hexenjäger were recently involved in slaying four fallen angels and preventing Armageddon. Who knows, you might even find that you will learn some things from them.'

Witch Finder Blackwood snorts derisively. 'If your Excellency believes so.'

My eyes flash with surprise, believing that our previous mission had been cloaked in secrecy. I exchange a baffled look with Armand and Francesca – both of whom had also taken part in the quest to locate and destroy the Tablet of Breaking – before turning to Bishop Henchman. 'How do you know of the Watchers?'

'It is my station to know such things,' the Bishop returns confidently, almost arrogantly. 'The Lord sees and hears everything, and I am the Lord's eyes and ears on earth.'

He looks at Armand. 'So, you will help us?' His tone suggests that he is not used to people refusing his requests.

Armand considers Bishop Henchman for some time, his brow heavy with thought, before glancing at von Frankenthal, Francesca and me. At length, the newly appointed Lieutenant is forced to give his first command decision and gives a solemn nod.

'Let's make it clear that I won't be held accountable for their deaths.' Witch Finder Blackwood gestures with a flick of his head towards us and stabs a finger on the table to emphasise his point. 'Nor of any political backlash that may result from when the Holy Roman Emperor asks as to why his Catholic witch hunters died in a Protestant land.'

'I will deal with the finer political matters,' Bishop Henchman says.

'As you always do, your Excellency,' Witch Finder Blackwood says, then withdraws into brooding silence.

Bishop Henchman relaxes back into his seat and attempts to smile. His stern features, evidently not used to the expression, strain against the effort and the resulting smile looks more like a lecherous sneer. 'But I very much doubt a report will be lodged concerning the deaths of these Hexenjäger. On the contrary, I imagine we will send a report on how they slew the Sons of Cain, prevented the coming of the False Prophet and saved England.'

Well, there's at least one vote of confidence. I don't think Witch Finder Blackwood shares his optimism, though. He is glaring at Francesca and me, as if questioning what use we could be to this mission, given our age and assumed lack of experience.

Noticing the Witch Finder's glare, Armand looks over at me and smiles reassuringly. But even he cannot mask his concern; his eyes, usually dancing with excitement, are narrow and troubled, as if he has just committed us to entering Hell.

CHAPTER EIGHT

'I hope you have made the right decision,' Francesca says to Armand once we have eaten and returned to my cabin. 'Wouldn't it have been prudent to receive permission from the Grand Hexenjäger before agreeing to join forces with the *Angeli Mortis*?'

'The decision has been made,' Armand says, taking off his hat and cloak, which he tosses upon the bed. He loosens the collar of the shirt beneath his tabard. 'Christian and I are now committed.' He looks across at Francesca and me. 'But you're not. Francesca, as you aren't officially part of our order, I'm giving you the chance to walk away. As this is not an official Hexenjäger mission, I'm also giving you, Jakob, the chance to say no. This has the potential to be the most dangerous mission we have ever been on. No one will think any less of you if you decide not to go ahead.'

Before I have a chance to respond, Francesca's jaw drops in shock and she plants her hands on her hips defiantly. 'What? And you'll think I'll do that – just walk away? Leave you to face the Sons of Cain by yourselves? I cannot believe you asked me that. I thought you knew me better, Armand Breteuil!' She spits his name as if it were poison in her mouth. 'I'm shocked to think that, after all we have been through, you still question my abilities because I am a *woman*.'

A hurt look crosses Armand's face, as if he has been wrongly chastened. He raises his hands, indicating that Francesca should calm down and takes a step towards her. 'I didn't mean to offend you. I no longer question your abilities. I haven't since the last mission we went on. You would be a welcome addition to our team.' He pauses and considers her for some time, his eyes soft. 'I just don't want to see you get hurt, that's all.'

Francesca stares at Armand, a blank expression on her face, as if caught off guard by the sincerity of his words. 'Well . . . you're worrying unnecessarily,' she says at length. 'I can take care of myself, so let's not discuss this matter again.'

I feel sorry for Armand. Having recently been appointed Lieutenant, he has been placed in the unenviable position of having to make decisions that could endanger the lives of those under his command. But in this particular situation, the people under his command are his friends.

'I won't turn my back on you either,' I say to Armand. 'We're in this together. And you made the right decision in saying that we would offer the *Angeli Mortis* our assistance. What else could we have done? We don't have time to seek the Grand Hexenjäger's consent. We've become terribly sidetracked from our original purpose of searching for my father, but a decision had to be made, then and there. Besides, we don't know for certain that the Antichrist is going to be summoned from the pages of the Devil's Bible. All we are basing this on is Witch Finder Blackwood's interpretation of Mother Shipton's prophecy. As you have already said, riddles are open for multiple interpretations. Perhaps this will amount to nothing.'

Armand rubs his chin in thought and paces the cabin. 'Our order firmly believes that this year, 1666, will herald the arrival of the Prince of Darkness. But we have been unsuccessful in trying to determine when exactly this will occur. Some Hexenjäger even travelled to Sweden last year to examine the Devil's Bible, believing the manuscript may hold some clue. For over a month they studied the codex, but found nothing.'

Von Frankenthal shakes his head in a frustrated manner. 'The leaders of our order have also spent a lot of time studying the stars, believing the Antichrist's arrival might be revealed through astronomy. Instead of searching for portents of doom in the heavens, they should have been keeping a close eye on what was happening down here on earth, and in particular, what their English counterparts were up to.'

Armand waves a hand dismissively. 'We cannot blame our leaders for not making this discovery. They have been anything but complacent. They just weren't aware of Mother Shipton or her prophecy. Had they been, I'm sure it would have given them cause to examine the Devil's Bible more carefully.' He stops pacing the cabin and clicks his tongue in thought, his expression grim. 'Perhaps Jakob is right, and the prophecy will amount to nothing. But what if it is true – and the Antichrist will be summoned from the pages of the Devil's Bible?'

'Then you made the right decision, and we are all behind you,' I say. 'Irrespective of whether we are here due to providence or chance, our blades are needed.'

Von Frankenthal, forever a supporter of swift, decisive action, tousles my hair in admiration. 'That's the spirit, lad. Just hearing about the Sons of Cain makes my blood boil. Even if this prophecy turns out to be a load of nonsense, we can at least slay these demonic soldiers. I'm not too sure about the *Angeli Mortis*, though. Their leader, Blackwood, doesn't seem too keen to join forces with us.'

'We will try to act independently of them,' Armand says. 'We will offer them our blades, but we certainly won't be placed under Blackwood's command. Let's make it very clear that none of you are to take orders from anybody but me.'

'I'm not going to argue about that,' I say. Just being in the same room as the *Angeli Mortis* makes me feel nervous.

'We share a common goal,' Armand continues, 'but I am wary of the *Angeli Mortis*. They are witch hunters, but they have been corrupted by the *Malleus Maleficarum*.'

'So the rumours are true?' I ask. 'Can some of them actually speak with the dead?'

Armand shrugs. 'I don't know. But the entire time we were seated at the table, Dorian kept looking around, almost as if he was watching ghosts move about the room.'

I cast a furtive glance around the cabin, wondering if there are indeed ghosts wandering aboard the *Royal Charles*.

'Why have they done that to themselves?' Francesca asks. 'They have received special powers, but at a terrible price.'

Armand plonks himself down on the edge of the bed and sighs. 'Our world is threatened by Satan's servants. The *Angeli Mortis* have merely armed themselves for the coming war.'

'But the Hexenjäger have not resorted to such lengths,' Francesca points out. 'You aren't covered in tattoos and piercings. Nor have you been corrupted by the *Malleus Maleficarum*.'

'The only reason we haven't been corrupted by the Hammer of the Witches is because we are wary of its powers,' Armand explains. 'Even its creators, the Inquisitors Sprenger and Kramer, were cautious of delving too deep into its secrets. Our order ensures that the text is studied under strict guidance and supervision. I, for one, will go nowhere near it.' He lies on the bed, yawns and rubs his eyes. 'Regarding tattoos and piercings, the Grand Hexenjäger has strictly forbidden such practices. Although witch hunters protect all that is good and fight the Devil's forces, there are many who are afraid of us. The Inquisition has left a bloody legacy, and many perceive orders such as the Hexenjäger and *Angeli Mortis* as merely other vengeful arms of the Church, finding evidence of witchcraft in every household and using torture to extract confessions from the innocent. Of course, we do no such thing – nor do the *Angeli Mortis* – but the appearance of the *Angeli Mortis* spreads fear amongst all who see them. Perhaps that is why they were placed under investigation by the Protestant Church. The Hexenjäger, on the other hand, want people to know that we can be trusted. Like the *Angeli Mortis*, we too use holy inscriptions in Latin. But rather than tattoo them across our foreheads, we reserve them for our blades and firearms; the very instruments we use to slay Satan's forces. As you are well and truly aware, the *Milites Christi* and the *Custodiatti* use the same practice.'

'Let that be a lesson to you, Jakob,' von Frankenthal says. 'I know that Captain Blodklutt has recently been instructing you in how to use the *Malleus Maleficarum*. Be careful. I won't even touch the text.'

I had no idea that the *Malleus Maleficarum* could corrupt its user to such an extent. I nod, heeding his warning. 'I just want to be the best witch hunter I can.'

Armand points a cautionary finger at me. 'I'm sure Dorian and Prayer will tell you exactly the same thing. Trust in your sword-arm. That's the one true thing you can rely on.'

'I'll be careful. But I was planning on getting a tattoo across my forehead,' I say, attempting some light humour, hoping to relieve the tension of the past hour. Instead, I receive curious looks from my companions. 'It was going to say *"Die dulci fruere"*, but the Grand Hexenjäger wouldn't allow it.'

Whilst Armand and von Frankenthal struggle to translate the words, Francesca giggles and shakes her head. 'Now that would be an interesting look for a witch hunter, having the words "have a nice day" tattooed across your forehead.'

Armand cannot help but laugh. 'You're a clown.'

'If you ask me,' Francesca says, gesturing at Armand, 'he's been hanging around you too long.'

'Although, I must say, a tattoo wouldn't be a bad idea.' Armand rubs his chin in mock thought and gives me a surreptitious wink. 'Now, what would I get? It would have to be something modest and refined – one that captures the essence of my nature.'

Francesca holds up a hand, signalling for him to stop entertaining the thought. 'Please, spare us. It's simple. Wouldn't you get *"Deliciae, num is sum qui mentiar tibi"*?'

'And what does that mean?' Armand asks, giving me a sideways glance as I burst into laughter.

'It means, "Sweetheart, would I lie to you?"' I say.

Armand suppresses a grin. 'That's not very nice. Hopefully the day will soon come, my dear Francesca, when you will finally start to appreciate me. Only then will you realise what you have been missing out on.'

Francesca laughs. 'Then I can only hope that day is a *long* way from coming.'

Glad to have relieved the tension of the last few hours, I move over to the window and stare out through the misty panes into the darkness of the night. 'I wonder how long it will be before we arrive in England?'

'The voyage across the Channel takes several hours, even in favourable weather,' von Frankenthal says. 'We should reach the Thames estuary shortly. It will then take another hour or so to sail up to London. By the way, how are you feeling?'

I reach up and touch my bandaged forehead. 'I had forgotten about it, given all the excitement. But now that you've brought it to my attention, I still feel a little light-headed.'

'Then you should rest,' Armand says. 'And that goes for all of us. I don't think we'll be getting much sleep once we arrive in London.'

'I wonder what the city is like,' I say. 'I've heard that it almost rivals Paris in size.'

'London is nothing to write home about,' von Frank-enthal mumbles, joining me by the window.

'You've been there?' I ask.

Von Frankenthal screws up his nose. 'Many years ago, and I'm not keen to return. Never before have I seen such an ugly city. Its houses, crammed along the banks of the brown smear of the Thames, are nothing more than shanties, seemingly built one atop the other, as if they are trying to escape through the permanent cloud of chimney-smoke that envelops the city. If you want my honest opinion, it will be no great shame if at least part of Mother Shipton's prophecy comes true and London does indeed burn to the ground.'

Armand points a finger in warning at von Frankenthal. 'You will keep such thoughts to yourself from here on. Do not make light of the prophecy. If we are to fail this mission and London goes up in flames, thousands of people will die.'

Francesca holds up a hand to signal us to stop talking. 'Listen! What's that noise?'

Armand pushes himself up onto an elbow and looks at her inquisitively. 'What noise? I can't hear anything.'

Francesca rolls her eyes. 'If you'd be quiet, then you might be able to hear. Now listen.'

As one, we fall silent and crane our ears towards the wall on the right-hand side of the cabin, from where we can discern muffled sounds coming from the adjoining room. We cast an uneasy glance at one another, and a cold chill crawls across my skin. For it is the sound of someone whipping themselves, in what I can only assume in an act of flagellation – a voluntary self-imposed punishment in which a person whips themselves across the back as an act of penance for sins committed. Their voice, struggling to hold back the pain, rises above the *slap* of the whip, chanting verses in Latin. We recognise it as that belonging to Witch Finder Blackwood.

Francesca looks at me, her expression grave, and whispers, 'What have we got ourselves into?'

CHAPTER NINE

I am woken gently by Francesca. Rubbing the sleep from my eyes, I sit up. It takes some time for me to take in my surroundings and register that I am still aboard the *Royal Charles*. Upon Armand's insistence that I get some rest, I had laid down upon our cabin's solitary bed. I must have drifted off to sleep, lulled by the rhythmic rocking of the ship.

'Wake up, sleepy,' Francesca says. 'We've reached London.'

'Already?' I question, believing I had only dozed off for a minute or two. 'What time is it?'

Francesca rises from where she had been sitting on the edge of the bed and slings her repeating crossbow over her shoulder. 'It's almost nine in the evening. You've been asleep for several hours.'

Armand straps on his weapons and opens the cabin door. 'You need to get ready. Prince Rupert wants us up on deck within five minutes. We're to go with the Prince, Sir Robert, the Bishop and the *Angeli Mortis* to the King's residence at Whitehall, where the Bishop will report directly to King Charles.'

Von Frankenthal whistles and raises his eyebrows. 'We had better be on our best behaviour then. The King of England – my, how we've gone up in the world.'

'I wouldn't get too excited,' Armand says. 'I very much doubt we will have a private audience with the King. Actually, I very much doubt we will even *see* the King. But it wouldn't surprise me in the least if we are sent to take care of the Sons of Cain at first light tomorrow morning.' He inspects the corridor beyond our cabin, closes the door, beckons us close and whispers, 'This may be our last chance to talk in private, so listen carefully. Things are going to be hectic over the course of the next few days. Stay alert and watch each other's backs. Although we have joined forces with the *Angeli Mortis*, do not place your trust in them. Blackwood has made it very clear that he doesn't want our help. Let's hope that he doesn't do anything foolish.' Armand draws his mortuary sword, kisses its blade and invites us to join our swords in a symbolic union of brotherhood.

'*Deo duce, ferro comitante*,' we say in unison, forming a ring of steel.

I find it hard to look into my friends' eyes as I wonder if this will be one of the last times I will see them alive.

✝

Emerging on the deck of the *Royal Charles*, I am immediately reminded that England is a country at war. Although it is night time, the Thames is host to an armada of battleships, their decks a commotion of activity, with crews lifting supplies of food, munitions and tackle aboard via pulleys stationed along the wharves. As far as I can see into the darkness, the surrounding dockyards are full to bursting with stores of barrels and sacks, roped together in large bundles to be lifted aboard ships and guarded by groups of soldiers armed with muskets and pikes.

And then there is the city of London itself, its houses spilling right down to the very banks of the Thames, its streets so twisted they could teach a contortionist a trick or two. As von Frankenthal had forewarned, the night sky is covered by a stationary grey haze; a permanent blanket of smoke produced by the thousands of household chimneys and brewhouses, and punctured by the hundreds of church steeples as they climb higher to Heaven in an attempt to flee from the earthly squalor below.

The *Royal Charles* is one of two ships moored along a wharf extending from a waterside gatehouse that gives entrance to an imposing castle, which I learn from Lieutenant Wolf is the Tower of London.

'Welcome to London,' von Frankenthal says sarcastically, standing by my side, his voice lowered so that none of the English crewmen around us can hear. 'A more seething warren of vice and corruption you won't find anywhere. Keep a careful eye on your purse and an even more careful eye over your soul, lad. If ever a city was designed to tempt even the most pure of heart into sin, then it is here.'

'I should feel right at home, then,' Armand says jokingly, patting von Frankenthal on the shoulder and receiving a roll of the eyes from Francesca. He moves across to the opposite side of the deck, where Prince Rupert, Bishop Henchman, Sir Robert Holmes, Lieutenant Wolf and the *Angeli Mortis* are preparing to disembark via a gangplank, which is being hoisted into position by some of the ship's crew. After a few words with Prince Rupert, Armand beckons us over, and we follow the Prince and his retinue down the now installed gangplank.

We are greeted by guards clad in leather doublets, who escort us off the bustling wharf through a raised portcullis set in the waterside gatehouse. Leaving the commotion of the Thames behind us, we make our way through the outer fortifications of the Tower of London to the two horse-drawn coaches that await us. After climbing inside, we are led out of the castle and taken through the cobbled streets of the city.

Some time passes before we enter what appears to be an aristocratic district, its refined apartments in stark contrast to the ramshackle, half-timbered hovels that characterise the sprawling metropolis. A massive cathedral – which I can only assume is Westminster Abbey – towers over the neighbouring buildings. Recalling Armand's earlier comment that Prince Rupert and Bishop Henchman needed to report to the King, it doesn't take me long to realise that this district of stately buildings must be the beginning of Whitehall, the King's residence in London.

We disembark before a three-storey mansion, where the Prince ushers us inside. We find ourselves standing in a lavish foyer, its floor of polished parquetry and its walls adorned with mounted deer antlers and intricately woven tapestries. A staircase, set against the left wall, leads up to a walkway that overlooks the foyer and leads to the rooms on the first floor.

'This is my private residence in London,' the Prince says, taking off his hat and cloak and handing them to a sallow-faced, elderly servant, who shuffles out from an adjoining room. 'And this,' he adds, gesturing towards the man, 'is my most loyal servant, Franz. He has been in my family's service for over sixty years now, long before my father was forced to leave Heidelberg at the beginning of the Thirty Years' War, and he still hasn't had the common sense to escape.'

'Only because the Prince keeps me locked up at night,' Franz says, his features deadpan. His tone, however, is familiar, suggesting that he and the Prince have an informal relationship and are accustomed to such palaver.

'I lock you up at night, do I?' The Prince laughs. 'Now that would be a sight to see. If I were to do that, though, I'd have to consider it a public service. I'd hate to think what mischief you'd get up to on the streets at night. Every father from St James Park to Whitechapel would have to keep their daughters inside.'

'Only if I could beat you to them, my Lord,' Franz says.

Prince Rupert slaps his thigh in laughter. 'Oh, Franz. What would I ever do without you?' He then turns to address us. 'I know you are no doubt tired and wish to rest, but there are urgent matters that we must discuss. Franz will show you to your quarters, where you can have half an hour to freshen up. We will meet in the drawing room afterwards, just through that doorway over there. An hour of your time is all I will require. Bishop Henchman and I will then need to report to the King. The rest of the night will be yours to do as you please.'

He says this in such a way as to suggest that we might like to take a tour of the city. But there will be no night-time tour of London for me, thank you very much. Given what Frankenthal has said, I know I'll be spending the rest of the night tucked up in bed, safe and sound, my swords and pistols within close reach.

No sooner has the Prince finished speaking than our heads snap in unison towards the front door. For somewhere in the extensive grounds of Whitehall comes the distant sound of yelling voices and gunshots.

CHAPTER TEN

'That can't be good,' Armand says, rushing to the door, his mortuary sword already drawn.

'Stay back!' Lieutenant Wolf orders Bishop Henchman, Prince Rupert and Sir Robert, and follows only a step behind Armand, his sword likewise ready for combat.

There's a hiss of steel as the rest of us draw our blades. My heart racing, I watch as Armand and the Lieutenant open the door and slip into the darkness outside. As von Frankenthal comes over to stand protectively beside Francesca and me, Dorian, having received a nod from Witch Finder Blackwood, produces the rifle from his shoulder, thumbs back the firing pin, and races up the stairs to disappear into one of the rooms overlooking the front of the Prince's mansion. Out of the corner of my eye I notice the Prince and Bishop exchange a knowing look.

More gunshots are fired, this time in closer proximity to the Prince's residence. Wary of being hit by stray shots, we brace our backs against the sections of wall between the foyer windows. An anxious minute passes, during which we hear more yelling and the stomping of boots and the clinking of weapons as groups of guards rush along the pathways that wind throughout Whitehall. Then, just as I'm about to ask the Prince what is happening, Lieutenant Wolf bursts into the room.

'Guards have spotted a man scaling down a wall below an open window in Lord Arlington's office,' he reports, struggling to catch his breath. 'The man appeared to have documents tucked into his belt. He also left a flower, a black violet, on Lord Arlington's desk.'

Prince Rupert's eyes flash with surprise and he turns to Bishop Henchman. 'A black violet! Congratulations, Bishop. Your information was indeed correct. The French rats were in London, and they took the bait. Now all that remains to be seen is if we can catch them. I must say, though, it's not going to be easy capturing the Ghost.'

'Catch *who*?' I ask.

Bishop Henchman looks across at the Prince and receives a nod of consent. 'As I am sure you are aware, the French are allied with the Dutch,' he says, his voice raised to compete against the shouts and gunfire. 'I had information come my way that suggested the French had sent members of the King's Secret – *Le Secret du Roi* – to infiltrate King Charles's court in London. Following these leads, I dropped a few hints that plans vital to the deployment of

English warships were being kept in a drawer in the Secretary of State's office. Of course, the plans were false, but the French didn't know that. For the past month, since we first started circulating the information concerning the battle plans, we have maintained a careful watch over Lord Arlington's office. And tonight the rats have come out of hiding and fallen into the trap. But we weren't expecting one of them to be the Ghost – *le Fantôme*.'

Prince Rupert produces one of the long-barrelled cavalry pistols from his belt. 'You have no doubt heard of the Marquis de Beynac and Horst von Skullschnegger,' he says, unaware that I had encountered them in Schloss Kriegsberg. 'They are two of the most famous members of the King's Secret. But whereas the Marquis is the mastermind controlling the French spy network and von Skullschnegger is his bodyguard, the most successful operative in the King's Secret is a man who is simply known as the Ghost. A master of disguise, he has infiltrated foreign courts, gaining the trust of those in power and learning state secrets. Before he can be detected he disappears, only to resurface again several months later in another part of Europe and with a different identity. But he is more famous as a professional thief. Only last year he snuck into the Queen's bedchamber, stole a kiss from the sleeping queen and left his calling card – a single black violet – on her pillow.'

'Why did he do that?' I ask.

Bishop Henchman shrugs. 'As nothing was stolen, we assume he did it to rattle our morale. Perhaps he also wanted to prove his skill as a thief. The queen's bed-chamber isn't exactly the easiest of places to break into.'

'We had planned on letting the French spies return to the Marquis with the fake plans,' Prince Rupert continues. 'It would give us a decisive edge in the war against the Dutch. But the Ghost is too great a prize to let slip through our fingers.' He pauses as he considers von Frankenthal, Francesca and me, a devilish glint in his eyes. 'How are witch hunters at catching ghosts?'

'We've never tried,' says a voice from the doorway, and we turn around to find that Armand has returned. 'But we've never been known to turn down a challenge.'

The Prince grins roguishly and grabs his cloak and hat from Franz. 'Now that's the spirit. Let's join the hunt before our quarry escapes.'

'Is that wise?' Sir Robert cautions, just as a musket ball shatters one of the foyer windows, forcing us to cover our eyes against the shards of flying glass. 'What in the Devil's name are those fools doing out there? They'll kill half of the English royal family before this night is over!'

'It's going to be a lot damned safer out there than what it is in here,' the Prince says, putting on his hat and cloak. 'Robert, stay here with the *Angeli Mortis* and protect the Bishop. Wolf and I are going to take the Hexenjäger on a hunting trip.' A cavalier grin crosses his lips as he looks at Armand. 'Is your team ready? Good – then let's go. The hunt awaits us.'

CHAPTER ELEVEN

Racing out of the Prince's apartments, we run into a group of four guards. One of them carries a lantern, its orange glow illuminating the pathways that run off to the left and right. Beyond the lantern's light all is hidden in darkness; a shadow-realm perfect for the Ghost to make his escape. Lieutenant Wolf says something in English to one of the guards, and receives an excited response in return.

'That way,' the Lieutenant says, looking back at us, and points with his sword to the right, where sounds of the chase resonate from the distance.

Untying the lantern hanging from the side of my pack, I go to light it, but Armand stops me. 'Best if you don't do that. You'll be lit up like a bonfire. The Ghost will see you coming a mile away. To catch a thief, it's better to stick to the shadows. Use the night to your advantage.'

'Sound advice,' Prince Rupert comments, already chasing after the guards, but moving deliberately over to the edge of the perimeter of light cast by the guard's lantern. Lieutenant Wolf, von Frankenthal and Francesca are only a step behind him.

'Come on,' Armand urges me, his eyes dancing. 'We don't want to fall behind.'

And we race off into the night, weaving our way through the pathways of Whitehall, passing stately mansions, court-yards and extensive stretches of garden. Eventually, we run across a large tract of open space, more like a public park or a parade ground than a garden, and join another group of guards. They have taken position behind a five-foot-tall wall, their pistols and muskets trained on the rooftop of a nearby three-storey-high building.

Joining them, we draw our firearms, aim at the rooftop and scan the area for movement. But the darkness betrays nothing. All I can see are chimneys silhouetted against the night sky like silent sentinels.

'I can't see any . . .' I say, but the words are caught in my mouth when three of the guards fire, the report of their firearms nearly making me jump out of my skin. And it's at that exact moment I see movement atop the building, and my eyes lock on the shadowy figure standing on the far left of the roof.

My heart racing, I nudge Armand and Francesca, who are standing on either side of me, drawing their attention to the figure. Trying to steady my breathing so as to not spoil my aim, and hoping to get a shot off before the figure moves, I level my pistol at the Ghost. The *BLAM!* of my pistol is followed not even a heartbeat later by the sound of smashing glass.

Armand shakes his head. 'Great shot, Jakob. That window won't live to see another day.'

'What?' I peer through the smoke created by my pistol to notice that I have hit one of the building's upper-storey windows. 'Oh.'

'I don't know why you persist in using those things. They are about as accurate as spitting into the wind,' Francesca says, producing the crossbow from her shoulder, slamming in a magazine of bolts and resting it on top of the wall to steady her aim. 'But this can hit a bullseye at eighty paces.'

Before she can get her shot off, her aim is distracted by the report of a firearm, and the figure atop the roof is hit by the impact of the ball. Snapping our heads to the right, we see Prince Rupert blow the smoke away from one of his long-barrelled cavalry pistols. He squints as he stares up at the roof.

'The Prince never misses,' Lieutenant Wolf boasts, looking across at us. 'He once hit the weather vane atop St Mary's Church in Stafford from a distance of over fifty yards. When the King questioned if it was merely luck, the Prince repeated the shot, again hitting the target. You might be able to hit a bullseye at eighty paces, Francesca, but the Prince could change the gender of a fly at fifty paces with one of his pistols.'

'My aim was true.' Prince Rupert draws our attention back to the rooftop. 'But it didn't kill the Ghost. Look, he still stands.'

As one, we look back at the rooftop, only to find that the Ghost is still standing. Strangely, despite being shot, he hasn't moved.

'Care for another try, my Lord?' Lieutenant Wolf asks. 'It seems as if the Ghost didn't get the message.'

Producing the remaining pistol from his belt, the Prince thumbs back the firing pin, takes aim and fires. Again, the figure is hit, its cloak ripped back by the impact of the ball.

'Remarkable!' von Frankenthal comments, admiring the Prince's marksmanship.

Prince Rupert lowers his pistol, a baffled look on his face. 'What's even more remarkable, though, is that the Ghost is *still* standing. That was a direct hit. He should have fallen.'

'Something is amiss,' Armand says, sheathing his mortuary blade. 'Cover me.'

He springs over the wall and races across to the building. He finds a vine snaking its way up the front wall and he climbs up to the roof. Drawing his mortuary sword and sabre, the French duellist then stalks across to the other side of the building. Using the chimneys as cover, he sneaks up to within ten yards of the figure, where he crouches behind the final chimney, his eyes locked on the Ghost – who still hasn't moved. Several seconds pass before Armand steps out from behind his concealment, his blades lowered, as if there is no threat. He walks across to the figure, reaches out and pulls off its cloak.

My jaw drops in surprise and von Frankenthal curses under his breath.

For it was all a trick. The cloak had been draped around a chimney stack, making us believe that the Ghost was atop the roof, when in fact it was stalling us whilst the spy made his escape.

Lieutenant Wolf lowers his sword in a defeated gesture. 'Don't we look like a pack of fools. Whilst we've been shooting at a chimney, the Ghost has been making his merry way out of here. He could be anywhere by now.'

Armand draws our attention with a shrill whistle. He points with one of his blades across at a distant rooftop, where, silhouetted against the eerie light cast by the crescent moon, we catch a glimpse of a darting shadow.

The Ghost!

No sooner have we spotted the French spy than Armand takes off in pursuit, racing to the end of the building and leaping across to the rooftop of a neighbouring mansion. A second later, Prince Rupert urges us to continue the chase, and we sprint out from behind the wall in hot pursuit of our fleeing quarry.

CHAPTER TWELVE

With Lieutenant Wolf leading, we hustle along a narrow pathway leading between elegant two-storey apartments. After fifty yards or so, we run through an archway and turn into a large courtyard, dominated by a central fountain. We assemble around the fountain and scan the rooftops for movement, searching for where we had last spotted the Ghost. But all is silent and still.

'Didn't we see the Ghost over there?' Francesca asks, pointing at one of the buildings to the left of the fountain.

'I think so,' I say. 'But it's hard to tell. The buildings here all look the same to me.'

'This is a fine mess we're in,' Lieutenant Wolf says, and points in the opposite direction to Francesca. 'I thought it was over that way.'

It's then that a shadow darts along the rooftops over-looking the courtyard, leaping deftly across the expanses that separate the buildings. Some of the guards snap their firearms up at the shadow and take aim, but they are stopped by Prince Rupert.

'Lower your weapons!' he orders. 'Are you that blind that you can't tell friend from foe? It's the witch hunter.'

Alarmed that I too was about to unknowingly take aim at Armand, I breathe a sigh of relief. I stare up at the shadow and realise that the French duellist is indeed recognisable by the moonlight glistening on the honed blades of his swords and the occasional glimpse of the crimson tabard beneath his billowing black cloak. Whereas we have lost track of the Ghost, Armand is hot on his trail, and again we are directed back on the hunt by one of his blades – this time pointing over to the left, to the rooftop of another distant building.

Again we give chase, racing through a narrow lane off the courtyard, eventually finding our way blocked by a ten-foot-tall wall.

'We've come to the end of Whitehall,' Lieutenant Wolf calls over his shoulder as he turns right and chases after the Prince and Francesca, who are following the course of the wall. 'We'd better be quick. We'll never be able to catch the Ghost if he makes it into the streets of the city. He'll disappear faster than a flea on a dog's coat.'

Following at the end of the company, I am overcome by a wave of dizziness. Before I have time to alert my friends, a thousand pinpricks of flashing silver assail my vision, and

I am forced to fall back from the others. Knowing that I should have remained at the Prince's lodgings and given my head wound time to fully heal, I rest my hands on my knees, suck in air and wait for the dizziness to subside. When I finally feel well enough to continue, I look up again. Only to find that my companions and the English guards have continued after the Ghost, and I'm left alone in the darkness.

I follow the course of the wall – hoping that it isn't too late to catch up to my companions – and feel my way through the darkness, careful not to over-exert myself. After some forty yards or so the wall ends at a fortified gate, its portcullis raised. Strangely, there is no sign of any sentries. Curious as to why this gate that leads from the city of London into the King's district of Whitehall should not be guarded, I peer into an adjoining guard room, wait for my eyes to adjust and get the fright of my life.

For I have discovered how the Ghost gained entry to Whitehall.

The sentries are lying at my feet in pools of blood, their throats slit from ear to ear.

I cross myself and stagger back from the gruesome scene, painfully aware of how dangerous this night's enterprise has become. Whereas I had initially considered the chase through Whitehall as a thrilling diversion from the greater peril awaiting us tomorrow, when we will be called upon to face the Sons of Cain, I only now realise how deadly and ruthless an opponent the Ghost is. He is not simply a glorified thief and spy, but a merciless killer.

Fearing that any shadow could harbour the Ghost – his eyes monitoring my every move, his dagger poised in preparation to slit my throat – I move warily through the portcullis and into the streets of London, praying to God that I can find my friends.

CHAPTER THIRTEEN

The instant I step through the portcullis, it is as if I've passed a portal into a different world. Gone are the stately buildings and extensive gardens of White-hall, replaced by the twisted squalor of the great metropolis. This is the London of which von Frankenthal had warned me: a city of vice and moral decay.

I find myself standing in a narrow alleyway, its floor of filthy cobbles, with a refuse-clogged gutter cut down its middle like some festering wound, its fetid stench almost making me gag. Perhaps I am projecting my fear of the night onto my surroundings, but the houses and build-ings here have a sinister feel to them. The timber-framed tenements and hovels lining the alley are ramshackle and twisted, as if they have been inflicted by a terrible disease that has retarded their growth. Their gables project out over the alley itself, giving the impression that I have entered the den of some great beast. There are no lanterns lighting the alley, nor does any candlelight escape through the hovels' shuttered windows – a realm of shadows perfect for cut-throats and footpads. All is quiet.

I am tempted to call out to my companions. Just one shout – that's all I would need. I'm sure they would hear my call and retrace their steps to find me. But I dread to think who else will answer my summons. And so, erring on the side of caution, I decide to follow the alleyway until I at least reach the first cross-street. If I haven't found my companions by then, I will return to Whitehall and try to make my way back to Prince Rupert's lodging.

My Pappenheimer rapier and a pistol readied for combat, I sneak down the alleyway and nearly jump out of my skin when someone belches from one of the overhanging gables. Wiping cold sweat from my brow, I regain my composure and continue forward. I search every shadowed recess, wary that it may conceal either the Ghost or some unsavoury denizen of the night.

The alleyway eventually joins a larger road, and I hurry instinctively over to a lantern hanging from the front of a nearby building. Somewhere in the distance I can hear evidence of life – a slamming door, voices raised in heated discussion, and a dog barking – but there is no sign of my companions.

Deciding that it will be prudent for me to return to Whitehall, I go to turn around. And it's at that exact moment a shadow drops from a rooftop only a yard or so over to my left. I whip up my pistol and take aim at the figure, who rises to their feet, their back turned towards me.

'Move and I'll shoot!' I threaten.

The figure freezes, then raises its hands and mumbles something in English; the voice revealing that it is a man, and he is terrified.

'Be silent!' I warn, believing by sheer luck that I have caught the Ghost, who has somehow managed to evade my friends and is trying to fool me into thinking that he is a common Londoner.

Again the man says some panicked words. Then he starts to turn around.

'Stop!' I try to make my voice sound as threatening as possible, which is not an easy task when my insides are churning with fear.

Unable to comprehend my commands in German, or at least pretending not to understand, the man continues to turn until he faces me. Seeing the pistol trained at him, he gives a startled cry, clasps his hands together and sobs for mercy. He is so convincing that I begin to wonder if I have been mistaken; that he is indeed some startled Londoner – perhaps some amateur footpad whose path I have inadvertently crossed.

As I study the man in the dim light cast by the nearby lantern, I am left with no doubt that he is no common thief. Although his features are concealed beneath a wide-brimmed hat, his breeches and shirt are of black silk. The rapier hanging by his side has an expensive bejewelled cross-guard. But the dead giveaway is the documents tucked under his belt.

'You can drop the facade,' I say, levelling my pistol straight at the man's face. 'I know who you are, *le Fantôme*.'

As soon as I say this, the man stops pleading and lowers his hands. I get the sense that his eyes – the cold and compassionless eyes of a slayer – are studying me from beneath the brim of his hat.

'And what are you going to do about it, boy?' he asks in fluent German, his tone confident, as if he has nothing to fear.

I feel my throat tighten. 'I won't miss at this range.'

The Ghost tilts back his head slightly, raising the brim of his hat just high enough to reveal the thin line of his lips. 'Your bravery is to be commended, but don't fool yourself. I'm not in the habit of taking lives, particularly of someone so young. Though if you don't lower that pistol, I'll have no choice but to kill you.'

My finger tightens on the trigger. 'Don't underestimate me. I am a Hexenjäger. Don't think you'll be the first person I will have killed.'

My words are intended to intimidate the Ghost, to make him second-think in trying to rush me. But I only achieve to make a mocking grin appear on his lips.

'Then so be it,' he says.

CHAPTER FOURTEEN

Believing that any second now the Ghost is going to launch himself at me, I snap my pistol down towards his right thigh in the hopes of crippling him. The instant I lower my firearm, however, he becomes a blur of motion.

With a speed that leaves me gaping, he springs to his left. Swinging my pistol after him, I panic and fire – at the same moment the Ghost lashes out with his right foot, kicking aside my firearm, the shot ricocheting off the cobbles several yards off to my right.

Capitalising on his attack, the Ghost draws his blade and lunges at my torso. I leap back from the skewering point of his rapier and flick up my Pappenheimer just in time to parry aside a second thrust, this time delivered to my thigh. I correctly anticipate the Ghost's next attack as a thrust to my face and step back and parry aside his blade to deliver a riposte, my sword snaking out at the Ghost's lower chest.

The Ghost swats aside my rapier and feigns to his left, drawing my blade after him. He then darts back to the right, the point of his rapier aimed at my neck. I cry out in alarm and stagger back, tripping on a cobblestone and dropping my sword in the process. I slam into the front wall of a house and, closing my eyes, brace myself for the cold bite of the Ghost's steel.

Only it doesn't come, and I open my eyes to find that the Ghost has stopped his attack just at the moment of impact, the point of his rapier pressed against the soft flesh of my nape.

'I told you that I don't kill boys,' he says, and I am shocked that such a cold-blooded killer can show mercy. 'There have been too many unnecessary deaths this night. Now go home to your mother.'

Withdrawing his blade, he steps back, wedges the toe of his boot under my discarded Pappenheimer, and flicks it up to catch it with his free hand. 'A fine blade,' he says, inspecting the sword. 'And imbued with holy inscriptions. The blade of a witch hunter. A rare prize indeed. Maybe one day we will meet again ... until then consider this sword mine.'

'But you can't!' I protest. Not only do I feel great senti-mental attachment to the sword, being the first blade I have ever owned, but I will need it more than ever when we face the Sons of Cain.

There's a flash of white in the darkness as the Ghost smiles. 'I can, and I will.'

Hearing the distant sound of people approaching – possibly my companions, alerted by the report of my pistol – and alarmed by the lamps turning on in the neighbouring houses as curious residents rise to see what the commotion is all about, the Ghost bows and makes his escape.

Only to stop dead in his tracks as a shadow detaches itself from a nearby doorway, its rifle trained on the French spy.

'Don't expect any mercy from me, French dog!' Dorian snarls in stilted German, stepping out into the middle of the road to intercept the Ghost.

'Nor from me,' says another voice with a strong Italian accent.

A smile crosses the Ghost's lips as Dorian and I look up to a neighbouring rooftop, barely ten yards away, where the moonlight glistens on the barrel of the pistol gripped in the hand of a cloaked figure perched on the edge of the roof.

A cold chill races through my skin at the realisation that not only does the Ghost have an accomplice, but that he might have watched my entire confrontation with the French spy, waiting for the right moment to intervene.

'It appears we have a stand-off,' the Ghost says, and starts to move slowly down the road.

Dorian raises his rifle to his shoulder to take aim at the Ghost's head. 'Don't move! Take another step and I won't hesitate to shoot.'

The Ghost pauses and considers Dorian for a few seconds. 'Black clothing. A face adorned with crucifixes. If I am not mistaken, you must be one of the *Angeli Mortis*.' He looks back at me. 'And working with the Hexenjäger. Something big must be brewing in London for rival Catholic and Protestant orders of witch hunters to join forces. But I hardly see how this has got anything to do with me. Why don't we do the sensible thing and lower our weapons. None of us really want to die here. Let's just walk away and forget that any of this took place. You can carry on with your business, and my companion and I will disappear into the night.'

Dorian snickers. 'I have no fear of death. And you won't be leaving this street alive.'

Realising that the Ghost's attempt to defuse the situation won't work with Dorian, I reach slowly for the second pistol tucked into my belt. I have barely moved, however, before the man atop the roof aims his pistol at me. I freeze, too afraid to even breathe.

'Try that again, and I'll send you straight to God,' he hisses.

'But not before I send the Ghost straight to Hell!' Dorian threatens, rolling a shoulder as he perfects his aim.

The Ghost lowers his head in a disappointed manner. 'Then it appears we have reached an impasse, and you leave me no choice.' He looks up at his companion, who whips his pistol back at Dorian. 'Do you have a clear shot?'

The cloaked stranger stares down the barrel of his pistol and nods. My heart racing, I watch helplessly as he takes aim at Dorian and fires.

CHAPTER FIFTEEN

There's a simultaneous flash and *BLAM!* as both Dorian and the stranger fire. Dorian takes the full impact of the stranger's shot, being knocked off his feet and smashing through the window of the house immediately behind him. Meanwhile the Ghost, having snapped his head to the side at just the last moment, manages to dodge Dorian's shot, the rifle ball smacking into the wall of a nearby house.

Snatching the pistol from my belt, I race to the cover of a nearby doorway recess and take a hasty shot at the cloaked figure, whose head jolts back. He clutches at his right ear – or rather, where his right ear *used* to be – removes his hand and stares at his blood-soaked palm. Then his eyes lock on me. Giving a savage cry, he springs from the roof and lands on all fours in the middle of the road, making the fifteen-foot drop appear effortless. He rises to his feet. There's a hiss of steel as he draws a dagger from his belt and stalks over towards me. My heart pounding, I produce my second rapier and prepare to face the enraged stranger.

'Spartaco, we don't have time for this!' the Ghost warns, racing over to grab his companion by the arm and drawing his attention to the crowd of onlookers, who have gathered at the windows of the houses on the street. 'We need to go – now!'

Spartaco shrugs aside the Ghost, mutters something furiously under his breath and continues to advance towards me. Believing my only chance of surviving this encounter lies in striking first, I assume an offensive stance and lunge forward. To my horror, Spartaco entangles my blade in the *S*-shaped cross-guard of his dagger. He produces a second dagger from beneath his cloak with his left hand and darts forward, thrusting at my chest. I give an involuntary cry of alarm and leap back, narrowly avoiding the blade, but finding myself trapped in the doorway recess.

Spartaco steps forward, a malicious sneer crossing his lips. My rapier is still caught in the dagger held in his right hand. But it is to his other dagger that my eyes fly, for it is drawn back in preparation to gut me like some stuck pig. My left hand reaches to the fold of my boot, searching desperately for one of my daggers, but I know that it is too late. Spartaco lunges forward, his glistening blade heading straight for my chest.

I brace myself for the impact – for the punch of steel that

will end my life. But then a firearm discharges, knocking Spartaco off his feet.

What?

I look to the left and blink against the impossibility of what I see. Dorian leans through the smashed window, a smoking pistol in hand. His other hand is clutching his chest, and his face, a lacerated, bloody mess, is contorted in pain.

But how is this possible? I had seen Dorian take the full impact of Spartaco's pistol. He should be lying dead in a bloodied heap, not coming to my rescue. Is it possible that the *Angeli Mortis* have delved so deep into the *Malleus Maleficarum* that they have learned how to cheat death itself?

I rush over to Dorian and help him climb through the window. I then turn around to face our opponents, only to find that the Ghost has dragged Spartaco to his feet and is supporting him with a shoulder as they scurry off down the road.

'Don't let them escape,' Dorian wheezes, pushing away from me and attempting to give chase. He barely takes three steps before he staggers and collapses to his knees. He produces the second pistol from his belt and hands it to me. 'Finish this.'

I thumb back the firing pin and take aim at the fleeing duo. But my shot is stalled when I hear voices from behind. Turning around, I lower the pistol and breathe a sigh of relief at the sight of my companions. They have just appeared at the far end of the street, some fifty or so yards away, illuminated in the wan glow of light cast by the guard's lantern. I can clearly make out Francesca and Prince Rupert at the front of the company, and the towering form of von Frankenthal bringing up the rear.

I am distracted for only a second or two, but by the time I turn around to take my shot, the Ghost and Spartaco are nowhere to be seen.

CHAPTER SIXTEEN

F rancesca is the first of the group to reach Dorian and me.

'Thank God we found you, Jakob,' she says, grabbing me by the shoulders and inspecting me for injuries. 'We hadn't even realised that you had become separated from us until we heard the gunshots. I had moved to the front of the group, and believed you were with von Frankenthal at the rear. He thought likewise.'

'I'm fine,' I say, somewhat embarrassed that Francesca is fussing over me when Dorian is too injured to even stand. 'But Dorian is hurt. He took a shot to the chest and crashed through a window.'

'Of course.' Francesca produces a handkerchief from her pocket and dampens it with some water from her stoppered flask. She kneels down to tend Dorian's wounds.

We are then joined by the rest of the group.

'What's happened?' Prince Rupert asks, noticing the smashed window and drops of blood on the cobblestone road. He inspects Dorian, flinching when he sees his lacerated face; the blood emphasised by the witch hunter's white makeup. 'You'll have some scars to show from this encounter. It looks as if the Ghost is a skilled fighter if he can take on one of the *Angeli Mortis* and a Hexenjäger.'

'He wasn't alone,' I warn. 'He had an accomplice. An Italian by the name of Spartaco.'

Prince Rupert purses his lips in thought and looks across at Lieutenant Wolf. 'Spartaco. I've never heard of this man before.'

Lieutenant Wolf shakes his head. 'Nor have I. He must be a hired-sword working for the King's Secret.'

'And a deadly sword at that,' I add. 'He carries dual daggers and knows how to use them. And thinking about it now, he was probably the one who slit the sentries' throats back at the gate leading into Whitehall.'

Prince Rupert nods. 'I didn't think that was the work of the Ghost. He's a talented spy and thief, but I've also heard that it's rare for him to take another's life. I believe he considers it an insult to his skill as a thief.'

'He could have easily killed me,' I confirm. 'He disarmed me and had the point of his sword pressed against my throat. But he let me go.'

'Damn!' von Frankenthal growls, pacing the road. 'If only I had been here.'

Dorian looks up and scowls. 'I had everything under control.'

Prince Rupert studies the trail of blood leading down the road. 'Well, at least one of them is injured. And this will make it easier for us to follow them.'

'I managed to take a shot at Spartaco, taking off his right ear,' I say. 'Dorian also shot him – where, I'm not sure, but he was hurt. The Ghost had to help him out of here.'

Prince Rupert stares down the far end of the road, where I had last seen the Ghost and Spartaco. 'Which means they won't get far.' He looks back at Dorian. 'Can you continue?'

I give a frustrated sigh. The longer we spend with Prince Rupert, the further we are being dragged from our original plan of finding my father. I don't even see how hunting down the Ghost will help us to locate the Codex Gigas. Fate has swept us terribly off course, now dragging us into matters of espionage and English national security during the Anglo–Dutch War. To make matters worse, I feel guilty for having dragged my friends into this. Had they not accompanied me into the Dutch Republic, none of them would be in this present predicament.

Dorian pushes Francesca away and climbs to his feet. 'Of course,' he sneers.

'But you were shot,' I say, wondering how he can carry on and why his clothes are not drenched in blood.

As if in answer to my unspoken questions, Dorian parts his shirt, revealing a steel chest-plate, its surface inscribed with crucifixes. There is a dent, directly above Dorian's heart, where Spartaco had shot him.

'A clever trick,' Francesca says. 'But you were lucky he didn't aim at your face.'

'It would make no difference to me,' Dorian scoffs as he goes to retrieve his rifle. He mumbles something under his breath as he climbs back through the smashed window, and the hairs on my arms stand on end.

Perhaps I am mistaken, but I am sure he said, 'For I'm already dead.'

'It's best if we move off,' Lieutenant Wolf warns. 'Not even the night watchmen dare patrol these streets at dark. The last thing we want is an angry mob coming after us, believing we have accosted one of their neighbours.'

Von Frankenthal snorts. 'I'm not running away from a couple of knock-kneed hags armed with broomsticks. Let them come. I'll teach them a lesson or two.'

'Brave words,' Prince Rupert says. 'But believe me, even you will run if they come, for they will do so in their hundreds.'

'Have the authorities no control?' Francesca asks.

'Over most of London, they do. But this area is notorious as a haven for criminals,' the Lieutenant says, looking warily over his shoulder to where a hovel door creaks open to reveal a brutish man armed with a cudgel. 'We had best leave before things get messy.'

'Where's Armand?' I ask von Frankenthal as we start to move down the road.

He shakes his head. 'I don't know. We haven't seen him since we last witnessed him atop the rooftops back in Whitehall.'

Wondering what has become of the Frenchman, I follow my companions.

✝

We race down to the end of the street until it forms a T-intersection. Mysteriously, the trail of blood suddenly ends.

Prince Rupert scans above the neighbouring houses. 'Did they take to the rooftops?'

'That's my guess,' I say, considering the Ghost's and Spartaco's penchant for using the roofs of the city to their advantage.

'But that's impossible.' Francesca directs us to consider the final drops of blood. 'The trail ends here – right in the middle of the road. There's no way they could have reached the rooftops from here.'

It's only then, kneeling down beside the former Italian tomb-robber to inspect the trail, that I work out what has become of the Ghost and Spartaco. I rise slowly to my feet, wondering how an earth we will ever catch them now.

'Francesca's right,' I say, drawing the group's attention. 'They didn't take to the rooftops.'

Lieutenant Wolf gives a baffled gesture. 'Then where did they go? They can't have just disappeared.'

I inspect the new road we have entered. To the right it runs into a dead end, but the other side stretches off into the night. 'They went that way,' I say confidently and point to the left. I jerk my chin at the pile of fresh dung located

101

only a yard away from where the trail of blood ends. 'And they've gone by horse.'

'Not only have they gone by horse,' Prince Rupert concurs, quick to follow my line of thought, and inspecting more mounds of dung further down the road, 'but they have gone by *coach*. Look, these have just been deposited and they have been squished by wheels.'

Lieutenant Wolf punches a fist in the air in frustration. 'Then they are as good as gone. We might as well give up.'

It is just then, however, that fortune smiles on us, and a horse-drawn carriage comes down the road we have just exited. We pull over the coach and order its occupants to climb out. Prince Rupert, Francesca, Dorian and I pile inside the cabin, leaving von Frankenthal and Lieutenant Wolf to climb atop the driver's seat. There's a crack of a whip as the Lieutenant spurs the two horses forward and we speed off into the night, leaving the guards who accompanied us out of Whitehall far behind.

CHAPTER SEVENTEEN

We race to the end of the road, where Prince Rupert leans out of one of the coach's windows and instructs the Lieutenant to head north.

'We'll be lucky if we can find them,' the Prince says, returning to his seat, his voice raised so as to compete with the noise made by the coach's metal-rimmed wheels as they roll over the cobbles. 'Our task would have been easier if we were within the heart of the old city, surrounded by its medieval walls. We could have intercepted them at one of the city gates. But we are in the western suburbs now. There are dozens of ways they can exit London. We'll head up Whitecomb Street, offering the most direct route out of the city. As the Ghost and Spartaco will be keen to escape London, hopefully they will take the same route.'

A minute or two passes, during which Dorian and I finish loading our firearms – not an easy task in the bouncing coach. No sooner have we returned our pistols to our belts than Lieutenant Wolf calls out.

As one, our heads snap up.

The Lieutenant announces that he had caught a glimpse of a speeding coach on the road directly ahead.

'Get us alongside them,' Prince Rupert yells out the window, his eyes wide with excitement. 'We need to take them out before they exit the city.'

A few sharp cracks of the Lieutenant's whip spurs our mounts even faster, and it isn't long before we can hear the racing wheels of the other carriage directly in front of us.

I lean out a window, trying to see past our horses to discern the identity of the black shape driving the coach. 'Are we sure it's them?'

Prince Rupert produces one of his pistols and cracks back the firing pin. 'They are making their way up White-comb Street and they are driving fast. That's good enough reason for me. Ready your firearms. We will draw alongside them shortly. I'll take out the driver. The rest of you deal with whoever is inside the coach.'

My heart racing faster than the pounding hooves of our horses, I draw both of my pistols and spare an anxious glance at Francesca, who smiles hesitantly in return. The next instant, Lieutenant Wolf brings us up along the left side of the other carriage. Being on the right-hand side of our coach, Dorian and I ready our pistols. We take aim at the window of the opposite coach – which is now no more than two feet away – when it swerves sharply to the left, slamming into us, knocking Dorian and me back into Francesca and Prince Rupert.

Dorian and I struggle to climb back to the right side of our cabin. No sooner have we regained our position, training our pistols out the window, than Spartaco appears at the opposite window. Before we have time to react, he slashes out with his dagger, knocking aside the barrel of my pistol and slicing a gaping wound across Dorian's forearm. The English witch hunter recoils in pain, clutching his arm. I whip up my second pistol, but we are side-swiped a second time and I'm knocked back into Francesca as our carriage grazes against the houses lining the street.

'Wolf, get the situation under control!' Prince Rupert roars.

'I'm onto it,' the Lieutenant yells back. Our coach swings sharply to the right, crashing into the side of the Ghost's carriage and forcing it across to the opposite side of the road.

Seizing the opportunity, Prince Rupert tucks his pistol into his belt and slides back-first out the window. He reaches up, grabs hold of the roof of our carriage and pulls himself up.

'Where does he think he's going?' Francesca yells. 'He'll get killed out there.'

'It's not much safer in here,' I shout, seeing the other carriage swerve back towards us.

I brace myself for the impact, but it is averted by the Prince, who leaps across to the rooftop of the Ghost's carriage. Miraculously managing to maintain his balance, the Prince pulls out one of his pistols and takes aim at the Ghost. But the French spy is faster. Twisting around in the driver's seat, he whips out a pistol and fires a hasty shot over his shoulder. The Prince drops on all fours, the pistol ball whizzing past him.

This is followed a second later by another *BLAM!* as either Lieutenant Wolf or von Frankenthal takes a shot at the Ghost, who ducks in his seat, somehow avoiding the ball, and pulls his carriage further across to the opposite side of the street. And it's at that moment I see Spartaco through the window of the carriage, the pistol in his hand aimed directly upward, preparing to shoot through the roof into the Prince's chest.

'Look out!' I yell, practically bursting my tonsils with the effort, fearing there is no hope for the Prince.

As if sensing what is happening in the cabin below, Prince Rupert responds instantly to my cry. He rolls to his right, bringing himself over to the very edge of the roof. Not even a heartbeat later, Spartaco fires, his pistol ball blasting a hole through the section where the Prince had just been.

But the Prince is not out of danger.

The Ghost turns to see what has become of his unwanted passenger. Pulling sharply on his reins, the spy swerves his carriage to the left, forcing the Prince to roll off the roof. Horrified, knowing that no one could survive a fall at this speed onto the hard cobblestones below, I lean out the window and search for the Prince's body.

But he is not there.

A terrible feeling of sickness wells in my stomach. I look back at the Ghost's carriage, where I fear the Prince may have become entangled in the wheels. My eyes are drawn to a flurry of movement *inside* the opposite cabin – to where Spartaco is trying to dislodge the Prince, who defied the odds to somehow grab hold of the coach's far window and is now trying to pull himself into the cabin. He has lodged an elbow on the inside of the door, his legs hovering above the speeding road below. The Prince has caught hold of Spartaco's dagger with his free hand and is trying desperately to fend off the Italian.

As if the situation could not get any worse, the Ghost steers his carriage to the right, intending to crush the Prince against the walls of the buildings on the street.

Not daring to shoot for fear of hitting the Prince, I kick open our carriage door, tuck my pistols into my belt, say a hasty prayer and, turning a deaf ear to Francesca's protestations, dive across the expanse between the carriages. I fly through the opposite window and crash heavily into Spartaco. Locking an arm around his neck, I drag him back, allowing Prince Rupert to pull himself through the window – just a second before the coach grazes against a building, showering the road behind us with sparks.

Thrashing about violently, Spartaco – who I only now realise has his left shoulder wrapped in a blood-soaked bandage from where Dorian had shot him – slams an elbow into my chest, making me release my hold around his neck. Through tear-filled eyes and gasping for air, I see

Prince Rupert slam a fist into the Italian's face, knocking him senseless.

'That wasn't too difficult, was it?' The Prince grins. He pries the dagger from Spartaco's hand and places the blade against the Italian's throat. 'Now we've just got the Ghost to deal with.'

'Which is easier said than done,' I wheeze, clutching my chest.

As the Ghost's carriage picks up speed, our attention is caught by the sound of footsteps atop our cabin. The Prince and I exchange bewildered looks and we lean out the windows to find that the Ghost is standing on the roof, preparing to leap off onto the extending gables of one of the neighbouring buildings.

That means only one thing: nobody is driving our coach, leaving us racing through the night, out of control.

CHAPTER EIGHTEEN

'He's not getting away again!' Prince Rupert snatches one of the pistols from his belt with his free hand and aims at the ceiling of the cabin. 'Let's see if the Ghost can dodge pistol balls.'

Just as he is about to squeeze the trigger, Spartaco comes to his senses. He barges his shoulder into the Prince and spoils his aim; the pistol ball blasts a hole through the front of the cabin.

'Don't give me an excuse!' Prince Rupert presses his dagger hard against Spartaco's throat.

Spartaco hardly seems frightened by the Prince's threat. I shudder when I see the Italian staring at me through the corner of his eye.

'Your days are numbered, boy,' he snarls in stilted German. 'You disfigured me. I swear to God you'll know the meaning of pain before I finish with you. You can run to the ends of the world, but you're as good as dead!'

The Prince applies more pressure on the dagger, silencing him. 'You're in no position to be delivering threats. You'll be dangling from a hangman's noose before the end of the week. That is, of course, after you spend some time in our dungeons. We have a guard who specialises in drawing information from spies. It will be interesting to see how long you can last before he extracts everything we need to know about the King's Secret.'

Spartaco stares defiantly at Prince Rupert. 'You have no idea who I am, or what I am capable of doing. You'll wish to God the day never came when you crossed my path.'

The Prince tilts his head in a disdainful manner. 'Oh, really?' He lashes out with his pistol, cracking its heavy butt across Spartaco's temple and knocking him out cold.

'Thank God for that,' I say, glad that I no longer have to listen to Spartaco's threats.

'There's no reason for you to fear him.' Prince Rupert tucks the Italian's dagger into a fold of his boot. 'He can't harm you now. Rest assured, he'll spend the rest of his short life under heavy guard in our dungeons. Then he will be hung.'

I try to take comfort from the Prince's words, but even with his assurances I have a terrible premonition that Spartaco will escape the hangman's noose – and that we will indeed meet again sometime in the future.

I am drawn from my thoughts by the squeal of steel on steel and I peer out the window, only to jolt back in surprise when I see that von Frankenthal and Dorian, his wounded arm crudely bandaged, have climbed atop their carriage. They are locked in a savage fight with the Ghost, who is still standing on the roof above the Prince and me.

Looking as stable as a house of cards in an earthquake, Dorian and von Frankenthal engage the Ghost in a deadly duel, their blades slashing at each other. Hoping to assist somehow, I lean further out the window and take aim at the Ghost with my pistol. The Ghost notices me and shuffles back to the far side of the roof, moving out of my field of vision. I curse under my breath and push myself out further, lodging a forearm on the roof for support – the cobbles a blur of movement beneath me; the combatants' swords a hissing blur of death only a foot or two above my head – and reach up with my pistol to take aim at the French spy. Only to have Dorian spoil my aim when he leaps across to the Ghost's carriage.

Having sheathed his rapier and drawn a dagger in preparation for close-quarters combat, Dorian grapples with the Ghost, grabbing his sword-arm and attempting to drive his dagger into the spy's side. But the Ghost manages to grab hold of Dorian's blade and overpowers him. Forcing Dorian's arms back to expose his torso, the Ghost drives a knee with bone-crunching force straight into the witch hunter's crotch.

Dorian doubles over and drops his dagger, which bounces off the roof and skitters down the road. Before any us have time to come to our companion's assistance, the Ghost grabs the English witch hunter by the scruff of the neck and throws him off the front of the carriage.

CHAPTER NINETEEN

Time seems to stall as Dorian flies through the air, his arms flailing wildly, before he disappears into the gap between the galloping horses. I turn my head away and squeeze my eyes shut, anticipating the sickening crunch of his body beneath the coach's iron-rimmed wheels. But it doesn't come, and I look to the front of the coach and find, to my utter amazement, that Dorian has somehow managed to grab hold of the leather straps tethering the horses together – with his feet! He is hanging, upside down, between the racing horses, suspended above the speeding cobbles by mere inches.

My eyes locked on Dorian, I fail to notice the sharp turn in the road ahead until it is too late.

'This isn't going to be good!' Lieutenant Wolf warns. He pulls hard on the reins and steers his mounts sharply to the right in an attempt to navigate the turn. 'Brace yourselves. This will be close!'

With nobody left to steer the horses on my carriage away from the Lieutenant's, the two sets of mounts slam into one another. The force of the impact almost throws von Frankenthal from the roof. At the last moment, he manages to drop to all fours, his hands locking like vices on either side of the roof, securing his hold. I notice the Ghost, quick to respond, do likewise.

But I'm not so lucky.

Fortunately, the Lieutenant's horses force ours around the corner, and both coaches fly around the bend – we avoid crashing into the neighbouring buildings by only a hair's breadth. But the inertia created by the sudden turn is too great. My heart practically popping out of my chest in fright, I lose my hold on the roof and fall backwards out the window.

I cry out in terror as I wait for my skull to crack like a ripe melon on the cobbles below. Just as the top of my hat is a mere inch or two above the road, strong hands grab hold of my ankles and hold me in place, preventing me from falling any further.

Dangling upside down along the side of the coach, a rear wheel of the other carriage a grinding whirr of death only a foot away from my face, I stare up at Prince Rupert.

'You didn't think you were going to get out of here that

easily, did you?' he says, grimacing as he pulls me back inside the carriage.

'I thought that was the end of me,' I gasp once I am back beside the Prince. 'I don't know how to thank you.'

'You can thank me later. We're not out of this yet. We've still got to catch the Ghost, and he's proving to be as crafty as a fox.'

'But he can't maintain this forever,' I say, only now realising that I didn't drop my pistol when I fell out the window. It is still clutched in my hand, ready to fire. 'His luck will run out sooner or later. Then we'll get him.'

It's then that fortune blows a raspberry in my face. For Lieutenant Wolf calls out, announcing that we have come to the end of the road.

I look out the window and notice that we have reached the northern limits of the sprawling metropolis. Beyond the row of houses the city ends, leading into country roads.

Leaving the city behind, we race along a dirt road, flanked by meadows and the occasional farmhouse, which appear as black monoliths in the distance. With only the moonlight to guide him, Lieutenant Wolf tries to keep pace with our speeding carriage. He is doing a commendable job, in fact, until we approach a river spanned by an old wooden bridge. Both carriages race towards the bridge at full speed, and it is only when we are some ten yards away that we make the terrible realisation that it is considerably narrower than the road, creating a bottleneck.

Anticipating a shocking crash, I pull myself back inside the cabin, tuck my pistol under my belt and brace myself.

'Look out!' Lieutenant Wolf cries, pulling hard on his reins.

But not even von Frankenthal's muscle-corded arms would be powerful enough to pull up the horses, and both carriages collide.

The horses go down fast – *hard!* – entangled in a mess of twisted legs and harnesses. And then the carriages crash into one another – just a second before they plough into the fallen mounts. The next instant, both carriages flip over the horses. I cry out, terrified, as we sail through the air, clipping the bridge's wooden railing, before we come to a jarring halt as we land roof-first in the river.

CHAPTER TWENTY

I lie on the inverted ceiling of the cabin for some time, amazed to have survived the crash with nothing more than a split lip. Prince Rupert is on top of me, disoriented, his features contorted in pain as he clutches his left shoulder. Of Spartaco there is no sign. I can only assume that the Italian was thrown clear when we sailed off the bridge.

With water flooding through the windows as the carriage slowly sinks into the river, I grab the Prince by the arm and scramble out of the cabin. I assist him in swimming a short distance across to the side of the river, and together we climb up the steep bank.

'Are you all right?' I ask, hearing the Prince moan in pain.

The Prince shakes his head. 'I think I've dislocated my

shoulder. But I'll be fine. Go and check the other carriage. The others may need your help.'

Desperate to find what has become of my companions, I return to the water and swim towards the other half-sunk carriage. I have only swum half the distance when I find that Francesca has already freed herself and is making her way over to the opposite bank to join a hulking figure, who I can only assume is von Frankenthal. Both of them appear to be uninjured.

I hear cries over to my right and move towards the bridge to find Lieutenant Wolf struggling to stay afloat. Hooking an arm under his shoulder, I assist him over to the river bank and drag him out. I gasp in shock when I see the length of wood, more than a yard long and an inch thick, impaled through his thigh.

'My God!' I exclaim, taking off my cloak and attempting to staunch the blood streaming from the wound.

'I've seen worse,' the Lieutenant says bravely. But his entire body is racked by convulsive shudders of pain. He passes out before I finish wrapping my cloak around the wound.

I leave the length of wood impaled in his thigh – for fear of causing greater blood loss if I were to try removing it – and call out to Prince Rupert, informing him that the Lieutenant is in urgent need of medical attention. As the Prince staggers over to join me, my attention is drawn to the darkness beyond the river bank, where I hear the sound of clanging blades.

What?

I tell the Prince to stay put and watch over Lieutenant Wolf. I then scramble over the bank, and my hand flies to my remaining rapier.

Dorian is alive!

The English witch hunter somehow managed to survive the crash on the bridge. But I fear he won't last much longer. Not when he's locked in a duel with the Ghost.

Whereas Dorian is covered in more cuts than an axeman's chopping block, the Ghost is uninjured. Having been positioned atop his carriage when it crashed off the bridge, he must have jumped to safety, landing in the river. He must have also rescued Spartaco, for the Italian is lying several yards off to the side.

I call out to alert my companions on the opposite side of the river, draw my blade and race over to assist Dorian. But I am too late. Just as I am within six yards of the combatants, Dorian lunges forward, his rapier aimed at the Ghost's heart. But the night has taken its toll on the witch hunter – his attack is slow and clumsy, as if he is being driven by instinct alone. The French spy deflects the attack with relative ease and, pushing off his rear leg, darts forward to hammer the guard of his rapier into Dorian's jaw. The witch hunter collapses to the ground, spitting blood, and leaves me to face the Ghost alone.

'It seems as if we are back where we started.' The Ghost positions the point of his blade under Dorian's chin, his eyes locked on mine. 'It's just you and me, boy. Only this time I hold a distinct advantage: I have two of your friends at my mercy.'

119

'Two?' I ask, for although Dorian is being held at sword-point, the rest of my companions are accounted for, either recovering or lying wounded by the river. But then a cold shudder races up my spine, as I only now realise why nobody has seen Armand since we last saw him atop the roof in Whitehall.

'Where is he? What have you done to the other Hexen-jäger?' I demand, taking a step towards the Ghost. He raises a finger in warning and applies pressure on his rapier, drawing a trickle of blood from Dorian's throat.

'Don't do anything rash,' the spy warns. 'Now go and bring me that remaining horse. Then I'll tell you where your friend is.'

Looking over my shoulder, I'm surprised to find that one of the horses survived the crash. It has wandered over to the end of the bridge, some ten yards away.

Dorian stares defiantly at his captor. 'Don't do anything for him, Jakob. Stall him until your friends arrive. Then kill him like the dog he is!'

The Ghost cocks his head to one side and considers the witch hunter. 'Now that's not helping matters much, is it? It would be best if you keep silent from here on, or I might be forced to slit your throat. In fact, there's no practical need for me to spare you. I already have my bargaining piece in the form of the first witch hunter I captured.'

Dorian breathes heavily and tilts his head back further, as if to offer the Ghost a clear target. 'Then do it.'

'No!' I say, not understanding Dorian's death wish. 'I'll get you the horse. But then you must let Dorian go.' I stare hard into the shadows beneath the Ghost's hat. 'And you must promise to tell me what you have done with the other witch hunter.'

The Ghost considers me for a few seconds before saying, 'I give you my word, but only on the condition that you give me yours that this is the end of the chase. Once I have that horse, you will let me ride out of here.'

'You have my word,' I say, concerned for only Armand's and Dorian's safety.

I bring the horse over to the Ghost, who orders me to pick up Spartaco and place him over the horse's back. Picking up the unconscious Italian, I do as instructed, then take several steps back.

The Ghost sheathes his blade and reaches down to take one of Dorian's pistols. He makes his way over to the horse, the pistol trained on Dorian the entire time. The English witch hunter rises gingerly to his feet, his eyes burning with rage.

Once mounted – and just as I hear the sound of footfalls reverberate on the bridge as Francesca and von Frankenthal make their way across the river – the Ghost looks at me. 'You will find your fellow Hexenjäger gagged and bound to a chimney near where we first met. He is unharmed.' He takes off his hat, sweeps it before him in a grand gesture and bows. Something falls from his belt and lands near the rear hooves of the horse. 'It has been a most eventful night. Until we meet again, young witch hunter.'

As the Ghost gallops off into the darkness, Dorian reaches for the remaining pistol tucked into his belt and takes aim at the French spy.

'No!' I knock aside the barrel of his pistol with my rapier. 'I gave him my word that I would let him go. Have you no honour?'

'There is no such thing as honour,' Dorian sneers. 'It is merely an excuse made by cowards to justify their actions – or rather, their *lack* of action.'

He raises his pistol to take aim again, but the Ghost has disappeared into the night. Dorian gives me a disgusted look, spits near my feet and stalks off.

Making a promise to myself that I will have nothing more to do with the English witch hunter, I sheathe my rapier. I walk over to collect the item that the Ghost had dropped and find that it is a small, leather-bound book. Curious, but knowing that my injured companions are in need of my help, I place it in a pocket on the inside of my cloak, intending to look at it later.

The chase finally over, I am overcome by a sudden wave of exhaustion. Adrenaline alone has kept me going, and I collapse to my knees. A thousand flashing stars besiege my vision for the second time this night, and I am vaguely aware of someone calling my name. I can also hear the sound of rushing feet. But then I succumb to a darkness deeper than the night and pass out.

⚔ CHAPTER TWENTY-ONE

I wake in a soft bed in an unfamiliar room, its furnishings sparse but of notable quality. Finding my weapons and a fresh set of clothes lying on a bedside table, I dress quickly, equip my weapons – cursing under my breath when I recall what has become of my Pappenheimer rapier – and pause to look out the room's solitary window.

I must be on the third floor. My gaze is drawn over the neighbouring rooftops to the Thames, which is little more than a stone's throw away, its brown surface a commotion of ships and barges. The docks and wharves lining its banks are covered in seamen, haggling merchants and dockyard workers, who are unloading cargo from ships via ramps and swing pulleys. Judging from the position of the sun and the absence of shadows around the neighbouring chimney stacks, it must be around midday.

London. I still can't believe I've ended up here, so far away from my new home. Hopefully when all of this is over, my friends and I will be able to return to solving the mystery as to who my father is. Right now, however, I need to find out what has become of Armand and my companions, and where I am – although I assume I am in a bedroom on the top floor of Prince Rupert's lodgings in Whitehall.

I exit the room and walk down a corridor. This eventually leads to a drawing room, where, to my relief, I find Francesca, von Frankenthal and Armand lounging in chairs. Armand is swirling a goblet of claret in his hand, and he smiles warmly when he sees me.

'Thank God you are all right.' I rush over to him and extend a hand in welcome. 'I was beginning to wonder if I'd ever see you again.'

The Frenchman's eyes lack their characteristic confident glint as he shakes my hand. 'That was one night I'd prefer to forget.'

'I didn't think anybody could get the drop on you,' I say, pulling up a seat.

'I'm only human.' Armand shrugs. 'And I was reckless. I was so focused on trying to catch the Ghost that I wasn't even aware he had an accomplice until it was too late. The first I saw of him was when he came at me from behind and put a knife to my throat.'

A cold chill runs over my skin at the mention of the Italian. 'That's Spartaco. He's a cold-blooded killer. You're lucky he didn't kill you then and there.'

'Believe me, he wanted to. But it was the Ghost who stopped him.'

'I'm not surprised to hear that,' I say. 'Although a professional spy and thief, he seems a man of honour.'

Von Frankenthal snorts derisively. 'A man of honour? He's nothing more than a glorified footpad.'

'No, he's not.' I shake my head, surprised by my willingness to defend the French spy. 'He had his sword pressed against my throat last night. He could have easily killed me, yet he let me live. He also had an opportunity to slay Dorian, but he didn't.'

'Well, I hope he and Spartaco don't expect any such mercy from me if we ever run into them again,' von Frankenthal says. 'They humiliated us – made us look like a pack of amateurs. We need to restore the honour of our order.'

I nod in agreement. 'They gave us a run for our money. But don't forget that we are witch hunters. We are trained in the art of slaying Satan's servants. Last night we chased a professional thief across rooftops. We charged blindly into *his* terrain – in a city that we don't even know. He held the advantage right from the beginning. I don't think we should be too hard on ourselves.'

Armand takes a sip of his drink. He savours the liquid for a few seconds before swallowing. 'Jakob is right,' he says at length, looking up. 'We were too hasty. We underestimated the Ghost and played right into his hands. Let this be a lesson to us: we need to watch each other's backs. It was foolish for me to have raced across the rooftops in pursuit. I should have taken one of you with me. If I had been more cautious, Spartaco would never have caught me.'

'Considering all that we went through, it's nothing short of a miracle that none of us were killed,' Francesca says. 'Although Dorian, Prince Rupert and Lieutenant Wolf came out worse for wear.'

'What's happened?' I ask. 'The last thing I remember is seeing the Ghost ride off into the night.'

'Christian and I saw you collapse, but you were unconscious by the time we reached you,' Francesca explains. 'Christian carried you back to the river bank to watch over you and Lieutenant Wolf.'

'The Lieutenant was badly injured,' I say. 'And so was the Prince. I remember that much, at least.'

Francesca nods. 'Prince Rupert pushed his shoulder back into place by slamming it against a tree trunk. As luck would have it, a group of night watchmen came out to investigate what had happened. One of them summoned a carriage, and you and the Lieutenant were taken back to the Prince's lodgings.'

'How did you find Armand?' I ask.

'Dorian led us to where the Ghost had said we would find the Frenchman. We found him bound and gagged, tied to a chimney stack. Then we returned to Whitehall.'

'And we've been here since, licking our wounds,' von Frankenthal says restlessly.

'How's the Lieutenant?' I ask, fearing for his life, given the severity of the injury he received when the coaches crashed.

'The Prince had the surgeon from the *Royal Charles* see to him,' Francesca says, her eyes downcast. 'He removed the shaft of wood, but Wolf had lost a lot of blood. He hasn't regained consciousness.'

'He's a tough career soldier,' Armand comments, offering us hope. 'I'm sure he'll pull through.'

There's a moment of silence before I ask, 'And what of Dorian?'

Armand shakes his head and smiles in an impressed manner. 'He's bruised and battered, but he's rearing to go after the Sons of Cain.'

'He's a brave one, I'll tell you that.' Von Frankenthal's eyes are full of admiration for the young witch hunter.

'He's brave, but he's also reckless,' I correct, lowering my voice, unaware of the whereabouts of the *Angeli Mortis* and wary that they may overhear our conversation. 'He has no regard for his personal safety. It's almost as if he has a death wish. I even heard him say that he considers himself already dead. What's that all about?'

'I suspect Dorian can *see* the dead.' Armand looks into his goblet, reaffirming the suspicion he voiced yesterday. 'He has been corrupted by the *Malleus Maleficarum*. Of that, I am certain. He may be a brave and skilled witch hunter, but I fear he has paid a terrible price to acquire those skills.'

'Death wish or not, I'd have him fight by my side any day,' von Frankenthal says.

'Well, I hope I'm never forced to pair up with him again,' I say, not placing the same emphasis as von Frankenthal

127

has on courage and fighting prowess, believing the qualities of friendship and trust to be more important. 'Dorian has no regard for the value of life – especially his own. He scares me.'

'There's no need to worry about that. We'll stick together from here on,' Armand says, and I am reassured by the conviction in his tone. 'I won't run off again, and we'll keep a close eye on one another, making sure that we watch each other's backs and that none of us get left behind. As Francesca said, we are lucky none of us were killed last night. We will need to be more careful when we go after the Sons of Cain.'

'And when are we planning on doing that?' I ask. 'Please don't tell me we're going after them today.'

Armand stares into his goblet again. 'We don't have the luxury of time. The Sons of Cain may already be in London, inside the Altar of Sun, preparing to use the Codex Gigas to summon the Antichrist. Before we pursue them, we need to remove the satchel from the Hanging Tree, free the bodies hanging from the gibbets and have a priest administer them their last rites. Only then can the Sons of Cain be killed.'

'And when do we plan on going out to the Hanging Tree?' I ask.

Armand drains the remnants of his drink and wipes a sleeve across his mouth. 'We'll be riding out with the *Angeli Mortis* within the hour. Which reminds me – Jakob, can you come with me? There's something we need to discuss.'

My mind reeling from the fact that we will be shortly heading out to the Hanging Tree, I shrug at Francesca and von Frankenthal, follow Armand back along the corridor and enter a bedchamber.

✝

'I'm giving you one last chance to remain behind,' Armand says, closing the door after us.

'What? And miss out on all the fun. Not on your life.'

Armand grins. 'Francesca is right – you have been hanging around me too much. But seriously, you've been hurt and are exhausted. Perhaps it's best if you sit this one out.'

I look Armand square in the eye. 'I won't turn my back on my friends. You can lock me in one of these rooms, but I'll find a way out and come after you. And you know I will. You were prepared to risk your life to help me find my father, and I want to repay the favour. You're only in this mess because I dragged you off to Rotterdam. How do you think it makes me feel to be asked to sit back whilst the rest of you go off to slay the Sons of Cain?'

'We have become terribly sidetracked from our original mission, and I intend to help you find out what happened to your father once all this is resolved. But I hope you don't think that you are in debt to me because I helped you break into the gaol. I did that out of friendship.'

'And it's that very bond that won't allow me to abandon you and the others,' I say, believing Armand has just backed himself into a corner in this discussion. 'Don't under-estimate its power. It's important to be skilled in the use of blades and firearms, and I know that you place sole faith in your ability to wield your swords. You told me as much when we were trapped inside Noah's Ark beneath the Dead Sea. But sometimes the only thing we can truly rely on is our friends. The main reason why none of us were killed last night during the coach-chase was because we were watching out for one another. And not even a minute ago you said that we wouldn't be leaving anybody behind from here on.'

Armand looks at me for some time before sighing in acquiescence. 'You present a convincing argument, young Jakob. You constantly remind me – both through your words and actions – that the biggest hero is not the one with the strongest sword-arm, but the one with the biggest heart.' He points a finger in warning. 'But don't be too upset when I position you at the rear of the group. I might even see if we can get you a rifle and put you on sniper duty.'

A smile so wide crosses my lips, it's a miracle it doesn't knock Armand off his feet. 'Then get me a rifle. Let me show the Sons of Cain what the Hexenjäger are capable of.'

Armand punches me playfully on the shoulder. 'What have I created?'

I smile back. 'I'm only following in your footsteps.'

Armand shakes his head. 'I know, and that's what's worrying. Come on, we should join the others.'

'I'm glad that you wanted to talk in private,' I say, preventing him from opening the door, 'as there's something I want to discuss with you.'

'What is it?'

'Please, don't take this the wrong way. But you have changed since your appointment as Lieutenant.'

Armand makes a curious expression. 'How?'

'I think you feel a great burden of responsibility for those under your command. You don't want to see any of us get hurt.'

Armand gives me a sheepish look, removes his hat and runs a hand through his hair. 'Is it that obvious?'

'It's nothing to be ashamed of,' I say. 'A good commander should look after his troops. They look up to him for leadership and guidance, but they should also know that he cares for them and will not commit their lives to foolhardy actions.'

'It's strange, but it never used to worry me,' Armand says. 'I was Captain of Louis XIV's Palace Cavalry for two years, and never once did I ever question the decisions I made. Though I think you're right – I have changed. I'm not worried about von Frankenthal. A building could collapse on top of him and I'm sure he'd crawl out with nothing more than a few scratches. But I'm concerned for both you and Francesca.'

'After what took place in Sodom, you should know by now that we can take care of ourselves.'

Armand sighs and plays absent-mindedly with his hat's crimson plume. 'I know. But that doesn't mean that I'm

131

not going to worry. Sometimes I wish I could be more like Captain Blodklutt. I know Francesca considers him to be heartless. She was very critical of his decision to leave you and me behind when we fell into that spider-infested pit back in Sodom.'

I shudder. 'Please, don't remind me. I still have night-mares about that.'

Armand places his hat back on his head and adjusts its brim. 'Well, heartless or not, the fact remains that Blodklutt does not hesitate when it comes to making tough decisions. I'm sure he'd have no qualms in committing both you and Francesca to go after the Sons of Cain.'

'But we trust you with our lives,' I say, and notice a faint smile cross Armand's lips.

There's a knock on the door, and Prince Rupert enters the room, his left arm supported in a sling.

'I'm glad to see you up and on your feet again.' He pats me on the shoulder and nods at Armand. 'I was worried that I might not have had the chance to say goodbye.'

'You're going somewhere?' Armand asks, unable to mask his surprise.

'I'm afraid so,' the Prince says. 'I've only just stepped out of a meeting with the King and his war cabinet. Reports are flooding in that a massive Dutch fleet is assembling in the Channel. I've been ordered back to sea.'

I shake my head in disbelief. 'But what of the Sons of Cain and Mother Shipton's prophecy?'

'As much as the King wants the Sons of Cain slain, he believes that my expertise will be better served with the

English fleet,' the Prince explains. 'And his Majesty is right. I would like to lead you to the Hanging Tree, but the English fleet will be in need of me more than ever in the ensuing battle against the Dutch. The commander of the Dutch fleet, de Ruyter, is throwing everything he has against us. This could well be the battle that decides the outcome of the war. Sir Robert has already set sail, and my orders are to follow after him aboard the *Royal Charles* within the hour.'

'These are indeed grave times for England, beset by both the Devil's servants and the Dutch,' Armand says.

Prince Rupert nods, his eyes restless. I wonder if he feels restricted by his duty as an Admiral of the English navy, and would prefer to come with us after the Sons of Cain. During the Civil War, he was renowned as one of the bravest and most impetuous soldiers in England. Perhaps the rescue mission in Rotterdam and the chase through London last night have sparked his passion to once again feel the weight of tempered steel in his hands and engage enemies in close-quarters combat.

'I must go immediately, but I could not leave without saying thank you and wishing you luck for the task ahead,' he says, shaking our hands in turn. 'And as a token of my gratitude for saving my life last night, when you dragged me out of the sinking carriage, I would be honoured if you were to accept this.' He draws one of the cavalry pistols from his belt and hands it to me.

I accept the gift and study the Latin engraving along its barrel – *bono malum superate*. Translation: overcome evil with good. The barrel itself is much longer than any other I have seen, perhaps twenty inches in length, looking more like a carbine than a pistol. A heavy ornamental metal boss is attached to the butt, to act as a counterweight against the massive barrel.

'It is one of the finest pistols I have ever fired,' the Prince says fondly. 'As you can see, its barrel has been inscribed with holy text. It has also been blessed by the Archbishop of Canterbury. I had that done as a precautionary measure during the Civil War in case I happened to come across the Sons of Cain. Although I never got to test it against them, it will serve you nicely, for not only can you use it against the Sons of Cain, but it will also be effective against witches.'

The Prince then leans in close and whispers in my ear so that not even Armand can hear. 'It is one of the pistols I used to shoot the weather-vane atop St Mary's Church in Stafford, many years ago during the Civil War. But it has a secret – its barrel has been *rifled*. You can clip the ear off a fox at fifty yards with that pistol.' He winks and taps the end of his nose. 'Let's just keep that to ourselves.'

I hold the pistol before me, turning it around in my hand, marvelling at it. 'I don't know what to say. I don't think I can accept such a gift.'

'It is yours to keep,' the Prince says, his words final. 'If it were not for you, I would have drowned last night.' He taps the remaining pistol tucked into his belt. 'Besides, I still carry the pistol's twin. From this day forth consider us bound by a union of firearms.'

I smile warmly. 'But we are already connected.'

The Prince's brow furrows. 'Oh, really. How?'

'My father served under your brother, Prince Maurice, during the Civil War,' I say, informing the Prince of what Dietrich had told me just after my return from Schloss Kriegsberg. I'm also hopeful that the Prince might be able to reveal something about my father's past; some clue as to how he is connected to Vicomte de Turenne. 'He learned much about cavalry tactics from your brother, which he later employed in the Low Countries, fighting for the Spanish against the French. He became a cavalry officer of considerable repute thanks to Prince Maurice's training.'

Prince Rupert tilts his head in an interested manner. 'I had no idea. What is your father's name?'

'Tobias von Drachenfels.'

'It rings a bell,' the Prince says, nodding slowly. 'But its chime is so distant, muffled by the passage of so many years, that I cannot put a face to the name.' He laughs. 'Besides, I have had many knocks to the head. Sometimes I think it's a miracle that I can even remember my own name.'

He turns to leave but spins on his heel, as if he has suddenly remembered something important. 'I was wondering. Francesca ... is she ...' He pauses, evidently searching for the right words. '*Involved* with any of you?'

'Yes,' Armand says quickly – defensively – putting an abrupt end to the topic.

'Oh, well. There was no harm in asking.' The Prince grins. 'Then it is goodbye for now. Hopefully we will meet again, under more favourable circumstances. Franz will see to your needs, and feel free to stay as my guests as long as you please. Godspeed, gentlemen.'

I give Armand a wry glance as the Prince exits the room. 'You genuinely care about her, don't you?'

'Francesca? No.' Armand gives me an awkward look. 'I only said that to save the Prince from getting a bloody nose if he ever tries to make an advance on her.'

'But the Prince won't be able to do that if he's leaving this very instant, going off to war,' I say. 'So don't lie to me. You like her, and I don't mean in your usual, superficial way. You care deeply for her. Don't deny it – for you confessed as much yesterday.'

Armand snorts and waves his hand dismissively. He goes to exit the room, then turns and says, 'And what if I do? What difference would it make? You're the one she cares about.'

'She cares for me in the same way she would a younger brother,' I point out, making Armand hesitate in the doorway. 'Yes, I have a strong bond with Francesca. But she's like a sister to me. We are close friends, but nothing more.'

Armand comes back inside the room, closes the door behind him and grins wolfishly. 'Then the hunt is afoot again.'

I shake my head and laugh. 'You cannot help yourself, can you?'

Armand assumes a hurt air. 'What? I'm a passionate man in the prime of his life. And it's not every day that you meet someone like Francesca. Although, I must say, I am more shocked than anyone that I could actually consider settling down with one lady.' He grabs me by the shoulder and his eyes narrow conspiratorially. 'You have her confidence and trust. Can you put in a good word for me; drop a few subtle comments about how devilishly handsome and charismatic I am? She barely says a word to me these days; I think I took the teasing a little too far.'

I roll my eyes. 'Perhaps you did. I will see what I can do, but I can't promise anything. Although, as a starting point, it wouldn't hurt for you to be a bit more modest in her presence.'

Armand makes a baffled gesture. 'I'm one of the most humble people I know.'

I shake my head in wonder, amazed by the irony of this entire situation – that I, a mere novice in the ways of women, should be offering advice to a man who is notorious for stealing women's hearts.

'So, can I rely on you?' Armand presses.

'As I said, I will see what I can do. But I'd like you to answer something first.' I pause for a few seconds, wondering how Armand will respond to my question. 'What is the significance of your handkerchief?'

Armand's eyes narrow defensively. 'Why?'

'You risked your life trying to retrieve it when you dropped it back in the monastery atop Meteora. I also noticed how you tied it to your sword and kissed it, almost as if it was the cheek of a loved one, before we faced the Musketeers in the dungeon in Rotterdam. You also said that you had some debt to square with the Musketeers. I cannot help but think that the handkerchief and the Musketeers are closely connected.'

Armand regards me, his expression sombre. 'You don't miss much, do you?'

'No,' I say.

Armand wanders over to the room's window and stares out across the rooftops for a few moments. 'We are all haunted by ghosts from our past,' he says at length, his back still turned towards me. 'Von Frankenthal was tormented by the loss of Gerhard, and you desperately want to know the truth concerning your father. But I'm haunted by an event that has plagued my sleep every night for the past two years. I fear that not even God will grant me His forgiveness for what I have done.'

'Nothing can be that bad,' I say dismissively, but dreading to hear what could cause Armand such torment.

Armand lowers his head and takes a deep breath. His entire body becomes rigid, and he squeezes his eyes shut, as if he is trying to keep some distant memory from invading his thoughts. 'The handkerchief belonged to a woman whom I once loved. But she was also loved by the commander of the Musketeers, Charles d'Artagnan, who we encountered in the dungeon in Rotterdam.' He drifts into silence for some time, and when he eventually turns to look at me his eyes have glassed over, almost as though he is fighting back tears. He walks past me, opens the door to exit the room but then pauses, his head lowered. 'And I accidentally killed her. Promise that you will never ask me of this topic again.'

'I promise,' I say, dumbstruck.

Armand steps out into the corridor, leaving me to listen to his footfalls. I stare blankly at where I had last seen him. It is a long time before I finally leave the room.

CHAPTER TWENTY-TWO

'Is everything all right with Armand?' Francesca asks when I return to the drawing room. 'He came through here some time ago, and he wasn't his normal confident, pretentious self. He seemed down, almost depressed.'

'I brought up a ghost from his past.' I feel terrible for having raised the issue of the handkerchief. Had I known it was going to cause him such pain, I would never have probed into its significance. Trust me to open my big mouth.

'Can I help?' Francesca asks.

'Thanks, but not this time,' I say, not wanting to betray the French duellist's trust. 'This is something Armand wants to deal with himself.'

'Well, if you ever change your mind, my offer's still open.' Francesca rises from her seat and slings her crossbow over her shoulder. 'But we have a more pressing matter to deal with. Before Armand wandered off with Christian, he told me that we need to find you a rifle. Which is easier said than done. What does he expect – that we'll just click our fingers and one will magically appear out of nowhere?'

No sooner has Francesca clicked her fingers to emphasise her point, than Franz walks into the drawing room and announces, 'Here is the rifle you requested.'

I exchange a baffled look with Francesca and accept the firearm.

'How did you know?' I ask Franz.

'I passed your commander in the stairwell a few minutes ago,' Franz explains in his monotone voice, and hands me a fresh bandolier and powder flask to replace my previous supply, which was destroyed when I fell in the river last night. 'He told me that you required a rifle, so I took this one from the Prince's hunting room. The Prince used this during the Civil War. Like all of the firearms he used back then, it had been blessed by the Church as a precautionary measure should he ever encounter the Sons of Cain. I don't know if it has ever been fired, though. The Prince much prefers pistols to cumbersome rifles.'

'So I get to christen it against the Sons of Cain.' I inspect the firearm, not knowing if I should feel honoured or terrified. 'Aren't I the lucky one?'

The rifle is long – perhaps a foot longer than those kept in the Hexenjäger armoury in Burg Grimmheim, Saxony, and with which I became very familiar during my first week in the order, when I spent hours polishing and oiling the order's arsenal of blades and firearms. But the most remarkable feature of the rifle is that it has *three* chambers just above the trigger, at the base of the barrel.

'How am I supposed to use this?' I have never seen anything like it before.

Franz takes back the weapon, gives me a reproachful look and points at the chambers. 'You load the chambers as you would any other muzzle-loaded firearm. The dog-head, or firing pin, needs to be cocked in order for each chamber to be discharged. Once the gun has been fired, you simply rotate the chamber until the next cylinder locks into place. There's no need to reload the chambers until all three have been fired.'

'You make it sound simple,' I say as he hands me back the rifle.

'That's because it is,' Franz says, matter-of-factly. 'Prince Rupert is somewhat of a hunting enthusiast. I'd be a very rich man if I had a coin for every time I have accompanied him on hunting trips. I once used a gun similar to this one, so I am familiar with how it operates. As with all firearms of this nature, its barrels have been rifled, giving the ball far greater accuracy. This should be capable of hitting a target at two hundred yards. That is, of course, when it is in the hands of a competent marksman.'

Which I'm not, I think sourly. I'm still not yet fully profi-cient in the use of my pistols, let alone a gun that looks as though it requires a one-hundred-page instruction manual to operate.

Two or three days before leaving Saxony to begin our journey to Rotterdam, Robert Monro – the Scottish marksman who had demonstrated his skill with a rifle against the witches back in Schloss Kriegsberg – had offered to take me deer hunting in the forests surrounding Burg Grimmheim. I had turned him down, preferring to spend my last few days with my friend Sabina, and not looking forward to spending an entire day with Robert, who speaks as often as a Benedictine monk who has taken a vow of silence. But I am now regretting that I didn't spend at least one morning hunting with the Scotsman. It would have been a golden opportunity to learn from a master sniper.

Francesca raises her eyebrows and whistles. 'Two hundred yards!'

'Do you want to swap?' I gesture at the repeating crossbow slung over her shoulder.

Francesca pats her weapon guardedly. 'Not on your life. But that rifle's powerful. Are you sure you are going to be able to use it?'

I shrug. 'We'll find out soon enough.'

'Thanks for reminding me,' she says. 'We should get moving. Armand said that he was going to tell the *Angeli Mortis* that we would meet them in the foyer. We'd best be on our way.'

Having thanked Franz for the weapon and assured him that I will guard it with my life, I follow Francesca down to the foyer. Armand and von Frankenthal have assembled with the *Angeli Mortis* and Bishop Henchman. There is also a cowled monk standing beside the Bishop. The holy men stand out like sheep amongst a pack of wolves, their absence of weapons in direct contrast to the witch hunters, who are decked out in enough steel to sink a galleon.

'I've organised for some horses to be brought over,' the Bishop says. 'As soon as they arrive, you will begin your journey.' He indicates the monk standing by his side. 'This is Brother Lidcombe. He will accompany you to the Hanging Tree and deliver the last rites to the Forsaken. He speaks fluent German, so communication will not be an issue. I would come, but I am needed here in London to oversee the search for the Altar of Sun.'

I snigger under my breath. How terribly convenient. The Bishop was prepared to ask for our help to destroy the Sons of Cain, but he is not prepared to risk his own life, choosing to send one of his underlings in his stead. Prince Rupert had no choice but to return to sea, but I feel the Bishop considers himself too important to take unnecessary risks. He'll happily pull the strings from a distance, but will never reveal himself to his enemies.

'How long is the ride?' Armand asks, the distasteful look on his face revealing he shares some of my resentment towards the Bishop. 'It's already past midday. We only have five hours left before it starts to get dark. The Sons of Cain might be guarding the Hanging Tree, and we don't want to get caught fighting them and their Hell Hounds once night falls. They will be stronger than ever then.'

'We will ride out of London and head south,' Witch Finder Blackwood explains. 'We should be at the Hanging Tree within an hour of leaving the city.'

'That's good.' Armand winks at me; an unspoken gesture signifying that all is well between us. 'I've had enough of waiting around here. My blades have slumbered long enough.'

'Why aren't we taking a larger force?' I ask, airing a question that has been on my mind for some time now. 'Surely there are more than three *Angeli Mortis*. Why aren't the rest here? And, no offence intended to Brother Lidcombe, but why is only *one* holy man accompanying us? Why aren't we sending a force of hundreds of soldiers and priests?'

'There are only twelve members of our order; a number chosen to represent the Twelve Apostles of Christ,' Witch Finder Blackwood explains. 'Three other *Angeli Mortis* are currently in London, but they are assisting Bishop Henchman in searching for the Altar of Sun. The other six are on missions throughout England. Besides, Prayer and Dorian are amongst the most skilled fighters in the *Angeli Mortis*. Their blades will more than suffice. It may seem strange to you, but I was also once a man of the cloth. I'm sure that Brother Lidcombe and I will be able to deliver the last rites to the Forsaken.'

My eyes narrow inquisitively. 'You were once a priest?'

'Yes, but that was a long time ago, before I rode with Witch Finder General Hopkins and John Stearne during the Civil War,' the Witch Finder says. 'England is infested to the core with the Devil's servants. I left the pulpit, believing I could best serve our Lord with pistol and blade, ridding the realm of evil.'

Bishop Henchman toys with his beard thoughtfully. 'We have kept our numbers to a minimum so as to avoid a national scare,' he says, his voice lowered, once again adopting the secretive tone that seems to come so naturally to him. 'London, in particular, is already in a perpetual state of war. Londoners live with the constant fear of the Dutch sailing down the Thames to plunder and burn their city – especially after Sir Robert Holmes's raid of West-Terschelling. If word ever got out that the Sons of Cain were going to enter London to summon the Antichrist, panic would seize the city.'

'We should also point out that not all Londoners are happy with King Charles's rule,' Witch Finder Blackwood adds. 'Should the people of London rise in rebellion, they would be well supplied with the stashes of gunpowder barrels hidden throughout the city, left behind from the Civil War. It was only five years ago that the Fifth Monarchists staged a rebellion.'

I cock an eyebrow. 'The Fifth Monarchists?'

'The Fifth Monarchy Men are a group of anti-Papist extremists who believe that God will punish England for the debauch and lecherous excesses of the King's court,' the Witch Finder says.

'So much for the divine right of kings,' Armand scoffs.

Dorian glances at Armand. 'You are not a supporter of monarchy?'

One of the reasons why Armand had gone into voluntary exile from France was to free himself from the libertine and hedonistic ways of the court of Louis XIV. Sick of the affectation of court life, he wished to cleanse his soul of the moral corruption to which it had been exposed.

'I believe that all men are born equal,' Armand answers, looking back at the English witch hunter. 'We are all equal – kings, queens, and beggars – in the eyes of our Lord.'

Dorian's stare becomes defiant. 'There are many in our country who share such beliefs. They are known as *Levellers*.' He says this word as if it were bile in his mouth. 'They are considered by the authorities as traitors to the realm, wishing to break down its social order. They should all be hunted down and killed.'

Bishop Henchman clears his throat, a deliberate diversion to draw Armand's and Dorian's attention before their argument becomes more heated. 'The Fifth Monarchists take their name from the Book of Daniel, which prophesises that a Kingdom of God would follow on from the great civilisations of Babylon, Assyria, Greece and Rome. They believed that the restoration of King Charles to the throne of England in 1660 would herald London's birth as the new Jerusalem, the fifth prophesied kingdom of righteousness. Believing the King had failed to create this kingdom, a group of the Fifth Monarchists staged a rebellion. After three days of fighting, it was suppressed.'

Dorian smiles sadistically. 'The heads of their leader, Thomas Veneer, and twelve of his followers now sit on spikes at the southern entrance to London Bridge as a warning to all who dare rise up against the King.'

'Although the rebellion was put down over five years ago, there are still thousands of supporters of the Fifth

Monarchists,' Bishop Henchman says. 'If word ever got out that the Antichrist was going to be summoned – beneath Saint Paul's Cathedral, of all places – it would provide the rebels with irrefutable evidence that God has abandoned the King's court. It would plunge the nation back into civil war. And that is why we are keeping our numbers to a minimum. We don't want to advertise the fact that something is amiss by having an army of hundreds of soldiers and priests descend on the Hanging Tree. London is an unlit bonfire, built upon an unstable platform of war and dissatisfaction with the King's rule. We don't want to initiate the spark that sets it alight.'

Armand nods in understanding. 'So what can you tell us about the Sons of Cain? We know they can only be killed once we have freed the Forsaken, given them their last rites and removed the satchel from the Hanging Tree. But we don't know much about them other than that they were cavalry soldiers during the Civil War and that their eyes bleed. What powers do they have? Can our weapons at least harm them?'

'Even weapons blessed by the Church and engraved with holy passages will only wound the Sons of Cain,' Witch Finder Blackwood says. 'After a few seconds, their injuries heal and they are back at full strength. As you know, there are four Sons of Cain, but they each have different abilities and powers. I was going to inform you of these during our ride out to the cemetery, but I may as well tell you now.

'The first of the demonic horsemen is Thomas Whitcliff. He rode with Haslerigge's Lobsters during the Civil

War. They were a unit of cuirassiers, heavily armoured cavalry who received their name from the gear they wore. Despite this, they were defeated by lighter armed harquebusiers at the Battle of Roundway Down, one of the earliest engagements of the war. Although we have no information as to the role played by Whitcliff during the battle itself, it was his actions afterward that earned him a reputation of notoriety. He tortured to death over twenty Royalist prisoners who were placed under his custody, and who were to be escorted back to London. He then started capturing and torturing supporters of the King, keeping them locked in a cellar beneath his hovel in Whitechapel. By the time his neighbours became suspicious and reported him to the authorities, he had killed over thirty people. Their remains were found in shallow graves in the cellar. Before he could be captured, Whitcliff escaped from London. He served under General Ireton for some time before becoming one of the Sons of Cain.'

'He sounds like a charming fellow,' von Frankenthal mumbles under his breath.

'Whitcliff still has the tri-bar pot helmet, chest-guard and metal gauntlets he wore when serving under Haslerigge,' the Witch Finder continues. 'He's also a crack shot with his pair of long-barrelled cavalry pistols. Legend has it that he perfects his aim by shooting at a crucifix, hanging from a wall in a crypt hidden somewhere within the cemetery adjoining the Church of the Holy Trinity, and which the Sons of Cain use as their lair.'

'I've heard of this practice before,' Armand says. 'The crucifix must be shot on Good Friday. The next shot fired from the pistol will hit the heart of its target. As the pistol ball is guided by the Devil, it never misses.'

Witch Finder Blackwood nods and clears his throat before continuing. 'The second member of the Sons of Cain is a Swedish mercenary, Nils Fabricius. He is a staunch, puritanical Protestant, who perfected his fighting skills whilst serving under the Swedish king, Gustavus Adolphus, during the Thirty Years' War. He also fought for some time in Flanders before crossing over to England. He joined Parliament's cause in the Civil War, believing King Charles's court was rife with Catholicism. He always dresses in black and is a master swordsman.

'He earned a reputation for daring and cruelty during his time in Flanders, often sneaking into enemy strongholds under the cover of night, and slitting the throats of anyone he came across. It is said that he can melt into shadows, becoming as one with the night. The first his victims know of his presence is the instant they feel the cold touch of his dagger's edge against their throat. He is also an expert tracker and hunter. It is said that no-one can evade him once he has found your trail.'

'He has also been active in London recently,' Bishop Henchman adds. 'There have been many recent murders around the area of Saint Paul's Cathedral. The victims have been found lying in pools of blood, their necks slashed from ear to ear, and inverted crucifixes scrawled in blood on their foreheads.'

Von Frankenthal tilts his head curiously. 'What is the significance of the crucifixes?'

'It is Fabricius's call sign,' the Bishop says. 'He leaves it on nearly all of his victims.'

'And what has been the purpose of these murders?' Francesca asks, shifting uncomfortably. 'Why would Fabricius draw unwanted attention to the fact that the Sons of Cain have some interest in the area around the cathedral?'

'By day, the bookstores and shops around the cathedral are bustling with activity,' the Bishop explains. 'But come evening, the shops close down, the streets deserted. Not even the town watch dares patrol that section of London anymore, for fear of running into Fabricius. And that is why he has been active around Saint Paul's. He has cleared the area, ensuring that there will be nobody on the streets to interfere with the Sons of Cain when they descend beneath the cathedral to summon the Antichrist from the Devil's Bible.'

Armand clicks his tongue in thought for a few seconds before asking, 'And who are the two remaining members of the Sons of Cain?'

'The third member is a former Protestant preacher from the town of Lower Slaughter,' Witch Finder Blackwood says. 'He is a puritanical maniac and was driven by an extreme religious fervour during the period before the Civil War – he wanted to rid England of all forms of iconoclasm and idolatry. Believing the King's court was rotten to the core with Catholic conspirators, he joined the Parliamentarians during the war. He may not look like much of a threat, being perhaps sixty years old, with long grey hair and being so emaciated that his clothes seem to hang from his body. But don't be fooled, for he's not bad with a pistol and sword. His real skill, however, lies in his ability to summon spirits and demons to do his bidding. Not surprisingly, he is known as the Warlock of Lower Slaughter.'

I swallow nervously and look across at Armand, fearful of the trouble we have placed ourselves in. We encountered a possessed witch hunter, Heinrich von Dornheim, on my very first mission, when we had been sent to Schloss Kriegsberg to eliminate the Blood Countess. He had used a grimoire to summon a demon, which we only managed to defeat because we fought it on hallowed ground. I know how strong and deadly an opponent a demon can be, and the mere thought of having to face another one terrifies me. But there is no sign of fear in Armand's eyes. On the contrary, he snickers and winks back at me, as though there is no cause for concern.

'And the final member of the Sons of Cain?' the Frenchman asks, looking back at Witch Finder Blackwood.

The Witch Finder holds Armand's stare for a while, almost as if warning him that he should brace himself for what he is about to hear. 'The final member is their leader, Alistair McClodden, the Demon of Moray Firth. He joined the forces of Parliament in the opening months of the Civil War, infuriated by King Charles's attempt to impose the Book of Common Prayer on his country. He's a giant of a man, standing nearly as tall as our friend here.' He pauses as he jerks his chin towards von Frankenthal. 'He has flaming red hair, wears a kilt and wields a massive, two-handed claymore. He also has the strength of three men and goes berserk in battle. Once he starts killing, he does not stop.'

'At least we now know what we are up against,' Francesca says sombrely.

Armand looks down at the floor for some time, his hands clasped on the hilts of his swords, and I wonder if he is questioning his decision to agree to help Bishop Henchman. At length, he looks up, stares hard at Witch Finder Blackwood, and asks, 'Can we beat them?'

The leader of the *Angeli Mortis* nods. 'If we can break the spell that makes the Sons of Cain immortal, then we can kill them.' He moves off with Armand, Bishop Henchman and Brother Lidcombe to the far side of the foyer, where they talk in hushed tones.

Dorian, meanwhile, notices the rifle slung over my shoulder and walks behind me to inspect the weapon. 'An impressive-looking rifle,' he says, then adds in a mocking tone, 'but can you use it?'

I notice von Frankenthal bristle at the English witch hunter's comment, but it is Francesca who intervenes. 'The Ghost and Spartaco can thank their lucky stars that Jakob didn't have a rifle on him last night,' she says. 'If he had, he would have put an end to them in a matter of seconds.'

I wish Francesca hadn't said that. I know she is just trying to look out for me, but there's no need to lie, particularly to someone who is evidently proficient with a rifle. Chances are Dorian will now want to challenge me to a shooting competition, and that's the last thing I want.

'So, you fancy yourself as a marksman?' Dorian asks, stopping in front of me and staring me up and down, his upper lip curled contemptuously. Despite being painted white, his face is riddled with cuts and lacerations, giving him a truly nightmarish appearance. 'Perhaps we could have a competition one day, to see who is the better marksman?'

My stomach tightens. Nice job, Francesca.

As if the situation could not get any worse, she then says, 'Just name the time and place. That is, of course, if you are prepared to put your reputation where your mouth is.'

'Oh, I am prepared to do that,' Dorian replies with smug confidence. 'Let's just hope that today Jakob shoots before he lets the enemy get away.'

In spite of his earlier comments commending Dorian as a brave and skilled fighter, von Frankenthal's eyes darken like a gathering storm. 'You're out of line,' he warns.

Dorian snorts and walks over to join Prayer. 'You hold no authority over me. I'll do – and say – as I please.'

Von Frankenthal takes a menacing step towards Dorian. 'You'll do *what*?'

I reach up, placing a restraining hand on von Frankenthal's shoulder. 'I'm certain Dorian means no offence. He is merely frustrated that he has been forced to work with a rival order. I'm sure we would feel the same if the *Angeli Mortis* turned up unannounced at Burg Grimmheim, bearing a letter from the Archbishop of Canterbury, informing us that we had to work with them. I, for one, would not be happy. I'd see it as a slap across the face; an insult, questioning my abilities as a witch hunter.'

A surprised look crosses Dorian's face, evidently shocked that I should demonstrate empathy for him. I actually believe I have a good understanding of his nature. He uses a rifle – a weapon preferred by snipers, solitary fighters who use stealth to blend into their environment to pick off their targets. They work best when alone, unhindered by less skilled companions, who may betray their presence. I also recall how last night Dorian went after the Ghost by himself. He did not accompany the rest of us through Whitehall. The first I knew that he had left the Prince's lodgings was when he emerged from the shadows, his rifle trained on the Ghost.

I have firsthand experience in seeing what rivalry can do between orders. Back in Sodom it almost cost Captain Blodklutt his life when he was inadvertently stabbed in the shoulder by the Spaniard, Diego Alvarez. Just for once, I would like to think that I could trust my companions, and not have to worry about whose blade – or *rifle* – I have to keep a careful eye on.

'Let's not lose sight of who the enemy is here,' I continue, believing my attempt at diplomacy is working and that Dorian will not snap the olive branch I am offering him. I also note that Prayer, standing beside Dorian, has lowered her eyes, as if embarrassed by her companion's behaviour. 'Should we fail, not only will London burn, but the Antichrist will be summoned from the Codex Gigas. That is why we have joined forces; not because we question the ability of the *Angeli Mortis*, but because the threat is so great. Should we fail, the greatest evil known to man will

155

enter the world. And we must stop that from happening at all costs. So let's keep our swords in their scabbards until we reach the Hanging Tree. It would be foolish for us to give the Sons of Cain an unfair advantage.' I look at Dorian. 'And I will accept your challenge in a game of marksmanship. But only after we have dealt with the Sons of Cain. And only as a friend, done in good will.'

'Now there's a future commander in the making,' Bishop Henchman commends, walking over to pat me on the shoulder. I was unaware that the others had finished their discussion and watched the entire affair. I feel the blood rush to my cheeks. 'Jakob is right. You need to bury your differences and work together. The price of failure is too great. Hexenjäger or *Angeli Mortis*; Catholic or Protestant. It matters not when we are facing the greatest evil to have ever threatened this world.'

'So, what's the plan?' von Frankenthal asks, the fuse of his rage having fizzled out.

'We shall assess the situation upon arriving at the Hanging Tree,' Witch Finder Blackwood says. 'We need to see who – or *what* – is guarding the satchel and gibbets. With any luck, the Sons of Cain won't be there, as I strongly believe they are already in London and have perhaps already made their way beneath Saint Paul's with the Codex Gigas. But the four Hell Hounds guard the tree, day and night. They will need to be slain, and they will not go down easily.'

A wry smile crosses von Frankenthal's lips. 'Four *dogs*, you say. How hard can that be?'

It is the Witch Finder's turn to give a wry smile. 'I take it you've never before encountered a Hell Hound?' When von Frankenthal shakes his head, he adds, 'Then prepare yourself to face four of the most dangerous beasts to have ever been spawned from Hell's bowels.'

While the Witch Finder's words do little to unnerve von Frankenthal, who cracks his knuckles in anticipation of the challenge, a terrible nervousness wells in my stomach. I am looking forward to this ensuing fight as much as a condemned criminal anticipates taking their final steps up the gallows to the hangman's noose. But I remind myself that my friends will be counting on me, and that it could be my blade or rifle that turns the tide in our favour.

There's a knock on the door and a guard appears, announcing that the horses are awaiting us. We head outside, mount up, bid farewell to Bishop Henchman and follow Witch Finder Blackwood through Whitehall into the bustling streets of London. I cannot help but feel that each clop of our horses' hooves on the cobbles is like a death knell counting down the time to our impending doom.

⚔CHAPTER⚔
TWENTY-THREE

We have only been riding through the city for a few minutes when I pull up my mount and stare down a shadow-filled laneway off to my left.

'What is it?' Armand asks, drawing up alongside me. 'You look as if you have just seen a ghost.'

'Not a ghost, but Justus Blad, the Witch Bishop of Aachen.'

I had met Justus earlier this year during a meeting held in Grand Hexenjäger Wrangel's office to discuss the secret location of the Tablet of Breaking. One of the Inquisition's most feared interrogators, Justus had asked how I knew of the relic's resting place. When Grand Hexenjäger Wrangel came to my defence, Justus cast suspicion over the security of our order, questioning if the Devil's servants had infiltrated the walls of Burg Grimmheim. The Bishop of Paderborn had been forced to intervene, assuring Justus that he was mistaken.

Believing the creation of the Hexenjäger would undermine the authority of the Inquisition, Justus has been a vocal opponent of our order. He finds evidence of the Devil everywhere he looks. Backed by the full authority of the Holy Roman Inquisition, he has sent hundreds of accused heretics and witches to be burned alive at the stake.

A doubtful look crosses Armand's face. 'That's impossible. What would a member of the Inquisition be doing in a Protestant land? And down that alley, of all places?'

Noticing that the rest of our company has stopped several yards down the road waiting for Armand and me, I swing out of my saddle and make my way quickly down the laneway. 'I don't know. But I'm sure I saw him. He disappeared into one of the doorways down here.'

Armand calls out to the others that he won't be long, dismounts and races after me. There are several two-storey, timber-framed buildings on our left, and we try their doors. All are locked, but I notice a symbol of three Xs carved into the wooden lintel of the last door we try.

Armand shrugs. 'Even if it was Justus Blad who you saw, we don't have time to go knocking on every door. Come on, Jakob. We're keeping the others waiting.'

I follow reluctantly after the Frenchman, join our companions and ride out of the city. All the while, I cannot shake the image of Justus Blad from my thoughts. Despite the improbability of the Witch Bishop of Aachen being in

London, I'm sure that it wasn't my imagination playing tricks. What would bring him this far away from Catholic lands, I cannot even begin to imagine.

An hour or so passes before Witch Finder Blackwood announces that we are only a mile from the cemetery in which the Hanging Tree is located. We stop to have a final check of our weapons, then continue up the road for a further half mile before the Witch Finder steers his horse off to the left, guiding us along a narrow trail.

I am drawn to a poster nailed to a tree bordering the trail, and I ride over towards it.

'It looks as if somebody is in trouble with the law,' I comment.

Armand leans over in his saddle to read the poster: 'Wanted dead or alive, Claude Duval, for armed robbery at Hampstead Heath.'

'I don't even know why they bother putting up these wanted posters,' Witch Finder Blackwood says, nudging his mount along the road, forcing us to follow after him. 'They'll never catch the Gentleman Highwayman.'

Armand raises his eyebrows in interest. 'The Gentleman Highwayman,' he says, savouring the sound of the title. 'I like it. But who is he?'

'Since the Civil War, highwaymen have roamed the byways and roads of this country, holding up stagecoaches and lone travellers,' the Witch Finder answers. 'Most are disgruntled ex-soldiers, short of coin since their military units disbanded. Being uncouth, cold-blooded killers, they'd sooner take your life than your money pouch. But there are a few who have acquired hero-like status, winning the hearts of women with their fancy clothing and charm. And of these gentlemen highwaymen there is none more famous than Claude Duval.'

'A fellow Frenchman,' Armand remarks, impressed.

Dorian snickers under his breath. 'Only last month he held up a coach near Hampstead Heath. There was a lady aboard who played a tune on her flageolet – I assume to demonstrate that she wasn't scared. Impressed, Duval escorted her out of the coach and, in front of her distraught husband and servants, danced with her. He then had the audacity to demand the husband pay for the performance.'

Armand slaps his thigh and roars with laughter. 'I like the man! He's a rascal by my own heart.'

Francesca steers her mount closer to mine, leans across in her saddle and whispers, 'As if the world isn't big enough for just one Armand.'

'I wouldn't get too excited, Frenchman, for it's only a matter of time before Duval is caught and dangled from a noose,' Dorian says, seeming to take a morbid pleasure from the deflated look he receives from Armand.

Witch Finder Blackwood looks back over his shoulder. 'How so? They've been trying to catch him for several years now and they've never got close.'

Dorian raises a finger to emphasise his point. 'But now the Thief-taker General has been hired to hunt him down.'

The Witch Finder makes a surprised look. 'I wasn't aware of that. Then I take back my earlier comment, for Duval is as good as hung.'

'So the Thief-taker General actually exists?' I ask.

Witch Finder Blackwood nods and I whistle in surprise. Even as far away as Saxony it's not uncommon for parents to warn their children that if they are not good the Thief-taker General will come and take them. Up until the age of ten I used to have nightmares about the man, believing that if I did not complete all my chores and keep my room clean, he would break into my bedroom at night and drag me off to some nearby gallows. As I got older, I started to doubt his existence, believing he was nothing more than a myth created by parents who wanted to get ill-behaved children off to bed at night. But it seems as if I was wrong.

Francesca makes a baffled gesture. 'Would someone care to tell me who this is?'

Witch Finder Blackwood sets his dark eyes on the Italian. 'His real name is Shannon Sharpe, and he is the most famous bounty hunter in England. He and his band of four trackers, known as the Grey Runners – a name they have acquired from the grey coats they wear – have tracked thieves, murderers and traitors all the way from the Scottish Highlands down to the pirate coves of Penzance. Once they start hunting you, they never stop.'

Dorian casts an askance glance at Armand and gives a sadistic smile. 'So much for the Gentleman Highwayman.'

Armand gives me a disappointed look and shrugs before we continue along the trail.

CHAPTER TWENTY-FOUR

Whereas the road initially wound its way through meadows and farms, we now find ourselves riding through a desolate landscape. The grass here is scorched, and the trees are twisted and black, their branches reaching out like those of charred corpses. The air carries a sickly stench of carrion, and tendrils of mist roam across the landscape like orphaned children searching for their parents after the sacking of a city. Soon it becomes impossible to see further than a hundred yards ahead, and an abandoned church materialises through the grey haze.

Having tethered our mounts in a copse of withered trees at the base of the hill, we follow the Witch Finder up to the church and pass through its iron-ribbed doors. We assemble in the nave, its floor littered with broken pews and debris. Ravens squabble above us, perched atop the rib cage of wooden beams supporting the broken-down roof, and rats the size of cats scurry away at our approach.

'This is the Church of the Holy Trinity,' Witch Finder Blackwood announces, his voice a low murmur that sounds alien and intrusive in this space. 'It was once richly decorated and held congregations of hundreds. That is, of course, until it was gutted by Puritan Roundheads during the Civil War. The service books were ripped apart and trampled underfoot, the altar used for musket practice, and horses were tethered in the aisles. But the final nail was hammered into this church's coffin when the Sons of Cain arrived, signing their pact with the Devil under the old oak tree in the neighbouring cemetery.'

'Charming.' Von Frankenthal screws up his nose as he looks around the church. 'But why have you brought us here?'

'I'll show you. Follow me.' The Witch Finder leads us into the northern transept, where he opens a heavy oak door and directs us up a narrow flight of winding stone stairs. Up and up we go, until we eventually reach a wall. There is a ladder set against it, leading to a trap door in the ceiling.

The Witch Finder looks back at us. 'We have reached the top of the church's tower. From here, we'll be provided with a bird's-eye view of the cemetery to the south. Not only will we be able to study its layout, but I'm hoping we can observe who is guarding the Hanging Tree. We'll be able to plan our attack before heading in.'

He then climbs up the ladder, opens the trap door and leads us out onto the top of the tower. Crouched low – so as to avoid being spotted by anyone, or *anything*, looking up from the cemetery – we sneak over to the southern wall, hide behind the battlements and slowly lift our heads up to spy over the wall.

The land to the south slopes down to what appears to be a forest, its perimeter – well over three hundred yards away – only visible for short periods, when wind parts the shroud of mist blanketing the land. Between the church and the distant forest lies the cemetery, its tombstones littered across the ground. The massive stone walls of the cemetery's few tombs tower over the forest of tombstones and crucifixes, looking like grey galleons trapped in a ghost-like sea. Over a hundred yards away, in the centre of the graveyard, stands a massive black oak tree, rising out of the sea of mist like some titanic beast.

The Hanging Tree.

Even from here we can discern the four gibbets dangling from its branches. The metal cages contain the skeletal remains of the four brothers slain by the Sons of Cain, left to rot for an eternity.

Scanning the cemetery, I can see no sign of the Sons of Cain or of the Hell Hounds. I breathe a sigh of relief, hoping that we might be able to make it to the Hanging Tree without incident. But then something *massive* stirs in the gloom over to the far right of the cemetery, and it takes every ounce of my willpower not to bolt in fear.

Dear God! What have we got ourselves into?

The beast looks like a wolf, but is as large as a *horse*. Even from this distance I can identify the slavering maw, armed with incisors over a foot long – it's a Hell Hound! Perhaps it is just a trick of my imagination, but smoke seems to rise from its fur and its eyes are ablaze with hell fire.

I point at the beast, unable to draw my eyes away from it. 'How are we supposed to defeat that?'

Armand fingers the pommel of his mortuary blade. 'Everything can be killed. Remember, too, that we are on hallowed ground, meaning that the Hell Hounds will be stripped of much of their power.'

'Look – there's another,' Prayer whispers, pointing over to the far left, where a second beast stalks through the mist, as if patrolling the perimeter.

'And the remaining two are over there, on either side of the Hanging Tree.' Francesca gestures with a nod to the black oak in the centre of the graveyard.

'So we know the location of the demonic wolves,' Witch Finder Blackwood says. 'But there is no sign of the Sons of Cain. As I said earlier, I think they may already be in London. That will make our task here easier.'

'Or they might be sleeping in their hidden lair,' Francesca remarks dryly.

'Either way, we should strike now, whilst the tree is guarded by only the Hell Hounds,' Armand says.

Brother Lidcombe gives Armand a terrified look, then sits with his back against the wall, chewing on his fingernails.

Armand regards him with concern. 'Are you going to be able to carry through with this?'

Brother Lidcombe swallows. 'Of course. I'm just a little nervous, that's all. But it will pass.'

'I hope so,' Witch Finder Blackwood says, his brooding eyes locked on the monk. 'Because a moment's hesitation could prove to be fatal when we are down there. We will need to move fast.'

Armand smiles reassuringly at Brother Lidcombe. 'We are all nervous. But we are Christ's warriors. He watches over us.'

Taking strength from Armand's words, the monk takes a steadying breath. 'Any ideas as to how we are going to do this?'

'This tower offers a perfect sniping position,' Witch Finder Blackwood says promptly, as if he has already assessed the layout of the cemetery and formulated a plan of attack. He sits down beside the monk, and the rest of us join them. 'Perhaps Jakob, Francesca and Dorian can take position up here, armed with their rifles and crossbow. They can provide cover for the rest of us as we make our way to the Hanging Tree. I also noted that the door providing entry into the tower can be locked from the inside. That could prove to be useful in keeping out the Hell Hounds should they decide to come after them.'

Dorian shakes his head. 'I work alone.'

I roll my eyes. Now how did I know he was going to say that? He's as predictable as the rising sun.

'Normally, yes,' Witch Finder Blackwood says. 'But not on this occasion. And I want no further discussion of this matter.'

Dorian considers the Witch Finder for some time before he shrugs. 'If that's the way you want it, then so be it. But how do you intend to reach the Hanging Tree? Those beasts aren't going to sit back and just let you walk up there. They'll rip you to shreds the second they detect you.'

'The wind is blowing from the east,' the Witch Finder says. 'So we'll enter the cemetery from the west. We don't want the Hell Hounds picking up our scent before we've even set foot in the cemetery.'

'Fair enough,' Dorian says. 'But what will you then do?'

'What would *you* do?' Armand asks, throwing the question back at the English witch hunter.

Dorian looks over the wall again, studying the layout of the cemetery and the location of the Hell Hounds. 'Two hounds guard the perimeter. The other two, however, don't seem to wander further than twenty yards from the Hanging Tree. And it's these two that will prove to be the problem. Whilst you will be able to slip between the outer pair without too much difficulty, you won't have any such luck with the hounds guarding the Hanging Tree. They will need to be drawn away from the area in order for you to reach the satchel and gibbets.' He pauses, deep in thought. 'One possible way of leading the hounds away is for one of you – and it cannot be the monk, for he will be needed to give the last rites to the skeletons in the gibbets – to reveal yourself, catching the hounds' attention, and then run like hell. With any luck, the hounds will give chase, allowing the rest of you to make it safely to the tree.'

'Pity help the sacrificial lamb,' von Frankenthal remarks dryly.

'Any other suggestions?' Armand asks the rest of us.

Dorian clears his throat. 'It's pointless having three of us stay up here in the tower. We'll need every person we can spare to cut down the gibbets. Let me remain here by myself. I will use my rifle to draw the beasts over to the church. As was noted earlier, the door to the tower can be locked. It will also be a tight squeeze for the hounds if they attempt to come up through the trap door. Hopefully I can buy you enough time to allow you to do what must be done at the tree.'

'That's assuming, of course, that you can draw all four Hell Hounds over to you,' Prayer says sceptically.

'Which will be impossible,' I say. 'You would never be able to reload your rifle in time. You would be lucky if you could get off two shots. And even if you did somehow manage to get off more shots and draw the hounds after you, how would you then make your escape? That door will not keep the beasts at bay forever. It would only be a matter of time before they break into the tower.'

'Well, I don't see anybody else coming up with any

better ideas,' Dorian says. 'So let me do it. It's the only way of drawing the beasts away from the tree.'

There's an awkward moment of silence as Witch Finder Blackwood and Armand contemplate Dorian's offer. At length, they nod reluctantly.

'It's a good plan,' Prayer says, interrupting the officers before they have a chance to comment. 'But it won't work – not as long as Dorian is the only person assigned to the tower. Jakob is right; Dorian will never get enough shots off in time. There needs to be a *second* marksman up here with him.'

I look across at Dorian and say reluctantly, 'I guess it's time to see what this rifle can do.'

'Don't be ridiculous. You've never fired a rifle before in your life,' Francesca says. She receives a surprised look from Dorian, evidently recalling the Italian's earlier comment that I was a crack shot. 'I'll do it,' she replies.

'No you won't,' Armand snaps. 'Neither of you are going to do any such thing.' He gestures for Francesca and me to follow him to the far side of the tower, where we can discuss the matter in private.

'This is not a good idea,' he says, his back turned towards our companions and his voice lowered so that they cannot hear. 'If Dorian's plan works, and the hounds are lured to the tower, it will become a death trap. I want neither of you up here when that happens. And don't you dare argue back that I am only doing this because you think that I am questioning your fighting ability. This is simply too dangerous. I wouldn't even allow von Frankenthal to stay up here as bait.'

Francesca plants her hands on her hips in defiance. 'But it's all right to condemn one of the *Angeli Mortis* to their probable death? That's courageous of you.'

'That's not fair,' Armand says, visibly hurt by her comment. 'That is Dorian's choice.'

'I'm sorry,' Francesca says. 'But you will never make it to the tree unless we manage to lure the Hell Hounds away. And irrespective of how skilled a shot Dorian is, he will not be able to do that on his own. I can get ten shots off with my crossbow in a matter of seconds. There will be enough of you down in the cemetery to free the gibbets, but Dorian will not be able to draw the hounds away unless he has my help.' She pauses and looks deep into Armand's eyes. 'Besides, it will be a lot safer up here than down in the cemetery.'

'Not when the Hell Hounds come after you – and mark my words, they will,' Armand says. He considers Francesca for some time before his eyes soften in acquiescence and he curses under his breath in frustration. 'I can't believe I'm going to agree to this, but you can stay here with Dorian. I'm only letting you on the condition that you give me your word that you will be cautious. I'll race back to help you the second we've finished doing what needs to be done at the tree.'

Francesca smiles, not only in gratitude, I believe, but perhaps because she is touched by Armand's genuine concern for her safety. 'Thank you. And yes, I give you my word that I will be careful.'

'Believe me, you won't be thanking me if Dorian's plan

works and the hounds come after you,' Armand mumbles under his breath as he returns to join the others and inform them of his decision.

Francesca turns after him, but I grab her by the hand, forcing her to look back at me. 'You're very brave. Are you sure you want to do this?'

'I'm no braver than you. Remember that you were first to offer to stay back with Dorian,' she points out. 'It's like you said – Dorian will never be able to do this by himself. He needs assistance, and I am proficient with my crossbow.' She pauses, and a wry smile crosses her lips. 'Besides, I'm not having you stay up here. You'd more than likely take off someone's head with your new rifle. Come on, let's join the others.'

Chuckling at Francesca's comment, I follow her back to our companions, where I take my rifle off my shoulder and hand it to Dorian. 'You'll have much greater need of this than I will. You'll get off three shots with this in a matter of seconds. Just make sure you don't miss.'

Dorian's eyes narrow determinedly as he accepts the rifle. 'Believe me, I won't.' He then turns to Witch Finder Blackwood. 'You'd best get going. Hide down in the fields over to the west. When you are in position, Francesca and I will start shooting. Once we draw the hounds after us, make your way to the tree.'

Armand turns to Francesca, evidently torn by his decision to allow her to stay. 'We'll be as fast as we can. And then we'll come to help you.'

She winks confidently. 'Just worry about yourselves.'

We move off, leaving Dorian and Francesca atop the tower. Just as I am going through the trapdoor, I notice Prayer linger behind. She talks briefly to Dorian in hushed tones, kisses him on the cheek and follows after us, tears in her eyes.

CHAPTER TWENTY-FIVE

Our pistols and blades gripped in our hands, we crawl across the scorched grass until we are some thirty yards or so away from the edge of the cemetery. Witch Finder Blackwood snaps up his hand, signalling for us to stop.

Only a few seconds later, a massive figure prowls through the tombstones directly ahead. I shudder and stare up at the Hell Hound. It appears even larger now, standing over seven feet tall, its eyes blazing like Hell's furnaces. Despite its size, it drifts silently through the mist, moving with the stealth of a cat stalking its prey.

We wait for what seems an eternity before the Hell Hound moves up to the northern edge of the cemetery. Breathing a collective sigh of relief, we stare up at the distant church tower, where Dorian waves his rifle above his head.

'That's the signal,' Witch Finder Blackwood whispers. 'It's time.'

The next instant, a crossbow bolt whizzes out of the mist, and I turn my head to look at the Hell Hound that only recently stalked past us. Its head jolts back, as if hit by a sledgehammer, taking the full impact of Francesca's shot. Staggering back, it shakes its head, disoriented. Before the beast has time to lift its blazing eyes up towards the tower, Dorian discharges his rifle. I nearly jump out of my skin at the sound of his shot, which blasts straight through one of the hound's eyes, exploding through its skull with a cloud of pink mist.

As the beast drops dead, I cover my ears against a blood-curdling growl. It starts from the centre of the cemetery, near the Hanging Tree, and is answered by a more distant call from the south, near the edge of the forest. This is followed a second later by the sound of the three remaining hounds tearing towards the church, leaving swirling trails of mist in their wake.

As soon as the Hell Hound to the south rushes past us, Witch Finder Blackwood leaps to his feet. 'They've taken the bait. Let's move!'

We follow after him and sprint towards the cemetery.

I just pray to God that we won't be joining the dead buried there.

We race into the cemetery, hurdling tombstones in our attempt to reach the Hanging Tree. Armand streaks ahead, his dual blades glistening in the mist. Then there's Prayer and me, some ten yards or so behind the Frenchman. Wrapped in the folds of her black cloak, Prayer is a blur of movement, barely detectable in the gloom. Following us are Brother Lidcombe and Witch Finder Blackwood. The witch hunter's face is set in a grim scowl, his eyes locked determinedly on the Hanging Tree. This is in direct contrast to the monk, whose eyes are wide with terror. He is frantically rubbing the crucifix hanging from his neck as if to give himself courage for the task ahead. Then, finally, bringing up the rear is von Frankenthal, a hulking mass of muscle, the rapier gripped in his hand looking like a toothpick protruding from a shoulder of ham.

Glancing over to my right, I see the Hell Hounds tearing towards the church and realise that the tower will indeed become a death trap. Having seen one of the beasts killed with relative ease, I had hoped that we had overestimated them, and that Dorian and Francesca would be able to dispatch the remaining three hounds even before they reached the church, picking them off with their rifles and crossbow. But it's only now I realise the peril they have placed themselves in. Whereas the first hound had been caught by surprise, Dorian and Francesca have lost the advantage, the remaining three beasts tearing through the mist with such speed that it almost defies comprehension.

Three more of Francesca's crossbow bolts *zip* through the air and Dorian, now armed with my rifle, lets off two shots in rapid succession. But the hounds are moving impossibly fast, and all of Francesca's bolts miss their targets.

Dorian's claim that he is a skilled marksman, however, was no idle boast.

His first shot is directed at the beast that had moved up from the south. The rifle ball punches into the beast's muzzle, forcing it to snap its head to the side and howl in pain. But rather than kill it, Dorian's shot only seems to enrage the beast, which now tears forward even faster than before.

His second shot hits one of the hounds that had been guarding the Hanging Tree, punching into its left flank, knocking it off its feet and sending it crashing into a tombstone. Before Dorian has time to ready his third and final shot, the hound scrambles up and races towards the church. It now uses the mist to its advantage, weaving left and right so as to avoid presenting an easy target.

Being the first to reach the Hanging Tree, Armand rips down the satchel and hacks it to shreds with his sabre and mortuary blade. He is joined a second or two later by Prayer and me, and we waste no time in sheathing our swords and scurrying up the trunk of the ancient oak. As the rest of our team assemble at the base of the tree, we climb out onto the branches and use our daggers to sever through the ropes tying two of the gibbets to the tree.

The iron cages crash heavily to the ground. I look over towards the church, fearing that the sound might have alerted the Hell Hounds to our presence. Seeing that the beasts are still racing towards the tower, I breathe a sigh of relief and climb over towards one of the two remaining gibbets. I look across at Prayer, who is following my lead and making her way over to the remaining iron cage, and smile victoriously, believing that we are actually going to pull this off. Von Frankenthal and Witch Finder Blackwood have already prised open the bars of one of the gibbets and extracted the skeleton. Having produced a Bible from his robe, Brother Lidcombe is now standing over the first of the Forsaken, delivering the last rites.

And it's at that moment I notice a cloaked rider watching us.

CHAPTER TWENTY-SIX

'**W**e've got company!' I warn. As one, my companions snap their heads to where I point, but the stranger is no longer there. It is as if the horseman has been swallowed by the mist.

'What did you see?' Witch Finder Blackwood asks.

'There was a man mounted on a black steed, some fifty yards down to the south,' I say.

The Witch Finder closes his eyes, as if fearing the worst. 'And what is he wearing?'

'A leather buff coat and a tan cloak,' I say promptly, surprised that even though I only caught a fleeting glimpse of the rider, their image is burned into my memory. 'He also has long, grey hair and a purple sash wrapped around his waist. A pair of pistols are holstered by the sides of the mount and a heavy blade is sheathed by his side.'

Witch Finder Blackwood curses under his breath, produces the *Malleus Maleficarum* from the leather case slung over his shoulder and moves to the southern side of the Hanging Tree. 'He wears the clothing of a Parliamentarian cavalry soldier from the Civil War. As uniform coats were not worn, officers often issued sashes to soldiers under their command as a means of identification. Purple was the colour chosen by General Ireton. And from the man's grey hair, it's safe to assume that it is the Warlock of Lower Slaughter. The Sons of Cain are here!'

'I only saw the one rider,' I clarify. Although I am glad to be up the tree, I look around fearfully, expecting the Warlock of Lower Slaughter to come charging out from behind a tomb. 'What do we do now?'

'You carry on with the gibbets.' Armand moves over to stand beside Witch Finder Blackwood. 'Leave the Son of Cain to us.'

As if in answer to Armand's bold statement, a gunshot rings out. I turn and see the Son of Cain guide his mount out from behind a thick patch of mist only twenty yards away, a smoking pistol gripped in his hand.

Witch Finder Blackwood slumps to his knees. He clutches his chest, then removes his hand to stare at his blood-stained palm. My eyes wide in disbelief, I watch, horrified, as the commander of the *Angeli Mortis* topples forward to lie face-down on the ground.

CHAPTER TWENTY-SEVEN

All hell breaks loose.

Holstering his pistol, the Warlock of Lower Slaughter draws his heavy broadsword and spurs his mount towards us. At the same moment, one of the Hell Hounds, alerted by the Son of Cain's pistol shot, turns back from the tower and tears through the mist, coming straight for us.

Whereas I cling to the branch, too afraid to move, Prayer drops from the tree. Rolling across the ground to break the impact of the fall, she leaps to her feet and darts over to stand guard before the Witch Finder, who lies motionless in an ever-widening pool of blood, the *Malleus Maleficarum* clasped in his outstretched hand.

Von Frankenthal orders me to stay put and moves to guard Brother Lidcombe. But it's Armand who leaves me gaping, for in an act that I can only describe as suicidal bravado, he races forward to intercept the Son of Cain.

Stepping aside from the thundering hooves at the last moment, Armand deftly dodges the rider's humming blade. In the same fluid motion, the Frenchman lashes out with his own arc of death, trying to take off the Son of Cain's head with a savage back-slash of his mortuary blade. Missing his target by a mere inch, Armand comes to a grinding halt and stabs his mortuary blade in the ground. He snatches the pistol from his belt, spins on his heel, takes aim, and fires at the rider. At such close range, the damage inflicted by the pistol ball is devastating. It punches straight through the Son of Cain's back to his chest, its exit point marked in the front of his buff coat by a small ragged hole that quickly pools with blood.

But the Son of Cain doesn't even flinch, riding forward to his target – which I only now realise is Brother Lidcombe; the only remaining member of our team qualified to deliver the last rites and break the unholy spell making the Sons of Cain invincible. Heaving back his broadsword in preparation to cleave the monk in two, the Son of Cain thunders towards his victim, who stands frozen in fear. Just as the rider draws within striking range of the monk, von Frankenthal – who has moved back several yards – gives a tremendous roar and charges, shoulder-first, into the mount's right flank. Von Frankenthal's heavy frame slams into the horse, almost dislodging the Son of Cain from his saddle. Abandoning his attack, the demonic rider struggles to keep his mount under control and pulls hard on the reins.

Before the horse can regain its balance, von Frankenthal capitalises on his advantage by reaching down and grabbing its rear right leg. In a Herculean feat of strength, he lifts the leg off the ground and pushes with all of his might against the horse's flank. The veins practically pop out of the witch hunter's muscle-corded neck as he forces the horse to teeter. Turning his head to the side so as to avoid the heel of the Son of Cain's kicking boot, von Frankenthal is able to make the horse lose its footing. It crashes heavily to the ground, but its rider somehow manages to leap free at the last moment. Before the Son of Cain can ready himself for combat, von Frankenthal clambers over the horse and dives at the fallen rider, crash-tackling him to the ground.

Grabbing hold of the Son of Cain's sword-arm, von Frankenthal wrestles atop his opponent. The witch hunter then slams his fist repeatedly into the rider's face with bone-crunching force. After ten or so punches, von Frankenthal pauses to catch his breath. No sooner has he stopped than the Son of Cain snaps his head up to stare into von Frankenthal's eyes, as if the witch hunter's barrage of blows has had no effect at all. The Warlock of Lower Slaughter's hand shoots out to lock around von Frankenthal's throat. Struggling to breathe, von Frankenthal tries to pull away from the vice-like grip, but even he is not strong enough to break free. His face turning purple, the witch hunter reaches down to the fold in his boot, draws his dagger and plunges it – hilt-deep – into the Son of Cain's torso. The demonic soldier lifts his head to stare down at the dagger embedded in his side and laughs sadistically. He looks back at von Frankenthal and continues to squeeze the life from him.

Knowing that it will only be a matter of seconds before von Frankenthal is killed, I leap from the tree. I land awkwardly, grazing my shoulder against a tombstone and fumble at the hilt of my rapier, hoping to reach von Frankenthal in time to sever the hand locked around his neck. Before I can race over to the combatants, Armand collects his mortuary blade and streaks across to deliver a savage kick to the Son of Cain's lower torso, forcing him to release his hold of von Frankenthal.

No sooner has von Frankenthal staggered to his feet, gasping for air, than a massive grey form crashes into him and sends him flying for over twenty feet before tumbling across the ground in a tangled mess of flailing limbs. Dazed, von Frankenthal clambers to his feet. The Hell Hound carries on with its attack, tearing after the witch hunter and launching itself at him, its jaws open in preparation to rip him to shreds.

I cry out in warning, but the situation is hopeless.

This will be the end of von Frankenthal!

Now only two yards away from von Frankenthal, the Hell Hound opens its jaws wider, targeting the witch hunter's head. I race forward, my rapier drawn back, ready to drive it into the beast's rear, yet knowing that I will never reach my friend in time.

But then I come to a sudden halt as a bolt of blue lightning slams into the side of the beast, knocking it away from von Frankenthal and sending it crashing into a tomb.

Smoke trailing from its scorched flank, the hound roars in pain and twists its head around, searching for the person responsible for the attack. Finally, it spots Prayer. The fire in its eyes blazing with rage, the beast advances slowly towards her.

The English witch hunter is standing protectively in front of Witch Finder Blackwood, who still lies motionless on the ground. Having sheathed her rapier, she is reading from the opened pages of the *Malleus Maleficarum*, which she has prised from her fallen commander's grasp. She is deep in concentration, preparing to cast another spell.

Crouched on its haunches, the muscles in its rear legs bunched to spring into action, the hound stalks towards Prayer, who extends the fingertips of her outstretched hand. A bolt of rippling blue lightning shoots forth from her fingertips. But this time she misses; the beast darts to the side, the bolt of lightning shoots harmlessly off across the cemetery.

With a speed that leaves me gaping, the Hell Hound suddenly springs forward, tearing across the cemetery towards Prayer, who reaches for the pistol tucked into her belt. Again I race forward, hoping to reach Prayer in time. I have only taken two steps when a shot rings out, hitting the beast in the side of the head and knocking it off its course.

Looking in the direction of the gunshot, I spot Dorian atop the tower, smoke trailing from the rifle he has levelled at the beast. The remaining two hounds are nowhere to be seen, and I can only assume that they have raced inside the church and are trying to gain access to the tower.

A demented roar draws my attention back to the Hell Hound in the cemetery. It shakes its head in pain, the fur below its right ear matted in blood, and continues advancing towards Prayer.

Having tucked the *Malleus Maleficarum* under her belt and drawn her pistol, the English witch hunter is still standing by her fallen commander. Her lips drawn tightly in a savage snarl, no fear evident on her features, she yells something in English at the beast, her tone defiant, then takes aim with her pistol.

Again, the Hell Hound comes at her, launching itself off its powerful rear legs, its jaws wide open. I cry out in warning. But Prayer refuses to move. Levelling her pistol at the beast, which is now only some three yards away, she fires. Her pistol ball hits one of the hound's dagger-like teeth, shattering it into a thousand shards, before carrying on into its gullet. The beast roars in pain, blood streaming from the sides of its blasted maw, but this time it doesn't stop. My heart caught in my throat, I watch as the beast crosses the remaining distance to Prayer.

Luckily, von Frankenthal intercepts it at the last moment. Having regained his senses, he charges into the beast. The hound's jaws slam shut a hair's breadth to the side of Prayer's head, but the momentum of its attack knocks her off her feet and sends her sprawling on the ground near Witch Finder Blackwood.

Drawing her rapier, she scrambles across the ground, her eyes locked on the beast, which comes at her again, its eyes ablaze. The beast's jaws snap wildly, showering her in a mixture of blood and saliva. But von Frankenthal comes to her rescue again, wrapping his powerful arms around the hound's throat in a choke-hold so tight that it could stop the flow of sap through the trunk of an ancient oak tree. His muscles knotting with the effort, he manages to restrain the hound, holding it away from Prayer, who scrambles back to safety and regains her feet. Von Frankenthal heaves with all his might, raising the beast's head and exposing its torso to Prayer. She responds instantly, lunging forward with her rapier, its blade sinking hilt-deep into the hound's chest and piercing its heart. Only a second later I join my companions and drive my own sword deep into the hound's torso until only a hand-span of steel remains.

The Hell Hound shudders violently and gives one final blood-curdling roar. It drops to the ground, convulsing in its death throes. Extracting our blades, Prayer and I step back from the hound, amazed that it is finally dead and look across at von Frankenthal. Physically drained, he staggers back from the beast, his chest heaving as he sucks in air.

'Thank you,' Prayer says to von Frankenthal and me. She smiles for the first time since we met her aboard the *Royal Charles*. 'You saved my life.'

Von Frankenthal waves a hand dismissively. 'Think nothing of it. You did the same for me, using magic from the *Malleus Maleficarum* to distract the beast. But we've got a long way to go. That's only two of the hounds taken care of – and we still have to deal with the Son of Cain.'

I look around to where I had last seen the demonic rider over near the Hanging Tree. Brother Lidcombe has resumed delivering the last rites to the first set of remains freed from the gibbet. And, ten yards off to the Bishop's right, Armand and the Warlock of Lower Slaughter are locked in a deadly duel.

CHAPTER TWENTY-EIGHT

Armand is a master of a cosmopolitan fencing technique, combining elements of the French, Spanish and Italian schools of fencing. His body turned sideways so as to minimise the target presented to his opponent, he darts back and forth, his dual blades transformed into a maelstrom of steel.

In direct contrast to Armand's synchronised movements, the Son of Cain fights in a far more aggressive manner. His thrusts are delivered with less precision, but with a fury that could cleave a man in two, at times even wielding his heavy cavalry broadsword with both hands. Rather than tire, however, the Son of Cain only seems to become more enraged the longer the fight continues, his attacks becoming faster and more savage. He is also impervious to the wounds delivered by Armand's snaking blades

– a vicious slash across the neck and two puncture marks through the chest – and I fear that it will only be a matter of time before Armand is hit by one of the Son of Cain's attacks.

Noting Brother Lidcombe complete delivering the last rites to the first set of remains that had been inside the gibbet, I level my pistol – the one that Prince Rupert gave me – at the Son of Cain, awaiting an opportunity to help Armand. And I don't have to wait long.

As Armand ducks beneath a savage two-handed swipe intended to cleave his head clear from his shoulders, I take aim and fire, blasting the Son of Cain off his feet with a direct shot to the chest.

'Well done!' Armand commends, looking over his shoulder and noticing the smoking pistol in my hand. He steps back to catch his breath, and a victorious smile crosses his lips when he notices the second slain Hell Hound. 'With any luck, we will get through this yet. But we need to free the remains in the last two gibbets. Jakob and Prayer, I need you to take care of that whilst von Frankenthal and I delay the Warlock. Brother – hurry up and administer the last rites. I've seen mass delivered faster than what it's taking you to do this! We can't kill the Son of Cain until you've broken the spell granting him unholy powers!'

'I know, I know.' Brother Lidcombe stares fearfully at the Son of Cain and makes his way over to the second opened gibbet.

'Then let's end this,' von Frankenthal snarls.

Drawing his blade, he moves over to join Armand. Meanwhile, Prayer and I sheathe our swords, make our way over to the Hanging Tree and start to climb its trunk.

Suddenly a blood-choked voice – so evil that it could herald the arrival of the Devil – calls out something in English, forcing us to freeze and turn to stare at the Son of Cain, who rises to his feet. Whereas Brother Lidcombe falls to his knees in terror, fumbling at the crucifix hanging from his neck, Armand takes a bold step towards the demonic soldier. The Frenchman snorts contemptuously, says something in return and slashes his sabre through the air in a defiant gesture.

'What did the Son of Cain say?' I ask Prayer, fearful of what she will tell me.

'That he knows what we are trying to do, and that we shall fail. Despite our efforts, the Antichrist will be summoned. He also said that the world will know such pain and suffering that Heaven itself will shed tears of blood.'

I swallow nervously. 'And what did Armand reply?'

Prayer shoots me a concerned look. 'He said that he loves dancing in the rain.'

Hoping that Armand's response does not make the Son of Cain any angrier – if that is indeed possible – I scurry up the tree, Prayer following close behind me. We straddle the branches from which the remaining gibbets hang and make our way out, our daggers drawn in preparation to sever the ropes. And it's then that a desperate cry for help, which I recognise instantly as Francesca's voice, forces us to look towards the church, where one of the remaining

Hell Hounds has climbed its way up to the tower, trapping Francesca and Dorian.

'Armand!' I call out, believing that they may be in need of our assistance and hoping he has some answer to our predicament.

His eyes flashing in alarm, Armand takes a hesitant step towards the church. He is evidently torn between his promise to help Francesca and his need to keep the Son of Cain at bay for just a few minutes longer, which will grant us enough time to destroy the source of the demonic horseman's power.

'Jakob, carry on with the gibbets,' he orders before pointing his mortuary blade at Brother Lidcombe. 'And you had better get started on the Forsaken. Be quick about it. This has dragged on long enough.'

'But what about Francesca and Dorian?' I ask.

'I'm sure they are capable of taking care of themselves for a while. Once we finish with the Hanging Tree, we'll go to their . . .'

Armand stops mid-sentence when the Son of Cain raises his hands, chants something in a diabolical language and casts a spell.

CHAPTER TWENTY-NINE

At first nothing happens. I turn about fearfully, wondering how the Son of Cain's spell will manifest itself. When I see that no demon has been summoned, I glance warily at my companions, fearing that one of them may have been possessed and turned into a pawn of evil. It's only a second later that I catch movement in the corner of my eye. Uncertain of what I had seen, I stare hard at the tombstones over to my right, where I had caught the blur of movement.

But the mist betrays no secrets.

Thinking that it was a trick of my imagination, an illusion born from my own fears, I go to look back at the Son of Cain. But I catch myself when I see movement again, this time both to the left and right. Although unable to see what is out there, I can feel its presence: a palpable aura of evil that seeps through my skin to freeze my heart with its ice-like touch. My companions also stare in the direction of the movement, dispelling any doubt that it is my imagination running wild. Armand, von Frankenthal and Brother Lidcombe then draw back to the Hanging Tree, the witch hunters forming a protective circle of steel around the ancient oak.

'There's ... there's something out there!' Brother Lidcombe stammers, his entire form trembling.

'Don't waste your breath telling us something we already know,' von Frankenthal growls. He scans the cemetery, trying to get a lock on whatever it is that is out there. 'All I want to hear from you is the last rites being read to the Forsaken.'

'Prayer,' Armand calls out, refusing to take his eyes off the mist surrounding us, 'can you cast a protective aura around us?'

Prayer returns the dagger to her belt and produces the *Malleus Maleficarum*. 'I can try.'

Noticing that Brother Lidcombe has still not moved, Armand grabs him by the arm and directs him over to the second set of remains freed from the fallen gibbets. No sooner has the monk knelt down beside the iron cage than a ghost-like form materialises only a yard away from him. It comes out of nowhere, taking its form from the mist itself, catching even Armand by surprise. Its spectral, clawed hand rakes out of the gloom, slashing the monk deep across the throat.

Armand's sabre darts out at the spectral figure not even a heartbeat later, but it is too late – the ghost disappears back into the mist, the Frenchman's sword humming harmlessly through the air. The next instant, Brother Lidcombe collapses on the ground, blood spraying from the gaping claw-marks across his throat.

His blades held defensively before him, Armand turns around in a circle, ensuring that the ghostly figure has indeed withdrawn. He kneels down to inspect the monk, curses under his breath and moves warily back to the Hanging Tree.

'He's dead,' he announces.

'Well, that didn't go down as well as we had hoped.' Von Frankenthal wipes the sweat and grime from his forehead with his sleeve. 'Any idea as to what we should do?'

Armand chews his bottom lip for a few seconds before shaking his head in a defeated manner. 'There's no point in staying here now that Brother Lidcombe has been killed. We can no longer destroy the spell granting the Sons of Cain their powers.' He turns to stare at the church tower. 'But we can help Francesca and Dorian. Jakob and Prayer, you had best come down here. Upon my command, we are going to bolt over to the church.'

Prayer looks down from the opened pages of the Hammer of the Witches. 'What about the spell I was going to cast?'

'I don't think we have time for that now,' I say, casting my eyes about fearfully, wondering what has become of the Son of Cain, but still finding no sign of him, nor of his black mount.

Armand tightens the buckles of his baldrics in

preparation for the sprint. 'Our situation has taken a turn for the worse. We have lost this fight. All that remains is to see if we can escape with our lives. And we aren't abandoning Francesca and Dorian.'

'I had no intention of leaving without them,' Prayer says determinedly as she follows me down from the tree. 'Even if you had all been killed and I was left here alone, I would not abandon them.'

I consider Prayer with newfound respect. She obviously places a high value on the bond of friendship.

Von Frankenthal is also impressed. He looks at Prayer admirably. 'There's more to you than meets the eye. I'm beginning to like you.'

'There will be plenty of time to sweet-talk the women later,' Armand says, making me smile nervously in spite of the severity of our situation. His eyes scanning the tattered sheets of mist – which, if I am not mistaken, appear to have drifted around us in an ever-tightening circle – he moves over to inspect Witch Finder Blackwood. After a few seconds he shakes his head and returns to join us.

Prayer stares at the still form of her former commander. 'I had hoped that he would still be alive. I cannot believe he is dead.'

I, too, find it hard to believe. Along with his former companions, Witch Finder General Matthew Hopkins and John Stearne, Israel Blackwood was one of the most revered witch hunters in English history. Yet he was killed in the opening stages of this fight by a single pistol shot to the chest – killed by an assailant he never even got to lay his eyes upon. His sudden death a harsh reminder of the perilous path followed by witch hunters, I say a silent prayer, hoping that no more of my companions are destined to fall in this cemetery.

'He taught Dorian and me all we know about hunting witches,' Prayer adds softly.

'Then his legacy will live on,' Armand says respectfully. 'You should feel honoured that he taught you all he knew. He obviously saw great potential in you and Dorian. And by the looks of it, he did a great job in training you.'

Prayer looks at Armand and smiles sadly. 'Thank you.'

Armand turns his attention back to the tower, where Francesca and Dorian are still fighting off the Hell Hound. 'It's time we go. Follow my lead. And whatever happens, do not fall behind. Once we reach the church we'll barricade the doors, then head straight up into the tower.' He looks at me and smiles encouragingly. 'We'll save our friends yet.'

It's just as we are about to begin our sprint up to the church, however, that the spectral figure that slew Brother Lidcombe materialises out of the mist, blocking our path up to the church. Its face resembles that of an old hag, its wrinkled features twisted in hatred and set beneath a mop of long grey hair strands, which drift in the air like snakes. The spectre appears to have taken form from the mist itself and from the waist down tapers off into nothingness, floating some three feet above the ground. From its gaping, slavering mouth rises a haunting, tortured wail that makes me cringe. The air has also become bitingly cold, forming clouds of condensation when we exhale.

'What is it?' Armand asks, moving protectively to the front of our group.

'It is a fury,' Prayer says. 'A ghost-like hag usually sent by witches and warlocks to scour over battlefields, searching for the souls of recently slain soldiers to take down to Hell. I've never seen one before, but Witch Finder Blackwood told me that he encountered one in Cornwall many years ago. It is exactly as he had described.'

'Can it be killed?' I ask, my terrified eyes locked on the spectral hag, my resolve shattered by the fact that we have yet another opponent to deal with.

There's a hiss of steel as Prayer draws her rapier. 'Witch Finder Blackwood slew it with his sword.'

'Then let's send it straight back to where it came from,' von Frankenthal snarls.

Just as we are preparing to rush the spectral figure, several *dozen* more emerge from the grey veil of mist. They encircle us, blocking any possible means of escape, and flex their claw-like fingers in preparation to rip us to shreds.

God help us!

✦ CHAPTER
THIRTY

Armand darts forward to meet the furies with his swinging blades, his mortuary sword and sabre carving hissing arcs of silver through the air, slicing through the spectral forms as easily as a blade passes through smoke. The furies hit by his blades lose their form, their remains swirling in the wake of his swords like tattered sheets. An instant later, the scraps of mist come together again, taking shape until the furies re-emerge, unaffected by Armand's slashing steel. They lash out with their claws at the French duellist, screeching wildly, tearing through clothing and flesh, leaving him cut and bleeding from multiple wounds.

'Our swords are having no effect against them. They cannot be killed!' I race forward to join Armand, determined to help him in any way possible.

Knowing that the best I can do is forestall the furies for a few seconds, I slash out with my Solingen rapier at one of the spectral forms coming up from behind Armand, my blade slicing it in half. Even before I can strike out at a second advancing fury, the first one I attacked reforms. Its clawed hands shoot out: one grabbing hold of my wrist, preventing me from using my sword; the other latching around my neck. Fingers as cold as ice start to squeeze the life out of me. I try to free my sword-arm, but I cannot break away from the fury's vice-like grip. Choking, I stagger back and stare helplessly into the eyes of the demonic face that materialises only a foot in front of me, its features twisted in a sadistic snarl.

Just as I begin to fear that this is where I will die, a hissing dagger slashes out at the hand locked around my throat, severing it at the wrist. As the fury recoils, screaming in pain and clutching at the stump of its hand, the blade snakes out again and cleaves the fury's head from its shoulders. Rather than reform, the severed head and torso turn into ash and scatter across the ground.

It's only now I realise that the dagger is being wielded by Prayer. 'How did you do that?' I ask, sucking in air, my throat burning with pain.

'They *can* be killed.' Prayer grabs me by the arm and pulls me back to join von Frankenthal, who is standing with his back against the Hanging Tree so that he can only be attacked front on. She brandishes her dagger at the furies, keeping them at bay. 'But not with your blades. Only *silver* weapons can slay these spectres.'

'That's fine as long as you have a silver blade – which we *don't*,' Armand says sourly, having fought his way clear of the furies and joining us by the tree. 'It might have been nice to have been told this before I charged into them.'

'I'm sorry,' Prayer says. 'But when I saw that your blades were having no effect I remembered the Witch Finder's rapier is fitted with a silver blade, explaining why he could kill the fury he encountered in Cornwall. We're just lucky that all of the *Angeli Mortis* carry silver daggers and I could come to your rescue.'

'Still, that leaves us only one weapon to defend ourselves with,' I point out, rubbing my throat.

Prayer shakes her head. 'No, we have *three* blades: the one I carry, and Witch Finder Blackwood's rapier and dagger.' She races over to her commander's corpse, where a fury tries to intercept her. But Prayer drives her dagger into its chest, turning it to ash. She then collects the Witch Finder's blades and runs back to join us.

'Here,' she says, handing the rapier to Armand and the dagger to von Frankenthal, leaving me, the least skilled in swordplay, to fend for myself.

Armed with his mortuary blade in his left hand and the Witch Finder's rapier in his right, Armand pays an anxious look over at the church tower. I follow his gaze and my stomach tightens with dread when I see no further sign of combat. I pray that Francesca and Dorian have either killed the Hell Hounds or escaped back into the church.

'We've delayed long enough,' Armand announces. 'We need to go right now.' He turns to me. 'Stay by my side.

I'll see that nothing comes near you. Don't worry – we've been through worse than this. I'll get us out of here yet.'

I swallow nervously, trying to take strength from Armand's promise but dreading the run up to the church. 'Believe me, I won't be leaving your side.'

Armand gives me an encouraging wink before turning his attention back to the furies. 'Prayer will take point. Jakob and I will come up in the centre. Von Frankenthal, you've got the rear. May God be with you.'

Then we race for the church.

CHAPTER THIRTY-ONE

We sprint through the cemetery, Prayer's long-bladed dagger carving a path through the furies, which swirl around us in a maelstrom of slashing claws. But Prayer's and Armand's blades are faster, severing the ghost-like limbs that swipe out of the mist, turning them to ash before they can rip into us.

Racing by Armand's side, I hurdle a tombstone and quickly glance back to see how von Frankenthal is faring. Not as fast as the rest of us, he has already fallen a few yards behind. The dagger in his hand, however, is a slashing arc of silver, dispatching all of the furies that dare come near him.

Onward we press, racing as fast as our legs can carry us, determined to reach the church and find out what has become of Francesca and Dorian. Just as we are halfway to our objective, Armand thrusts at a fury coming at us from the right. At that exact moment, out of the corner of my eye, I see a blur of grey come shooting at me from the left. A cry of warning caught in my throat, I lash out desperately at the fury with my sword, hoping to cut it in half and delay it long enough for Armand to send it back to Hell with his silver rapier. But the fury avoids my attack, rushes forward and swipes at my face.

I pull back instinctively, just as clawed fingers – as sharp as razors – swish only a hair's breadth past my left cheek. Unbalanced, I trip over my feet and slam into Armand. We go down in a mess of flailing limbs and blades, and roll across the ground for several yards before tumbling down a lengthy flight of stairs and stopping before the metal door of a tomb.

Sprawled on the stone floor, I raise my rapier and stare anxiously up the stairs, expecting the furies to swarm after us. Seconds drag by, but the spectres do not give chase, the sounds of pursuit carrying on towards the church.

'We need to go back to the others,' I say, shaking Armand, who lies face down by my side, his blades lying a yard or two back up the stairs.

He only mumbles incoherently, and I roll him over to find that he is barely conscious. His eyes are closed in pain and a terrible lump has formed on the left-hand side of his forehead. Cradling his head in my lap, I pull the stoppered leather bag from my belt and pour water over his face in an attempt to bring him back to his senses. He coughs and splutters, shakes his head and opens his eyes.

'What happened?' he asks, and tries to lift himself up onto a shoulder. Finding the effort too great, he slumps back into my lap. He winces in pain as he clutches his right arm, his primary sword-arm, tightly against his chest. 'This isn't good.' He gestures with a nod of his head to his arm. 'I think I've broken it. Either that, or I've severely sprained my wrist. It also feels as if I've cracked my head open. What in God's name happened?'

'A fury came at me,' I say, feeling immense guilt in being responsible for Armand's injuries. I look back up the stairs once more, hoping that the furies do not return and pursue us. 'I accidentally knocked you over. We fell down this flight of stairs leading to a tomb. That's when you sustained your injuries. We're just lucky that the furies didn't follow us.'

'Lucky for us, but not for von Frankenthal and Prayer. I'm also worried about Francesca and Dorian,' Armand mutters sourly. He looks about desperately, as if in search of something. 'My swords! I need my swords.'

'They're here, on the stairs.' I scurry over to collect them and hand them to the French duellist.

Armand sheathes his mortuary blade and grips the handle of his recently acquired rapier. I feel the tension in his body drift away, the feel of steel in his hands evidently as comforting as a priest's absolution to a sinner at death's door.

'It's a fine mess we're in now, Jakob,' he says, shuddering against a spasm of pain in his arm. 'Let's just hope that the furies don't come after us. I don't think I'm any state to fight them off.'

I lower my head in shame. 'I'm sorry. This is my fault. If I hadn't run into you none of this would have happened.'

Despite his injuries, Armand attempts a smile. 'We're alive. That's all that matters for now. I'll just need to rest here for a few minutes, then we'll carry on.' He closes his eyes and takes some deep, controlled breaths. 'I have to get to Francesca. I won't abandon her.'

'We'll save her yet,' I say determinedly.

Looking up to Heaven, praying that Francesca has fought her way past the hounds and is currently hiding somewhere in the church, I see something that makes my heart freeze in fright. For a figure has appeared at the top of the stairs.

The Warlock of Lower Slaughter!

He reins in his mount and stares down at us through blood-filled eyes. Dismounting, he draws his broadsword from its scabbard with a deliberately accentuated hiss of death. He comes towards us, his stride painstakingly slow, our deaths an absolute certainty.

CHAPTER THIRTY-TWO

'**G**et up!' I cry, dragging Armand to his feet. 'We need to escape.'

The Frenchman pushes me aside. 'Leave me here.' He leans against the tomb door and raises his blade in his left hand in preparation for combat; his features visibly strained by the effort, his sword trembling. 'I've had enough of running. It's time to stand and fight.'

I look at Armand in disbelief. 'Don't be ridiculous. You know the Son of Cain cannot be killed. And you're injured. It will be a massacre!'

Armand stares grimly at the Warlock of Lower Slaughter, who has descended a quarter of the way down the stairs. 'It's nice to see you have such faith in me.'

'What? How are you going to last longer than a few seconds?'

Armand shakes his head defeatedly. 'I'm in no condition to run, Jakob. If this is where I am going to fall, then so be it. But, believe me, I will not fall easily. I'll buy you the time you need to escape. Just promise me that you'll go and save Francesca.'

My heart beating wildly, I grab Armand by the shoulders and stare at him hard in the eyes. 'None of us are going to die here – not you, nor me. We're going to find a way out. I'll even carry you if I have to. Then we're going to go to the church and save Francesca together. You made a *promise* that you would help her. And I understand you too well to know that you would never break your word. We've been through so many adventures for us to die here. So stop talking as if you've given up, and start thinking of a way to get us out of this mess before it's too late.'

Armand's eyes flash with renewed purpose. 'I'm not well enough to race past the Son of Cain. Which means our only option is to get into this tomb. We can barricade ourselves inside. Once I've had time to check my injuries and prepare myself, we'll break out. With any luck, I will have only sprained my wrist. I may only need a few minutes for it to get better. Then I'll show this accursed servant of Satan what a witch hunter can do.'

'That's the spirit,' I say. 'Now give me a hand with this door.'

Finding the metal door unlocked, we push our shoulders against it, prising it open just far enough for us to slip into the darkness beyond. Leaning my sword against a nearby wall, I reach into the inside pocket of my cloak and

209

produce the spare length of cord I had used to detonate the gunpowder barrels in the dungeon. I lie it on the ground and ignite it with my tinder and flint, illuminating the tomb with a soft, flickering light. Armand and I then close the door, and I wedge one of my daggers in the gap beneath it. I brace my shoulder against the door in anticipation of the Son of Cain.

I breathe a nervous sigh of relief, comforted by the fact that there is now a heavy metal barrier separating us from the Son of Cain, but I cannot shake the final image of the demonic rider from my mind. For just as the door was about to close, I noticed that the Warlock of Lower Slaughter had stopped several yards from the tomb, his sword lowered and his features set in a sadistic smile – it's as if we had escaped from a wolf by running blindly into its den. And it's with a cold shudder of dread that I recall Bishop Henchman's earlier comment that the Sons of Cain had a lair somewhere within the cemetery.

'I don't think he's coming after us,' Armand says after what seems to be an eternity. He slumps against the door, squinting against the pain in his forehead and arm. 'Thank God for that. I was not looking forward to that fight, given my present state.'

'It might be a little premature to be thanking God,' I warn, reaching down to break the lit cord into two pieces.

I tie them around the blades of our rapiers, just above the cross-guards. 'The Warlock seemed to take a morbid pleasure from the fact that we had run into this tomb. I don't think he had any intention of coming in here after us. Bishop Henchman said that the Sons of Cain slept inside coffins in a lair within the cemetery. I hate to say this, but I think we may have just found it.'

Armand stares at me blankly and swallows nervously. He raises the glowing length of cord wrapped around his sword. Dreading what we are about to find, we inspect our surroundings.

The tomb is some twelve feet wide but stretches back for over twenty yards, where it gives access to two closed doors, set in opposite sides of the chamber. In its centre, lying perpendicular to the long side walls, are four stone caskets, their lids removed. A four-foot-tall crucifix hangs on a wall, its wooden beams pockmarked by dozens of small holes that resemble pistol-shot impact craters, suggesting the crucifix has been used for target practice. The air is a pungent mixture of dust and death, as if there is something rotting within or behind the caskets. Strangely, a fresh pile of horse dung lies only a yard off to the left.

'I have a very bad feeling about this,' Armand whispers, his eyes locked on the caskets. 'I'm going to have a quick look around. Stay here and guard the door.'

I reach out and grab Armand by the sleeve. 'Are you up to this? Only a minute ago you were questioning if you had the strength to walk. Let me do it.'

Armand smiles at my concern. 'The pain in my head is subsiding, and I can still use my left hand. I'll be fine. Now make sure that nothing comes through that door.'

A terrible nervousness welling in my stomach, I brace my back against the door and watch Armand stalk down the tomb, his blade held before him, warding back the darkness with the wan light of the lit cord. Creeping stealthily towards the first casket, he draws back his rapier in preparation to thrust it into whatever might lie within. I watch with bated breath as he leans over the casket, expecting a corpse-like hand to spring out at any moment.

I breathe a sigh of relief when Armand lowers his blade. Perhaps we have worried unnecessarily, the tomb being home to nothing more than horrors conjured by our own imaginations. But then I catch myself – the cold hand of fear squeezing my heart – as Armand whips up his rapier and recoils abruptly from the second casket.

The point of his blade aimed at the stone coffin, he quickly walks backwards to join me. 'We've got a problem,' he whispers, refusing to take his eyes off the casket. 'One of the Sons of Cain is lying in the second casket, and I'm sure we'll find the other two in the remaining coffins.' He turns to me. 'We've discovered their lair.'

☩CHAPTER☩ THIRTY-THREE

I look down at the floor in despair, only now realising that the sandstone slabs are covered in what appears to be drops of *dried blood*. Following my gaze, Armand reads the telltale signs of passage left by what we can only assume are the Sons of Cain's bleeding eyes.

I look up at Armand. 'What are we going to do?' I whisper.

Armand shakes his head, his expression grim. 'Death awaits us outside.' He clicks his tongue softly in thought and observes the far side of the tomb. 'We need to see what's behind those two doors. One must lead to where the Sons of Cain have their mounts stalled, judging from the fact that there is a fresh pile of dung just over there. I also noticed several dried clods down past the caskets and got a waft of manure and hay. I'm hoping that the second door might provide access to another exit from the tomb.'

My eyes narrow in question. 'What makes you say that?'

'It's not uncommon for tombs to have a rear escape passage, in the off-chance that someone was entombed alive and woke to find that the front door was locked.'

Entombed alive. That's exactly how I feel right now – trapped in the darkness with little chance of escape. We have been in perilous situations in the past, but we have always been able to rely on Armand's sword-fighting skills to save us. Now the Frenchman has injured his primary sword-arm. Our only hope lies in one of the doors at the rear of the tomb leading to a way out.

'Then let's do this before the Sons of Cain awake,' I whisper, my stomach churning in nervous anticipation of having to sneak past the caskets.

I remove my shoulder tentatively from the door, testing that it is not being pushed from the other side, and produce my remaining pistol with my free hand. I'm not sure what use my rapier and pistol will be in a fight against the Sons of Cain, but I take strength in knowing that they have been blessed by the Church, reminding me that we are champions of Christ and that He watches over us.

Praying that the dagger I wedged beneath the door will be enough to prevent it from being opened, I follow after Armand. We creep cautiously down the tomb, keeping close to the right-hand wall, shying away from the caskets. Wary of making even the slightest of noises, we take each step with extreme care on the stone floor so as to avoid betraying our presence. Like Armand, I use my cloak to shield the light of the lit cord away from the sleeping Sons of Cain.

It seems to take an eternity before we reach the far end of the tomb. I wipe the sweat from my brow and follow Armand over to the door set in the opposite wall. Having handed me his rapier, Armand tries the handle. He looks back at me and winks encouragingly when it turns without making a sound. When he pushes against the door, however, its rusted metal hinges make a high-pitched creak.

Wincing, our hearts pounding, we stare anxiously at the caskets, expecting the Sons of Cain to rise. Pools of sweat form on the palms of my hands. I stare back at the stone coffins, too afraid to even breathe. Saying a silent prayer when nothing stirs from within, I turn to Armand and shake my head as a warning to be more cautious.

Raising his good hand to indicate that I have nothing to worry about, Armand pushes the door open a further six inches, this time being careful not to make a sound. I hand him back his rapier, and he raises the lit cord to reveal the chamber that lies beyond.

The room is roughly the same dimensions as the one in which we are presently standing, but with a major difference: it has been converted into a makeshift stable. Three sleeping mounts, as black as the Devil's soul, are tethered to metal rings set along the walls. Six lidless caskets, of similar design to the ones in which the Sons of Cain are sleeping, are arranged in a row in the centre of the former tomb, serving as water and food troughs. Saddles, harnesses, coils of rope and sacks of supplies and food are piled in the far left corner of the chamber, illuminated by a lantern hanging from the wall.

Armand closes the door gently, wary of disturbing the mounts. 'Well, we're not getting out that way, are we?' he whispers. 'We've got one last chance. Let's hope the second door offers us a way out of here. If not, we'll have no option but to go back out the way we came in.'

I shudder at the mere mention of this. That would mean facing the Warlock of Lower Slaughter again, and I'm looking forward to that as much as volunteering to be a test subject for the Inquisition's latest torture devices.

'Come on.' Armand gestures with his sword for me to follow him across to the remaining door.

We creep stealthily across the tomb. It's just as Armand is about to open the second door that we freeze, our hopes of escaping the tomb suddenly dashed. For three consecutive *clangs* resound against the tomb's metal entry door, as if the pommel of a sword is being hammered against it from outside. In the confined space of the tomb, the sound resonates like a church bell being rung.

I stare fearfully at the caskets, my blood turning to ice.

The Sons of Cain are sitting upright in their stone coffins and lock the bloody pools of their eyes on us.

CHAPTER THIRTY-FOUR

'**M**ove!' Armand yells, positioning himself protectively in front of me. 'Get out of here. I'll be only a step behind you.'

Opening the door, I race through into the darkness beyond, Armand shadowing my every move. I glance back and see the three Sons of Cain climb out of their caskets and reach for their swords.

One of the demonic soldiers is Thomas Whitcliff, identifiable by his chest-plate and tri-bar pot helmet. A pair of long-barrelled cavalry pistols is tucked into his belt.

The Son of Cain to his left is evidently the Swedish slayer, Nils Fabricius. He is clad in a dark cloak, black leather gloves and a wide-brimmed hat. His blade is an English swept-hilt rapier, its ovoid pommel adorned with a ruby.

The remaining Son of Cain is their leader, Alistair McClodden, the Demon of Moray Firth. He is a giant, standing over a foot taller than his minions. He has flaming red hair that falls past his shoulders, and is wearing a battle-scarred leather buff coat and a kilt. His primary weapon is a massive, two-handed Scottish claymore, which he draws from the scabbard strapped across his back. He points the blade at us and roars a command. The next instant, his two companions heave back their swords and tear after us.

Armand and I barely have time to close the door and brace our shoulders against it before the Sons of Cain slam into it. The door shudders, the rusted nails holding its hinges in place are almost torn free from the frame, but it doesn't break. I look desperately over my shoulder, searching for some means of barricading the door, and notice that we have entered a narrow passageway. It is barely one yard wide and only six feet high, dug through the rock and earth beneath the cemetery, and stretches away into darkness. Like a mine, its ceiling is comprised of slabs of wood, propped in place at regular intervals by heavy upright wooden beams. Hundreds of cobwebs stretch from one side of the tunnel to the other, and the air is stale, suggesting the passageway has not been disturbed in many years. I can find nothing, however, that will be of any use in bolstering the door.

'Get ready!' Armand warns, hearing a rush of movement coming from inside the crypt.

No sooner has he said this than we hear the swoop of a descending blade. We step back instinctively just as one of the Sons of Cain's sword smashes through the door, showering us in splinters of wood, and stops only when it hits a metal crosspiece. Barely a second after the blade is wrenched free, one of the Sons of Cain kicks the door in, knocking Armand and me to the ground.

We scramble to our feet and duck beneath a savage swipe from Thomas Whitcliff. His broadsword hums through the air an inch above our heads and thuds into one of the tunnel's upright wooden support beams, which showers us in a cloud of dirt and dust. Unable to wrench his blade free, the Son of Cain places a foot against the wall and pulls with all his might, blocking his companions from coming after us. Seizing the advantage, Armand shoves me down the tunnel and sprints after me. Praying that the passage is indeed an escape route, my blade raised to shield me from the spider webs, I tear through the darkness.

We race as fast as we dare along the tunnel, ducking and weaving past the projecting wooden support beams. Some of them creak precariously as we inadvertently knock them, as if they might come crashing down, burying us beneath a tonne of earth and rock. But we carry on regardless, determined to put as much distance as possible between us and the Sons of Cain. We can hear them chasing after us, the spurs on their knee-length cavalry boots clanging with each step across the stone and earth floor. Their cries and curses reverberate along the passage, giving the impression that they are only a yard behind us. Every time I pay a terrified glance over my shoulder, all I see behind Armand is an empty stretch of tunnel, giving me hope that we may somehow survive this nightmare.

I'm not sure how far we have run – it must be close to fifty yards – when I come to an abrupt halt, my hope of escaping sinking faster than an anchor.

'We are done for!' I moan. 'What are we going to do now?'

Armand pulls up behind me, staring over my shoulder at the collapsed section of tunnel blocking our path.

'I don't know,' he says, nursing his injured right arm, his breaths coming in ragged gasps. 'But we'd better think of something fast, because in a few seconds the Sons of Cain are going to catch us. Then we'll have no option but to face them. And with my hand out of action, I don't think I need to tell you how that will end.'

I move forward to inspect the collapsed section of tunnel and notice that there is a narrow gap between the roof and the pile of rubble. It is wide enough for me to stick the hilt of my sword in and illuminate the space with my lit length of cord, revealing that the fallen section of roof only extends for some two yards. Beyond that, the tunnel continues.

'We can still escape, provided we can dig through to the other side,' I say hopefully.

Armand shakes his head. 'But we won't have time to do that.'

'Then we need to buy ourselves the time,' I say. 'We have to stop the Sons of Cain from reaching us, to give us enough time to make it through.'

'And how do you plan on doing that?' Armand stares

defiantly back down the tunnel. He flicks his cloak free from his left arm so that it won't interfere with his rapier. 'Unless we can bring down the tunnel, I don't see how we are going to do it.'

'That's it!' I race back down the passage, studying the wooden beams that support the ceiling, searching for a weak spot. 'I don't think this tunnel is very stable. All it might take is a good kick to one of the beams to bring down a section of the roof.'

'But how do you know it won't bring down the *entire* roof?' Armand calls after me.

'I don't.' I lead Armand to what appears to be an unstable section of the tunnel. Dirt falls between the creaking wooden beams holding up the roof, as if they will give way at any moment. 'But I can't see any other way out this.'

Armand shakes his head sceptically. 'I've got a bad feeling about this. Look what happened the last time we tried doing it.'

'But we were using gunpowder back then,' I point out, my mind flashing back to the prisons beneath Rotterdam. 'This should be a lot safer.'

No sooner have I said this than the Sons of Cain appear at the edge of the perimeter of light cast by our lit lengths of cord. They are crouched low so as to avoid hitting their heads, their swords held menacingly before them. Then, as the leading demonic soldier produces a pistol from his belt and takes aim at me, I deliver a kick with the heel of my boot at one of the wooden columns holding up the roof – instantly causing a cave-in.

CHAPTER THIRTY-FIVE

I barely have time to dive back before a section of the roof collapses and crashes down with incredible force. A massive pile of earth and rubble fills the tunnel from floor to ceiling, preventing the Sons of Cain from coming after us. Coughing and wheezing, I cover my mouth with my sleeve and shut my eyes tightly against the dust and dirt as I crawl along the ground. Finally Armand drags me to safety.

'That was one of the most dangerous things I've ever seen you do,' he says, sitting me against the tunnel wall and making me drink from his water-skin. 'But it worked. I've always thought that our Lord has a soft spot for you. Now I've got no doubt at all.'

'Soft spot or not, I think it will be a long time before I try doing that again,' I say, thankful that the liquid is clearing my throat, allowing me to breathe once more. Dusting myself off, I look back through the settling cloud of dirt at the mound of rubble. 'But that should buy us the time we need to dig through to the other side.' I hand back the water-skin and climb to my feet. 'Come on, let's get started.'

We have barely walked back to the collapsed section of tunnel when Armand raises a hand in warning. Stopping dead in our tracks, we turn to look back down the passage, where we can hear the Sons of Cain digging their way through the rubble.

'Don't they ever give up?' I whisper, my adrenaline pumping, knowing that it has now become a race to see who can dig through their section of collapsed tunnel the fastest.

Armand leans his blade against the wall and wastes no time in removing the earth and rocks with his good hand, attempting to enlarge the gap beneath the ceiling. 'We only need to make this wide enough for us to crawl through. It shouldn't take too long.'

'Let's just hope that we can beat the Sons of Cain,' I mutter. I drop my weapons and join Armand, using both hands to scoop away the earth.

We dig frantically for several minutes until we are caked in a sick mixture of sweat and dirt. Armand, finding the narrow tunnel too cramped and evidently noticing that I am a more efficient digger since I'm not injured, moves back and allows me to crawl forward on my chest. Scooping the earth back behind me, I make quick progress, and it isn't long until I make it through to the other side.

Armand passes me our weapons, and I offer him a hand and start to pull him through. Halfway through the hole he suddenly stops and stares at me with terror-filled eyes. The next instant, he is ripped free from my grip and dragged back.

Snatching up my pistol and rapier, I lift the length of lit cord attached to my blade to reveal that Armand has used his elbows to wedge himself in the hole. He is trying desperately to kick himself free from Thomas Whitcliff, who has grabbed hold of his ankles.

Yelling out to Armand to stay still, I raise my pistol, take aim past the Frenchman and level my barrel at the Son of Cain, whose blood-filled eyes lock onto mine, his features set in a malevolent sneer.

'Are you sure about this?' Armand tries to shift as far away as possible from my pistol. He squeezes his eyes shut in anticipation of the *BLAM!* from the firearm, which is only a few inches away from his head.

'Trust me,' I say, firmly believing that I can make the shot and taking aim down the barrel. 'Just don't move.'

'You hardly need to tell me . . .'

I blast away, knocking Whitcliff off his feet with a direct shot to the head, just below the visor of his helmet. I reach into the hole, grab hold of Armand and drag him through to safety.

Pausing only to pick up Armand's rapier, we set off again. The faint light of the fuses tied to our swords guide us as we sprint along the tunnel, spurred by the enraged cries that echo from the darkness behind us. Onward we press, wheezing like punctured bellows, our mouths as dry as wrung-out dishcloths, until we reach the end of the tunnel.

Finding a ladder leading up through a vertical shaft, we sheathe our blades and climb up. I follow behind Armand, who is forced to use his right elbow instead of his injured right hand. I kick down hard on each of the aged wooden rungs, snapping them off, preventing the Sons of Cain from coming after us. After having climbed some twenty feet, we reach the end of the shaft and push aside a stone slab. We scramble out, caked in enough dirt to fill a grave, and find ourselves standing in a shadowed alcove in the southern transept of the Church of the Holy Trinity.

We push the stone slab back in place to seal the tunnel and sit back against the alcove wall, exhausted.

'I can't believe we made it back to the church,' I say after a few minutes of rest.

'I thought it was strange that the tunnel went for so long, but it now makes sense,' Armand says, using water from his stoppered leather bag to clean his face. 'I think the underground passage was made during the Civil War so that priests and possibly even their congregations could escape from bands of marauding soldiers should the church ever be attacked.'

'Well, they say that the path to salvation is through the Church.' I remove the now smoking length of cord from my rapier. Believing that this is only a moment of reprieve and that we are far from out of trouble just yet, I start to reload my pistols.

Armand tests his right hand tentatively and winces in pain when he tries to bend his wrist.

I look up from my pistols. 'How is it?'

'I don't think it's broken, but I've severely sprained it,' Armand answers dismally. 'It's going to be a few days before I can wield a sword again with my right hand.'

'Let this be a lesson to you that there are times when you cannot rely on your blades,' I say, hoping that Armand takes heed of my words. 'Even Captain Blodklutt, the most talented swordsman in our order, has his copy of the *Malleus Maleficarum* to fall back on. Sometimes all we can rely on is our own resourcefulness and the bond of friendship we share. That's what gives us the edge over our enemies – the fact that we know we have one another.'

'That,' Armand smirks, holding up a finger to emphasise his point, 'and the twenty-inch barrel of a cavalry pistol.' He rubs his ear in jest, referring to when I fired past him to hit the Son of Cain who had him by the ankles. 'But talking of relying on one another, we need to find out what has become of Francesca. The fact that this church is as silent as a grave does not bode well.'

I nod grimly. 'I was just thinking that. I was also wondering what has become of von Frankenthal and Prayer.' I am fearful that they may have been cut down by the furies before reaching the church.

Armand shakes his head. 'I don't know, but let's first find out what's happened to Francesca and Dorian. Then we can look for the others.'

I load my pistols, then we climb to our feet and stalk through the shadows of the southern transept, scanning the church for evidence of our friends. We cross over to the opposite transept, and our hope sinks when we find the door to the tower ripped off its hinges. I position myself a yard or two behind Armand to cover our rear and follow the French duellist up the stairs, glancing warily over my shoulder every few yards. We try to move as silently as possible, but the faint, inadvertent scuffing of the soles of our boots across the worn stone steps resounds as loudly as cannons being fired – in my mind at least. Finding the trap door at the end of the stairwell smashed to pieces, we exchange a grim look. We are about to climb to the top of the tower when a series of three gunshots ring out in swift succession.

Armand freezes, his eyes flashing with hope. 'That had to have been the rifle you gave Dorian! No other firearm could be fired so quickly.'

'And the shots came from outside the church – down where we left our mounts,' I say.

'If Dorian has survived, then there's a good chance that Francesca might have too.' Armand pushes past me and races down the winding stairwell four steps at a time.

Praying that she is indeed still alive, I chase after Armand, my rapier readied for whatever horrors await us.

CHAPTER THIRTY-SIX

We bolt out of the stairwell, tear through the church and burst out its front doors. Heading in the direction of the gunshots, we sprint down the hill, towards the copse of trees where we had tethered our mounts. It isn't long before we find out what has become of Francesca.

She and Dorian have somehow fought their way out of the church and made it down to our horses, all the while, apparently, hunted by the two remaining Hell Hounds. Armed with her *talwar*, Francesca is keeping one of the beasts at bay. Having positioned herself beside a tree to protect her rear, she wields her *talwar* in a two-handed grip, her crossbow slung over her back. She breathes heavily, the point of her sword held low to the ground, as if attempting to conserve energy. Despite her exhausted state, she does not appear to have been injured.

Conversely, the Hell Hound – which is crouched on its haunches as it stalks to the left and right, searching for an opening in Francesca's defences – is bleeding freely from several deep cuts, its fur matted with blood. Rather than have scared the beast away, these wounds seem to have only fed its rage, the fire in its eyes blazing.

Dorian is facing the second Hell Hound, several yards deeper in the copse of trees, and is positioned protectively in front of our terrified mounts. His rapier is a humming streak of silver that leaves its signature as bleeding puncture wounds on the massive beast, which momentarily withdraws to yelp and lick its wounds. Like Francesca, Dorian does not appear to have been wounded, but his chest is heaving with each laboured breath. The white makeup on his face is blotched and streaked with sweat and dirt, which gives him the appearance of a revenant that has clawed its way out of a grave.

And then – much to our surprise and relief – we see von Frankenthal and Prayer, who have almost fought their way down to Francesca and Dorian, but are now surrounded by the furies only thirty yards from the copse of trees. Standing back to back, they are engaged in a savage fight with the remaining furies. Only a dozen of the spectral hags remain, but both of our companions have been injured. Von Frankenthal's back looks as if it has been subjected to a flogging: his cloak, tabard and shirt are shredded and wet with blood. Prayer, meanwhile, is sporting deep gashes across the left side of her face and is limping on her left foot.

Armand tosses me his silver rapier in mid-stride and instructs me to go to the aid of von Frankenthal and Prayer. Drawing his mortuary blade, he races around the furies and makes a direct line for Francesca.

Armed with my rapier and Witch Finder Blackwood's blade, I tear into the furies from behind, slicing two of them in half and turning them to ash before they are even aware that I am upon them. Momentarily distracted by my attack, a number of the other furies snap their heads towards me. Both Prayer and von Frankenthal are quick to seize the advantage, their blades snaking out to take out a further three of the spectral hags, and clear a path for me to race over to join them.

'Jakob! I can't believe you're alive,' von Frankenthal exclaims. 'What happened?'

'It's a long story,' I say, adding my blades to theirs to form a ring of steel. 'I'll tell you later. Let's just get out of here first.'

'I'm all for that.' Prayer looks anxiously over her shoulder at Dorian, who is being attacked again by the Hell Hound. 'Let's finish this!'

Prayer ducks a wild swipe at her head by one of the seven remaining furies, dives forward and rolls across the ground, drawing two of the spectral hags after her. Leaping to her feet, she pulls her head back sharply and recoils from a second attack. She then lashes out, her dagger a flash of silver, severing one of the fury's arms. Even before the detached limb turns to ash, Prayer delivers a back-hand slash across the fury's throat, her blade moving faster than a shooting arrow to dispatch the spectral nightmare.

The second fury to come after her weaves to the side, moves away from Prayer's blade and rakes out its claws, intending to rip Prayer's torso open. Catching the fury as a blur of movement in the corner of her eye, Prayer tries to dodge the attack. But she is not fast enough – the fury's claws carve through her side like razors. Prayer cries out in pain, twists around to face the fury and lashes angrily with her dagger. The blade drives deep into the spectre's chest, turning it to ash. Prayer moves from the fray and drops to her knees, inspecting the severity of her wound.

Seeing her injured, von Frankenthal gives a tremendous roar and launches himself at the remaining furies, his dagger slashing wildly, tearing them apart. I follow after von Frankenthal, doing my best to cover his rear. But it's as if my help is not needed, for in only a few seconds he carves through the spectres. He then staggers over to slump down beside Prayer and tends to her wounds. Having applied some salve from a phial tied to his belt, he starts to bandage her torso with strips of cloth torn from his cloak.

I race over to join Armand, who has already engaged the Hell Hound attacking Francesca and has drawn it away by delivering a deep cut to its flank. My dual blades readied, I pull up beside Armand in a stance taught to me by the French duellist. But he pushes me away with a flick of his sword, as if he has the situation under control – or possibly, I find myself wondering, if he fears I lack the skill to face the beast and will only get in his way. Withdrawing from the fight, my blades still drawn, I watch him lure the beast after him.

Although not fighting with his favoured hand, his wounded right hand held close to his chest, Armand is no stranger to wielding a blade in his left. Raising his mortuary sword above his head, he waits for the Hell Hound to pounce at him. He darts to his right the instant it attacks – the beast's jaws slam shut a good two feet away from the French duellist. Before the injured hound can even twist its head around to set its blazing eyes on Armand, his blade comes down like a bolt of lightning, cleaving through flesh and bone, and severs the beast's head clear from its body.

'That's one way to put an end to them,' Armand mutters, already racing over to assist Dorian.

I sheathe my rapier and draw one of my pistols, awaiting an opportunity to get off a shot at the remaining Hell Hound. Facing both Dorian and Armand, the already wounded beast doesn't stand much of a chance. As Armand rushes in from the left, drawing the hound's attention, Dorian weaves forward, driving his blade hilt-deep into its chest. Rising up on its rear legs, the Hell Hound howls in pain and thrashes its head about. Armand rushes in, plunging his blade deep into the hound's lower torso. With a blood-gargled roar, it falls to the ground, its legs twitching like those of a dead man hanging from a gallows. Dorian produces a pistol from his belt, pins the beast's head to the ground with his boot and shoots it at point-blank range, finally bringing an end to the last of the Hell Hounds.

CHAPTER THIRTY-SEVEN

My breath coming in laboured gasps, I lower my weapons. 'I can't believe we slew them.'

Armand extracts his blade from the hound and nods grimly. 'We are lucky to have survived this fight. It could have ended badly.' He flicks his mortuary sword free of blood, sheathes it by his side and walks over to Francesca.

'That's the first and last time I want to face a Hell Hound,' she says, her voice trembling. Francesca's blade is still raised, its point directed at the beast, as if she expects it to leap to its feet again.

I join Armand and hand him Witch Finder Black-wood's rapier, which he tucks under his right armpit. He then places his one good hand on Francesca's and eases her blade down. 'It's over. The beasts are dead. There is no need to fear them any longer.'

Francesca closes her eyes and exhales heavily. 'And what of the Sons of Cain?'

Armand shakes his head. 'They were too strong for us. We only managed to destroy the satchel and deliver the last rites to one of the Forsaken. But we didn't kill any of the Sons of Cain.'

'Then it's not over,' Francesca says bluntly, her eyes snapping open. 'And we should get out of here before they come after us.' She looks gratefully at Armand. 'I knew you'd come back for me. Thank you.'

Smiling softly in return, Armand touches her gently on the cheek. She flinches initially, almost as if out of instinct. But she gradually succumbs to his caress, reaches up to hold his hand and closes her eyes.

'Not even Hell's legions could have stopped me,' Armand whispers.

'I'll vouch for that,' I comment. 'I think the vow he made to you was the one thing that kept him going.'

For a moment they stare into each other's eyes. At length, Francesca clears her throat and jerks her chin at Dorian. 'But I only made it off the church tower thanks to Dorian. He drew the beasts after him, allowing me to escape.'

Dorian? I can hardly believe my ears. Perhaps I have misjudged him.

Armand turns to the English witch hunter, who is cleaning his sword by the carcass of one of the dead Hell Hounds. 'You did well. Your plan worked, luring the hounds away from the Hanging Tree.'

Dorian scoffs contemptuously. He looks dismissively past Armand. 'Where's Witch Finder Blackwood?'

Armand lowers his eyes respectfully. 'He fell.'

Dorian stares hard at Armand, his lips curled in distaste, as if he is about to make some curt comment, possibly blaming the Frenchman for the Witch Finder's death. 'You have his sword,' he says, noticing the silver rapier tucked under Armand's arm. He crosses over and extends a hand. 'What is this? A free-for-all, where we scavenge what trophies we like from the dead? He would have wanted me to have that. Give it to me.'

What? The English witch hunter had better be careful. One does not skate on such thin ice with Armand. He does not take affronts to his honour lightly.

I realise that I have not misjudged Dorian. He is arrogant and self-centred, believing the world revolves around him only. It is interesting that he did not ask what had become of Brother Lidcombe. I'm sure he considered the monk expendable, reconfirming my belief that he cares little for anyone. I'm shocked, in fact, that he even asked about his commander. It may be that the only reason he assisted Francesca escape from the church is because he thinks she can serve some use in fighting the Sons of Cain. Perhaps he is also drawn to her because of her beauty, and believes he could win her over by saving her life. Good luck to him, I scoff. He'd have as much chance of winning her heart as the Catholic Church renouncing the Bible.

Armand's eyes flash with anger and he returns Dorian's stare. Then, much to my surprise, he gives a cold smile and hands over the sword. Without even so much as a word of thank you, Dorian shoulders past Armand and walks over to inspect Prayer's wounds. Having spent no more than a cursory ten seconds with her – during which Prayer's initial smile fades to sadness – he crosses to the edge of the copse of trees, where he turns his back to us and starts to reload his rifles.

With Witch Finder Blackwood now dead, I'm sure Armand has realised that it will be up to him to lead this team. He's hardly going to be able to win the respect of the *Angeli Mortis* by taking offence at Dorian and driving a blade into his heart.

Francesca notices the way in which the Frenchman is nursing his right arm. 'You're hurt. We have a few basic medical supplies in one of the saddle bags. You should let me have a look. And Christian and Prayer should come over here, too. It appears as if they have both sustained serious wounds.'

'It will have to be fast,' Armand says. 'The Sons of Cain are still out there somewhere. We should get out of here whilst we still have the chance.'

As Armand calls out to the others to assemble by the horses, I look up at the church, wondering what has become of the demonic horsemen. I get the scare of my life when I see three of them assembled on the crest of the hill to the left of the church, stationary on their black mounts, staring down at us.

CHAPTER THIRTY-EIGHT

'The Sons of Cain are here!' I call out, drawing my companions' attention to the horsemen, who now spur their mounts down the hill and thunder towards us.

'We'll return down the track to the main road.' Armand readies his horse and climbs into his saddle. 'Then ride like Hell back to London.'

Whilst the rest of us untie our mounts, swing into our saddles and ride out of the copse, Dorian remains standing by the edge of the trees; Prince Rupert's rifle, now primed and loaded, gripped in his hands.

'Dorian!' Prayer yells, pulling hard on her reins. She steers her mount around and heads back towards her fellow English witch hunter. 'What are you thinking? They cannot be killed!'

As von Frankenthal calls out after Prayer and turns his horse after her, Dorian raises his rifle and takes aim at the Sons of Cain. 'We may not be able to kill the riders,' he says coolly, his eyes narrowing as he stares down the rifle's massive barrel, singling out Nils Fabricius, the closest of the horsemen, 'but we *can* stop them from following us.'

BLAM! Dorian takes his first shot, taking the horse out from under the rider, who crashes heavily to the ground. Rotating the rifle's chamber and thumbing back the firing pin, an action that takes no more than two seconds to complete, Dorian brings the rifle back up to his shoulder and fires. This time Thomas Whitcliff comes crashing down, flying over the head of his dead horse. Then, having reloaded the final chamber of the rifle, Dorian levels the firearm at the remaining Son of Cain – Alistair McClodden.

Turning his horse sharply to the left just as Dorian shoots, the rifle ball whizzes past the Scotsman's mount and brushes through its flying mane. Now only forty yards away from us, the massive Scotsman draws his claymore, locks his eyes onto Dorian and thunders towards him.

In an act of suicidal bravado, Dorian taunts the Son of Cain with a crude remark. He then grabs his rifle by the barrel and turns it upside down so as to club the rider from his mount. Fearing that this will be the end of Dorian – and possibly also Prayer and von Frankenthal, who have just dismounted alongside Dorian, their swords drawn in preparation for combat – I snatch Prince Rupert's pistol from my belt.

Recalling the Prince's comment that this pistol can clip the ear off a fox at fifty yards, I pull up my horse, thumb back the pistol's firing pin and take aim at the Son of Cain. When Alistair McClodden is no more than twenty yards away from von Frankenthal and the *Angeli Mortis*, I fire.

The Scotsman clutches his chest and is knocked from his horse. Seizing the advantage, Prayer and von Frankenthal remount, and Dorian races over to swing into the saddle of his own horse. I follow them along the trail to join Armand and Francesca, and as one we spur our mounts along the main road back to London.

†Chapter† THIRTY-NINE

The Sons of Cain do not pursue us, and we arrive back at Prince Rupert's lodgings an hour before it gets dark. Armand immediately calls upon Franz to summon a surgeon to tend to our wounds. Having sutured von Frankenthal's and Prayer's cuts, the surgeon examines Armand's wrist and concludes that it is sprained. He binds it in linen and advises the French duellist to rest his hand for the next few days. We then bathe and have a quick dinner.

It isn't long before we are joined by Bishop Henchman, to whom Armand gives a full report of the fight. The Bishop informs us that he had been unsuccessful in locating the temple beneath Saint Paul's Cathedral. After assuring us that the guards he had positioned around the cathedral will alert us should the Sons of Cain appear, we retire for the night.

I wake early in the morning, dress and have a light breakfast with my fellow Hexenjäger down in the dining room. We converse sparingly, feeling the worse for wear. I spend the remainder of the day resting in my room, checking my weapons. It isn't until after dinner that there is a knock on my door, and Armand informs me that Bishop Henchman has called a final meeting.

It is now late afternoon, the sun sinking into the west. Soon the denizens of London will be blowing out their candles and going to bed. But there will be no sleep for us. For tonight the Sons of Cain will attempt to summon the Antichrist, and we must do everything within our power to prevent this from happening.

We gather in the Prince's study: a spacious room on the third floor, dominated by a central table surrounded by chairs, and often used by the Prince to host councils of war. In addition to the Bishop, Prayer and Dorian, we are joined by the three *Angeli Mortis* who have been searching for the altar beneath Saint Paul's Cathedral.

The first of the English witch hunters to be introduced is Richard. He is perhaps in his mid-twenties and is clad in the black clothing typical of his order. A brace of three pistols is strapped across his chest. These are complemented by the swept-hilt rapier sheathed by his side, and a pair of thin-bladed throwing knives tucked into a leather sheath strapped to his left forearm. Like Prayer, a Latin inscription is tattooed across his forehead, but only its lower half is visible beneath the wide brim of his hat, which makes it impossible to read. Twin crucifixes are tattooed on his cheeks. He is quite portly, and has the ruddy complexion of someone who has taken a strict set of marriage vows to a tankard of claret.

The second of the *Angeli Mortis*, introduced as Jebediah, is perhaps forty years of age and studies everything with the alert eyes of a hawk. Apart from the long-barrelled pistol equipped on his belt, the only other weapon he carries is a heavy wooden cudgel, over four feet in length and as thick as von Frankenthal's forearms. Its notched and scarred surface testifies that it has seen many battles.

The final English witch hunter, Valentine, is only a few years older than me. He has the look of a jester, with eyes that seem accustomed to laughter and lips that appear to be struggling to keep a smirk at bay. He reminds me of a friend I once had back in Dresden, a boy who could see the humorous side of any situation, however dire. Armand has trained my eye to note that the hilt of the rapier jutting between the folds of Valentine's cloak, with its 'S' shaped cross-guard in the form of a snake and its engraved pommel in the shape of an apple – perhaps symbolic of Adam's temptation in the Garden of Eden – is the type of blade carried only by a consummate swords-man. The worn state of the leather on the inside of the thumb and the outside of the index finger on Valentine's right glove, where it has rubbed against the blade's cross-guard, are testament that the rapier rarely slumbers in its scabbard.

Beneath the black cloak he wears a thick leather doublet, capable of withstanding a direct thrust from a blade, and a blood-red scarf is tied around his neck. His face is painted white and twin crucifixes dangle from his ears, but I can see no evidence of tattoos on the exposed skin of his face and neck. The outline of a pipe sticks out from the inside of his cloak. He obviously puts this pipe to good use, for the smell of tobacco hangs heavily on his breath.

'So we're in the same situation we were in before we rode out to the cemetery,' von Frankenthal says dismally, sitting forward in his chair, favouring his sutured and bandaged back. 'And all we've got to show for our efforts are a load of injuries.'

Prayer raises her palm commiseratively. 'Don't forget that we destroyed the satchel and delivered the last rites to one of the Forsaken, meaning that one of the Sons of Cain has lost its unholy powers and can be killed.'

'But at a terrible price,' Bishop Henchman says bleakly in German, evidently still shocked by the deaths of Witch Finder Blackwood and Brother Lidcombe.

Armand rises from his chair, walks over to one of the room's windows and observes the neighbouring rooftops leading down to the Thames. 'And are you any closer to locating the hidden temple?'

Bishop Henchman rubs his eyes wearily and gestures at Richard, Jebediah and Valentine. 'We have only just returned from conducting yet another search, but we can find no trace.'

'Are there any building plans kept on record?' I ask.

Armand nods in an impressed manner. 'That's a good point.'

The Bishop shakes his head. 'We've already checked. But the plans show nothing of a secret temple buried beneath Saint Paul's. All that we can now do is keep a careful watch around the perimeter of the cathedral. Hopefully the Sons of Cain will lead us to the Altar of Sun.'

Armand chews his bottom lip in thought. 'That's risky. What if they slip past us?'

'Then we will need to be extra vigilant,' the Bishop says.

'We seem to be forgetting that the Sons of Cain *can* be killed,' Dorian announces, still looking out the window, his back turned towards us. 'All that needs to be done is for the remaining Forsaken to receive the last rites.'

'You make it sound easy,' Francesca says. 'But we've already tried that, and look what happened to us.' She nods at von Frankenthal and Prayer, the left side of her face a stitched and swollen mess. 'We're lucky that any of us survived.'

'I'm not keen to go back to the cemetery,' I say in her support.

'Nobody asked you to go,' Dorian says bluntly, turning around, seemingly perceiving my caution as fear. 'I'll go by myself and complete what *you* failed to finish.'

I look away from Dorian, tired of his attitude. Conversations with him are comparable to eating something foul that lingers on the palate.

'And how do you plan on doing that?' Armand asks. 'It's not as if you're just going to be able to walk unchallenged down to the Hanging Tree.'

'It might be as easy as that,' Dorian says. 'I no longer have to worry about the Hell Hounds. And I'm sure that the Sons of Cain are going to be in London tonight, performing their black ritual in the temple.'

Armand clicks his tongue in a cautionary manner. 'That's one hell of a gamble you are prepared to take, riding out there alone. What if Alistair McClodden orders one of the horsemen to guard the tree? I'd do the same if I were in his position.'

Dorian shrugs. 'Then I only have to deal with *one* of them. If I head off now, I can ride out to the cemetery, do what needs to be done, and return to London within two or three hours. Hopefully I will be back in time to help you locate the Altar of Sun. All I need is a priest to accompany me – someone who can deliver the last rites to the Forsaken.'

'You won't be riding out there with only one priest to assist you,' Prayer objects. 'I'll come too.'

Dorian shakes his head. 'No you won't. I work best alone. You know that better than anybody here. Besides, you're injured. All you'll do is slow me down.'

Prayer stares at Dorian for some time, a hurt expression on her face. 'Then may God protect you, Dorian. Because there will be nobody else there to watch your back.'

Dorian snorts contemptuously at her remark. He looks at Bishop Henchman and asks, 'So can you organise a priest?'

'I can see to that,' the Bishop says, then turns to Armand. 'I say we let him do it. It will be our last chance to kill the Sons of Cain. What do you think?'

Armand twirls an edge of his moustache, his eyes deep in thought. 'If you think he can pull this off, then I have no objection.'

'But how will we know if Dorian has been successful?' I ask.

'When we stab the Sons of Cain and they don't get back up again,' von Frankenthal says dryly.

'We'd best get started.' Bishop Henchman rises from his seat and crosses over to the study door, Dorian following after him. 'It will be dark soon, and we don't have much time. I have in mind a particular priest who will be up to the task of accompanying you out to the cemetery.' He looks back at Armand. 'There are some matters we still need to discuss. I'll return once Dorian has set off.'

Armand catches Dorian before he exits the room. He extends a hand in good luck and says, 'Godspeed.'

There was a time when the Frenchman would have demanded satisfaction for the rebuke Dorian had made out at the cemetery, and only considered the matter resolved when he drew the English witch hunter's blood. But Armand has demonstrated great restraint in how he has dealt with this matter. Perhaps his appointment as Lieutenant has had a sobering effect on his cavalier attitude.

Pausing in the doorway, Dorian looks down at the proffered hand, a contemptuous expression on his face. 'I'll be back in a few hours,' he says, refusing to shake Armand's hand and exiting the room. 'Try to see to it that no more of my order die in my absence.'

CHAPTER FORTY

'I must apologise for Dorian's behavior,' Prayer says once Armand returns to his seat. 'He gives the *Angeli Mortis* a bad reputation. We aren't all as uncivil as he is.'

Armand waves a hand dismissively. 'You need not apologise for that. He is responsible for his own actions. Besides, one bad apple does not destroy the barrel. I'd be glad to have someone of your qualities join our order.' He pauses as he jerks his chin at the three other members of the *Angeli Mortis*, who sit opposite us and have remained silent since joining us in the study. 'And I'm sure your fellow witch hunters likewise do your order proud.' He then says something in English to the three members of the *Angeli Mortis*, and they laugh softly in return.

'As I am sure you have already worked out, none of my companions speak German,' Prayer says.

Armand smiles. 'Don't worry. I won't hold it against them.' He gives a troubled look. 'But I am concerned about Dorian. He obviously has a lot of pent-up anger. Why?'

I look expectantly at Prayer. With the possible exception of Bethlen and Diego Alvarez, a Spanish swordsman who tried to take Armand's life during our mission to recover the Tablet of Breaking, I have before never met such a ruthless person as Dorian.

Prayer nods in agreement. 'Yes, he does. But his real problem is that he *loves* too much.' When she sees the confused looks on our faces, she elaborates: 'Dorian was not always as he is now. Whilst you see him as cold and merciless, he was once a beautiful soul, at peace with himself and the world. But that was before the death of his wife and child. Dorian had everything he wanted in life. And then, in one fell swoop, he lost it all – everything he loved.'

There is a moment of silence before Armand says, 'I'm sorry to hear this. When did it happen?'

'Two years ago,' Prayer says. 'His wife and newborn son contracted the plague. Believing that God had sent the illness to punish humanity for our sinful ways, Dorian prayed for his family to recover. I have never seen anyone pray so hard. He didn't leave the church for a week. He barely ate or slept. But that alone wasn't enough to save his family. And when they died, Dorian blamed God for their deaths. I'm sure too, although he will never admit it, that he also blames himself, believing he wasted his time in prayer, when he could have been consulting apothecaries and searching for a way to save his family. And now he is determined to cross the divide into death, to bring back his wife and child.'

Armand lowers his eyes and absent-mindley fingers an end of the handkerchief tucked up his right sleeve. 'Some divides are not meant to be crossed. And that is one of them.'

Prayer shrugs defeatedly. 'Try telling that to Dorian. Sometimes I think his sole reason for joining the *Angeli Mortis* was to learn how to uncover the spells hidden within the *Malleus Maleficarum*. It is said that the text holds the secret to the Resurrection itself. I'm sure that's what Dorian searches for, and he will not stop until he finds it.'

'Isn't that dangerous?' I ask.

Prayer nods. 'Very. Last year I tried to help him unlock some of the mysteries of the *Malleus Maleficarum*, but at a terrible price. The tome enacts a heavy toll on those who are game enough – or foolish, I now think – to open its pages. Ever since that fateful day, my sleep has been haunted by tormented spirits. They come to me almost every night, lurking in the corner of my dreams, caught between Heaven and Hell.' She pauses, tears welling in her eyes. 'But Dorian's price was greater still. He tried to raise the spirit of his deceased wife, except the spell went terribly wrong. Not everybody who dies rests peacefully. Some tortured souls are doomed to roam this earth for an eternity. Dorian now sees these ghosts everywhere, but he cannot communicate nor interact with them. He lives in a permanent nightmare.'

We sit in silence for some time, shocked by what we have heard. Francesca reaches across the table and places a comforting hand on Prayer's arm. 'You obviously care a lot about Dorian.'

'How can I not?' A tear rolls down Prayer's cheek. She smiles sadly, rises from her seat and says something in English to the rest of the *Angeli Mortis*. They then make their way out of the room, but Prayer pauses in the doorway and looks back at us. 'We have some preparations to make before we head off to Saint Paul's. We will meet you at the foyer in an hour. Please do not take Dorian's insults personally. He's not angry with you – he's angry with God. And the reason I care so much for him is simple: he is my younger brother.'

She exits the room and her companions follow after her, leaving us sitting in the uncomfortable silence.

⫷ CHAPTER ⫸
FORTY-ONE

Wrapped in the folds of my cloak, as if to shelter me against the enormity of the task we face, I exit Prince Rupert's lodgings. I sit down on a stone bench, which is set against a hedge in the private section of a small garden close to the Prince's apartments. I need some time to distance myself from all that is going on, and I am hardly able to do that back in the study, where Armand and von Frankenthal are checking their firearms and honing the edges of their swords. Each *schlick* of von Frankenthal's blade on his whetstone reminds me of the perilous task that awaits us, eating away at my resolve like some cancerous growth.

A hot, dry wind has risen, coming from the east, rustling the leaves in the garden and sending clouds racing across the darkening sky. It also brings with it the salty, seaside waft of the Thames, and carries the distant commotion of dockyard workers loading and unloading ships and the banging of unlocked shutters on distant windows. The gloom of the approaching night reflects my solemn mood perfectly, and I pull my cloak tightly around my neck and shuffle along the bench into the darkest section of the garden.

It's only now I remember the book that the Ghost had dropped. I pull it out from my cloak and discover that it is an anthology of poetry printed in German. I flick through its creased and worn pages, pausing when I notice a message written on the inside cover. I tilt the book in the direction of the lamp hanging from above the front door of Prince Rupert's lodgings. Leaning close, I read the note: *To my dearest husband. May these poems comfort you during the long hours we are apart. With eternal love . . .* The name at the bottom is obscured by a dark smudge, possibly blood or dirt.

I reflect on how this glimpse into the private life of the spy has altered my opinion of him. He has a wife somewhere, no doubt waiting anxiously for his return. I wonder if she is even aware that he is a member of *le Secret du Roi*, or if he has kept his true identity from her. Perhaps he is also a father, with a son just like me who dreams of following in his footsteps.

I return the book inside my cloak and think of my own father. The deeper I dig into his past, the greater the mystery surrounding his life and identity becomes. I honestly believed that I was going to find him in the

Devil's Bowels, and that we would be united once more. But I was greatly mistaken. All I discovered is that his past is clouded in secrecy. Rather than getting closer to learning the truth about him, he seems to be slipping further away from me like some elusive ghost. I desperately want to uncover some clear answers as to who he is; if anything, to help me understand who I am. But that will have to wait for the moment, for I need to remain alert, focused and prepared for the monumental task that faces us tonight.

Half an hour must have passed. I am staring down at my feet, smiling softly as I think of what Sabina is doing back at Burg Grimmheim, when I look up to find a cloaked figure standing in front of me.

'I hope I didn't scare you,' the figure says, and I realise that it is Francesca. 'You seemed deep in thought, and I didn't want to disturb you.'

'Scare me? Don't be silly.' I'm relieved that the darkness has concealed the startled look on my face.

'Well, I'm glad I've found you.' She gestures for me to shuffle over some more before sitting down beside me. 'It's been a long time since we've chatted. And I owe you an apology.'

'An apology?' I say, surprised. 'For what?'

'For not thanking you for coming back to save me at the church. I thanked Armand, but not you. It was very rude of me.'

I shrug dismissively. 'Think nothing of it. And, for the record, nothing was going to stop Armand from returning to help you.'

Francesca raises an eyebrow. 'I'm no fool, Jakob. He didn't do it all by himself. You can't tell me he fought his way back to Dorian and me singlehandedly, what with his sword-hand injured. So, to make it official, thank you.'

I smile. 'So we haven't scared you off joining the Hexenjäger just yet?'

'Not on your life. What you do is so special. It's dangerous work – even more so than sneaking into trap-riddled tombs. But we fight in the name of Christ, and there is no greater cause.' Francesca pauses as she looks across at Armand and von Frankenthal, both of whom have just exited the Prince's lodgings to stretch their legs and get some fresh air. They talk in hushed tones, their cloaks pulled tightly around them, and are bathed in the orange light cast by the lantern above the front door. 'Besides,' she adds, watching Armand out of the corner of her eye, 'things just got more interesting.'

'You like him, don't you?' I say, my voice lowered so that the others won't hear.

Normally, I wouldn't inquire into a lady's personal affairs, particularly concerning matters of the heart. But I had given Armand my word that I would assist him in courting Francesca. And now that the subject has been broached, this seems as good a time as any to try to find out where he stands, and how much of an effort I need to make on his behalf.

Francesca shakes her head in a confused manner and sighs. 'I don't know what to think anymore. It's strange, when I first met Armand I considered him to be the most presumptuous, conceited person I had ever met. He'd sooner fall in love with his own reflection than another person. But I was wrong, and it's only now that I'm starting to see that. Yes, he is flamboyant, and he thinks he's the most handsome man to have ever walked the earth, but there's no denying that there's an endearing roguish charm about him. He is fiercely protective of his friends, and he has a sense of personal honour rarely seen in people. When he gives his word, it is set in stone.'

'He's a loyal friend, and a good person,' I say. 'I'd trust him with my life.'

Francesca nods slowly, her eyes still studying the French duellist. 'There's certainly a lot to be admired in him.' Then, seeing Armand produce his handkerchief and flourish it in such a manner you'd think he was conducting an orchestra, she adds, 'That is, of course, once you take away the love affair he has with himself.'

'That's not fair,' I object, knowing the deeper meaning of his handkerchief.

Francesca cannot help but laugh at her comment. 'I'm sorry. That was quite cruel.' She grins and pats me on the thigh. 'But enough of Armand. How are things with you and Sabina?'

I smile warmly at the mention of her name. 'Good.'

Francesca looks at me expectantly for some time. 'Well, that's hardly fair, is it?'

'What?' I ask.

Francesca sighs. 'I confide in you how I feel about Armand – open my heart, as it were. And all you can tell me about Sabina is that things are going "good". Honestly, Jakob. It's not going to break your back to tell me a little more, is it?'

I shrug. 'I would if I could. But there's not really much to say, other than that things are going . . . well, good.'

Francesca regards me flatly and shakes her head. 'I'd sooner be able to draw blood from a stone than get a man to disclose their true feelings. Men! You are a breed apart.'

'We might be,' I smirk and nudge Francesca with my elbow. 'But you can't live without us, can you?'

Francesca gives me a shocked look. 'You have *definitely* been hanging around Armand too much.' She wraps an arm around my shoulder, putting me in a headlock, then knocks off my hat and tousles my hair. 'And he's starting to corrupt you, my poor, sweet Jakob.'

Laughing, I wrestle free, fix my hair and replace my hat. I do feel bad for not revealing more about my relationship with Sabina. But I've always found it hard to talk about such private matters. Perhaps it's because I lost my parents at such a young age, and I'm extremely protective and guarded of those for whom I care deeply.

'At least tell me this –' Francesca's tone is serious '– Sabina doesn't think much of me, does she?'

I smile dismissively. I had been wondering when Francesca would broach this subject. It's no secret that Sabina dislikes the former Italian tomb-robber. The looks she sometimes shoots at her are drenched in enough poison to wilt every tree in the Black Forest.

'I wouldn't say that,' I reply. 'She just doesn't know you yet, that's all.'

'I'm not concerned. I'm just curious if I've done anything to offend her.' Francesca sits forward and toys a rock with the toe of her boot. 'But, I must say, most women behave like that in my presence. It's almost as if they feel threatened by me. It's sad. It just goes to show how little effort they make to get to know me. And I wish I could be friends with Sabina. There's no reason for there to be any tension between us. I know we spend a lot of time together, but surely she knows that we are just good friends.' She smiles and looks up at me. 'So, are you still considering getting "have a nice day" tattooed across your forehead?'

'No.' I laugh in return as I glance across at our companions. Armand is flexing his bandaged hand, and von Frankenthal is standing as stiff as a pole, favouring his sutured back. 'But I am worried about what's going to happen tonight.'

Francesca smiles encouragingly. 'We've faced tougher opponents than the Sons of Cain. We'll pull through this. We may have lost Witch Finder Blackwood and Brother Lidcombe, and we're all bruised and battered, but we've now got three fresh blades. Richard, Jebediah and Valentine seem as if they can take care of themselves. And I'm hopeful that Dorian will succeed in his mission.'

'I know,' I say. 'It's just that I feel this is all my fault. If I hadn't insisted in searching for my father, none of you would have been placed in this situation.'

Francesca leans forward, forcing me to look at her. 'Nothing would have stopped us from accompanying you, Jakob. Friends stand by one another through both good and bad times. That's why I know we'll get through this.' She shuffles back and stretches her legs. 'Have you thought much about your father?'

I'm sure Francesca asked the question in an attempt to distract my thoughts, and it works. I give an exasperated sigh. 'I haven't had time. Things have spiralled out of control since we joined Prince Rupert. But what you and Armand told me has been lurking in the back of my mind.' I lower my eyes. 'All the evidence suggests that my father is a spy, working for the French. He might even know the Ghost. They might be the closest of friends.'

'You should just stick to the facts. At least your father didn't die in the gaols of Rotterdam. That's something.'

I shrug half-heartedly. 'I suppose so. But it doesn't bring me any closer to finding him. And I'm not too sure if I want to anymore. It might have been for the best if he had been executed back in Rotterdam. At least then I would have had some form of closure on the matter.'

'Don't wish him dead, Jakob. Never do that. Not until you have had a chance to learn the truth of who he is.' Francesca gives me a gentle prod with her elbow. 'Besides, I don't know about you, but I find the entire affair very exciting.'

'What do you mean?'

Francesca gives a conspiratorial glance at Armand and von Frankenthal to ensure that they cannot overhear us.

'You might be the son of a famous French spy – perhaps a member of the King's Secret. How many people do you know who can make such a claim?'

'But if what we have heard is true, then he betrayed his allies and the men under his command. He is a traitor. I could never do that to my friends.'

Francesca cocks an eyebrow. 'That's all just a matter of perspective. In the eyes of the French, he might be a national hero; one of the most famous members of the King's Secret.'

While I believe the Ghost to be a man of honour, there wasn't much to admire about Bethlen. He, too, was a member of the King's Secret, and he was one of the most merciless people I have ever met. He made my first week with the Hexenjäger a living hell, teasing me relentlessly and playing malicious practical jokes. He was also a ruthless killer, driving his blade through the back of Klaus Grimmelshausen, one of the Brotherhood of the Cross. The mere thought of my father being similar in nature to Bethlen is anything but exciting. It makes me feel sick.

'What are you two doing hiding over there?' Armand asks, finally spotting us.

'I came out to get some fresh air,' I say, rising from the bench. Francesca follows, and we walk over to join Armand and von Frankenthal.

'I wanted to thank Jakob for saving me back at the church,' Francesca says.

Armand looks at me proudly. 'He saved my life, too.'

Von Frankenthal tousles my hair. 'It seems as if I'm next on your list.'

'That will be the day.' I find it hard to imagine that von Frankenthal, who is as sturdy as a fortress, would ever need my assistance.

Our attention is drawn by the sound of an approaching horseman. We look to the right and see a rider emerge from behind a wall of hedges at the far side of the garden. Clad in clothing similar to the English guards we met when we chased after the Ghost, the man guides his mount along the cobbled pathway that runs around the perimeter of the garden, pulls up in front of us, dismounts, and asks something in English, to which Armand responds. The rider then removes a large canvas-covered bundle from the side of his mount. Lying this on the ground, he unties its cord straps and brings back the canvas to reveal a pile of swords and some leather pouches. With a courteous bow, the guard remounts and rides back down the pathway.

Armand kneels down to inspect the weapons. 'Complements of Bishop Henchman. Apparently he sent that guard to the royal armoury to find us some silver blades.'

'I won't say no to one of these.' Von Frankenthal reaches down to select a sabre and removes it from its scabbard. He tests the weight of the sword and has a few practice swings, its silver blade glistening in the dull lantern-light. 'I wasn't looking forward to facing the furies again. But these will even the odds somewhat.'

Armand distributes the rest of the swords and hands me a swept-hilt English rapier and a leather pouch. I open the pouch and find a dozen or so silver pistol balls. 'You should be comfortable with that blade, Jakob,' he says. 'You'll find it similar to your Pappenheimer in weight and design.'

'Let's just hope that the Ghost doesn't steal this one from me,' I say dryly, strapping the blade by my side and tying the pouch to my belt.

Francesca draws her new weapon, a stout-bladed hunting sword, a few inches from its scabbard to inspect the quality of the blade. She nods in a satisfied manner. 'I wouldn't worry too much about him. I don't think we'll ever see him or that Italian sword-for-hire again. After all, they don't call that French spy the Ghost for nothing.'

'I hope you're right,' I murmur, but again I feel a terrible premonition that I will indeed meet both of them sometime in the not too distant future. 'Why is it that only silver blades can harm furies?'

Armand straps the silver-bladed broadsword he selected from the pile by his side. 'Silver is a pure metal. Many of the Devil's servants can only be killed by silver blades or pistol balls. It is also not uncommon for priests to use silver nails to seal shut the coffins of people of evil repute and of those who died unbaptised.'

'Why?' I ask.

'To ensure they won't rise from the dead,' Armand says matter-of-factly.

I shake my head in disbelief. 'Really? Why am I only being told this now? And why don't we all carry silver blades, like the *Angeli Mortis*?'

'Many of the Hexenjäger *do* carry silver weapons,'

Armand says. 'You obviously haven't noticed, but Robert Monro and Captain Blodklutt only ever use silver balls in their firearms. The legendary Spanish captain Alejandro De la Cruz uses a cup-hilt rapier with a silver blade, fashioned by the most famous swordsmith in Toledo, a region in Spain renowned for the quality of its swords. One of the sabres I normally use is made from a combination of steel and silver.'

'Then why didn't you bring it with you?' I enquire.

'Because I had no reason to.' Armand gives me a playful cuff over the back of the head. 'I thought we would be going to Rotterdam to break into a gaol. Had I known that we would be facing an enemy such as the Sons of Cain, I would have come prepared with a very different arsenal of weapons.'

We are joined shortly by the *Angeli Mortis* and Bishop Henchman, who opens the door to the Prince's lodging and ushers us into the foyer.

CHAPTER FORTY-TWO

'Is everything ready?' Armand asks.

The Bishop nods. 'We are fortunate that Saint Paul's lies within the medieval heart of London, which is itself surrounded by the old Roman wall. The only way into the old city is through the eight gates set in the wall, or by coming up from the south and crossing over London Bridge. I have placed guards at all of the gates and along the bridge. In order that they won't be spotted by the Sons of Cain, they are positioned on rooftops and will use signal lanterns to relay a message to Saint Paul's, where a further four guards are hiding atop the cathedral's tower. They will alert us when the Sons of Cain have entered the old city and are on their way to the cathedral. The number of lantern flashes will correspond with how many of the Sons of Cain there are and from which direction they are coming.'

Francesca purses her lips in thought. 'And where will we be positioned?'

'A wall surrounds the entire cathedral precinct,' Bishop Henchman says. 'The cathedral and its surrounding churchyard can only be entered via the six gates set in this wall. You will be positioned at the gates, making sure that all access points to the cathedral are guarded.' He produces a handful of small tin whistles from his pocket and distributes them amongst us. 'As soon as the Sons of Cain reveal the hidden entrance to the temple, blow your whistle to raise the alarm. The rest of you will then rush to that location. I will be waiting inside Saint Paul's with a company of armed guards. We will also come to your assistance.'

Armand places his in the small leather pouch tied to his belt. 'You said before that you wanted to keep this secret, to avoid a mass panic. But won't the guards be suspicious?'

'As far as they know, they are monitoring the arrival of four foreign spies who have plans to rendezvous with an English informant at Saint Paul's. The guards have been provided with a physical description of the Sons of Cain, so they will be able to identify the demonic soldiers the instant they make their way into the old city. Not only have the guards been instructed not to approach them, but they are to avoid being spotted at all costs, lest the spies abandon their secret meeting.'

Armand strokes his chin in thought. 'That's clever. I'm sure that word of what happened two nights past, when we encountered the Ghost, has spread throughout the city.

It wouldn't take much to convince the guards that more spies are on the prowl in London.'

'They were my thoughts exactly,' the Bishop says. 'If all goes to plan, the Sons of Cain will lead us straight to the hidden temple.'

Von Frankenthal cracks his knuckles. 'And that's when the fun truly begins.'

Bishop Henchman crosses to one of the windows and stares out into the night. 'We have also imposed a curfew around the cathedral. There will be no civilians getting in our way.'

'How did you manage that?' Armand asks.

'I don't know if you recall this, but I once told you that Fabricius has been stalking the area surrounding the cathedral, slitting the throats of anyone foolish enough to wander the streets alone at night. The townsfolk are terrified. Come evening time, the streets around Saint Paul's become deserted.' The Bishop folds his arms across his chest and turns to face us. 'If the Sons of Cain are carrying the Codex Gigas, we will engage them before they reveal the location of the temple. According to Mother Shipton's prophecy, the Antichrist must be summoned from the pages of the codex this very night, between the stroke of midnight and the rising sun. If we can steal the book from the Sons of Cain, then we can prevent this from happening.'

Prayer looks shrewdly at the Bishop. 'But how are we going to tell if the Sons of Cain have the codex on them? We'll be hiding in gateways leading into the cathedral precinct, concealed in darkness. How are we supposed to see if one of them is carrying the book?'

'That won't be an issue,' the Bishop says. 'The Codex Gigas is the largest known manuscript to have ever been created. It is over a yard in length. It's not as if one of the Sons of Cain will have it tucked under his belt. Even if they have it wrapped in cloth and strapped to the side of a horse, or concealed beneath a cloak, its outline will be blatantly obvious.'

Prayer scratches her head in thought. 'That's all fine. But what if the Sons of Cain have already placed the codex within the temple? Won't that be cutting things a bit fine?'

Bishop Henchman purses his lips and nods. 'It will be. And in that case, we will have to move swiftly. As soon as the Sons of Cain reveal the entrance to the hidden temple, we will have to go straight after them – literally confront them the second they reveal the entrance. But remember that, even if Dorian has succeeded in breaking the spell granting the Sons of Cain their powers, our objective is not to kill them. It is the *codex* that we are after.'

'And I assume the plan is to destroy the Devil's Bible once it is in our possession?' von Frankenthal asks.

Bishop Henchman shakes his head. 'I wish it were that simple, but the codex cannot be destroyed. It is protected by powerful dark magic. You cannot even make a tear in one of its pages. All we can do is try to hide it from the Sons of Cain. If we can prevent them from using it between the stroke of midnight and dawn, then they would have missed their chance to summon the Antichrist.'

Von Frankenthal gives an exasperated sigh. 'There's always a catch, isn't there?'

Armand grins roguishly. 'It would be no fun if there wasn't.' He grips the silver-bladed broadsword strapped by his side. 'It's time we do this.'

✦CHAPTER✦
FORTY-THREE

alf an hour later, Francesca and I are positioned at the largest of the gates giving access through the churchyard wall. Located at the west end of the cathedral precinct, it spans Ludgate Street, which runs uphill from Ludgate, one of the eight fortified gates set in the old Roman wall encircling the medieval heart of the city. We are hidden in the darkness a few yards back from the gate, wrapped in our cloaks. It is a perfect position, offering us a clear line of sight through the opened churchyard gate to the cathedral and its tower, atop which the four guards, equipped with signal lanterns, are located.

The largest church in London, Saint Paul's dwarfs the neighbouring buildings, its tower soaring into the night sky like an enormous siege belfry. Almost six hundred feet long, the cathedral is surrounded by a wide open space. The stores and markets that have spilled over its walls into the cathedral precinct itself have closed down several hours earlier, leaving the area silent and drowned in darkness.

Before taking position in the six gates set in the cathedral wall, we had taken the precautionary measure of extinguishing all of the street lamps within the grounds and neighbouring alleyways. This provides us with the cover we need to catch the Sons of Cain off-guard. We don't want any innocent bystanders being injured, and the deserted alleyways and cathedral grounds offer us the perfect stage on which to engage the Sons of Cain. No audience. No witnesses. Just the cold hiss of drawn steel to applaud us in our endeavour. That's all we ask for.

Following Francesca's lead, I have pulled the folds of my cloak tight around me, concealing my weapons in the off-chance that the glimmer of moonlight on the honed edge of a drawn blade might betray our presence. Every now and then I cast a nervous eye up at the cathedral tower, anticipating the guards' signal that the Sons of Cain have entered the old city.

Each of the five other gateways leading into the cathedral precinct is monitored by members of our team, ensuring that all access points to the cathedral are covered. In an alleyway off to the north, running down to the cathedral from Paternoster Row, the primary road running east–west to the north of the cathedral, Armand is keeping watch. Meanwhile, von Frankenthal is hiding in the shadows of the narrow road some two hundred yards off to the Frenchman's right, over near Saint Paul's Churchyard. The remaining four entrances to the cathedral are guarded by Prayer, Jebediah, Richard and Valentine. Bishop Henchman, along with a personal bodyguard of two dozen soldiers, has taken position within the cathedral itself.

It's not surprising that Francesca and I, both being the least experienced in fighting Satan's forces, should be assigned to guard the same gateway. I'm sure that Armand wants the peace of mind in knowing that we are together, watching each other's backs. And I was greatly relieved, I must confess, when I had heard that Francesca was going to be my partner. Granted, neither of us has dared whisper a word since taking position near the gateway and beginning our silent vigil, but that doesn't mean that I haven't taken comfort in having her – and her repeating crossbow and *talwar*, for that matter – by my side.

The wind has risen considerably since we left Prince Rupert's lodgings, producing a haunting whistle as it funnels through the alleyways and roads, and driving clouds across the night sky like tattered ghosts. Or rather, I find myself thinking ominously – my hand reaching instinctively for the hilt of my new silver-bladed rapier – like furies.

As we stand in the shadows, my back pressed up against the wooden facade of a hovel, and Francesca waiting as silent as a statue on the opposite side of the road, it's hard to gauge the passage of time. I reckon several hours must have passed before I stare up at the tower, where the dark figure of one of the guards keeping watch catches our attention. He flashes a lantern twice and points to the south-east, in the direction of London Bridge.

My blood freezes.

The signal!

Two of the Sons of Cain have entered the old city.

CHAPTER FORTY-FOUR

'This is it,' Francesca whispers. She slips through the shadows and gestures for me to follow her to the end of the street, where we take position in the gateway.

From here we have an unobstructed view of the front of the cathedral, its columned portico resembling the bars of a giant prison cell. We can also see down either side of the cathedral, although with the exception of pale moonlight, all is blanketed in darkness.

I pull up behind Francesca and reach beneath the folds of my cloak to draw one of my pre-loaded pistols. But I keep it concealed, conscious of the possibility of moonlight glistening on its barrel. 'They are coming from the direction of London Bridge,' I whisper. 'Who is guarding that approach?'

'The *Angeli Mortis* are monitoring the alleyways to the south and east,' Francesca says over her shoulder. 'Are you nervous?'

'Me? I've got nerves of steel,' I reply, putting on a brave air, but thankful that Francesca can't see my trembling hands.

'So, I take it you have no objection in being the first to run out to face the Sons of Cain?' Francesca says wryly.

I give her a nervous pat on the shoulder. 'I'm quite comfortable right here.'

I glance up at the tower atop the cathedral, wondering why the guard signalled that only two of the demonic horsemen had entered the city. What has become of the other two? As Armand had speculated, perhaps some of them remained behind at the Hanging Tree? But then, just as I'm about to scan the darkness on the southern side of the cathedral, a lantern flashes from the tower and answers my suspicions.

It flashes once, indicating that the third Son of Cain has entered the old city. Only this time, the signal indicates that the demonic soldier is coming from the *west*.

I spin around to stare into the darkness at the end of Ludgate Hill, my heart racing. There is only one approach into the old city from the west: the fortified gate, Ludgate, lying only a hundred yards or so down the street in which Francesca and I are hiding.

I stare into the night, knowing that one of the Sons of Cain is coming straight towards us.

'We should move!' Francesca whispers, grabbing me

by the hand and pulling me around the side of the gate, into the cathedral grounds. Repositioning ourselves against the side of the building, our chests pressed up against its wooden wall, we peer back down the road and scan for movement.

At the far end of the road, I can see the battlements of the old Roman wall rising above the roofs of the hamlets as black silhouettes stark against the night sky. But there is no sign of movement beneath the extending gables that stretch down the road and form a dark tunnel through which the Son of Cain must pass, and into which not even the ghostly moonlight can penetrate.

Wary of the fact that the other two Sons of Cain are approaching from the south-east – and that Francesca and I, having relocated to the outskirts of the perimeter of open space surrounding the cathedral, are now exposed to them – I sink down into my cloak. I pull it up around my cheeks and lower the brim of my hat.

Anxious seconds pass, our ears tilted towards the hot, dry, moaning wind in hope that it will carry warning of the demonic soldier's approach. I know he is there somewhere in the darkness, stalking closer with each passing heartbeat. But still there is no sign of him.

I shiver and place a finger on the trigger of the pistol beneath my cloak, determined to get off an early shot. 'Can you see anything?' I whisper in Francesca's ear, too nervous to remain silent any longer.

She raises a hand for silence. Her entire body tenses. For the wind is now carrying the sound of footfalls advancing along the cobbles of the road. Perhaps it is a trick played by the breeze, the sound magnified in the tunnel created by the gables. But the noise is impossibly close, as if the Son of Cain is merely yards away from us.

Following Francesca's lead, I pull back from the gateway and retreat into the dark recess of a doorway of one of the small shops located on the inside of the cathedral wall. Pressed up against the door, we part our cloaks, draw our silver-bladed swords and wait with bated breath for the Son of Cain to emerge from the road. I feel an irresistible urge to produce the tin whistle from the pocket of my shirt and raise the alarm, but I can't do that yet – not until we can see that the Son of Cain is carrying the Devil's Bible.

A few more agonising seconds pass before the footsteps suddenly stop. There is a short pause, followed by a hollow, grinding sound, as if a heavy stone slab is being dragged back. There is a longer pause before the grinding sound is repeated. After a few seconds, this, too, stops, leaving only the sounds of the moaning wind and the distant barking of a dog.

After what seems to be an eternity, I look at Francesca. 'What's happened? What was that sound?'

She shakes her head. 'I'm not too sure, but I have a bad feeling about this. And we need to find out what's happened. Come on, let's check it out.'

I grab Francesca by the hand, holding her in place. 'Do you think that's wise?'

'No,' Francesca says calmly, and I am reminded of how she once told me of how she tries to distance herself from events, so that she can consider all options with a clear mind. 'But we aren't going to find any answers merely hiding here, are we? You can stay if you like, but I'm going to have a look.'

I shake my head adamantly. 'I'm not letting you wander off by yourself. I don't like your idea one bit, but I'm coming with you.'

Summoning every ounce of courage, I follow her out of the recess. Our backs braced against the side of the dwelling, we stalk through the darkness and eventually reach the gateway. Taking a breath to steady my nerves, my pistol raised in preparation to fire, I press up against Francesca's back and peer over her shoulder into Ludgate Street.

I scan the area for movement, but I can see no sign of the Son of Cain.

'Where is he?' I whisper. 'It sounded as if he was almost upon us, and now he's disappeared.'

Francesca studies the darkness for some time before being certain that the coast is clear and stepping out from behind the corner. 'He didn't disappear.' She gestures with a jerk of her chin for me to follow after her. 'The grinding noise we heard was the sound of a stone slab being pushed aside – a sound I have heard dozens of times before in tombs and crypts. If what I fear is indeed true, then the Son of Cain has opened a stone door, perhaps a concealed entrance granting access to a hidden passage.'

'Like a tunnel?' I scan the cobbled road and fail to find any such dislodged stone slab. 'But where?'

'It won't be on the road.' Francesca moves off to the side to inspect the facades of the dwellings and points for me to search the opposite side. 'But we need to find it fast. The Son of Cain may have entered an underground passageway that leads to the temple beneath the cathedral. That would explain why the Bishop failed to find the hidden entrance – he was looking within the cathedral itself, searching in the wrong place.'

A terrible thought makes the hairs on my arms stand on end, and I peer back over my shoulder. 'If you're right, and the entrance to the temple is located somewhere here, then that means . . .'

Francesca looks back at me, her eyes flashing with alarm in the grey moonlight. 'That the other Sons of Cain will make their way to this exact location.'

CHAPTER FORTY-FIVE

I reach for my whistle. 'Should we call the others?'

Francesca raises a hand, signalling for me to stop. 'Not just yet. We need to make sure that there is indeed an entrance to the temple somewhere here. We should wait until then.'

I stare determinedly into the darkness on my side of the road. 'Let's find this passage before the other Sons of Cain make their way here.'

Without a further word, we move down the road, searching for the elusive entrance. Most of the dwellings lining the road are constructed of wood – yet what we heard sounded distinctly like a stone slab being drawn back. Keeping this in mind, I study the ground outside the dwellings, focusing on the stone steps leading up to their doorways. But nothing resembles an entrance to an underground passage.

That is, until, having moved some twenty yards down the road, I discover a narrow strip of land, barely three yards wide, stretching back between two ramshackle tenements. At first I thought it was an alleyway, but peering into the darkness, my eyes having become acclimatised to the night, it doesn't take me long to learn that I was wrong. I signal eagerly for Francesca to join me.

'I think I've found it!' I point with the tip of my rapier into the gap between the dwellings, where, some five yards back from the road, there is a small graveyard. Its three graves, marked with headstones, are made of ancient stone and rise a foot above the ground, resembling small sarcophaguses. They are sealed with stone slabs, one of which has been pushed aside and then hastily put back in place.

'This is it, all right.' Francesca moves stealthily over to the sarcophagus with the askew lid. She leans down to inspect the headstone, running a finger over its worn inscription. 'Look at the date on this headstone: in the Year of Our Lord 746. This is an Anglo-Saxon burial. It's nothing short of a miracle that these graves weren't destroyed centuries ago to make way for some alley or dwelling.'

I move over to join Francesca by the grave. 'Miracle or not, we should notify the others that we've found the hidden entrance. For all we know, a Son of Cain was carrying the Devil's Bible, and he's now reached the Altar of Sun and started to summon the Antichrist.'

'I wouldn't do that just yet,' a voice whispers from behind us. We nearly jump out of our skin and turn around to see a cloaked figure, armed with a large staff, standing at the graveyard's entrance.

CHAPTER FORTY-SIX

I react instantly, surprising myself with the speed of my response. Fearing it is one of the Sons of Cain, I place myself instinctively in front of Francesca and whip up my pistol to take aim at the figure's torso – the part of their body offering the largest target.

The figure raises the length of wood it carries, gestures for me to lower my pistol and whispers calmly, 'Surely you don't want to blast me away, Jakob? That would be a terrible crime. Imagine how many broken hearts would lament my departure.'

'Armand?' Francesca and I say in unison, recognising the French duellist's voice.

'The one and only,' he whispers in return, and sneaks over to join us. 'Now, lower that pistol before you accidentally blast a hole through my chest.'

Wary of drawing unwanted attention, we continue to talk in hushed tones.

'Sorry.' I do as instructed. 'It's just that you were the last person we expected to find here. I thought one of the Sons of Cain had snuck up behind us.'

'You're lucky it was only me.' Armand kneels down beside us. 'Otherwise, I'm sure you'd both be dead by now. You need to be more careful.'

'Thanks for the vote of confidence,' Francesca snorts. 'And I don't think you're in any position to be telling us to be cautious. Why have you left your post? No one has raised the alarm. You shouldn't be creeping around. And you're the one who should consider yourself lucky. Jakob might well have taken your head off with his pistol. Either that, or you might have run into the Sons of Cain yourself. What would you have done then, all alone, and with your injured hand?'

'Point taken,' Armand answers, a lot humbler now, and pays a wary look over his shoulder. 'But I had to find you. Something's gone terribly wrong.'

'What do you mean?' I ask.

Armand gestures for Francesca and me to come closer. 'When the guards atop the cathedral signalled that two of the Sons of Cain were approaching from the south-east, I made my way quickly around to the south of the cathedral, believing the *Angeli Mortis* might be in need of my assistance.' He pauses, his expression grave. 'I went to check on Richard. I found him lying dead in an alleyway, his throat slit from ear to ear.'

'What?' I gasp.

'It gets worse.' Armand shows us the length of wood he is carrying, and I feel my stomach sink as I discover that it is Jebediah's staff. 'I found Jebediah in the next alley, having suffered the same fate. Both bodies were stone cold, indicating the *Angeli Mortis* had been killed some time ago, perhaps only moments after they had taken position in the gateways and long before the guards atop Saint Paul's signalled that two of the Sons of Cain had entered the old city.' He pauses again and stares grimly at us. 'Both Richard and Jebediah had inverted crucifixes on their foreheads, scrawled in blood.'

'Fabricius!' I stammer.

Armand nods. 'I fear that he is stalking these streets, hunting us. You will need to be on your guard more than ever. The *Angeli Mortis* had been taken by surprise. Neither Richard nor Jebediah had the chance to draw a weapon.'

I look fearfully past Armand, back towards the street, expecting to see the Swedish mercenary suddenly materialise out of the darkness. 'Remember what the Bishop told us about Fabricius when he had campaigned in Flanders?' I whisper. 'He snuck into enemy strongholds under the cover of night and slit the throats of his enemies. It was as if he could blend into the night. He could be out there somewhere this very instant, sneaking right up on us. We wouldn't even see him coming until it was too late.'

'As I said, we will need to be extra vigilant.' Armand's tone is calm and controlled.

'But how did Fabricius get past the sentries placed at the gates in the old wall?' I ask.

Armand shrugs uncertainly. 'Perhaps he was already inside the old city before the guards took position. He might have also climbed over the city walls, correctly anticipating that the city gates would be watched.'

'Have you warned the others?' Francesca queries.

'I was able to find Prayer and Valentine,' Armand says. 'They have taken to the rooftops and are waiting for the first two Sons of Cain to come up from London Bridge. The last I saw of von Frankenthal was when he was heading off to the alleyway to the north-east of the cathedral more than an hour ago.'

'Then anything could have happened,' I say, concerned. 'Shouldn't one of us go and check on him?'

'I planned on doing that straight after I had warned you.' Armand jerks his chin at the stone lid that sits ajar on the grave. 'But it seems as if you have made an important discovery.'

'We are certain that the Son of Cain who came up this road disappeared down here,' Francesca says. 'We think this grave gives access to an underground tunnel that leads to the temple.'

Armand's eyes flash in alarm and he gestures for us to help him lift the heavy stone slab off the grave. Placing it on the ground, we peer into the hole and detect a roughly hewn, narrow flight of stone stairs burrowing into the earth. They descend for some fifteen feet before leading into a tunnel, which is illuminated by the wan glow of a distant light, as if a lantern or torch has been lit some-where down below.

Armand places Jebediah's staff on the ground and parts his cloak to draw his mortuary blade with his left hand. 'Nice work,' he commends, staring down the flight of stairs. 'I'm sure this is the entrance to the temple. But we're not going to raise the alarm just yet.'

Francesca's eyes narrow suspiciously. 'What do you have in mind?'

Armand clicks his tongue in thought for a moment. 'If we raise the alarm, our companions will rush to this location. But it will also draw the Sons of Cain straight to us. And we still don't know where the Devil's Bible is. It might be being carried by the two Sons of Cain approach-ing from the south-east, and we don't want to tip them off that Prayer and Valentine are awaiting them. But it might also have already been taken into the temple by the Son of Cain who descended these stairs.

'Perhaps it is better for us to go down into the tunnel by ourselves. We can sneak up on the lone Son of Cain and see what he is up to. I'm hoping that he will have the Devil's Bible on him. And if that's the case, then we'll take it. Whilst two of us keep him occupied, one of us should be able to escape with the codex. With any luck, that person will be able to make it out of the tunnel and disappear into the streets of London before the remaining Sons of Cain arrive here.'

'But what if we don't make it out in time, and the Sons of Cain trap us down there?' I ask.

Armand gives me a confident look. 'London Bridge is a considerable distance from here. My guess is that the other two Sons of Cain who have entered the city are still several minutes away from us. If we are quick, we can pull this off.'

'But shouldn't there be a person to keep watch?' I persist. 'To warn the others if anyone approaches the tunnel entrance, hopefully giving them enough time to make their way out?'

Armand shakes his head. 'I don't think it's wise for any one of us to remain, given what happened to Richard and Jebediah. A Son of Cain has evidently gone down this passage. It may have been Fabricius. But for all we know the Swedish slayer is still stalking the night, hunting us. I fear he would kill whoever stayed behind before they even knew he had snuck up on them. I know this sounds strange, but it will be safer down in the tunnel. Now, are you with me?'

Francesca and I exchange a brief look, during which I see the resolve mirrored in her eyes. 'Of course we are,' I say for the both of us, knowing that neither Francesca or I would allow Armand to venture into the tunnel alone, particularly with his primary sword-arm injured. I'm so nervous that it takes every ounce of self-control to stop my voice from trembling.

Armand smiles proudly, pulls his cloak behind his shoulders to grant his arms greater freedom of movement and – with his mortuary sword raised warily before him, its blade held parallel to the angle of the stairs – enters the grave. 'Stay behind me and make no sounds,' he whispers, his eyes trained on the glow of light in the tunnel below. 'We're going to catch this abomination off-guard and give him a yard of steel for supper.'

Well, at least one of us is confident, I think to myself as I follow two steps behind Armand. For I doubt the French duellist is going to be serving any meals of steel. On the contrary, I fear the Son of Cain is going to feast on a banquet tonight, and we're going to be the main course.

⊹CHAPTER⊹ FORTY-SEVEN

We descend the stairs with extreme caution, fearful of even breathing too loudly lest it echo along the tunnel and alert the Son of Cain. Reaching the end of the stairs, we find ourselves staring down a long, narrow tunnel, its walls and roof made of large blocks of stone. Fortunately, the floor is made of compacted earth, which absorbs and muffles the scuffing of our boots. As we had observed from the graveyard, the tunnel is illuminated by a distant light, but we still cannot discern its source for, some twenty yards ahead, the passage turns sharply to the right.

We follow Armand and eventually reach the turn. Signalling for us to stop, Armand braces his back against the wall and spies around the corner. After a few seconds he pulls back, raises a finger to his lips and motions for Francesca and me to have a look.

Brushing past the Frenchman, we peer around the corner and I recoil instantly. The tunnel extends for a further forty yards before leading into a small chamber, its walls pockmarked with small niches in which dozens of lit candles are set. A stone altar stands in the centre of the room, upon which is set a massive leather-bound book – the Devil's Bible! Kneeling in front of it, his back turned towards us and his head lowered as if in prayer, is a man wearing a metal chest-guard and pot-helmet.

Thomas Whitcliff.

Armand motions for us to follow him several yards back from the corner. He jerks his thumb at his chest, then points at his drawn blade, indicating that he is going to face the Son of Cain. He points at Francesca and me, makes a grabbing gesture and points back at the stairs, signifying that we are to snatch the Devil's Bible and run for our lives. We nod in understanding and sheathe our blades, preparing ourselves for when we will have to carry the heavy codex.

Armand gives one of his reassuring smiles, produces his handkerchief and ties it around the cross-guard of his sword. With a flick of his blade, he motions for Francesca and me to follow him around the corner.

Wrapped in the folds of our black cloaks in an attempt to blend in with the shadows, we sneak along the tunnel, our eyes locked on Whitcliff, fearing that he will turn around at any moment and spot us. When we are halfway to the chamber, the Son of Cain suddenly stands. Armand flicks up a hand, signalling for us to stop. My heart racing,

I watch the demonic soldier reach into a pocket and place something on the altar. He then reassumes his position, kneeling before the Devil's Bible.

We breathe a collective sigh of relief, and Armand motions for us to continue moving. It seems to take an eternity before we reach the entrance to the chamber, where Armand rolls his shoulders in preparation for combat. He spares a brief glance at us, ensuring that we are ready. Then he raises his blade, kisses its honed edge and, in the blink of an eye, darts into the temple, catching the Son of Cain off-guard.

The impetus of Armand's charge and his swinging blade – which hacks into Thomas Whitcliff's lower neck, in the gap between his helmet and body armour – sends him sprawling into the altar, which crashes heavily to the ground. Francesca and I race past Armand and the Son of Cain, who is lying motionless on the floor, and collect the Devil's Bible. We race out of the temple.

With Armand trailing only a few yards behind us, covering our retreat, we hasten down the tunnel. Francesca and I find it too difficult to carry the codex between us in the narrow passage, so the Italian draws her *talwar* and falls back to join Armand. Perhaps it's just a figment of my imagination, but the codex seems to emit an aura of evil. Touching its worn leather surface makes me feel as though I'm in the presence of one of the Watchers. It fills me with such a profound sense of foreboding that my stomach knots in fear and the hairs on my arms stand on end.

Turning the corner, we reach the base of the stairs, believing that we may be able to escape with both the codex and our lives. The fact that Whitcliff has not given chase makes me hopeful that perhaps Dorian was successful at the Hanging Tree, and Alistair McClodden and his three demonic henchmen can now be killed. When we are halfway up the stairs, however, a blood-curdling roar reverberates up the tunnel from the temple.

Thomas Whitcliff has regained his senses. And he's going to come after us with a fury that would send Hell's legions scurrying.

CHAPTER FORTY-EIGHT

Armand chases Francesca and me out of the small graveyard and points with his sword westward, towards the distant fortified gate set in the Roman wall encircling the medieval heart of the city. 'Head that way. Disappear into the streets, then hide the Devil's Bible and guard it until dawn. By that time it will be too late for the Sons of Cain to summon the Antichrist.'

Carrying the codex between us, Francesca and I start to race down towards Ludgate, but we have only moved a few yards when I pull up sharply and stare back at Armand, who has not moved. He stands in the middle of the street, looking back at the graveyard, his whistle held between his lips, its silver surface glistening in the darkness.

'Aren't you coming with us?' I ask, already knowing the answer I will receive.

Armand shakes his head and removes the whistle. 'I'm going to buy you the time you need to make your escape.' His eyes are still locked on the entrance to the temple. 'I'm going to draw Whitcliff – and hopefully all of the Sons of Cain, for that matter – after me.'

'But they'll kill you!' I protest. 'The simple fact that Whitcliff is still standing after the blow you dealt him is irrefutable evidence that Dorian was not successful. The Sons of Cain are still immortal. You won't stand a chance against them.'

'Not on my own, I won't,' Armand says, finally looking back at Francesca and me. 'But if I can summon von Frank-enthal, the remaining *Angeli Mortis*, and Bishop Henchman and his guards to help me, then hopefully we'll be able to lure the Sons of Cain over to the opposite side of the city, far away from you and the Devil's Bible. With any luck, we'll be able to lose them. By that time, you and Francesca should have hidden the codex. We'll then all meet at Prince Rupert's lodgings at dawn. Now go, my friends, before it is too late.'

'Be careful,' Francesca warns.

Despite the severity of our predicament, Armand gives one of his trademark roguish grins. '"Careful" is my middle name. Now go.'

Not wanting to abandon Armand but aware that his plan offers us with the best possible chance of success, Francesca and I race reluctantly down the street, lugging the Devil's Bible between us. We are only halfway down towards the Ludgate entrance when a shrill, piercing sound cuts through the night.

We stop and turn towards the cathedral, where Whitcliff has emerged from the tunnel and Armand has blown his whistle in an attempt to draw the Son of Cain after him. When we hear the sound of what appears to be two sets of feet sprinting away in the opposite direction, we know that Armand's ruse has been successful.

'Let's hope he makes it back to Prince Rupert's lodgings,' Francesca whispers, her eyes locked on the far end of the street, where we had last seen the French duellist.

'If anyone can outrun the Sons of Cain, it will be Armand,' I say. 'But he wouldn't be happy knowing that we are just standing here in the middle of the street. Come on. We need to find somewhere safe to hide the codex.'

We move further down the street. It isn't long before we pass through the fortified gate in the medieval wall and head down the street that lies beyond. Although we have no idea as to where we are going, we know that we must take the Devil's Bible as far away from the Sons of Cain as possible.

We continue westward through the city, feeling exposed and vulnerable in the yellow pools of light cast by the street lamps. Finally, we reach a narrow bridge across a filthy stream, which runs northward from the Thames and cuts through the city like a brown scar. Half-timbered houses line its banks and their extending gables jut out over the water, in some parts coming so close that they give the appearance of a black tunnel, encompassing the water. Noticing a rowboat moored to one of the bridge's wooden pylons, I steer Francesca over to the side of the street, just where the bridge begins.

I peer down at the rowboat and note a small wooden jetty at the base of the embankment. 'I've got an idea.'

'What do you have in mind?' Francesca asks, following my line of sight.

Having placed the Devil's Bible on the ground, I climb over the bridge's side rail. 'It mightn't take the Sons of Cain long to learn of Armand's diversion.' I make my way down to the boat. 'They'll then start searching the streets for us, and I don't relish the thought of being hunted through the twisting alleyways of London by Fabricius. But what if we don't take to the streets? What if we rowed out into the Thames and travelled downstream? We could sail right out of London and pull up in a secluded section of the countryside. Not even Fabricius would be able to track us then. The Sons of Cain would never find us.'

Francesca nods eagerly. 'Better still, we could even just stay in the boat, floating in the middle of the river further downstream.'

'So you think it's a good idea?' I ask.

'Jakob, I think it's brilliant,' Francesca says excitedly. 'Let's do it.'

We are soon rowing down the stream, gliding beneath the archway of overhanging gables, slowly but steadily making our way through the darkness towards the Thames. Whilst I row, Francesca sits in the rear of the vessel, looking over her shoulder back at the bridge to ensure that we have not been followed.

'This is too easy,' she whispers at length, shifting into a more comfortable position. The Devil's Bible lies at her feet. 'It feels as if we are cheating. I'm so glad you thought of this.'

'I figured it would be the easiest and safest way for us to disappear out of London,' I say, feeling quite proud of myself. 'We'll reach the Thames shortly. Once we've reached the middle of the river, we'll head west. Even if the Sons of Cain are clever enough to search the Thames, I very much doubt they'd be able to see us. It's pitch black out there. And even if they do, they'll never be able to spot the Devil's Bible at the bottom of the boat. I . . .'

The words are caught in my mouth when I see a swirling black cloud emerge from the street we had exited. Alerted by the look on my face, Francesca turns around quickly, and we watch the cloud pull up sharply at the side of the bridge, right where we climbed over the rail to reach the jetty. We blink against the impossibility of what we are witnessing – the cloud transforms into a *man* wrapped in the folds of a black cloak and wearing a wide-brimmed hat. He swings over the bridge rail in one fluid motion and lands on the jetty, then kneels down to inspect the pylon to which the rowboat had been fastened. The man rises to his feet, turns and stares down the stream towards us, scanning the darkness for movement.

CHAPTER FORTY-NINE

'This can't be good,' Francesca whispers, readying her repeating crossbow. 'Who is it?'

Having stopped rowing the instant the cloud appeared so as to not make any noise and give away our position, I stare fearfully at the cloaked figure. I recognise him as one of the Sons of Cain I encountered in the crypt beneath the cemetery. 'It's Fabricius.'

We sit with bated breath, unable to remove our gaze from the Son of Cain, who hasn't moved and stares across the water like a hunting dog scanning a thicket for game. Then, as the gentle current pushes us slowly down the stream, we glide beneath a break in the overhanging gables and enter a pool of moonlight. I pull desperately on the oars, steering us out of the patch of light, and back into the darkness.

But it is too late.

Fabricius snaps upright, transforms back into the billowing black cloud and shoots towards us, flying a foot above the surface of the stream.

'Jakob, get us out of here!' Francesca yells, snatching the crossbow off her shoulder and slamming in a cartridge of bolts.

'I'm doing my best.' I heave desperately on the oars, trying to increase our speed, but knowing that we will never be able to outrun Fabricius, who is gaining on us fast.

I look frantically over my shoulder and consider our options. We are still some fifty yards or so from where the stream joins the Thames, meaning that we won't make it to the river in time. And the stream offers nowhere to hide or any means of escape: no jetties bordering its sides; the timber-framed walls and the stone foundations of the hovels lining the water's edge offering nowhere to climb out. My great idea of using the rowboat has suddenly backfired, becoming a deathtrap.

'All we can do is try to make it to the Thames,' I say through clenched teeth, pulling with all my might on the oars, attempting to gain as much speed as possible. 'Hopefully we can find a jetty or wharf where we can escape on foot. But we'll never be able to make it unless you can work out some way of stalling Fabricius.'

'It's not going to be easy.' Francesca twists around to take aim with her crossbow at the billowing cloud of smoke, which is now no more than ten yards away.

She unloads the entire cartridge of bolts at Fabricius, but they zoom straight through the smoke, disappearing up the stream. That is, all but *one*, which thuds into something solid within the cloud, bringing it to a sudden stop. Amazed that one of Francesca's bolts managed to hit the Son of Cain, we hesitate, waiting to see what damage it inflicted.

Our eyes become acclimatised to the dark, and we see the cloud move haltingly over to the stone hovels lining the stream, the area illuminated by a shaft of moonlight, which lances through a break in the canopy of extending gables. The cloud then transforms into Fabricius. Chest deep in the water, he hangs onto the building's foundations with his left hand, his right clasped around the shaft of the bolt lodged deep in his left shoulder. Biting back the pain, he pulls the bolt free, buries his head into his shoulder and screams in pain. But his scream soon turns into a roar of rage and he looks up to stare at us, his eyes burning with hatred.

'We should move!' I pull on the oars again, propelling us further away from the Son of Cain.

'That shot did more than simply halt Fabricius for a few seconds,' Francesca says, staring at the Swedish mercenary. 'He's wounded, and he's not recovering.'

My heart fills with hope. 'You're right. Dorian must have been successful at the Hanging Tree. That, or the spell that Brother Lidcombe broke was the one that made Fabricius immortal.'

Francesca clips in a new cartridge of bolts into her crossbow. 'Either way, Fabricius can now be killed.'

'Perhaps we should finish him off.' I release one of the oars and reach for a pistol tucked into my belt.

'Not with your firearm,' Francesca warns. 'The report will alert all of London to our presence, and certainly draw the remaining Sons of Cain to this location.'

'I never thought of that.' I grab hold of the oar once more. 'Then why don't you finish him off with your crossbow?'

In answer to my question, Francesca takes aim with her weapon and shoots a single bolt at Fabricius. Her shot is true, zipping through the darkness, heading straight for his heart. But Fabricius whips up his hand, palm open, and mutters a diabolical command. Just as the quarrel is about to thud into his chest, the air immediately in front of Fabricius shimmers and ripples, protecting him like an invisible force-field. The bolt comes to a jarring halt and drops harmlessly into the water. Fabricius uses the stone foundations of the hovel to drag his way after us.

Francesca slings her crossbow over her shoulder. 'I think I was lucky before. Perhaps he wasn't even aware that he could be injured. But he won't be making that same mistake again. This is far from over. Get us out of here as fast as you can!'

I heave on the oars and we reach the Thames. Abandoning my initial plan of heading westward, I steer the boat over to the east, where a small jetty provides access into the city's streets through an archway. Some thirty yards further down to the east, however, there is a second, larger jetty, extending from a narrow wooden platform that runs along the riverside for a short distance before ending at a shadowed gateway. And it is towards this second jetty that I start to row.

'Shouldn't we get off here?' Francesca asks as I steer the boat past the first jetty.

I shake my head. 'I'm sure Fabricius thinks we'll do exactly that. But we're going to trick him.'

'What do you have in mind?'

'Just trust me on this,' I say, my heart pounding as I row the boat down to the second jetty and throw out the Devil's Bible. Francesca and I then climb out. But before we pick up the codex, I slide on my stomach off the edge of the jetty and give the rowboat a firm shove with my feet, sending it back towards the first jetty. I hope that my simple ruse will fool Fabricius into believing that that is where we abandoned the boat. We pick up the codex and hasten across to the wooden platform, determined to disappear back into London's labyrinth of twisting alleyways before Fabricius emerges from the stream and spots us.

We race over to the gateway. Finding it unlocked, I say a silent prayer that we make it in time, then follow Francesca off the walkway as we head up the narrow alleyway beyond.

✠CHAPTER✠ FIFTY

After running for what must be over a quarter of an hour, Francesca and I pull into the doorway of a warehouse. Hidden in shadow, it offers a good hiding spot; the closest source of light being a streetlamp on the corner some distance over to our right.

'We need to stop for a while,' Francesca pants. 'I can't go on any further until I catch my breath.'

I lean the Devil's Bible against the wooden doorway. Sucking in air, my hands planted on my knees, I nod in agreement. I stare down the laneway, scanning the area illuminated by the streetlamp for movement. After a while I slump on the ground and rest my back against the door.

I look up at Francesca. 'We must have lost Fabricius by now. It feels as if we've run halfway across the city. Even I don't know where we are anymore.'

Francesca inspects the night sky in an attempt to get our bearings. 'I think we've headed east, but I can't be sure. These alleyways twist and turn so much, it's impossible to tell which direction they head.'

I tilt my head in question. 'East? I thought we'd headed north?'

Francesca removes her crossbow and massages her shoulder. 'I'm sure we did at first, but then, back at that intersection by the tavern, where you were certain you saw Fabricius chasing after us, we started heading east.' She pauses as she wipes a sleeve across her forehead. 'But I wouldn't be so convinced that we've lost Fabricius. I've never seen anybody track like him before. I'm sure he's there somewhere, following our trail, narrowing down our lead.'

I shake my head in bewilderment. 'How can he do that? It's not as if we've been making our way through a forest, leaving footprints in the earth and snapping branches for him to follow. And I doubt my trick back at the jetty fooled him for a second. I might as well have left a trail of breadcrumbs.'

Francesca shrugs uncertainly. 'Perhaps it's a skill he acquired from the Devil. But I don't think we're going to be able to find somewhere to hide the codex; not with Fabricius tracking our every move.'

'Then we'll keep moving, until dawn if need be.' I push myself back up to my feet, but wince at the mere thought of having to continue running. A drop of rain falls onto my shoulder, and I look up curiously into the night sky, surprised that this would happen on such a hot, dry night. 'He can't get his hands on the Devil's Bible if he can't catch us.'

Francesca raises a hand, signalling for me to wait. 'Just give me a few more seconds.'

My fingers cramped from carrying the heavy codex, I use this opportunity to massage some life back into them, and wonder what has become of our companions. I thought, not too long ago, that I heard the sound of steel clanging on steel, carried by the breeze from somewhere not too far away. But then the wind abated; the night disturbed only by the sounds of our heavy breathing and our footfalls on the cobbles. I'm hopeful that Armand found our remaining companions and informed them of his plan to lure the Sons of Cain away from Francesca and me. Perhaps we had heard one of our friends facing the demonic soldiers, locked in a savage fight. But now, in a cruel twist of fate, we are lost within the city and being hunted by Fabricius. I don't think things could be much worse.

As I go to tell Francesca we should continue moving, a cloaked figure, their features hidden beneath a wide-brimmed hat, skids to a halt at the illuminated intersection at the far end of the laneway. The stranger looks both left and right, as if considering their options, before racing straight towards us.

CHAPTER FIFTY-ONE

I n less than a heartbeat, Francesca and I have our crossbow and pistol locked on the figure, who comes towards us at breakneck speed, their drawn sword glistening in the moonlight.

'I'll hold him off,' I say, believing it is Fabricius, and stand protectively in front of Francesca. 'You need to escape with the codex.'

Francesca grabs me by the shoulder and shoots me an incredulous look. 'What? And leave you to face him on your own? Not on your life!'

'You don't have a choice!' I pull myself free and step out from the darkness of the doorway to take position in the middle of the laneway. I stare down the barrel of my pistol, taking aim at Fabricius's heart. 'You need to leave right now. *GO!*'

'Forget it, Jakob.' Francesca rushes over to join me. 'I'm not leaving you.'

I go to push her back, but catch myself when the cloaked figure – now only some ten yards away – lifts their head as if to inspect what lies beyond in the shadows. Moonlight falls across the features beneath their hat.

Breathing a sigh of relief, Francesca and I lower our weapons.

For it is Valentine.

The English witch hunter gets the fright of his life when he finally sees us, pulling up sharply and whipping up his blade. It's only when I call his name that his eyes flash with recognition and he lowers his sword. He clutches a hand over his heart to emphasise the shock we gave him, and comes over to pat us on the shoulders. Having evidently been running for some time, he plants his hands on his hips and takes some deep breaths. He stares fearfully over his shoulder.

'What is it?' I follow his line of sight down the laneway, only now realising that he was running away from someone – or *something*.

Valentine cannot speak a word of German, but he infers the meaning of my question when he sees me staring past him, my pistol held uncertainly in a half-raised position. He produces his own pistol and aims the barrel at the far end of the laneway. Alarmed, Francesca and I do likewise, and the three of us stand there, staring at the illuminated intersection. Some time passes before the English witch hunter relaxes and thumbs his pistol's firing pin back into a half-cocked position, satisfied that he is no longer being pursued.

But then a figure appears at the end of the laneway – the distant streetlight glistens on the edge of the massive two-handed claymore gripped in their hands.

It is Alistair McClodden.

Valentine hurries Francesca and me into the warehouse's doorway, where we peer at the leader of the Sons of Cain. He has stopped in the middle of the intersection and is staring down the laneway, as if searching for Valentine. Bracing our backs against the door, we once again conceal our weapons beneath our cloaks so that they won't glisten in the darkness and give us away. We wait with bated breath, hoping that the night will hide us and that the Scotsman will continue along the adjacent street. After a few agonising seconds, McClodden decides to do just that, and I breathe a sigh of relief when he disappears around the corner.

Certain that the coast is clear, I step out from the recess. Another drop of rain falls, this time landing on my hand, and runs in between my fingers. Surprised by its slimy texture, I raise my hand up to my eyes, only to realise that it is not rain at all – but blood!

I step back in shock and accidentally knock over the Devil's Bible, which I had propped up against the door. It hits the cobbles with a dull thud.

Staring at the intersection, I see McClodden tear around the corner and thunder towards us, his two-handed sword heaved back over his shoulder, ready to cut us down.

Another drop of blood splatters on the brim of my hat.

I look up and recoil in shock when I come face to face with the black-cloaked shadow perched on the gable directly above me, blood dripping from its eyes.

'You honestly didn't think you could outrun me, did you?' Fabricius hisses in stilted German, his voice sounding like a blade being drawn from a scabbard. 'You've run your race. Now it's time to die!'

CHAPTER FIFTY-TWO

Fabricius drops from the roof and lands on the cobbles on all fours. He lashes at me with a kick, making the wind explode from my chest and sending me crashing into the warehouse door. Before I have time to recover, there is a flash of silver as Fabricius draws a stiletto from the inside of his boot, springs to his feet and thrusts the blade at my torso. With a speed I never knew I possessed, I dart to the left, narrowly avoiding the blade, which thuds into the door. But I don't see Fabricius's right elbow lash out until it is too late – it thuds into the side of my head and sends me staggering down the laneway, my vision swimming.

Stunned but at least having the presence of mind to raise my pistol, I spin around and take aim at the Son of Cain, only to find that Francesca has come to my rescue.

She forces Fabricius to withdraw back up the laneway with several wild swipes of her *talwar*. And then there is Valentine, whose pistol is aimed at McClodden. The Son of Cain tears towards the English witch hunter with his claymore now held above his head in preparation to deliver a devastating blow.

With my line of vision to Fabricius blocked by Francesca, I redirect my pistol at the Scotsman, blink some clarity back into my eyes, take aim and fire. Valentine discharges his gun only a split second after me, and McClodden's massive frame spasms as he is shot twice in the chest. Rather than drop dead, he gives a blood-curdling roar born of rage and pain, crosses the remaining distance to Valentine and heaves his sword. It swipes through the air like the vane of a windmill spun by an immense gale. But the attack is slow, and Valentine ducks beneath the blade, allowing it to hum through the air a hand span above his head. As McClodden follows through with his attack, his sword sweeping around him in a wide arc, drawing up behind his head again, Valentine whips out his rapier and counter attacks. As I had correctly surmised when I had first noted the worn section of leather on the inside of Valentine's glove, he is a skilled swordsman. His blade snakes out, cutting a deep gash across McClodden's right thigh, delivering a wound that would mark the certain incapacitation of any normal opponent. But McClodden, the Demon of Moray Firth, is not just any *regular* opponent, and he drives the knee of his injured leg forward, slamming it into Valentine's face, and sends him sprawling on the ground.

Valentine scrambles back, trying to regain his feet, his rapier held defensively before him, but McClodden is thirsting for blood. The Son of Cain kicks Valentine's sword aside, twists his claymore around so that it is pointing blade down and drives it at the English witch hunter. At just the last moment, Valentine parts his legs, and the point of the heavy sword strikes sparks on the cobbles between his thighs. Valentine tries again to scramble to his feet, but McClodden moves forward and drives the heel of his boot into Valentine's chest, knocking him back to the ground, where his head hits the cobbles with a sickening thud.

As McClodden draws back his blade, I snatch the second pistol from my belt, palm back the firing pin, take aim at the Scotsman and fire. The pistol ball hits McClodden in the left shoulder, spins him like a top and forces him to drop his sword, which clatters on the ground. Seizing the opportunity, Valentine retrieves his rapier and climbs to his feet. He staggers back to join me, too dazed to continue the fight, wincing in pain as he rubs the back of his head.

Still holding back Fabricius with her swinging *talwar*, Francesca glances over her shoulder and spots the Devil's Bible lying on the ground near the warehouse door. 'Jakob – the codex!'

As I rush over to collect the Devil's Bible, Fabricius's eyes lock on me, then on the codex gripped in my hands. Dancing effortlessly away from Francesca's blade, he positions himself over near McClodden. He parts his cloak and, with his lips set in a malicious sneer, draws his rapier.

He performs this action slowly, as if savouring the hiss made by the blade as it clears its sheath.

'Get away from him!' I warn Francesca, recalling Witch Finder Blackwood's comment that Fabricius is a master swordsman. I am also alarmed that Fabricius has only now decided to draw his sword, as if he had considered Francesca's efforts to kill him as nothing more than an entertaining distraction.

Francesca rushes back to join Valentine and me, sheathes her *talwar* and produces her repeating crossbow. 'Look at McClodden,' she says. 'His wounds are not healing.'

'Dorian must have succeeded at the Hanging Tree,' I say, believing for the first time that there might be a slim chance of surviving this encounter. Blood is flowing freely from the deep gash across McClodden's thigh, and his buff coat is stained by two spreading pools of blood where he was shot.

McClodden raises a hand, points at us and growls a command to Fabricius. The Swedish slayer advances towards us, his stride measured and controlled, his eyes locked on the codex held in my hands. His blade is held low, its point trailing down near his boots, suggesting that facing us will prove to be no challenge at all.

Valentine barks some command in English to Francesca and me, and points to the far end of the laneway, indicating that we are to escape in that direction. He then steps forward to confront Fabricius.

I turn to Francesca. 'We can't leave him to face the Sons of Cain by himself!'

She shakes her head and pushes me down the path. 'We've got one last chance to escape with the Devil's Bible. We can't fail this time. We have no choice but to run.'

I do as instructed, but I can't take my eyes off the combatants. Valentine and Fabricius stop in the middle of the laneway, leaving a gap of several yards between them. Whilst Valentine paces slowly to the left and right, his rapier raised and locked on Fabricius's eyes, the Son of Cain just stands still, his sword lowered by his side.

Springing forward off his left leg, the Swede whips up his rapier with a speed that leaves me gaping, and thrusts it at Valentine's torso. But Valentine is equally fast. He parries aside the attack and answers Fabricius's thrust with a riposte that forces his opponent to weave to his right, lest he be left gagging on the yard of steel that almost punctured through his neck.

Withdrawing several steps, his blade held horizontally to keep the witch hunter at bay, Fabricius rolls his wounded shoulder testily and spits angrily. He reaches behind his back and produces a thin-bladed dagger with an extended cross-guard, drawing it up near his neck in preparation to strike. Not wanting to face an opponent armed with two blades, Valentine neutralises the Son of Cain's advantage. The English witch hunter unfastens his cloak, wraps it around his left forearm and transforms it into a makeshift buckler, with which he will block incoming strikes. He says something to the Swede, his tone haughty, which makes Fabricius's lips draw tightly in rage. The comment having achieved its desired effect – to anger Fabricius and provoke him to make a mistake – Valentine then leaps forward, determined to end this fight.

His rapier transformed into a slashing streak of silver, Valentine tries to find a weakness in Fabricius's defences, forcing the Swedish slayer to use both his rapier and dagger to parry aside his attacks. Noting that his opponent is favouring his wounded left shoulder, Valentine focuses on Fabricius's left side. The witch hunter delivers a series of thrusts and strikes that force the Swede to wheel around towards the warehouse until his back is pressed up against the wall. Their blades momentarily entangled, Valentine pushes in close towards Fabricius until their noses are almost touching. In a daring gesture designed to infuriate the Son of Cain, Valentine frees his left hand and pats the Swede on the head with his makeshift buckler.

By this time, Francesa and I have reached the end of the laneway. I wish Valentine luck, then follow after Francesca, the howling wind soon drowning out the sounds of combat.

✦CHAPTER✦
FIFTY-THREE

The crossbow slung over her shoulder, Francesca assists me in carrying the codex, and we race through the twisting streets of London for several minutes. Eventually we stop, breathless, at the gateway of a small church. It is set several yards back from the road and hidden in darkness; the closest source of light being a streetlamp some distance over to our right. Dropping the codex, we rest our backs against one of the stone walls flanking the gate and spend a minute or so resting.

I peer anxiously at the shadowed entrance of the road we had just exited. 'I hope Valentine has managed to stop the Sons of Cain from coming after us.'

'I wouldn't put anything past the Sons of Cain, especially Fabricius,' Francesca says sceptically. 'He's managed to find us twice already. I've a bad feeling that we haven't seen the last of him. Valentine is skilled with a sword, but he's facing two supernatural enemies. I just don't know how long he will be able to hold them off for. They may now be mortal, but they are incredibly strong fighters. Did you see how many wounds we inflicted on McClodden? And he was still standing!' She gives me a faint, sad smile, as if in pity of what we have gone through this night – and what yet awaits us. 'You should use this opportunity to get your pistols ready. We'll need to continue moving.'

I kneel down, untie the gunpowder flask attached to my belt and start to reload my weapons. It's not an easy task in the dark, particularly with my hands trembling nervously, and it is some time before I rise to my feet, my primed pistols tucked into my belt.

'So what's the plan?' I move alongside Francesca and peer back across the road.

Francesca studies the rooftops of the neighbouring buildings. I reach instinctively for one of my firearms, fearing she has spotted Fabricius. 'What is it?' I whisper, trying to follow her line of sight, but unable to detect the Swedish killer's black silhouette.

'I'm sure I recognise this area from when we passed through here the other day, when we rode out to the Church of the Holy Trinity,' Francesca says, much to my relief, and nods her head in the direction of a distant laneway. 'That lane should lead us down to London Bridge. If we can make our way across to the southern suburbs, we may be able to steal some horses from one of the many farms located on the fringe of city. We could then escape from London, hit the country roads and keep riding until dawn. The Sons of Cain would never catch us. What do you think?'

'Anything sounds good as long as it doesn't involve us carrying this accursed codex for much longer.' I rub my back to emphasise my point. 'But seriously, I think it's a great idea.'

Picking up the Devil's Bible, we continue making our way through the streets of London and head south. It is when we are hurrying down a dark laneway – which I happened to notice is called Pudding Lane, as indicated by the crooked street sign hammered onto the wall of one of the corner houses – that we pull up sharply, place the codex on the ground and press our backs against the wall of the closest building. For we have been alerted by the sound of footfalls coming from behind.

Somebody is racing after us.

Our hearts pounding, we stare into the darkness to see a cloaked figure enter the laneway. A bloodstained, makeshift bandage is wrapped around their wounded left shoulder, and their drawn stiletto and rapier glisten in the moonlight.

'Oh, dear God!' Francesca gasps, whipping aside her cloak and drawing her *talwar*. 'It's Fabricius!'

CHAPTER FIFTY-FOUR

Spotting us the instant we step out into the middle of the laneway, Fabricius laughs sadistically. He slows down to a brisk walk and slashes his sword through the air in a frustrated manner, no doubt incensed that we have managed to evade him twice this night, and determined that he will not make the same mistake again.

'Your friend squealed like a pig as I slashed his throat,' he taunts with a malicious smile.

'You're lying!' I growl, hoping that Fabricius somehow managed to slip past Valentine, who is alive and well, keeping McClodden busy.

'Am I, boy?' Fabricius stares lasciviously at Francesca and licks his lips, as if savouring some morsel he is about to devour. 'I won't be taking her life too quickly. I have other plans in store for her.'

Enraged and repulsed, I swear under my breath, stand protectively in front of Francesca and draw Prince Rupert's pistol. I take aim at Fabricius's head and shoot. Only to have the Son of Cain raise his left hand – the one holding the stiletto – and utter the same diabolical command he used when we first encountered him back at the stream. The pistol ball hits the rippling magical force-field directly in front of his head and ricochets off onto the cobbles.

Some people in nearby houses cry out in alarm, woken abruptly by the report of my firearm. But I don't care. We're now fighting for our lives, and I intend to do anything I can to stop the Swedish slayer.

Cursing in frustration, I nonetheless notice that the air shimmered only immediately in front of Fabricius's head and torso. I produce my remaining pistol, level it at one of Fabricius's thighs and fire, hoping to cripple him.

But the firearm misfires, sending hissing, hot gunpowder over my hand. Crying out in pain, I toss aside the pistol. It lands amidst a stack of barrels half-concealed beneath a waxed-cloth cover, stored in a recess between two hovels on the opposite side of the laneway. With Fabricius only ten yards away from us now, I draw my rapier and am about to step forward to face the Son of Cain, when Francesca grabs me by the arm and pulls me back.

'Jakob!' she yells, her eyes wide with terror. She points at the barrels.

My heart misses a beat when I notice that my pistol, having landed atop one of the barrels, has ignited what appears to be a small pile of black powder on its lopsided lid.

'Please don't tell me that's *gunpowder*?'

Francesca responds to my question with swift, decisive action. She snatches up the Devil's Bible and pulls me after her down the laneway, trying to gain as much distance as possible from the stack of gunpowder barrels before they explode.

We sprint desperately down the narrow laneway, the sound of footfalls behind us revealing that Fabricius is giving chase. But Francesca and I have covered little more than fifteen yards when – *KABOOM!* – the barrels go up, knocking us off our feet and filling the night with fire, smoke and debris. Sprawled on the cobbles, we cover our heads to shield ourselves from the storm of stone and wood that shoots through the air like canister shot from a cannon.

✦CHAPTER✦
FIFTY-FIVE

I t seems to be an eternity before the air finally clears. I clamber to my feet, bleeding and aching from dozens of small lacerations and grazes, amazed to have even survived the blast. Francesca stirs by my feet, covered in lengths of shattered wood, too dazed to pick herself up and mumbling incoherently. She holds the side of her head, where she appears to have grazed herself on the cobbles.

Looking back up the laneway, I am horrified to see the result of the explosion. It is utter pandemonium. The houses flanking the recess in which the gunpowder had been stored have been obliterated, and the neighbouring buildings are ablaze. Whipped into an inferno by the hot, dry winds, the fire has already leapt across to nearby rooftops, which also catch alight.

In stark contrast to the deserted silence that had previously smothered the sleeping city, a crowd of confused Londoners have emerged. Some are screaming hysterically, terrified of the fire, which burns fiercely and uncontrollably and threatens to engulf their homes. Others are barking orders, trying to coordinate some sense of order in combating the flames, and are attempting desperately to put out the blaze with blankets and buckets of water. I cannot understand a word they are saying, but I can read the horror and fear on their faces. London is a city comprised of wooden buildings. If the fire is not contained and brought under control, it will spread as quickly as a spark ignited in a hay stack.

The smell of gunpowder hangs heavily in the air. A billowing trail of smoke is being blown across the night sky, appearing as a grey smear, laden with sparks and glowing cinders that threaten to set alight the shingled rooftops and timber facades of distant buildings. All is illuminated by a hellish red glow.

I shudder, realising that one part of Mother Shipton's prophecy has come true – London will burn. I never thought in my wildest dreams that *I* would be the one responsible for starting it. And so much for not bringing any attention to ourselves. Even the dead would have been woken by the explosion. It's best if Francesca and I make a quick exit.

I remove the debris covering Francesca, then drag her away from the blaze until she is out of harm's reach. I remove her cloak and, using it as a makeshift pillow, prop her against the wall of the closest building. It's only then that I remember the Devil's Bible, and I scan the cobbles for where we must have dropped it. Unable to find it, I study the people hurrying about the lane, fearing that one of them may have taken the codex. Alerted by the cry of an elderly lady who has just been knocked to the ground, I spin around and finally spot the Devil's Bible – gripped in Fabricius's bloody hands as he barges his way down the laneway. He had been directly opposite the gunpowder barrels when they exploded and he took the full impact of the blast. His clothing is shredded, revealing exposed patches of scorched and bleeding skin. He drags his left foot, leaving a dark smear of blood across the cobbles.

'Go after him!' Francesca groans.

'But what about you?' I'm torn between going after the Son of Cain and leaving her.

Francesca makes an impatient gesture, silencing me. 'I'll be fine. I just need some time to rest. But you can't let him escape with the Devil's Bible. Now go, Jakob, before it's too late.'

'I'll come back as soon as I can,' I promise. I brush aside her matted hair to inspect the wound on her face, making sure that it is safe for me to leave her. Noting the injury is a graze and that Francesca is only concussed, I rush over to retrieve my rapier. I pause to check that the lady knocked over by Fabricius is not injured, then chase after the Swedish slayer.

In spite of his injuries, Fabricius is able to make it down to the end of the laneway and halfway up the next street before I catch him. Dropping the codex, he roars in frustration and whirls around to face me; his rapier and stiletto already drawn, glistening blood-red in the hellish glow cast by the distant inferno. I recoil in shock when I see the terrible state of his face, which is burnt almost beyond recognition.

'Damn you to hell!' he cries, capitalising on my moment of hesitation and lunging with his sword, its point aimed at my heart.

Surprised that he can still move with such speed, I barely manage to parry aside his attack, then shuffle back a few steps, granting me an extra second or two to read and respond to his moves. Drawing on the months of fencing practice I have had with Armand – and knowing that I should at first ascertain the extent to which Fabricius's injuries have impacted on his fighting skills – I assume a defensive stance. I raise my rapier up to my chin, its blade horizontal to the ground, and its point directed at Fabricius's eyes. I take an extra three steps back, ensuring that I am well out of striking range, then use the same tactic employed by Valentine: roll the folds of my cloak around my left hand to form a makeshift buckler to counter any thrusts from Fabricius's stiletto.

Seeing the rage in Fabricius's blazing eyes, I try my best to deliver a reckless smile, followed by a mocking laugh. Enraged, Fabricius pounces forward, almost catching me by surprise, each swish of his blade accompanied by a tirade of curses. As aggressive as his attack may be, it lacks its former precison, and I give ground easily, parrying aside his sword. But it is his stiletto that I really have to watch. The Swede is holding it before him, ready to entangle the blade of my rapier within the stiletto's elongated cross-guard. And if that were to happen, this fight would be over in a second, ending with me lying on the ground, a yard of steel driven through my chest. But I am fortunate that Armand has been an excellent teacher in the art of swordplay. His rigorous training sessions have prepared me for an encounter with an opponent such as Fabricius, instructing me how to use my cloak to counter an enemy's left-handed dagger.

As Fabricius lumbers forward, hindered by his injured left leg, and thrusts with his rapier at my chest, I dart to the right and wrap the fold of my cloak around his blade, entangling it. Our eyes lock. With a savage snarl, Fabricius then whips up his stiletto and drives it at my neck.

Anticipating such an attack, I dodge back to the left, drawing Fabricius past me. Carried forward by the momentum of his attack, I give a sharp tug on his entangled blade and, sticking out my right foot, trip him over. As soon as he hits the ground I lunge at his chest with my rapier, intending to skewer him. But Fabricius somehow manages to roll to the side, avoiding my blade, which strikes sparks on the cobbles.

Fabricius regains his feet with surprising speed and slashes his rapier at my head. I duck – the blade swishing through the air only an inch above my head – and retaliate with a swipe directed at Fabricius's belly. Drawing back at only the last instant, standing on his toes, sucking in his stomach and arching his upper torso forward, he manages to avoid the attack.

We withdraw a few paces, our blades lowered as we catch our breath. Fabricius's left shoulder is slumped, the bandage drenched in blood, and he is carrying his weight on his right leg. Having sustained such terrible injuries, it is nothing short of a miracle that he can still stand and wield a blade. But his eyes are still blazing with rage and, in an attempt to catch me by surprise, he lunges forward, crossing the distance between us with startling speed, his sword darting out, its point aimed at my chest. A month or two ago I'm sure this attack would have ended my life, but Armand has taught me how to counter such a thrust, and I flick up my rapier, swatting aside Fabricius's blade. In the same fluid motion, I riposte, plunging my rapier forward, its point aimed at Fabricius's neck. The attack is instinctive – a manoeuvre practised well over a hundred times with Armand in the training hall at Burg Grimmheim – and I stare in awe as my blade punches through Fabricius's neck, leaving him gagging on a foot of steel.

Marvelling at the idea that I have slain the Swedish killer, yet sickened by the sight of his convulsing form, I extract my blade. The Son of Cain falls to his knees, his blades slipping from his fingers to clatter on the cobbles. He is at death's door, but with his dying breaths he manages one last malicious sneer.

'You may have ... killed me, boy,' he gurgles in stilted German, his blood-choked words barely comprehensible.

'But the ... Order of Judas is coming. They will hunt and ... exterminate every last ... one of you.'

He shuffles on his knees in an attempt to reach the Devil's Bible. A final spasm racks his body and his eyes roll back. He slumps to the ground, dead, his outstretched hand reaching for the codex.

CHAPTER FIFTY-SIX

Having sheathed my rapier and retrieved the Devil's Bible, I make my way back to the laneway. Much to my surprise, I find Francesca supporting herself with an outstretched hand against one of the corner buildings. She has cut a makeshift bandage from the hem of her cloak and tied it around her forehead. She is breathing through the sleeve of her shirt, which she uses to filter the smoke that has engulfed the area. She looks exhausted, but her eyes have regained their alert spark.

'You shouldn't be up.' I prop the codex against the building and support Francesca with my shoulder.

'It's too dangerous to stay in this area.' She looks back at the inferno, which has spread to even more houses. 'The exploding gunpowder barrels would have woken up the entire city.'

Finding it difficult to breathe, I raise the hem of my cloak to my mouth. 'But you're hurt.'

Francesca lowers her sleeve and smiles bravely. 'I'm going to have a cracking headache tomorrow, but the dizziness is subsiding with each passing minute. I'm fine to move, as long as I take it easy.' She looks down at the Devil's Bible and exhales in a relieved manner. 'You caught Fabricius. I hope you weren't hurt?'

I shake my head. 'I'm fine. But Fabricius was badly injured from the explosion.' I pause for a moment, shivering as I think back to the final moment of the battle, when I plunged my rapier through his neck. 'I don't think you could have called it a fair fight.'

Francesca gives me an earnest look. 'Don't underestimate your skill with a sword. A little over a month ago I'm sure Fabricius would have escaped with the codex, and I would have found you lying dead in some street. But you've become a skilled fighter, Jakob. I wouldn't have told you to go after him if I didn't think you had it in you.'

'You're just being polite,' I say.

'No, I'm not,' Francesca says, and I am stirred by the conviction in her voice. 'I've seen you train with Armand and Alejandro de la Cruz. I've heard them talk about how quickly you learn, and how far your fencing skills have progressed in such a short period of time. They think you have the making of a great swordsman.' She pauses and gives me a sheepish look. 'Truth be known, I'm actually quite jealous, because you've already surpassed my skill with a blade.'

Armand has often praised me, calling me a model student. But I never knew that both he and Alejandro saw such promise in me. Perhaps I have underestimated my ability after all. Reflecting back on the fight with Fabricius, I had remained calm the entire time, and many of my attacks and ripostes had been instinctive.

'Armand is an excellent instructor,' I say modestly, but swelling with pride. I pick up the codex, hook it under my left hand and help Francesca down the next street.

We head south, moving through the gathering crowd of people drawn out by the fire, and it isn't long before we reach the banks of the Thames and London Bridge. Although I had seen the bridge when we first arrived in London, there had been so many sights for my eyes to behold that I had only paid the bridge a cursory glance. It is only now, in fact, standing before the landmark, and having spent the last hour being chased through the city's twisting warren of alleyways and streets, that I can appreciate its size – and it is awe-inspiring.

The bridge stretches from one side of the Thames to the other. It is set above the river on twenty massive arches, which are buttressed on stone piers that rise out of the dark water and are surrounded at water-level by wooden pontoons. A number of waterwheels are constructed alongside some of the pontoons, utilising the flow of the river to grind grain or pump water into wooden tubes that appear to lead back into the city.

Constructed atop the bridge is a crowded mass of timber-framed shops and houses, most reaching six storeys high, and with projecting terraces, gables and balconies that jut out over the river. The roadway burrows through the ground floors of the buildings, forming a tunnel through which pedestrians are forced to pass. The area is illuminated every dozen or so yards by lanterns, hanging from metal poles set above the doorways. Although the bridge is now deserted, wagons, carts and stacks of barrels line the roadway; evidence that the bridge is one of the city's principal areas of commerce and trade. Punctuating the mass of buildings are three sections of open space, the largest being in the middle of the expanse, where a drawbridge, lowered over the central arch, serves as part of the roadway.

A small group of guards – no doubt the sentries assigned by Bishop Henchman to alert us when the Sons of Cain crossed London Bridge – have taken position at the beginning of the bridge roadway. They are looking worriedly to the north, staring up over the rooftops at the distant fire and are barring entrance onto the bridge, possibly as a means of preventing the spies they believed to be in the city from escaping. A few people, alarmed by the fire and hoping to flee south, have already made their way down to the Thames, only to be turned away by the guards, one of whom accompanied Francesca and me during our chase after the Ghost. He recognises us and allows us to pass.

We head out across the bridge, passing through the tunnel beneath the buildings. Making slow but steady progress, we eventually reach the section of open space containing the lowered drawbridge. Deciding to take a brief rest, we carry on into the opening of the next section of the tunnel, where we stop in a dark recess between two wagons parked along the shopfronts. It offers a perfect resting spot, set several yards back from the perimeter of light cast by the closest lantern and sheltered from the howling wind. As Francesca sits down to wipe her face with a damp handkerchief, I place the Devil's Bible on the ground, pace back and forth restlessly, and massage some life back into my left hand, which has gone numb from carrying the codex.

'I wonder how Armand and the others are faring.' I glance through the burrowing roadway, to the old medieval heart of the city. 'We might have made it out alive, but they're still back there, running and fighting for their lives.'

'They stand a much better chance of surviving now that the Sons of Cain can be killed.' Francesca closes her eyes and squeezes the water from her handkerchief over her face. 'But I wouldn't get too confident just yet; we're still not out of the city.'

'At least we're already halfway across the bridge,' I say optimistically, looking southward, 'and it won't be long before –'

'What is it?' Francesca asks, alarmed.

I take a step deeper into the shadows and reach for my silver-bladed rapier. Rising warily to her feet, Francesca follows my line of sight down through the tunnel, where, at the southern end of the bridge, she finally spots what has made me freeze.

A swarm of furies have amassed on the bridge. They are commanded by the grey-haired figure who stands several yards behind them, his form visible in the lantern-light that streams from a bracket on a nearby wall.

'The Warlock of Lower Slaughter!' Francesca gasps.

CHAPTER FIFTY-SEVEN

'How did he know that we would come this way?' Francesca asks, dumbfounded.

I shake my head. 'It's almost as if the Sons of Cain can follow the Devil's Bible. I don't know if you can feel it, but the book emits an evil aura. I noticed it the second we stole the codex. Just touching it makes my skin crawl.'

Francesca swallows nervously. 'I felt it too, but I didn't say anything as I thought it was just a figment of my imagination.'

'We aren't imagining it, Francesca. The codex is a portal through which the Antichrist will enter our world – a gateway to Hell. I fear the Devil is trying to reach through the text, drawing the Sons of Cain to it. That would explain why Fabricius could track us. He was following the evil *aura* of the codex.'

Francesca looks anxiously at the Devil's Bible. 'And if that's the case, then we've got no chance of hiding it from the Sons of Cain.'

'Well, however they are managing to track us, it doesn't seem as if we'll be getting out of London that way,' I mutter, staring at the Warlock of Lower Slaughter and his furies. I pick up the codex in preparation to run back across the bridge. 'I don't think the Warlock has seen us yet, judging by the fact that he hasn't sent his furies after us. And we're not going to hang around long enough to let him spot us. Are you okay to move?'

Francesca gives a dogged nod. 'I'm going to have to be. It's not as if we have many options.'

I sneak out from behind the wagons. 'Good, then let's get going. Keep out of the lantern-light.'

But I jolt back when I look northward and find that a cloaked figure has somehow snuck past the guards that are still redirecting people away from the bridge. The person has already advanced a quarter of the distance across the bridge, their black metal chest-plate, tri-bar pot helmet and the metal barrel of their drawn cavalry pistol glistening in the light of a nearby lantern.

'The Devil take us!' I curse. 'It's Thomas Whitcliff. The Sons of Cain have us trapped!'

-✠CHAPTER-
FIFTY-EIGHT

'We need to find a way off the bridge.' Francesca moves over to the doorway of the nearest building and tries the handle. Finding it locked, she puts her shoulder against it. 'If we can get inside this building, we'll be able to climb its staircase up to the roof. From there, we should be able to make our way across the rooftops until we reach the southern end of the bridge.'

Having been left with a severe aversion of heights from my experiences atop the keep at Schloss Kriegsberg and the cliff-top monastery of Varlaam, I race out onto the lowered drawbridge. Determined to find an alternative means of escape, I move to the side. I place the codex on the ground and peer over the wooden railing to scan the river below. The water is illuminated by the hellish red

337

glow of the distant fire. I hope to find a boat moored along one of the wooden pontoons at the base of the stone piers. When I discover nothing but a waterwheel and an adjoining wooden shed, I start to reload my pistols, planning to get off two shots at the Sons of Cain before they reach us.

Turning to the south, I notice that the Warlock of Lower Slaughter is walking slowly towards us, past the lanterns on the bridge roadway, his furies keeping pace alongside him. As I look in the opposite direction, however, I'm alarmed to find that Whitcliff has obviously spotted us – perhaps detecting our silhouettes cast by one of the lanterns to our rear – and is sprinting along the bridge.

'How are you going with that door?' I call out to Francesca.

'Not good,' she yells back, now trying to kick it open, and glancing over her shoulder at Whitcliff. 'He's going to be on us in no time at all!'

'I know.' I tuck my loaded pistols back into my belt and retrieve the Devil's Bible.

As I'm about to move back to help Francesca, I see something that fills me with sudden hope. For two figures – having evidently been allowed onto the bridge by the guards – are racing towards us, their blades drawn and their cloaks billowing behind them. As they pass through the light cast by the tunnel lanterns, I notice that the figure on the left – who is of a slender build and dressed entirely in black – is struggling to keep pace with their companion, whose fluid running style and crimson tabard I recognise instantly.

'We'll get out of this yet,' I say to Francesca. 'Armand and Prayer are on their way!'

'They'll never reach us in time,' Francesca says, noting that our companions are over fifty yards behind Whitcliff. Giving up on the door, she starts to load her crossbow.

I look hurriedly to the left and right, assessing our situation. 'It's only Whitcliff that we need to worry about for now. With any luck, you'll be able to take him out. Just be careful that none of your bolts miss him and hit one of our friends.'

'That's what I'm concerned about.' Francesca moves over to join me and raises the crossbow to her shoulder to take aim at the Son of Cain, who is now no more than forty yards away. Steadying her breathing so as to minimise the movement of her weapon, she pulls down on the release lever with her free hand and sends a bolt zipping down the tunnel – only to have Whitcliff twist sharply to the left at the last moment. The bolt flies past his head and continues on its course to thud into the wall of a building behind him, and which Armand races past only a second or two later.

'Be careful!' I warn Francesca.

'You don't need to tell me that.' Francesca levels her second shot, her left eye closed as she stares down the crossbow's sights. Again she shoots – this time the bolt zooms towards the larger target presented by Whitcliff's torso. But the Son of Cain sidesteps to the right, and the bolt is deflected by his cloak to skitter along the cobbles only a few paces behind him. Then, in the same fluid motion, just as he exits the tunnel and enters the open space above the drawbridge, he raises one of his pistols and levels the barrel at me.

Recalling Witch Finder Blackwood's comment that Whitcliff uses cursed pistols guaranteed to hit the heart of their target, I whip up the Devil's Bible and use it as a shield. Whitcliff fires, and the codex jolts back, taking the full force of the hissing ball. The impact of the shot knocks me back against the bridge railing, which gives way. With a cry caught in my throat, I topple over the side.

CHAPTER FIFTY-NINE

Dear God!

I let go of the Devil's Bible and claw desperately in the air, searching for something to grab hold of, afraid that I will crash onto one of the wooden pontoons located at the base of the stone piers. I see the underside of the bridge fly past me, then the front of one of the stone piers. I try to turn around to see if I will land in the water, when, having fallen only half the height of the bridge, I land, back-first, on something solid, making the wind explode from my chest. I lie there for a few seconds, stunned. I rub the back of my head, unsure of what has happened but vaguely aware of a grinding sound coming from somewhere beneath me. Perhaps it's just a trick played by the blow I took to the back of the head, but it feels as if I am slowly rolling backwards.

341

Blinking hard in an attempt to bring some clarity back to my blurred vision, I force myself up onto an elbow, only now realising that I landed atop the massive waterwheel. Looking across and down to my left, I see the Devil's Bible lying open on the edge of the opposite pontoon where it landed. From above and over to the right, I hear the sound of nail-studded boots rushing closer, no doubt made by Whitcliff as he races across the remaining twenty yards to reach me.

I turn around and crawl along the waterwheel, wincing in pain as I keep pace with its slow rotation, wary of slipping between the one-foot-wide gaps between its wooden cross beams. Before I've started to contemplate what I'm going to do next, the nail-studded boots stop directly above me. I stare up fearfully, expecting to find Whitcliff peering over the broken bridge rail with his remaining pistol trained at me.

But it's then that I hear a second pair of rushing feet, which I'm guessing is Francesca, judging from the direction of the footfalls and the lighter sound they make. This is followed by the swish of a blade, the clang of steel on stone, a thud and a whimper of pain. Fearing that Francesca has been hurt, I search desperately for a means of regaining access to the bridge and find a ladder, set in the pier over to my right, and onto which the waterwheel and the adjoining wooden shed are attached. I clamber forward, trying to negotiate my way across the waterwheel with as much speed as possible, determined to reach the ladder and help Francesca, when some sixth sense warns me that I am being watched.

I freeze.

I look up at the bridge to find Whitcliff staring down at me, drawing the remaining pistol from his belt.

Another set of rapidly approaching footfalls sounds from the right – no doubt belonging to Armand – which momentarily distract Whitcliff, forcing him to look over to his left. I burst into action, throwing myself backwards and snatching Prince Rupert's rifled pistol from my belt. Just as my back hits the wooden slats, I take aim and fire.

It's a hasty shot, and I cannot believe my luck when Whitcliff jerks back his right hand and curses as my pistol ball hits him in the forearm. He drops his weapon, which falls and hits the slanting roof of the wooden shed, then ricochets off into the Thames. With a roar of demented rage, Whitcliff leaps over the remnants of the broken bridge rail. Landing on the waterwheel on all fours, he climbs to his feet and, biting back the pain in his wounded forearm, draws his heavy broadsword. Scrambling to my feet, I tuck my pistol into my belt, produce my Solingen rapier, ensure I am well balanced, and prepare to meet the Son of Cain's attack.

He swings his broadsword savagely at my head, putting his full weight behind it, and I duck beneath the silver arc of his blade. The momentum of the attack almost forces Whitcliff to lose his footing, and I counterattack, concerned that if I do not press forward and keep pace with the revolving wheel, I will eventually be thrown off into the water. Lunging forward, but wary of over-pressing the attack and losing my balance, I almost manage to skewer

Whitcliff through the left thigh. He shifts to his right at the last moment, avoiding the thrust, hoists back his own blade and sends it streaking at my head again. Retreating with a cautious step and deftly pulling back my head, I move beyond the reach of his swing and answer with a hasty slash intended to prevent Whitcliff from pressing forward. As he shuffles back, almost losing his balance when the heel of his right boot slips on one of the wooden cross beams, I seize the advantage.

I take two sudden steps forward and drive my blade at Whitcliff's torso, certain that this attack will end his life. With surprising speed, the Son of Cain whips around his broadsword, deflecting my attack. Then, reaching out with his gauntleted left hand, he grabs hold of my blade, takes one step back, twists his body to the right and gives a tremendous yank on my rapier. Losing hold of my blade, I stumble forward and fall down one of the gaps between the wooden slats. With a cry of alarm, I reach out, locking my elbows around the closest cross beam, preventing me from falling into the waterwheel.

Which leaves me at the complete mercy of Whitcliff.

With Whitcliff now holding my rapier, I support my weight with my left elbow, reach down to my belt and pull out my remaining pistol. Before I have time to take aim, Whitcliff kicks my hand away, and the pistol flies off to the left, hits the neighbouring pier and splashes into the river. Whitcliff draws back my rapier, and I'm about to let go of the cross beam and try my luck in the churning inside of the waterwheel, when a blur of red and black leaps from the bridge. It crashes into the Son of Cain and knocks him off the waterwheel, my rapier flying from his hand to clatter beside the Devil's Bible on the nearby wooden pontoon.

The blur of movement is Armand!

I watch in shock as both figures fall in a twisted mess of limbs and plunge into the river. Believing Armand may be in need of my assistance, I pull myself free from the waterwheel. I crouch on the cross beams, draw a dagger from my boot and dive in after the Frenchman.

✦ CHAPTER ✦
SIXTY

I surface in the river and, surprised by the speed of the current, swim towards the pontoon on which my sword and the codex lie, and beside which Armand and Whitcliff are engaged in a savage fight. Armand has grabbed hold of the pontoon with his bandaged hand and is trying desperately to fend off the Son of Cain. Meanwhile, Whitcliff has lost his broadsword in the fall and is somehow managing to stay afloat in spite of his armour. His right forearm is locked around Armand's neck in a vicious choke-hold.

Reaching the combatants, I swim up behind Whitcliff and drive my dagger into his side, in the unprotected area beneath his chest plate. He roars in pain and lashes out with his left arm, but I pull back just in time, his fist flying through the air only an inch before my face. Breaking free from Whitcliff, Armand draws a dagger from his belt with

346

his free hand, holds it blade-down and drives it into the Son of Cain's neck.

Whitcliff twists to his left at the last moment, avoiding Armand's attack, then slams his right fist into the Frenchman's jaw, knocking him back against the pylon. Wrestling the dagger free from the dazed witch hunter, Whitcliff draws back the blade in preparation to plunge it into Armand's torso. Gasping in alarm, I propel myself forward, throw my left arm around Whitcliff's neck, pull him back, and drive my dagger once more into the unprotected area on his lower right flank. His body spasms in pain and the dagger slips from his fingers. Rather than sink dead into a watery grave, he twists around to face me. His left hand shoots out to lock around my neck, forcing me to drop my dagger. His eyes blazing with fury, he pushes me back towards the churning waterwheel.

I try to wrestle free, but he is too strong. Just as my head is within inches of being fed into the revolving wooden beams, something whistles past me. Whitcliff suddenly jolts back, clutching at the bolt lodged in his throat. He releases his hold of me and turns to look at Francesca, who is standing on the bridge, high above us, her crossbow targeting the Son of Cain. She shoots four more bolts in swift succession at Whitcliff, each finding its mark in the unprotected area just above his chest plate, in the nape of the neck.

I swim away from the waterwheel, leaving Whitcliff to sink, dead, into the black waters of the Thames. Reaching Armand by the pylon, I assist him out of the river, collect

my Solingen rapier and the Devil's Bible, and look gratefully up at Francesca.

'Must I always be the one to save you two?' she calls, her
crossbow rested against her left shoulder, her right hand
on her hip in an exaggerated manner.

Armand pats me on the shoulder and softly chuckles.
'Now that's what I call a woman.'

CHAPTER SIXTY-ONE

'I gave you an order to head westward out of London.' Armand gives me a stern look and wrings the water out of his tabard. 'You and Francesca were the last people I expected to find here. You're just lucky that Prayer and I decided to head this way to escape the fire. What are you doing here, of all places?'

'Fabricius found us not long after you left us back near the cathedral,' I explain, returning my rapier to its scabbard. 'We had no choice but to make our way back into the city. We were hoping to head southwards across London Bridge, but got cornered by Whitcliff and the Warlock of Lower Slaughter.'

Armand gives me a concerned look. 'The Warlock of Lower Slaughter is here, too?'

Surprised that Armand did not see the furies approaching from the south, I point in their direction. The Frenchman must have been so focused on Whitcliff that he failed to see them.

'He's down at the southern end of the bridge, slowly making his way up here,' I say calmly, believing we still have time to climb back up to the bridge and escape into the city. My confidence has also been bolstered by the fact that we have now killed two of the Sons of Cain, and that Armand and Prayer have joined us.

'The Warlock's not that far away now,' Francesca calls, an alarmed edge to her voice. She looks to the south and reloads her crossbow with a fresh cartridge of bolts. 'The gunshots must have alerted him, and I'm sure he's seen us by now. He and his furies are rushing this way.'

Prayer appears beside Francesca and takes a few steps to the south. She produces the *Malleus Maleficarum* from the leather case slung over her shoulder and starts to search through its pages. 'You'd better get back up here quick smart. Francesca is right; they've seen us. I reckon we've got about a minute before they'll be on us.'

I'm about to ask Armand if he knows what has become of the other members of our team, particularly von Frankenthal, when he draws my attention to a wooden ladder that scales the face of the stone pier in front of us and provides access back up to the bridge.

'There's no rest for the weary, is there?' Armand mumbles, rubbing his throat and massaging the area where Whitcliff had choked him. He points at the ladder. 'Youth before beauty.'

Francesca comes down to assist me with the Devil's Bible. We climb as fast as we can, but it's a difficult undertaking, hoisting the codex between us, and by the time we gain the bridge the Warlock of Lower Slaughter and his furies have reached us. Fortunately, Prayer has been able to use the Hammer of the Witches to cast a spell, summoning a luminous blue force-field to surround us, keeping the furies at bay.

At first the ghost-like hags amass to the south, raking their dagger-like fingernails against the magical barrier, probing for weaknesses. But then some of them move to the left and right, floating over the side of the bridge to encircle us upon the lowered drawbridge. There must be over two dozen of the spectral hags, and they fill the night with their horrific wails and cries. I notice people staring fearfully through the windows of the nearest buildings, alarmed by the earlier report of my firearm and the cries of the furies. Rather than come to our assistance, they shutter and bolt their windows, scared for their lives.

'This could get better.' I shudder in fear as I place the Devil's Bible in the centre of the bridge, and around which we form a ring.

'Nobody said this was going to be easy.' Armand brandishes his newly acquired silver-bladed broadsword at the furies. 'Remember, they can only be killed by silver weapons.' As Francesca and I draw our silver-bladed swords, he glances over his shoulder at Prayer, who is reading frantically from the pages of the *Malleus Malefi- carum*. 'And be ready to use them; I don't know how much longer Prayer can hold them off. She's already been forced to summon the magic of the *Malleus Maleficarum* several times tonight. It's taken a toll on her.'

Francesca readjusts her grip on the leather-bound handle of her hunting sword in preparation for combat. 'Then let's finish this,' she snarls. 'I've had enough of running.'

Armand gives a dogged grin and turns to face the furies. 'My thoughts exactly. Let's show them what the Hexenjäger, a former member of the *Custodiatti* and one of the *Angeli Mortis* can do.'

Just then the furies move to the south part, revealing the Warlock of Lower Slaughter lurking in the shadows in the tunnel that burrows through the bridge buildings. His lips are set in a malicious sneer as he produces a long-barrelled pistol from beneath his cloak. He mutters some Satanic spell, and a small breach appears in Prayer's force field, providing an opening just large enough for him to shoot through.

Being the only one of our party to be facing the south, I reach instinctively for one of the pistols tucked into my belt, hoping to kill the Warlock before he can shoot. But I stop when I remember that not only do my pistols need to be reloaded – my gunpowder is also wet, rendering my firearms useless. Before I have time to warn my compan- ions, the Warlock takes aim and – *BLAM!* – fires.

I flinch instinctively, expecting to be blasted off my feet. But it is not me that takes the pistol ball. As the breach in the force field closes, I look to my right in horror as Francesca gives a cry of pain, takes two teetering steps forward, and drops to her knees.

CHAPTER SIXTY-TWO

'Francesca!' I rush to her side to support her with my shoulder, fearing that she has been mortally wounded.

Her teeth clenched in pain, she clutches her right thigh, her fingers turning red with the blood spilling from the wound left by the pistol ball. 'I-I've b-b-been hit, Jakob!' she stammers, sliding out from beneath me to lie on her back, her eyes wide with shock.

Armand is only a second behind me, and he pries away Francesca's fingers to tear open a section of her breeches to inspect the severity of the wound. 'You'll be all right,' he says after a few anxious seconds. He breathes a sigh of relief, and produces a dagger from the inside of his left boot. He cuts a strip of cloth from the hem of his cloak, which he uses to tie a tourniquet around the wound. He then takes off his cloak, folds it several times to create a pad, and instructs me to hold it firmly against Francesca's thigh.

'You're lucky,' he says, looking down at Francesca and stroking her cheek. 'The ball's entry and exit wounds reveal that it travelled straight through your leg. We just need to staunch the wound and stop the bleeding. The tourniquet and bandage will take care of that.'

'Thank you.' Francesca shudders against the pain in her leg. She then looks over at the Warlock of Lower Slaughter, her eyes widening in alarm when she sees him reloading his pistol. 'He's going to pick us off one at a time. We've got to stop him!'

Armand clicks his tongue as he looks around the bridge, considering our options. His gaze eventually stops on a single-storey building located to the north, a few yards beyond the perimeter of Prayer's force field. It is positioned off to the left of the roadway, just before it burrows into the buildings. A small wooden crucifix is located atop its roof, signifying that it is some sort of chapel.

He points at the chapel. 'Prayer, can you move back up the bridge until your force field covers that building over there?'

Still chanting her spell, Prayer spares a sideways glance at the building and nods.

'Everyone's going to pull back to the chapel,' Armand announces. 'Once inside, you're going to barricade the door, preventing the furies from coming in after you. And if they do break inside, at least you'll be facing them on hallowed ground, giving you the advantage.'

My eyes narrow in concern. 'And what about you?'

Armand rises to his feet, stares at the Warlock of Lower Slaughter and slashes his broadsword angrily through the air. 'Me? I've got a score to settle.'

'What? You'll never be able to beat the Warlock and the furies! There are far too many of them.'

Armand gives a reckless smile as he considers the screeching mass of ghost-like hags. 'Really? I would have thought that the odds were on my side.'

I shake my head, not impressed by his foolhardy bravado. 'You can't –'

But Armand stops me with a raised hand. 'I want no arguments, Jakob. Do as I have instructed and we still may have a chance of getting out of this alive. Now help Francesca to her feet. Prayer has already started moving back.'

Not liking this one bit but unable to think of a better plan, I sheathe my rapier and hook the Devil's Bible under my left arm. I then support Francesca with my right shoulder and assist her to her feet. Staying close to Prayer, who is still deep in an incantation, her eyes locked on the opened page of the *Malleus Maleficarum*, we move slowly over to the chapel.

Reaching its iron-ribbed door, I try the handle and say a silent prayer when it turns. I push the door open and usher Prayer inside. Then, just as Francesca and I are about to follow after her, I look over my shoulder to see that the Warlock has reloaded his pistol and created another breach in the force field – his firearm is locked on us. I position myself protectively in front of Francesca to shield her from the shot, but Armand, still standing in the middle of the lowered drawbridge, waves his bandaged hand at the Warlock and draws his attention.

'Over here, ugly,' he taunts, stepping over towards the opposite side of the bridge, luring the pistol away from Francesca and me.

An enraged sneer on his face, the Warlock takes the bait and redirects his pistol at Armand. He fires ... and I stare in disbelief as Armand is blasted off his feet and lies in a twisted heap on the drawbridge.

CHAPTER
SIXTY-THREE

Letting go of Francesca – who staggers into the chapel, unaware of what has just transpired behind her – I take a hesitant step towards Armand, struggling to comprehend what I have just witnessed. A silent cry caught in my throat, I stare at him, willing the duellist to climb back to his feet and give me one of his cavalier grins. But he lies motionless, his eyes closed, his legs splayed awkwardly, and his broadsword still gripped in the lifeless fingers of his outstretched hand. Refusing to accept that Armand has been killed, I throw the Devil's Bible into the chapel and am about to sprint over to his side when Prayer's force field falters.

As the furies come tearing towards me, I scream out in frustration and rage, retreat to the door and close it behind me. The instant before it slams shut, I pay one final look at my fallen friend, only to see his eyes flicker open and give one of his trademark roguish winks.

Believing that Armand was not even hit by the Warlock's shot but is only acting dead – perhaps as a ploy to catch the Son of Cain off-guard – I pull across the metal bolt on the inside of the door, locking it and sealing Francesca, Prayer and me in complete darkness. Only a few seconds later the furies hit the door, tearing into it with their dagger-like fingernails, trying to rend the wooden beams apart. But for the moment, at least, the door holds firm, and I stumble further into the chapel, groping in the dark, searching for some means of creating a light.

Prayer utters a strange incantation somewhere over to my right, and a soft blue light fills the chapel, revealing that the English witch hunter is standing near the altar at the far end of the chamber. The light is coming from the opened pages of the *Malleus Maleficarum*, which she has placed atop the altar. Francesca is sitting on the floor a yard over to her left, her back propped against one of the chapel's four pews. She holds Armand's folded cape tightly around her injured thigh, applying pressure to the wound.

'I'm sorry, but I couldn't hold the force field any longer.' Prayer's voice is strained from the effort of summoning the magic of the Hammer of the Witches.

'We wouldn't have made it to the chapel if it wasn't for your magic,' I say, scanning the interior of the chamber for some means of bracing the door. 'And now you've provided us with light. So please, don't apologise. In fact, we should be thanking you for saving us. But we're not going to last long if the furies break into here. So I'm going to need your help in moving that up against the door.' I point at one of the wooden pews aligned in two parallel rows before the altar. 'Do you think you have the strength?'

Prayer gives an exhausted nod. 'It's not going to do it itself, is it? Come on.'

Despite being only three yards long, the pew is constructed of heavy oak, and it takes us several attempts to position it against the door. We then move back to join Francesca at the far side of the chapel, our eyes locked on the door, which shudders against the furies' relentless efforts to break inside. In addition to the wraiths screeching and clawing at the entrance, we can discern the sound of clashing blades.

'Armand has engaged the Warlock of Lower Slaughter!' Francesca says, sitting upright.

I shake my head, my frustration building, feeling an irresistible urge to pull back the pew and burst out of the chapel to help Armand. 'This isn't right. We can't just leave him out there!'

'As much as I hate this, Armand gave us an order,' Francesca says. 'Perhaps he believed we would only get in his way, distracting him from slaying the Warlock and the furies. He can hardly kill them if he is forced to protect us. Besides, you need to stay in here, Jakob. I can barely stand, let alone wield a sword, and Prayer is exhausted. If the furies break inside here, we'll be counting on you to guard the codex.'

'She's right.' Prayer leans against the altar, so tired that she can barely stand. 'The *Malleus Maleficarum* has sapped the strength from me. We'll be in need of your blade to protect us.'

Knowing that Prayer and Francesca are right, I curse under my breath and pace back and forth, listening to the sounds of combat outside. I pray that Armand will survive.

For what seems to be an eternity we wait in the chapel, staring anxiously at the door, our ears assailed by the screaming furies and the squeal of steel on steel. As I'm about to move over to the door and brace my shoulder against it for added support, the sound of shattering glass forces me to spin around. I stare in disbelief at the fury that has just smashed its way through the stained-glass window behind the altar – a window that up until now I had failed to notice – and is tearing towards Prayer.

'Look out!' I yell, hurdling over a pew and racing towards Prayer.

She snatches her silver-bladed hunting knife from her belt and slashes instinctively at the fury, cleaving it in half with a back-handed swipe. Even before the fury has turned to ash, several more scream through the shattered window, and we find ourselves fighting for our lives.

I pull Prayer away from the opening and push her to the opposite side of the chapel, where I believe it's safe. I then stand protectively beside Francesca, who struggles to her feet, draws her hunting blade and tries in vain to slash out at the swirling hags. Sending the closest fury recoiling with a swipe of my silver rapier, I'm forced to dodge deftly to my right, almost knocking over Francesca, and narrowly avoid a raking claw that seems to come out of nowhere. My training taking over, I deliver a lightning-fast thrust at this second wraith, my blade puncturing through its neck, to send it back to Hell.

The next instant, there is a massive *KABOOM!* from just outside the chapel, and the walls and floor vibrate. Distracted, wondering what on earth has just happened, I catch movement in the corner of my eye and duck as razor-like fingers tear out of the gloom and slice through the air only an inch above my head. I slash out wildly with my blade, cleaving the fury in half and turning it to ash. I carry through with the momentum of the attack, spinning on my heel, my blade transformed into a streak of silver as it slices through the neck of a wraith coming from behind Francesca.

Noticing how easily the furies are being dispatched, I start to believe that we will be able to fight our way out of this. But a cry of alarm catches my attention, forcing me to turn to my right. Over on the far side of the chamber, near the pew that is braced up against the door, Prayer has been knocked to the ground. She clutches a deep gash across her left shoulder, and her blade lies uselessly several yards beyond her reach. To make matters worse, the four remaining furies to have burst into the chapel are tearing towards her, their fingers bared in preparation to slice her apart.

I snatch Francesca's hunting blade and race across the chapel, catching two of the spectres by surprise by coming up behind them and slaying them with synchronised swipes of my swords. Still some distance away from the remaining furies, which are on the opposite side of the chapel, and knowing that I will never reach Prayer in time, I wedge the toe of my boot beneath her hunting knife. I call out her name in warning, drawing her attention, and flick the blade towards her. She catches the knife and slashes desperately over her right shoulder, cleaving through one of the furies. But the remaining wraith twists to the left, narrowly avoiding Prayer's knife, which it sends skittering across the stone floor with a swipe of its hand. The fury grabs Prayer by the hair, forces her head back exposing the English slayer's neck, and draws back its clawed hand. A desperate cry caught in my throat, I streak forward and dive onto the pew braced against the door. The momentum of my charge allows me to slide on my belly across the pew, and I plunge my rapier through the fury's chest, killing it instantly, its dagger-like fingers turning to ash only an inch away from Prayer's throat.

Prayer raises a hand in a gesture of gratitude. 'That was close,' she says, wincing against the pain in her wounded shoulder. 'I didn't think you were going to reach me in time.'

I kneel down beside her and give her a reassuring pat on the back. 'Believe me, I'm not going to let anything happen to you. Your brother would never forgive me. I'd rather face a thousand furies than have *him* come after me.'

Prayer cannot help but smile. 'That's a valid point.' She looks around the chapel. 'I think that was the last of them.'

'We got them all – or rather, *Jakob* got them all,' Francesca confirms, using the pews to support herself as she hobbles over towards us.

'But that doesn't mean that more won't come,' I warn, assisting Francesca as she joins us over near the barricaded door that, located on the opposite side to the shattered window, has become the safest part of the chapel.

I retrieve Prayer's hunting knife and inspect her shoulder. Believing the deep gash will need to be sutured but lacking the means of doing this, I follow Armand's example: I cut a length of material from the hem of my cloak, which I then tie as a makeshift bandage around the wound. Returning Francesca her sword, I step into the middle of the chapel, wipe a hand across my forehead, face the window and prepare myself for the next onslaught.

'I don't think any more will come,' Francesca says after a few anxious seconds.

'What makes you think that?' I ask.

Francesca jerks her chin towards the door. 'Listen. You can't hear them. It's almost as if the furies have moved off or been killed.'

I had been so focused on defending the chapel, I had failed to notice that it has become deathly quiet outside. Not only can I no longer hear the screeching furies and their clawing at the door, but the distinct clang of blades has also ended. All that can be heard is the haunting, wailing wind.

'You're right.' I move over to the door and press an ear against it. 'Perhaps we should check outside?'

Eager to find out what has become of Armand, I don't even wait for a response to my question. I place my sword on the ground, crouch down, brace my shoulder against the pew that blocks the door and push with all my might. After several efforts, I manage to move it a few feet. I then retrieve my sword, pull back the iron latch and open the door a few inches. I peer outside.

From the light cast by a nearby lantern, I can see that the bridge roadway is deserted. The only evidence that this area had been host to a recent fight are the claw marks all over the exterior of the door and the piles of ash left behind by the slain furies. Even these are quickly disappearing, being blown away by the wind. Alarmingly, there is no sign of Armand, nor of the Warlock of Lower Slaughter.

Wondering what has happened to my friend, I step cautiously outside, and my eyes are drawn immediately over to the drawbridge – or rather, to where the drawbridge *used* to be. All that remains of it is the left-hand section of bridge railing, spanning across the newly created thirty-yard-wide chasm on a heavy wooden support beam. On the opposite side of the breach, a ten-yard-long section of the drawbridge hangs vertically against the side of the far pier, dangling from two thick lengths of rope tied around twin stone pylons on the edges of the bridge roadway.

Realising that this was the source of the terrible crashing sound that had assailed my ears, but curious as to what could have possibly caused this to happen, I walk warily over to the chasm. I get the shock of my life when I see two figures, barely visible in the darkness of the void, hanging from the end of the dangling section of drawbridge.

CHAPTER SIXTY-FOUR

'Armand?' I call out, my heart racing, believing that one of the shapes must be the French duellist.

'Jakob!' the figure on the left yells back.

I breathe a sigh of relief, recognising the voice as Armand's. On closer inspection, I notice that he has hooked the heel of his right boot onto a projecting wooden beam, and is holding onto the bridge with his left hand, his bandaged right hand held against his chest. Looking across to the other side, I see that the Son of Cain is hanging from the lowest section of the bridge and is slowly making his way over towards Armand.

'How can I help you?' I scan the dangling drawbridge and the remaining section of bridge railing, trying to work out how to make my way down.

Armand shakes his head. 'I don't think you can. I injured my hand again in the fall. There's no way I can climb up.' He curses in frustration. 'I had killed the furies and had everything under control until the Warlock cast a spell that smote the drawbridge in two. As we happened to be fighting on it at the time, it's nothing short of a miracle that I didn't fall to my death.'

'There has to be something I can do,' I say, refusing to give up.

'Whatever you are going to do, you'd better do it fast.' Armand looks across at the Warlock, who is now only six yards away from him. 'And don't you dare think of climbing down. It's too dangerous. If you fall from here you'll smash onto the broken sections of drawbridge caught between the piers beneath us. You'd never survive.'

'We'll worry about that later,' I say, already moving over to the narrow bridge railing and testing my weight on it. Believing it will be able to support me, I take a firm hold on the hand rail, use it to keep my balance and shuffle out across the void. Terrified of looking down, I lock my eyes on the far side of the bridge and make my way over as quickly as possible. I am only halfway across, however, when I hear the sound of clanging swords. Forcing myself to look down, I find that the Warlock of Lower Slaughter has climbed across to reach Armand. The Son of Cain is hanging from the bridge with his left hand. He has drawn his blade with his right and is attacking Armand. Needing his one good hand to defend himself, the French duellist has somehow hooked his legs over the projecting wooden beam and is now hanging *upside down*, parrying aside the Warlock's blade with his mortuary sword.

Fearing Armand won't last long, I search desperately for a means of assisting him, and spot the wagon that Francesca and I had previously rested behind. Only now do I notice it is stacked with small barrels. Racing over to the wagon, I grab one of the barrels, hasten back over to the edge of the broken drawbridge and take position above the Warlock.

'Armand, look out!' I yell, alerting him to the barrel poised in my hands, ready to drop on the Warlock of Lower Slaughter.

As Armand twists his body away from the Son of Cain – who is so caught up in his attempt to kill the Frenchman that he hasn't even noticed me appear above him – I drop the barrel. Just as the Warlock draws back his sword in preparation to deliver a swipe guaranteed to cleave Armand in two, the barrel crashes onto the Son of Cain's head and knocks him from the bridge. Thrashing and screaming, he plummets down the side of the pier to crash – flat on his back – onto the jagged remains of the drawbridge that lie snagged to the wooden pontoon at the base of the pier. There is a sickening crunch, then the Warlock's lifeless form slides into the Thames to be swept away by the current.

✦CHAPTER✦
SIXTY-FIVE

'That's one problem dealt with.' Armand swaps his sword into his right hand. With considerable effort, he swings himself up to grab hold of the drawbridge. He sheathes his blade. 'But I've still got to get back up to the bridge. And I don't think I've got the strength in my right hand to do that.'

'I'll find a rope and pull you up,' I say encouragingly, glancing back at the wagon. 'There's bound to be one around here somewhere. Just don't go falling into the river before I return.'

Armand flexes the fingers of his injured hand. 'I wasn't planning on taking another dip in the Thames tonight.'

Before I can respond we suddenly hear a loud *snap*. I look down at Armand, who grabs hold of the bridge with both hands.

The suspended section of bridge then groans and plummets down the side of the pier.

My heart caught in my throat, I watch helplessly as the right-hand side of the bridge slides into the chasm. Armand holds on for dear life, his eyes wide with terror. The bridge only drops a few yards before it comes to a jarring halt, almost dislodging Armand, who screams out in pain and nurses his right hand against his side.

For a few anxious moments I stare down at Armand clinging to the now lopsided dangling section of drawbridge. When he resumes a two-handed grip on the wooden beams and I am confident that he won't fall, I try to find out what happened.

As I had previously noticed, the bridge is being held in place by two lengths of rope tied to small stone columns located on opposite sides at the southern edge of the chasm. But it's only now I realise that each section of rope is actually comprised of *two* separate ropes that have been wound together to form a single, stronger length. One of the wound sections of rope over to the right has snapped, causing the bridge to suddenly drop, and leaving one, frayed remaining length of rope to support its weight.

'This isn't good, is it?' Armand asks desperately.

I shake my head. 'All that's keeping the drawbridge from falling are two ropes. I don't think we have long before one of them snaps.'

Armand glances down at the water racing past the shattered remnants of the drawbridge. 'It's just one thing after another, isn't it? If only I could use both hands, I'd be able to climb back up.'

'Maybe you don't need to use your right hand,' a familiar voice says. Armand and I look across to the opposite side of the bridge and see Francesca sitting at the edge of the chasm. She aims her crossbow at the dangling drawbridge, slightly above Armand's head. 'Don't move,' she instructs, steadying her breathing and staring down the crossbow's sights. Prayer is standing off to her side, the Devil's Bible resting at her feet and the *Malleus Maleficarum* held in her hands, its blue light illuminating the night.

'It's not as if there are many places I can go,' Armand says dourly, burying his head in his shoulder. 'I think I know what you have in mind, Francesca. Just don't miss.'

'Trust me,' Francesca says softly, deep in concentration. 'Prayer, can you give me more light?'

Prayer nods and utters an incantation. The light emanating from the codex intensifies, eventually basking Armand in a soft blue glow.

'How's that?' she asks.

Francesca's eyes narrow. 'Perfect.'

She then fires all twelve bolts, raising her crossbow a fraction after each shot and alternating her aim to the left and right, to create a series of handholds for Armand to use. When she is finished, she lowers her crossbow, exhales heavily and massages her injured thigh.

'You should be able to go up now,' she says.

Armand reaches up, hooks his right forearm around the closest bolt and tests his weight on it. Satisfied that it will hold, he climbs up the suspended length of drawbridge. In spite of his injured hand, he moves with surprising speed, and it doesn't take him long to climb within two yards of the top of the pier.

'It appears as if I'll get out of this mess yet.' He looks up and gives me a triumphant grin.

I kneel by the edge of the drop and reach down to offer Armand a hand. 'Let's not start celebrating just yet; not until you have your feet firmly planted on the bridge.' I cast a wary glance over at the frayed section of rope. Only to find that it has been worn down by the sharp edge of the pier to nothing more than a few straining strands.

'Armand! The rope's about to give way!' I lie on the edge of the pier and reach down as far as I can, but my outstretched fingers are still a good yard above the Frenchman.

The grin vanishes from Armand's lips. Then the rope snaps.

—✦Chapter—
SIXTY-SIX

The right-hand side of the dangling drawbridge falls down the side of the pier. A second later, the length of rope attached to the stone pylon on the opposite side of the bridge, unable to support the weight of the structure, also snaps.

The entire section of remaining drawbridge plummets down the chasm.

And it's at that moment, when all hope seems lost and Armand is destined to fall to his death, that the duellist makes a desperate leap, his outstretched left hand reaching for mine.

For a split second, time seems to freeze.

Then our hands lock in a monkey-grip. Wary of being pulled over the edge, I grip the remaining yard of rope attached to the pylon with my free hand. Biting my lip, struggling to support Armand's weight, I hold on for dear life.

There's a tremendous *CRASH!* as the drawbridge smashes into the river. But I am too drained to save Armand from the same fate. Just when I fear that I'm not going to be able to hold on for much longer, Armand's feet find purchase in the grooves between the stone slabs on the side of the pier, allowing me to pull him up. We crawl away from the edge and lie on our backs, breathing heavily.

'That was close,' I say at length, sitting up.

'Too close,' Armand says. 'Yet again, I owe you my life, Jakob. I don't know where I'd be without you.'

'You'd more than likely be dead at the bottom of London Bridge,' Francesca says. Surprised, we look up to find that she and Prayer have traversed the chasm via the remaining section of handrail. What is even more surprising is that, despite their wounds and fatigue, they somehow managed to carry the Devil's Bible across with them.

'I thought for a terrible moment we were going to lose both of you,' Francesca continues.

I make a dismissive gesture at the tomb-robber as she and the English witch hunter sit down beside us. 'We're Hexenjäger. We don't go down that easy.'

Armand smiles proudly. 'Spoken like a true witch hunter.'

As Francesca rolls her eyes, I massage some life back into my left arm and shoulder, the muscles strained from saving Armand. 'Mind you, I think my arm's an inch or two longer now.'

Armand winks playfully. 'Then think yourself lucky, Jakob. Your extended reach will give you an unfair advantage in swordplay from here on.'

We laugh for a while at his comment, relieved to have made it through the night. Noticing my gunpowder flask is wet, Prayer kindly hands me hers, and I tie it to my belt.

'Well, that's three of the Sons of Cain dealt with,' I say. 'There's only Alistair McClodden left.'

Armand sits up, tilts his head and frowns. 'Aren't you forgetting about Nils Fabricius?'

I shake my head. 'He's dead. I slew him with my sword.'

Armand gives me an impressed look. '*You* killed Fabricius? Well done, Jakob. That's good news. Good news, indeed. I knew that all that sword-training would pay off.' He produces his water-skin and takes a long draught, then, with a proud smile, passes it to me. I take a drink and hand it back.

'What's become of von Frankenthal?' I ask. 'I thought he would have been with you and Prayer.'

Armand wipes his sleeve across his lips. 'I found von Frankenthal not long after I left you back at the graves.' He rises to his feet and looks to the north. 'We managed to draw McClodden and Whitcliff after us. We led them on a wild-goose chase through half of the city before they finally caught us. While I fought Whitcliff, von Frankenthal paired off with the Scotsman.'

'I bet that was one hell of a fight.' I envisage the encounter between the two massive warriors.

Armand nods. 'It was, but not even McClodden could match von Frankenthal's strength. The Son of Cain was forced to withdraw down a laneway, and von Frankenthal tore after him. That was the last I saw of them.'

I cannot help but smile at my valiant, powerful friend. 'We don't call him Revelation 6.8 for nothing, do we? Although, McClodden must have managed to evade him.'

'What makes you say that?'

'We ran into Valentine, and he was being chased by McClodden.'

'How long ago was that?'

I shrug uncertainly. 'Maybe half an hour. Possibly a little longer. But I'm worried about Valentine. Fabricius said that he had killed him.'

'Then Fabricius had been lying,' Prayer says. 'For we saw Valentine moments before we followed Whitcliff onto the bridge. He bolted past the end of our street, but he was gone by the time we got down to where we had seen him.'

I breathe a sigh of relief. Thank God for that. Whilst I was worried what had become of Valentine, I hold no such fears for von Frankenthal. A building could collapse on him and he'd walk out complaining of nothing more than a dull headache. I'm sure he's stalking through the twisting alleyways, still trying to lure the remaining Son of Cain after him.

Armand draws our attention to the distant inferno. 'I wonder how that started.'

Francesca casts me a cautionary glance and, when the others are not looking, raises a finger to her lips. She evidently does not want me to be blamed for starting the fire, even if it was an accident.

'I was hoping you might be able to tell us,' she says, looking at Armand and Prayer in turn.

Armand makes a baffled gesture. 'Not long after I escaped from Whitcliff, I ran into Prayer. She had joined up with Bishop Henchman and his guards, who had come out of Saint Paul's Cathedral to help us draw the Sons of Cain away from you and the codex. Prayer then joined me, and we were heading down the eastern bank of the Thames, past the Tower of London, when a massive explosion sounded from somewhere over to the west.'

Prayer rubs her eyes wearily. 'We made our way straight there. By the time we arrived, an entire laneway was up in flames. We also spotted Whitcliff heading south towards London Bridge. We thought it would be wise to follow him to see what he was up to.'

'I'm sure he was being drawn by the codex,' I say. 'It's been impossible for us to escape the Sons of Cain. Everywhere we run, they find us. And if McClodden is still alive, it won't be long before he comes after us.'

Prayer looks warily at the codex. 'Then we should move.'

Armand gives a concerned glance at Francesca and Prayer. 'Not before you have a brief rest. I also want to have a better look at your wound, Francesca.'

As Armand kneels beside the Italian and inspects her thigh, and Prayer lies down and closes her eyes, I rise to my feet and look towards the southern end of London Bridge.

Armand notices me chewing my bottom lip in thought. 'What's on your mind?'

'When we rode out to the cemetery, I'm sure I saw a stable just after we crossed the bridge,' I say. 'If we could get some horses, we'd be able to ride out of here in no time at all.'

Armand reaches into a pocket and hands me a small leather pouch full of coins. 'Then, what are you waiting for? There are more than enough coins in there to buy two mounts. And don't worry about waking up the owner to discuss prices, as we don't have time. Just take what you need and leave the pouch for the owner.'

'That's very honourable of you,' Francesca says. 'I'm sure, at this time of the night, Jakob could easily steal the horses.'

'I know I have my faults, but I'm no thief.' Armand looks at me. 'Now go.'

'I'll be as fast as I can,' I say, heading off across the bridge.

I eventually reach the far end and continue down the adjoining main street until finding, much to my relief, that there is indeed a stable. It's not as large as my uncle's business in Dresden, but set back from the main building are half a dozen stalls. My eyes acclimated to the dark, I move stealthily through the stable-yard and inspect the first of the stalls. Finding two horses within, I slowly open the gate and slip inside.

Having whispered soothingly in the horses' ears and gently rubbed their necks to earn their trust, I search along the walls until, as I had suspected, I find harnesses and bridles. Readying the horses in the darkness is not the easiest of tasks, and it is some time before I leave Armand's pouch hanging from a rafter and lead the mounts out across the cobbled stable-yard. The sound of their passage is muffled by the cloth bags, which I found on a shelf at the rear of the stall, that I wrapped around their hooves. Reaching the main road, I mount one of the horses and, holding the second by the reins, ride back to join my companions.

'This should make things easier.' I pull up before my friends and assist Prayer to climb up behind me.

Armand helps Francesca, her thigh wrapped in a fresh bandage, mount the second horse. He secures the Devil's Bible through the harness straps and swings up behind the Italian. 'It's time we get out of here.'

'Should we destroy the remnants of the drawbridge?' Prayer looks back at the handrail. 'That would prevent McClodden from coming after us.'

Armand shakes his head. 'Even if he is drawn after the codex, he'll never be able to catch us now. And it wouldn't surprise me if that fire consumes the entire city. The bridge may be the only way for thousands of people to escape from the flames. We're not going to leave them stranded on the other side.'

He kicks his mount into a canter and, with Prayer and me following close behind, we cross London Bridge, make our way through the southern suburbs and head out of the city.

✠CHAPTER✠
SIXTY-SEVEN

We ride at a steady pace along a country road, eager to get as far away from London as possible, but wary of pushing our horses too hard and causing them to stumble in the darkness. Having covered several leagues, Armand directs us up a narrow trail that branches off the central road. We pass over a bridge that crosses a small stream. The Frenchman then pulls off to the side of the trail, guides us across a stretch of open field and leads us to a clearing in a thick copse of trees.

We dismount and tether the horses to nearby branches. Armand quickly starts a fire, and it isn't long before we are warming our hands before the crackling flames.

'I know this is going to sound like a stupid question, but I suppose nobody has any food on them?' Prayer asks, huddled in her cloak, her face drained of colour.

'Sorry, but I left the picnic basket back in London,' Armand jokes, and prods the fire with a stick. He stares into the flames and clicks his tongue in thought, as if there is something troubling him.

'What is it?' I ask.

Armand waves his hand dismissively. 'I'm sure I'm worrying unnecessarily, but I cannot stop thinking about von Frankenthal and Valentine. Perhaps I should have remained in London to look for them.'

'Valentine is almost your equal with a blade, and von Frankenthal is big and ugly enough to look after himself. I'm sure they are all right,' I say, not wanting Armand to feel guilty for leaving our companions behind. Having witnessed Valentine's swordsmanship, and seen how von Frankenthal fought the witches back in Schloss Kriegsberg during my first mission with the Hexenjäger, I have little doubt that they are safe. I suspect Armand is just being over-protective again, feeling burdened by his position as leader of our group. 'I'm sure they've met up and are still going after McClodden. Perhaps that's why the Demon of Moray Firth hasn't come after us.'

Armand gives a faint smile. 'You're probably right.' He turns to Francesca. 'How's that bandage looking?'

Francesca has her wounded leg stretched and elevated before the fire. 'You did a good job,' she says, inspecting her thigh. 'It's stopped bleeding.'

'We'll get it checked properly when we return to Prince Rupert's lodgings in the morning,' Armand says. 'In the meantime, I suggest you get some rest. And that goes for all of you. I'm certain we're safe here, but I'll keep watch nonetheless.' To emphasise his point, he draws his mortuary blade and rests it across his thighs.

As Prayer and Francesca smile appreciatively and lie down by the fire, I start to reload my pistols.

Armand jerks his chin at my firearms. 'I don't think you'll need those again tonight.'

'It doesn't hurt to be cautious.' I ram a piece of wadding down the barrel of one of my pistols to keep the ball in place. 'I'll feel a lot more comfortable when I have these loaded.'

'Sound advice,' a voice says in German, but with a strong French accent.

What?

Armand and I spin around to see a masked man emerge from the darkness, the flames of the fire glistening on the barrels of his raised pistols.

'Now, isn't this cozy?' the stranger says, locking his pistols on Armand and me as we spring to our feet. He gestures at the weapons in our hands and makes a clicking noise with his tongue. 'Let's not do anything foolish. I think it would be best if you dropped those.'

The man has the aplomb of a gentleman, with his refined speech and having spared no expense on his wardrobe. He is clad in a scarlet shirt with embroidered silk sleeves. A velvet cape is slung over his left shoulder, and the lower half of his face is concealed behind a black silken handkerchief. Silver spurs are attached to the rear of his polished knee-length riding boots, and his wide-brimmed hat is adorned with a crimson plume.

As Francesca and Prayer rise warily to their feet, Armand signals for me to ignore the stranger's command. 'You seem to be at a disadvantage,' he says to the masked gunman. 'There are four of us, and only one of you.'

'You don't think I'd be so foolish as to approach you single-handedly, do you?' the stranger says.

We turn around as four other masked men emerge from behind trees that encircle the perimeter of our firelight. They brandish their pistols at us, and the outline of a smile forms beneath the gunman's mask. 'The Gentleman Highwayman never works alone.'

Francesca snorts contemptuously and looks at Armand. 'You finally get to meet Claude Duval. I hope you're impressed.'

As Armand makes a sour face, Claude laughs. 'Now, your weapons; drop them.'

There is a tense moment as Armand holds the highwayman's stare, his fingers twitching on the hilt of his mortuary blade. Licking his lips, Armand turns to look at us, his eyes lingering on Francesca's bandaged thigh and the unprimed pistols held in my hands. Having evidently decided that we are in no position to take on Claude Duval's band of highwaymen, he sighs resignedly and nods, signalling for us to do as instructed.

As we drop our weapons, Claude crosses over to Armand and uses the barrel of one of his pistols to draw aside the duellist's cloak. He raises his eyebrows in curiosity when he sees Armand's crimson Hexenjäger tabard. He then looks across at me, noting that I am similarly dressed.

'Isn't this interesting,' he remarks, stepping back. 'I happen to stumble across two Hexenjäger, a member of the *Angeli Mortis*, and their wounded friend. And if I'm not mistaken –' he nods to the north, where the night sky has turned red with the glow of the distant fire in London '– I'd say that London is ablaze.' He turns towards Armand. 'You're a long way from home, my friend. Would you care to tell me what this is all about?'

'Just take our money and go,' Armand says dourly.

'That's exactly what I plan on doing.' Claude flicks one of his pistols, directing one of his men to search our pockets. A second highwayman goes to inspect our horses and returns shortly with the Devil's Bible.

Claude notices my eyes flash with alarm and Francesca and Prayer glancing warily at one another. He motions for his accomplice to bring the codex over to him. Claude examines it, then looks back at us, his eyes narrowing suspiciously. 'Having observed how you reacted when we discovered this, I'd say there's a good chance that it lies at the heart of tonight's mysterious events. Am I right?' When we do not respond to his question, he chuckles softly to himself. 'I didn't think you would provide me with an answer, but the worried look on your faces betrays this book's importance.' He turns to the highwayman holding the Devil's Bible. 'Strap it to my horse.'

'But you can't take it!' I exclaim, furious that after all we have been through we are finally going to lose the codex.

'I can, and I will,' Claude says. 'You see, I'm not only an opportunist, but I'm also a very curious man. When you rode past our hideout several hundred yards back, it was my inner opportunist that compelled me to add your money pouches to my coffer. But now you have piqued my curiosity. Not only are three of your company witch hunters – which in itself I find fascinating – but London is on fire, and you have a strange codex in your possession. Noting your reaction, I'd say it is an object of consider-able importance. The opportunist in me also tells me that objects of considerable importance are often worth a considerable amount of gold.'

'You have an amazing intellect,' Francesca says wryly.

Claude dubs his hat in mock appreciation. 'Thank you. I'm afraid I have dallied here long enough. It's been a pleasure meeting you, but it's time for me and my men to go.'

'You won't be going anywhere!' a familiar voice snarls.

Startled, we all turn around to see a cloaked man armed with a rifle emerge from behind a tree trunk several yards over to the right.

I breathe a sigh of relief.

Dorian has come to our rescue.

CHAPTER SIXTY-EIGHT

D orian steps boldly into the clearing and aims his rifle at Claude. 'Order your men to drop the codex, or I'll drop you!'

'And what makes you think I'll do that?' the Gentleman Highwayman says calmly, not even bothering to look at Dorian. He points one of his pistols at me and shakes his head in warning when I attempt to reach down to collect my firearms. 'Don't move, boy. It would be a shame for this night to end in bloodshed.'

'That's exactly how this is going to end!' Dorian threatens, ignoring the two highwaymen who now have their pistols aimed at him. 'There's a large bounty out on your head, Duval. And I intend to collect it.'

Prayer takes a sharp breath when one of the highwaymen squints down the barrel of his pistol, perfecting his aim at her brother. 'Dorian, lower your rifle!' she pleads. 'There's just too many – you'll never be able to beat them.'

Dorian snickers recklessly. 'There are only five of them. I can't believe you let these men get the drop on you. I was coming up the road from the south, returning from the Hanging Tree, when I saw you turn off and head across that bridge back yonder. I was about to call out, but then I saw these highwaymen follow after you. I thought you might need my help.'

To my great surprise, Dorian curses under his breath and drops his rifle. He raises his hands above his head and steps towards the fire, pushed forward by the *sixth* masked highwayman who has snuck up behind him and placed a pistol against his back.

Claude crosses over to Dorian, takes his pistols and sword, and tosses them into the darkness. 'The first rule of the Highwaymen's Code: always have an accomplice waiting in reserve, watching your back.' He kicks our weapons away from us, then signals to his men that it is time to leave.

'Just promise me one thing,' Armand says, making Claude pause at the edge of the clearing. 'You won't take the codex anywhere near London tonight.'

'I haven't gone anywhere near London for the past two years, dear chap,' Claude says. 'I'd be recognised the instant I step into the city, and I'm rather fond of having my head attached to my neck. Rest assured, your codex will be safe with me. Once I've determined its value in gold, I'll be in touch. Until then, consider me as its caretaker.'

As much as I hate seeing the codex stolen from us, I begrudgingly acknowledge that it is most probably safest now with Claude and his band of thieves. It is only several hours until dawn. Once the sun rises, McClodden would have missed his opportunity to summon the Antichrist from the Devil's Bible. The most famous highwayman in England, Claude has not been caught in the past two years. He probably has dozens of hideouts all over the country. Who better than him to become the codex's next guardian?

Claude bows low and sweeps his hat before him. 'Adieu, dear witch hunters.'

The Gentleman Highwayman and his henchmen then disappear into the night.

'What are we going to do now?' I stare into the darkness where I had last seen the highwaymen.

'We're going to collect our weapons,' Armand says, already moving off to retrieve his mortuary sword.

'And then we're going after Duval!' Dorian says determinedly.

Armand shakes his head. 'If you want to ride after Claude, go ahead. I won't stop you. But you will be riding off by yourself.' He sheathes his sword and hands Dorian his rifle. 'I'm sure Claude and his men have returned to the main road. As he's not keen to head towards London, he'll follow the road south. And we'll be keeping vigil by the road, making sure that McClodden doesn't come after him.' He pauses and looks at each of us in turn. 'Fate has decided that the codex be passed on to new minders. All we can do is ensure that, for the next few hours, the remaining Son of Cain doesn't go after Claude.'

When Dorian doesn't object, we retrieve our weapons and mount our horses. We ride back to the main road, where we hide behind a thicket. As Francesca and Prayer lie down to rest, Armand, Dorian and I maintain a silent vigil for the remainder of the night.

I spend most of the time marvelling at how sidetracked we have become from searching for my father. Surprisingly, it was only a few days ago that Armand, Francesca, von Frankenthal and I rode into Rotterdam. So much has occurred since we first met Prince Rupert and his English soldiers as we all prepared to enter the Devil's Bowels. We've chased spies through the streets of London, battled Hell Hounds, found a secret, subterranean temple, fought the Sons of Cain and been held up by highwaymen. Perhaps, when all of this is over, I may be able to resume the search for my father. As determined as I am to solve the mystery of his identity, I don't think I'll begin my quest until after I have returned to Burg Grimmheim. I desperately need some time to rest and think through all that I have learned. I also want to spend some time with Sabina.

The hours drag by, long and tedious, but not a single soul passes by. At the first light of dawn, Armand wakes Francesca and Prayer.

Francesca rubs her eyes wearily and looks to the east, at the first grey traces of the approaching day. 'It looks as if we did it. We prevented Mother Shipton's prophecy from coming true.'

Armand stands by her side and smiles. 'It's not every day you get to stop the Antichrist from being summoned. Not bad for a night's work, I'd say.'

We mount our horses and ride slowly, lethargically, back towards London, staring up at the red glow created by the distant inferno. I smile tiredly, recalling the comment made by von Frankenthal when we first sailed to England: that it would be no great pity if London were to burn to the ground. How prophetic his words turned out to be. I'm sure he'll laugh his head off, though, when I tell him how the fire started.

Eager to see my towering friend again, I trail after Armand.

CHAPTER SIXTY-NINE

Standing at the rear of the *Royal Charles*, I watch the White Cliffs of Dover slowly fade into the night. Two weeks have passed since London was set ablaze. For four days the fire raged out of control, spurred by the dry, easterly winds. Whilst the inferno did not reach Whitehall or London Bridge, and the southern part of the city was spared, the old medieval heart of London was completely destroyed. Not even Saint Paul's Cathedral escaped the blaze; all that remains of the city's largest church is a burned-out shell.

We returned to Prince Rupert's lodgings the morning after facing the Sons of Cain. No sooner had Franz called for a surgeon, who cleaned and sutured our wounds, then we were joined by Bishop Henchman. He commended us for our efforts in fighting the Sons of Cain and preventing the Prince of Darkness from being summoned. He had also asked if we knew anything about the fire. Wary of the truth being revealed and of the possible political backlash against our order, Francesca and I had acted ignorant. Armand suspected that the Sons of Cain had started the fire in an attempt to fulfill Mother Shipton's prophecy. The Bishop had agreed that this was most likely and made us swear to secrecy. As he had previously told us, London was a political hotspot. The country could revert to a state of civil war if the King's enemies were to learn that the Antichrist had almost been summoned in the capital. Instead, it would be recorded in history that the fire had been started accidentally in a baker's shop in Pudding Lane.

I had informed my companions of what Fabricius had said about the Order of Judas, but nobody had heard of this organisation before. Armand decided that he would discuss the matter with Grand Hexenjäger Wrangel, hoping that the head of our order would be able to shed some light on the topic.

Valentine returned to Whitehall the morning after we battled the Sons of Cain. Although Fabricius had slipped past him during the fight in the alleyway, the English witch hunter had managed to delay McClodden. Despite delivering several wounds to the massive Scotsman, the leader of the Sons of Cain refused to fall. His sword-arm tiring, Valentine had been forced to withdraw. McClodden then chased him through the streets of London for the remainder of the night. It was not until dawn that Valentine managed to lose the Scotsman.

Even the priest who had accompanied Dorian to the Hanging Tree met us back at the Prince's lodgings. He had been forced to travel back to London by himself, once Dorian had spotted Claude Duval and his band of highwaymen ride after us.

But none of us have seen von Frankenthal since the Devil's Fire engulfed London.

Armand, Francesca and I remained in London to search for our companion. Once the fire had died down and it was safe to investigate the old city, Armand took us to where he had last seen von Frankenthal. We wandered the scorched and blackened streets for days, searching through the gutted remains of the city for our friend. Accompanied by Prayer, Valentine and Prince Rupert, who had returned to London after battling the Dutch fleet, we questioned Londoners if they had seen or heard what had become of the witch hunter. But we could find no answers. We had been forced to reluctantly end our search earlier today, conceding that von Frankenthal had most likely been slain by McClodden, and his remains incinerated in the great fire. There was nothing more that we could do. And so we decided to make the long journey home to Burg Grimmheim.

'I'm glad we've seen the last of England,' Armand announces, joining me by the ship railing. 'Although I'm going to miss Prayer, Valentine, Prince Rupert and Lieutenant Wolf.'

'The Prince's surgeon believes that the Lieutenant will make a full recovery,' I say, having visited the Lieutenant in the infirmary this morning. 'That is, of course, if he rests for the next few weeks.'

Armand rubs his chin and scoffs. 'Which will be no easy task. Soldiery is in Wolf's blood. I think it's nothing short of a miracle that he didn't drag himself out of bed to come and join us when we fought the Sons of Cain.'

I smile sadly and lower my eyes. 'We've made some good friends, but at a terrible price. I don't ever want to return here. I wish I'd never asked you to accompany me to Rotterdam. If that were the case, von Frankenthal would still be alive.'

Armand pats me on the shoulder. 'We can't turn back time, Jakob. And you certainly can't blame yourself for what happened to von Frankenthal. Even if he had known that it was his destiny to fall, I'm sure he still would have come to England. Besides, it was *my* decision to assist the *Angeli Mortis*. I just never thought that anything would have happened to von Frankenthal.'

From the moment von Frankenthal didn't return to Prince Rupert's lodgings, I have been overwhelmed by grief and guilt. It eats away at me, keeping me awake at night, dominating my every thought. It was *my* decision to search for my father in Amsterdam, and I had eagerly accepted my friends' offer of help. I had been selfish, believing no harm would come to my companions, particularly von Frankenthal. Never before have I met such a powerful fighter. Even when we had ridden out of London, just before we were robbed by Claude Duval, Armand had expressed concern for our companion and wanted to return to the city to search for him. Believing that Armand was feeling burdened by the responsibility of command, I had convinced him that he was worrying unnecessarily. Perhaps if I had allowed Armand to return, von Frankenthal might still be alive.

My greatest criticism of people like Captain Blodklutt is their belief that the mission must be given priority over all other concerns, and that people are expendable. But friends do not abandon one another. I have lived by this creed my entire life. But I abandoned von Frankenthal. I had believed that he was in no real danger. The last anyone had seen of him was when he had given chase after Alistair McClodden. I had firmly believed that he would hunt down and slay the leader of the Sons of Cain. But I was terribly wrong. In leaving my friend behind in London, I signed his death warrant.

Von Frankenthal was more than a mere friend to me. During my first mission to Schloss Kriegsberg, he was assigned to act as my protector. When I had killed the Blood Countess and freed von Frankenthal from her spell, he had sworn that he would gladly lay down his life to protect me. From that moment on, I had absolute trust and faith in him, that he would always be there to save me. At times I had found his promise to act as my guardian overwhelming, and wished he would show greater faith in my abilities.

But I overestimated von Frankenthal's fighting skills.

I wish that I could turn back time and offer him a helping hand when he so desperately needed it. I blink back the tears welling in my eyes. 'You had no choice. We had to help the *Angeli Mortis* defeat the Sons of Cain.'

Armand pulls the folds of his cloak tight around his neck and stares into the night sky. 'I know.' He smiles and points at a shooting star. 'Some people believe that when one of God's loyal followers dies, He sends a shooting star across the heavens, signalling their entrance into His kingdom.'

I smile, comforted by Armand's words. Until I have closure on the matter, however, I will never stop wondering what happened to von Frankenthal.

We hear the sound of approaching footsteps and turn around to find Francesca crossing the deck.

'I was wondering where you two ended up.' She joins us and looks over her shoulder expectantly.

'You seem anxious,' Armand observes. 'Is everything all right?'

'Everything would be just fine if only Prince Rupert would keep his hands to himself,' Francesca says. 'Honestly, he's done nothing but chase after me since we boarded this ship. I don't know what's gotten into him. He certainly wasn't like this before. I'm beginning to wonder if he took a knock to the head during the recent naval engagement with the Dutch.' She points an accusing finger at Armand. 'And I have you to blame for this!'

Armand raises his hands defensively. 'Me? How?'

Francesca's eyes narrow and she takes a threatening step towards the duellist. 'Don't you dare act ignorant, you rogue! You told the Prince that I am your significant other. What were you thinking?'

Armand makes a baffled expression. 'Me ... I did no such thing. Jakob, do you know anything of this?'

Francesca pokes the Frenchman in the chest. 'Don't try worming your way out of this by dragging Jakob into it. And don't you dare lie to me, Armand Breteuil! The Prince told me so. When I corrected him, telling him that there was nothing between us, he took that as an open invitation to start chasing after me.'

Armand gives a defeated sigh. 'You're right. I did tell the Prince that we are together, but only to save you from having him come after you. Don't tell me you haven't seen the way he looks at you. I only did it to save you.'

Francesca folds her arms across her chest and turns her back on us. 'Well, it's a fine mess you've placed me in now.'

Armand smiles wryly, evidently happy with how Francesca is avoiding the Prince's advances and finding the entire incident quite funny. 'I thought it was every woman's dream to be swept off her feet by a prince.'

Francesca snorts. 'Well, you thought wrong, you great oaf.'

Armand winks at me. 'At least think on the positive side of this, Francesca, you've only got to evade the Prince for a few more hours. How bad can that be?'

The Italian turns and elbows Armand in the ribs. 'Thanks a lot.'

Armand places a hand on Francesca's shoulder. 'Don't worry. I'll keep you safe from the big, bad Prince.'

'I'm glad you can see the humorous side of this,' Francesca says. In spite of herself, she cannot help but smirk.

'You've become quite attached to that, haven't you?' she adds, gesturing at Prince Rupert's rifle slung over my shoulder. 'Ever since Dorian returned from the cemetery and handed it back to you, it has barely left your side.'

'The Prince told me that I can keep it,' I say. 'Having seen how proficient Dorian is with rifles, I intend to master it.'

Armand points at the pistols tucked into my belt. 'You're turning out to be quite a consummate marksman.'

'I just prefer taking out Satan's forces before they get too close,' I say. 'I'm hoping Robert Monro can instruct me in the finer skills of shooting.'

Armand nods. 'Robert is forever going on hunting trips around Burg Grimmheim. It wouldn't surprise me if he was the person responsible for eliminating every deer within several leagues of the castle. I'm sure you'll have many opportunities to perfect your aim.'

'Although, it's not as if you need to become solely dependent on your skill with firearms,' Francesca says. 'You are a talented swordsman.'

Armand tousles my hair. 'Only because he learns from the best.'

Francesca is about to respond when she starts at the sight of Prince Rupert. He crosses the deck to join us, smiling delightedly at the Italian.

'I was wondering where you had run away to,' he says.

Francesca sidles up beside Armand, loops her arms through his and whispers, 'Help me, please!'

Armand raises his eyebrows in mock surprise and looks down at their entwined arms. 'Well, I never! Isn't that a little presumptuous? What type of man do you take me for? What on earth will people think?'

As Francesca stomps on Armand's toes, the French duellist shoots me a smile that suggests he has just won the greatest treasure in the world. I cannot help but grin.

Historical notes

As is customary, I have included this section for readers who want to learn more about the world of The Witch Hunter Chronicles.

HISTORICAL SETTING

Seventeenth-century Germany was very different to the country we know today. The country, in fact, was not even known as 'Germany', but comprised several hundred independent states, principalities and cities, the borders of which were constantly changing. Referred to as the 'German states' or the 'German-speaking lands', these territories were part of the larger Holy Roman Empire. With its capital set in Vienna, and ruled by the Habsburg Holy Roman Emperor, this was a vast and cosmopolitan empire, stretching from Hungary in the east to the Netherlands in the west, and from the North Sea to present-day Italy.

During the period in which The Witch Hunter Chronicles takes place, the boundaries of the Holy Roman Empire had been established by the Treaty of Westphalia of 1648. This treaty, which effectively brought an end to the Thirty Years' War, saw the Holy Roman Empire lose much territory and power. Of particular importance to The Witch Hunter Chronicles, this treaty saw the Netherlands gain independence from the Holy Roman Empire, resulting in the creation of the Dutch Republic. Jakob's father was one of thousands of German soldiers who fought alongside the Spanish against the French in the Netherlands.

LOCATIONS

The Devil's Bowels: These medieval dungeons beneath Rotterdam are fictitious.

ORDERS AND MILITARY UNITS

The Hexenjäger: This is the German term for witch hunters, who were operating in every state of Germany during the seventeenth century. These members of

the Catholic and Protestant Churches were responsible for sending thousands of innocent people to be
burned alive at the stake. You may be dismayed to learn
that there was no specific unit called the 'Hexenjäger':
this is purely fictitious. Sadly, Burg Grimmheim and
the members of the Order – yes, Jakob and Armand,
too – were also given birth in the misty realm of my
imagination.

The *Custodiatti*: Although this is a fictitious unit of
professional tomb-robbers, the Vatican Museums,
founded by Pope Julius II in the early sixteenth century,
contain thousands of rare manuscripts, sculptures and
works of art. This impressive collection of antiquity has
been acquired from archaeological sites, private collec-
tions and purchases from other museums.

The Inquisition: This was an institution created by the
Roman Catholic Church to eradicate all forms of heresy.
The Inquisition used torture to extract confessions from
suspected witches, heretics and apostates. Tens of thousands of suspects, including Galileo and Joan of Arc, were
interrogated by the Church throughout the medieval
and early modern periods. Justus Blad, the Witch Bishop
of Aachen, did not exist.

The Grey Musketeers: This group was known to be one of France's most revered military units. At the time of the Witch Hunter Chronicles, they were commanded by their sub-lieutenant, d'Artagnan.

The *Angeli Mortis*: The Angels of Death (English translation) are an order of witch hunters from England. They are a product of my imagination.

The Grey Runners: The Thief-taker General Shannon Sharpe and his bounty hunters are fictitious.

HISTORICAL PERSONALITIES

Prince Rupert: A German Prince who commanded the royalist cavalry during the English Civil War. He was banished from England after the fall of Bristol and became a pirate in the Caribbean. He returned to England during the Anglo–Dutch Wars, during which he served as an Admiral of the English fleet.

Claude Duval: A highwayman who robbed coaches along the byways around London. He was famous for his refined manners and extravagant clothing.

Swords: The primary weapon favoured by the Hexenjäger is a rapier. The use of these long-bladed duelling swords became less common by the late seventeenth century, as changes in fashion impeded their effective use.

Jakob uses two rapiers: a Pappenheimer rapier, named after Count Gottfried Heinrich, Graf von Pappenheim, one of the most daring cavalry officers fighting on the side of the Catholic League during the Thirty Years' War; and a rapier from Solingen, a town in Germany famous for the quality of its blades. Swords from this town were often engraved with a running wolf.

Sabres, such as that wielded by Armand, were commonly used in the seventeenth century. Heavier than rapiers, these robust, curved-blade broadswords were used by cavalry; the combined impetus of the charging horse and swinging blade delivering a devastating blow.

Armand also uses a mortuary sword. These basket-hilted broadswords were common during the English Civil War. Their hilts were engraved with human heads believed to represent King Charles I and Queen Henrietta.

Francesca uses a *talwar*: a heavy, single-edged sword from India. The curved blade of this sword was usually heavily decorated with inscriptions.

Firearms: The pistols and carbines used by the Hexen-jäger are equipped with a flintlock firing mechanism. This was a new invention in the 1600s, and proved much more effective than the matchlock pistols and carbines, which used a lit length of cord to ignite the powder pan, and for this reason tended to malfunction when it rained. A further advantage of the flintlock pistol was that it could be preloaded; the firing pin, or cock, could be pulled back into a half-locked position. This allows Jakob to have his pistols tucked into his belt, ready to blast at the first witch, demon or undead minion to rear its head.

Repeating crossbows: The crossbow used by Francesca is inspired by bows used in China at the time. These had far greater power, speed and accuracy than smoothbore European firearms.

Duels: I have taken some liberties here. The Witch Hunter Chronicles depicts Europe, in particular the French capital, as besieged by duellists who draw their swords at the slightest provocation; every street corner hosts some matter of honour that could only be satis-fied through drawn steel. Whilst this had certainly been the case in the early seventeenth century, edicts passed by the French monarchs had outlawed duels in France long before the 1660s. It was more than likely that duels still occurred in the French capital, but not to the extent that I present in these stories.

THE FORCES OF DARKNESS

Witchcraft: The seventeenth century was a period in which people believed in the Devil and witchcraft. Tens of thousands of heretics (people who did not follow, or criticised, the doctrines of the Roman Catholic Church) were condemned to death as witches. These victims of the Inquisition came from all sectors of society. In The Witch Hunter Chronicles a distinction is drawn between those who have been wrongly accused of witchcraft, and the 'real' witches and demons who the Hexenjäger battle.

The Sons of Cain: Four fictitious demonic soldiers from the English Civil War.

Malleus Maleficarum: Arguably the most infamous book written in history, the *Malleus Maleficarum* – the Hammer of the Witches – existed. Created by the Inquisitors James Sprenger and Heinrich Kramer, this text was used throughout the sixteenth and seventeenth centuries as the Inquisitor's handbook on how to detect witches. In The Witch Hunter Chronicles, the text is riddled with cryptic passages that, when deciphered, unlock powerful spells.

The Codex Gigas: This thirteenth-century text actually exists. It is more commonly known as the Devil's Bible: a name it receives from an illustration of the Devil that appears inside the manuscript. Legend has it that the monk who wrote the book sold his soul to the Devil in order to scribe the text in one single night. It is currently stored in the National Library of Sweden.

EVENTS

The English Civil War: Lasting from 1642 to 1651, this conflict divided the English nation, forcing people to side with either Parliament or the King.

The Anglo–Dutch Wars: A series of naval engagements between England and the Dutch.

The Great Fire of London: This fire raged out of control for four days, destroying the medieval heart of London. It started in a baker's shop in Pudding Lane.

SELECT BIBLIOGRAPHY

Ackroyd, Peter, *Thames: Sacred River*, Chatto and Windus, London, 2007

Hanson, Neil, *The Dreadful Judgement: The True Story of the Great Fire of London*, Corgi, London, 2002

Tinniswood, Adrian, *By Permission of Heaven: The Story of the Great Fire of London*, Pimlico, London, 2004

Withers, Harvey J.S., *The Illustrated Encyclopedia of Swords and Sabres*, Alto Books, London, 2008

Acknowledgements

I would like to thank the following people for all their support and patience: the truly wonderful team at Random House Australia, particularly Zoe Walton, Cristina Briones, Sarana Behan, Dorothy Tonkin, Nerrilee Weir and Justin Ractliffe; my family and friends; the students and staff at International Grammar; and a special thanks to Ben Rekic, who planted the seed for this adventure.

About the Author

Stuart is a History teacher in a private high school in Sydney. Inspired by the works of Dumas, Pérez-Reverte and Matthew Reilly, and drawing upon his knowledge of the English Civil War and the Thirty Years' War, he has long considered writing an action-packed adventure series set in the seventeenth century. His biggest fan – and critic – is his six-year-old daughter, who can often be found sitting on his lap in his study as he types away on the next title in The Witch Hunter Chronicles.

THE WITCH HUNTER CHRONICLES

BOOK ONE: THE SCOURGE OF JERICHO

No reprieve. No surrender.
This is the Hexenjäger.

It's 1666, and the forces of darkness are spreading across
Europe. Dreaming of wielding a blade in epic battles like
the father he never knew, Jakob von Drachenfels falsifies
a letter of introduction to join the Hexenjäger – an elite
military order of witch hunters. He soon learns a lesson
in the dangers of ambition when he finds himself selected
for a team sent to recover a biblical relic from a witch-
infested castle. But when the team is betrayed from within,
what was already a difficult mission turns into a desperate
struggle for survival.

Out now!

(Also available in ebook format)

THE WITCH HUNTER CHRONICLES

BOOK TWO: THE ARMY OF THE UNDEAD

Darkness spreads. Evil rises.
The Hexenjäger prepare for battle.

The Watchers have roamed the earth for millennia, searching for the Tablet of Breaking. If they find it, they will destroy the world. Jakob and his witch hunter companions are sent on a mission to locate the relic before it falls into the hands of the four fallen angels.

From the cliff-top monasteries of Meteora to a trap-riddled mausoleum lying at the bottom of the Dead Sea, the Hexenjäger must stay one step ahead of the fallen angles and their army of undead – for the cost of failure is Armageddon.

Out now!

(Also available in ebook format)